CONTESTED HERITAGE

Contested Heritage: Global Perspectives on Stakeholders' (Dis)Harmony at Heritage Locales explores the intricate relationships surrounding heritage, emphasizing the diverse, often contradictory, meanings attributed to heritage sites, historic towns, and museum objects by various stakeholders.

The book is structured into four parts, beginning with foundational contributions from leading scholars that set the context for understanding conflicts affecting heritage. Subsequent sections present case studies from around the world, including Europe, Africa, and the Americas, documenting how various heritage sites and historic towns experience conflict and its implications for sustainability. Topics range from the pressures of mass tourism and urban regeneration to the impacts of mining and community contestations, revealing the conflict and negotiations that often arise between and among stakeholders. By addressing tensions at heritage sites, historic towns and in museums, the book offers pathways for sustainable heritage practices that promote inclusive growth and community resilience. Through its diverse case studies, globally, it enhances an understanding of the silent tensions at heritage locales and underscores the importance of collaborative approaches in heritage management.

This comprehensive volume is essential for anyone interested in heritage management, offering fresh insights and case studies that illuminate the challenges and opportunities in this vital field. This volume is particularly valuable for academics, students, heritage practitioners, and policymakers, as it provides original research and practical strategies for fostering cooperation and mitigating conflicts.

Elgidius B. Ichumbaki is Associate Professor in the College of Humanities at the University of Dar es Salaam in Tanzania. He is also Visiting Professor in the School of Archaeology, University College Dublin, Ireland, a Senior Research Associate at the British Institute in Eastern Africa as well as Adjunct Professor in the Division of Heritage Convergence, College of Culture and Sports, Korea University, South Korea.

CONTESTED HERITAGE

Global Perspectives on Stakeholders' (Dis)Harmony at Heritage Locales

Edited by Elgidius B. Ichumbaki

Routledge
Taylor & Francis Group

LONDON AND NEW YORK

Designed cover image: Orthographic image generated from digital twin data for Bagamoyo, Tanzania, captured in May 2022. This dataset comes from a joint research initiative between the Universities of Bradford, Dar es Salaam and St Andrews, funded by the AHRC (Grant No. AH/W006723/1). Wilson, A.S., Ichumbaki, E.B., Sparrow, T., Gaffney, C., Bates, C.R. (2026). Visualising Heritage: Reimagining Townscape Heritage in Bagamoyo, Tanzania. University of Bradford. https://doi.org/10.82200/mx2e-dg23

First published 2026
by Routledge
4 Park Square, Milton Park, Abingdon, Oxon OX14 4RN

and by Routledge
605 Third Avenue, New York, NY 10158

Routledge is an imprint of the Taylor & Francis Group, an informa business

British Library Cataloguing-in-Publication Data
A catalogue record for this book is available from the British Library

ISBN: 978-1-041-03412-4 (hbk)
ISBN: 978-1-041-03411-7 (pbk)
ISBN: 978-1-003-62372-4 (ebk)

DOI: 10.4324/9781003623724

Typeset in Times New Roman
by Apex CoVantage, LLC

This book is dedicated to my daughter Katarina Kalungi Ichumbaki

This book is dedicated to our ... our Kangaroo ...

CONTENTS

FIGURES

TABLES

CONTRIBUTORS

Richard Nandiga Bigambo is a Tanzanian archaeologist and Senior Lecturer in the Department of Archaeology and Heritage Studies at the University of Dar es Salaam. He earned his bachelor's and master's degrees in Archaeology, both from the University of Dar es Salaam in 2011 and 2013, respectively. In 2020, he completed his PhD in Cultural Heritage at the University of Birmingham, focusing on the safeguarding of intangible cultural heritage in Tanzania. His research interests include analyzing policies, strategies, and practices for managing both tangible and intangible heritages, as well as community-based methods for protecting cultural heritage and the significance of cultural expressions in shaping and sustaining community identity. He advocates for participatory approaches that actively engage local communities in the safeguarding and management of their cultural heritage.

Colin Breen is Associate Professor and Head of School of Geography and Environmental Sciences at Ulster University in Northern Ireland. He teaches aspects of conflict geographies, environmental and landscape change, and development on the geography and environmental science degrees. His research focuses on historic landscape and societal change, environment and conflict, and the historical archaeologies of past maritime societies. He is currently engaged in research across the Middle East and Africa, as well as across the Atlantic maritime zone of NW Europe.

Mariam Joseph Bundala is Lecturer in the Department of Archaeology and Heritage Studies, University of Dar es Salaam, Tanzania. She is an archaeologist who specializes in phytolith analysis. She is a co-author of four peer-reviewed publications. She has 14 years of experience doing archaeological research in Tanzania and ten years of undergraduate teaching in class and field schools. Her fundamental research objective focuses on understanding the environmental context in which early humans are living in East Africa, both kinds of recent human ancestors and early representatives of *Homo sapiens*. She worked at various sites in the northern and the southern highlands of Tanzania.

Sonia Menéndez Castro holds a Master's degree in Archaeology from the Complutense University of Madrid, a bachelor's degree in History from the University of Havana, and a Diploma in Cultural Anthropology from the National Center for Cultural Development, Havana. She is a specialist in Historical Archaeology at the Archaeology Office of the Office of the Historian of Havana. She is the general coordinator of the team for archaeological heritage management in the historic center of Old Havana. She leads a research area focused on developing a Preventive Archaeology model for urban archaeological heritage management. She has been a collaborator at the Cultural Heritage Management Research Group (Universidad Complutense) since 2010. In this line, she has been part of the work team on the projects The archaeological dimension in world heritage cities: Advances in heritage management in Alcalá de Henares, Puebla and Havana (HAR2013-46735-R) and City, Heritage and Museums in Spain and Latin America: contributing to the challenge of social cohesion (PR87/19-22584).

Nekbet Corpas Cívicos is a specialized research technician at the Institute of History of the Spanish National Research Council and a member of the research team EST-AP on landscape archaeology. Also, she is an external collaborator with the Cultural Heritage Management Research Group (Universidad Complutense). She holds a master's degree in Mediation, Negotiation and Conflict Resolution (Universidad Complutense) and Archaeological Heritage and Museums (University of Cambridge). Her PhD in History and Archaeology was granted by the Universidad Complutense de Madrid and focused on heritage conflicts in historic urban landscapes in Spain and Mexico. During her postdoctoral research, she analyzed disputes involving archaeological heritage in several World Heritage Sites and proposed processes to address them drawing on the field of conflict analysis and resolution.

Juan Martin Dabezies is Adjunct Professor at the Department of Agricultural Systems and Cultural Landscapes of the Centro Universitario Regional del Este, Universidad de la República, Uruguay; Member of the National System of Researchers of the National Agency for Research and Innovation of Uruguay; and Research Assistant Professor in the Department of Geographical Sciences, University of Maryland, USA.

Mesut Dinler is Assistant Professor at the Interuniversity Department of Regional and Urban Studies and Planning (DIST) at Politecnico di Torino. He has been actively involved in numerous international conservation projects and is a member of the International Council for Monuments and Sites (ICOMOS) Italy. His research lies at the intersection of cultural heritage and climate change, exploring how heritage can contribute to a sustainable and resilient future. By framing heritage as a community praxis of engaging with the past in a spatial context, he integrates digital tools and data-driven methodologies to develop innovative approaches that connect conservation with broader social and environmental challenges.

Lars Frühsorge is Anthropologist and Director of the Museum "Collection of the Cultures of the World" in Lübeck, Germany. He has traveled to 80 countries and performed extensive fieldwork in North and Latin America. His research focuses on memory culture, the history of museums, colonialism, tourism, and spirituality.

Elgidius B. Ichumbaki is Associate Professor in the College of Humanities at the University of Dar es Salaam in Tanzania. He is also a Visiting Professor in the School of Archaeology, University College Dublin, a Senior Research Associate at the British Institute in Eastern Africa as well as Adjunct Professor in the Division of Heritage Convergence, College of Culture and Sports, Korea University.

Alicia Castillo Mena is a University professor and archaeologist specializing in cultural heritage management. She serves as co-director of the Cultural Heritage Management Research Group at the Complutense University of Madrid (https://www.ucm.es/gpc/). Her main work has been focused on social aspects, the relationship between urbanism and archaeology, World Heritage in Europe and Latin America. She is an expert member of ICOMOS: International Committee of Archaeological Heritage Management (ICAHM) and International Working Group Our Common Dignity, which advances a Heritage Rights Based Approach.

Ryoko Nakano is Professor of International Relations at Kanazawa University in Japan. Her research interests encompass a wide range of themes such as security and foreign policy, identity politics, and global governance. She has made significant contributions to the field of heritage and international politics by exploring the political dynamics of heritage production and promotion in East Asia. She is the editor of a special issue titled "Mobilizing Nostalgia in Asia" (*International Journal of Asian Studies* 18:1, 2021) and the author of the book "Beyond the Western Liberal Order: Yanaihara Tadao and Empire as Society" (Palgrave Macmillan, 2013). Her scholarly articles have been published in prestigious journals such as *International Affairs*, *International Journal of Cultural Policy*, *Cambridge Review of International Affairs*, *Contemporary Politics*, *The Pacific Review*, *Journal of Current Chinese Affairs*, *GR2P*, and *International Relations*.

Özgün Özçakır is an architect by training who specializes in the conservation of cultural heritage. He is an associate professor and the director of the Graduate Programme in Conservation of Cultural Heritage at Middle East Technical University.

He earned his PhD from the same program with a dissertation titled "In-Between Preservation and Economics: Establishing Common Ground Between Socio-cultural and Economic Aspects for the Sustainability of Urban Heritage Places in Turkey." A member of ICOMOS Turkey, the ICOMOS Sustainable Development Goals Working Group, and the ICOMOS International Scientific Committee on Economics of Conservation, his research focuses on heritage values, intervention strategies in heritage places, conservation policies in Turkey, and heritage impact assessment.

Ana Pastor Pérez is Senior Project Specialist at the Getty Conservation Institute. She holds a PhD and an MA in Cultural Heritage Management and Museology from the University of Barcelona, a degree in Archaeological Conservation from the ESCRBC of Madrid, and a degree in History from the Autonomous University of Madrid. In 2011, she participated in ICCROM's course "Reducing Risks to Cultural Heritage," developing a holistic view of research and practice. Her PhD focused on Social Archaeological Conservation, integrating ethnographic techniques and sustainable conservation strategies. Prior to the GCI, she worked as a postdoctoral researcher at the Norwegian Institute of Cultural Heritage and the Autonomous University of Barcelona, leading different community-based projects. At GCI, Ana works with archaeological collections to fill knowledge gaps and highlight the work of conservation from an inclusive and contextualized perspective. Ana is an active collaborator at the Cultural Heritage Management Research Group (Universidad Complutense).

Constanza Segovia Quinteros is a research technician for the PID2021-1272480B-I00 CIPAMUR project. She holds a master's degree in Cultural Heritage in the 21st Century: Management and Research (Complutense University of Madrid). She holds a degree in History from the Pontifical Catholic University of Chile and a diploma in Cultural Management. She is currently a predoctoral student at the UCM, where she researches networked management of cultural heritage from the study of SNA and the perspective of social cooperation and participation.

Citlalli Reynoso Ramos holds a PhD in Anthropology, with a specialization in Archaeology, from the National Autonomous University of Mexico (UNAM). She graduated from the University of Calgary with a Master's degree in Archaeology. Currently, she is a full-time professor in the PhD and master's degree program in Socioterritorial Studies at the Institute of Social Sciences and Humanities "Alfonso Vélez Pliego" at the Benemeritus Autonomous University of Puebla. She is part of the National Researcher's System of México (SNI-SECIHTI). She is a collaborator at the Cultural Heritage Management Research Group (Universidad Complutense).

Craig Ross has over 27 years of civilian and military experience covering built environment design, heritage protection, counterterrorism, and irregular warfare.

He is working on PhD research at the University of St Andrews, investigating unconventional warfare and cultural heritage destruction; he has lived and worked in the Middle East for ten years. His home is in Riyadh, Saudi Arabia, where he works as Associate Director for Security Strategy and Design at Diriyah Company.

Munyaradzi Elton Sagiya is Lecturer in Culture and Heritage Studies at Bindura University of Science Education, Zimbabwe, and a visiting research fellow at the Centre for Advanced Study | inherit. Heritage in Transformation, Humboldt University of Berlin. He holds a BA from Midlands State University and an MA and PhD from the University of Zimbabwe. Previously, he was a curator of archaeology for the National Museums and Monuments of Zimbabwe and stationed at the Great Zimbabwe World Heritage Site. His research centers on decolonizing heritage management through African Indigenous frameworks, challenging Western epistemologies. He is an alumnus of TheMuseumLab fellowship program, and he has also been a visiting researcher at the University of Cologne and University College London-Qatar. In 2023, he led a heritage documentation project under the Endangered Material Knowledge Programme hosted by the British Museum. He serves on the Editorial Board for the *Journal of the Institute of Conservation.*

Melathi Saldin is Lecturer in Cultural Heritage & Museum Studies at Deakin University, Australia. She is ICOMOS International Member and Co-Chair of the Sri Lanka ICOMOS National Scientific Committee on Intangible Cultural Heritage. An archaeologist and critical heritage scholar, she researches the politics of heritage and the role of heritage in building resilient communities in post-disaster spaces. She is the co-editor of the *Routledge Handbook of Heritage Destruction* (2023).

Eloisa Pérez Santos is Professor of Psychological Assessment and Psy.D. at the Faculty of Psychology of the Complutense University of Madrid (UCM). She serves as a teacher and researcher in the field of audience studies in museums and other contexts of cultural heritage interpretation. Co-director of the Cultural Heritage research group (UCM) and member of the Audience Studies Forum, a platform for dialogue and socialization made up of professionals and researchers in Audience Studies in the Ibero-American context. Driving force and scientific coordinator for over 10 years of the Permanent Laboratory of Museum Audiences of the Ministry of Culture (Spain), where she has directed more than twenty research projects on audiences and evaluations of social and educational programs in Spanish state museums.

Gabriel de Souza is Anthropologist, Researcher, and Lecturer in Tourism Studies at FHCE UDELAR, where he also serves as Coordinator of the Academic Unit for Tourism Studies. Also, he coordinates projects in Visual Anthropology http://www.antropologiavisual.org.

José Antonio González Zarandona was born in Puebla (Mexico), where he studied Communications Sciences at the University of the Americas-Puebla. He was awarded an MA and a PhD at the University of Melbourne, Australia. He has received fellowships from the British Academy and Columbia University. He is currently Reader in Heritage Studies at Newcastle University, where he leads the Global Heritage Management postgraduate program. His research interests are the destruction of art, heritage, and iconoclasm. He has published on destruction of heritage in Australia, Myanmar, Mexico, Syria, Iraq, video games, and Google. He is a co-editor of the *Routledge Handbook of Heritage Destruction* (2024).

ACKNOWLEDGEMENTS

This volume would not have been possible without the contribution and support of various friends, colleagues and collaborators. I am grateful to all the contributors for accepting my invitation to participate in this book initiative. Accepting to contribute their original research in this book was not only an honour to me, personally, but also a vision they have for seeing peace and harmony excel among the diverse stakeholders in the heritage sector. My sincere thanks go to the chapters' anonymous reviewers for sharing their expertise. Their insightful comments strengthened each chapter, resulting in coherence seen in this volume.

I also thank the University of Dar es Salaam, University College Dublin (Ireland), Korea University (Republic of Korea), the University of St Andrews (UK), University of Bradford (UK) and the British Institute in Eastern Africa (Kenya) for the invaluable support. My affiliation with these institutions provided me with a platform for international visibility, which has elevated me from a mere Tanzanian scholar to, as Professor Claire Smith notes in the foreword, one of the leading global voices in the decolonisation of heritage studies.

I appreciate the contribution of my mentors Professors Bertram Mapunda (Jordan University College, Tanzania), Peter Schmidt (University of Florida, USA), Innocent Pikirayi (University of Pretoria, South Africa), Shadreck Chirikure (Oxford University, UK), Claire Smith (Flinders University, Australia) and Chaprukha Kusimba (University of South Florida, USA), for encouraging and pushing me to 'go global.' I would also like to extend my appreciation to my friends at the University of Dar es Salaam, specifically Professors Thomas Biginagwa, Michael Andindilile, George Kahangwa, and Dr Dominicus Makukula, whose regular engagements and discussions at the staff club (UDASA) continue to shape my academic work. I want to extend my sincere thanks to Prof. Andindilile for proofreading some of the chapters.

The University of Dar es Salaam's *Urithi Wetu* (Our Heritage) Research Group which I happen to be the Founder and Leader of, has been helpful in linking me up with various scholars and students from the region and beyond. Some of these fellows are contributors to this volume. My long-time research collaborators and friends, Richard Bates and Donald Herd (University of St Andrews), and Dr Edward Pollard (Discovery Programme, Ireland), have always supported my academic initiatives, and I thank them for this. My collaboration with the University of Bradford team resulted in, among other outputs, the image on the cover of this book—the twin view of the historic town of Bagamoyo.

Last, but not least, I appreciate the patience of my families in Dar es Salaam, Dodoma and Kagera. I am aware that my academic commitments, including frequent travel, take away time from them. Sincerely, I value their understanding and support over the years.

FOREWORD

I am delighted to endorse this important new volume, edited by Elgidius Ichumbaki, which focusses on place-based global perspectives of contested heritage. While Ichumbaki and I have been in email contact for many years, we first met at the 9th World Archaeological Congress, which was held in Prague, in 2022. Ichumbaki was co-convening a theme with Australian Indigenous archaeologist, Wirradjuri woman, Kellie Pollard. The topic of the theme, *Landscapes, Forests, Groves, Rocks, Rivers, and Trees: Ontological Groundings and Seeking Alternative Theories*, marked Ichumbaki as a thought leader and innovative thinker. Subsequently, I followed his work with close attention. Accordingly, I was honoured when invited to write the Forreword for this volume.

This volume is pioneering, offering genuinely fresh perspectives on long-standing topics that are central to heritage scholarship. In shaping it, Ichumbaki consciously sought authors whose work widens current heritage scholarship. His approach includes a focus on interdisciplinary scholarship, which is required to address the challenges raised by the inter-connected and complex factors that underpin contested heritage. Recognising the value of diverse disciplinary perspectives, Ichumbaki commissioned chapters to encompass a wide range of viewpoints and expertise. The disciplines represented by the authors in this volume include archaeology, cultural heritage, architecture, urban studies and planning, international studies, cultural tourism, terrorism and violence, museum studies, arts and culture, and geography and environmental sciences. Each discipline brings a distinct perspective to a specific issue, shaped by a particular time and place. Themes that underpin this volume include 'silent conflicts' among stakeholders which would potentially result in heritage destruction and the 'dilemma of disharmony' where cultural heritage sites and museum objects are among the threatened parts of human culture.

The innovations of this volume are reflected in its case studies, which span diverse geographical, cultural and political contexts. The sites for the case studies encompass Western and Eastern Europe as well as Australia, Latin America, East Asia and Africa. Authored by scholars who are based in diverse countries, these chapters provide a much-needed counterbalance to current English-language scholarship which is dominated by scholars based in the United Kingdom and North America. These chapters provide new ways of thinking and a wider view of issues that are simultaneously global and specific to particular societies. Read together and cross-referenced, the chapters in this volume provide new insights and a holistic understanding of contested heritage. Lessons from one chapter can be applied to others. For example, there are wider learnings in chapter by Castillo Mena which documents how museums and archaeological sites can innovatively and proactively create resilient and peaceful communities. Similarly, Ryoko Nakano's analysis of the conflicts inherent in preserving Japan's imperial and World War II heritage concludes that the tensions that are integral to such heritage can be productively engaged by embracing plural understandings of a contested past. This lesson can be applied to contested heritage in many parts of the world. Each chapter in this volume offers insights that are useful to heritage practitioners in many parts of the world.

Finally, I suggest that this volume marks Ichumbaki's transition from an African leader of his discipline to a global leader who is embedded in Africa. The innovations of this volume are shaped by the editor's location at the University of Dar es Salaam in Tanzania, which has afforded him the particular insights, networks, and motivations that underpin its distinctive contribution to decolonising heritage studies. In putting together this volume, Ichumbaki has foregrounded forms of knowledge production, scholarly networks, and research priorities that are often marginalised in global heritage discourse. This volume not only consolidates Ichumbaki's leadership within Africa but also establishes his role as a leading global voice in decolonising heritage studies.

Professor Claire Smith A.O.
Flinders University
Adelaide, South Australia
29 December 2025

1

INTRODUCTION

Elgidius B. Ichumbaki

Heritage valorisation and sustainability

Globally, heritage locales (historic cities, archaeological sites, monuments, museums and their cultural objects) have different meanings to different stakeholders. Whether natural, cultural, tangible, intangible, movable or immovable, heritage is perceived and valued differently. The differences in valorisation depend on the stakeholders' interests, attachments, expectations, etc. For example, while researchers consider heritage sites, museums, art galleries and cultural objects as sources of scientific knowledge (Whitehead, Schofield, & Bozoğlu, 2023), tourists consider such locales as centres of pleasure, relaxation and enjoyment (see, e.g. Timothy, 2023). On the one hand, a few government officials and independent tour operators regard museums, archaeological sites and objects therein, art galleries and cultural centres, to mention a few, as sources of income, hence, engines of economic development (Pacelli & Sica, 2022; Larsen & Logan, 2018). On the other hand, individuals and groups of local people in the heritage site's vicinity consider cultural heritage locales as markers of identity and centres of various spiritual practices (Ichumbaki & Schmidt, 2021; Brosius & Polit, 2015). These varying meanings and interpretations cause contestations among stakeholders at locally, regionally and globally valued heritage sites, national monuments and UNESCO World Heritage Sites. Similar contests exist in museums, art galleries and at cultural centres where visitors may have different opinions about the displayed exhibitions including works of art.

These contests disrupt the sociocultural and economic stability in the communities around heritage locales and beyond. They can as well limit innovation and entrepreneurship opportunities that the respective heritage sites, cultural heritage centres and museums could offer unless the challenges force businesses to

DOI: 10.4324/9781003623724-1

be done in a different way – adaptive reuse. Some of the initiatives that could result in heritage sustainability alongside creating employment opportunities for the locals, especially youth and women, do not progress because of misunderstandings among stakeholders. For example, at some sites such as Kunduchi in Tanzania (Masele, 2012) and Domboshava in Zimbabwe (Chirikure & Pwiti, 2008), the conflicts between local communities and government authorities led to the destruction of investments intended to develop cultural tourism. Because of such scenarios, understanding the history and nature of contests at heritage sites, in museums and historical towns, and exploring the strategies to minimise and resolve these problems are relevant for the sustainability of the respective heritage assets.

For the past two decades, heritage sustainability has captured the interests of many heritage scholars and practitioners (Stubbs, 2004; Hidalgo-Sánchez et al., 2022). Such a move is not surprising because heritage – in all its forms ranging from tangible to intangible, movable to immovable and natural to cultural – belongs to humanity; both present and future generations must benefit from heritage. The archaeological sites, museums, historic urban landscapes, monuments, artefacts, oral traditions, ethnographic objects, etc., are public goods which, by all possible means, must be protected to benefit communities, today and in the future (Leeson et al., 2025). It is here where heritage becomes part of the UN discussions around sustainable development, calling for authorities to take steps to protect them (heritage assets) alongside exploring strategies to harness their economic potentials (Dehghan Pour Farashah & Pourzakarya, 2025).

In its totality, cultural heritage offers an opportunity to individuals and groups of people to reflect on their pasts, contemplate about the present and make plans for future (Holtorf, 2012). For the stakeholders to benefit from these heritage values, today and in the future, peace and harmony among the parties must prevail. Once all the stakeholders understand and embrace their diversities in heritage valorisation, they will be in positions to negotiate and renegotiate, and hence, reduce contests. With limited conflicts and continuous implementation of conflict resolution measures at heritage sites, inclusive exhibitions in museums and in art galleries, then the respective stakeholders will design relevant plans to make the assets beneficial to local communities, visitors, learners and other heritage stakeholders. Meanwhile, there are several instances whereby in the process of utilising heritage to bring inclusive growth while protecting it (heritage) for future generations, conflicts have been emerging and continue to resurface. *Contested Heritage: Global Perspectives on Stakeholders' (Dis)harmony at Heritage Sites* is designed to inform its audiences (academics, heritage practitioners, policymakers, heritage development partners, students, etc.) about the existing conflicts at heritage sites, in museums and in historic town alongside potential mitigation measures.

Conflicts involve two or more parties. These parties may be individuals, groups, organisations, nations or systems. In the analysis of any conflict, an identification of the parties involved is a primary issue. At the heritage sites, the parties involved in the conflict are the members of the surrounding community, tour guides, local government authorities responsible to preserve these sites, investors, religious leaders and other stakeholders who may have a stake in the respective heritage site. Comparatively, the parties that are involved in the conflicts are asymmetrical in terms of power, resources and perception. There are disparities between the parties involved in the conflict in terms of access to what the heritage sites offer, power and how the stakeholders perceive each other. The authorities involved in the management of the heritage sites (conservators, site managers, historic town planners, museum curators, etc.) and big investors have immense powers and resources compared to the members of the local community, tour guides and small-scale businesspeople around the site. This asymmetry leads to differences in how the involved parties view the intensity and magnitude of the conflicts.

Conflicts are both ubiquitous and inevitable; they are considered part of human beings' life. Mao Tse-Tung's philosophical outlook on contradiction best explains this, viewing contradiction as universal, absolute, existing in all processes of the development of things and running through all processes from the beginning to the end (Zedong, 1987). That, without contradiction, things seize to exist. The inevitability of conflicts, especially in human societies, including at heritage sites, is because they are related to scarce resources, access to resources and information, division of labour, social interaction and incompatible goals. Due to their inevitability, scholars of conflict studies hold that conflicts are not always bad, and, in some cases, they are necessary (Borcovitch et al., 2008; Dennen, 2005). A few discourses (e.g. see Al-Mamary & Hussein, 2019; Isa, 2015; Abiodun, 2014) link conflicts with creativity, mutual understanding, social and cultural reconfigurations, and improved communication settings, and satisfy specific psychological needs. While these contradictions are referred to as functional conflicts, it does not take away the fact that some of these conflicts have adverse effects on the psychology of the people and physical well-being. Some of the conflicts disrupt social relations, lead to the loss of legitimacy for a political entity, affect performance of tasks in an organisation and result in the decline of the economy of the responsible parties. These kinds of discords are known as dysfunctional conflicts (Abiodun, 2014).

Conflicts are not necessarily violent, and the absence of violence does not entail absence of conflicts. Violence is only one of the manifestations of conflict. Contemporary conflict studies have moved away from the traditional military outlook of conflicts which concentrates on violence to be a behavioural dimension which is based on the incompatibility of ideas and position on issues (Abiodum, 2014). At the centre of this behavioural dimension of conflicts there is perception. Subjective perception of individuals, groups and organisations may lead to a conflict when they believe that their needs or access to a certain value has been denied by others. Behavioural dimension of conflict is more suitable in understanding the nature of conflict at two heritage sites, in historic towns and in museums, globally. In the context of heritage management, perception of actors may lead to conflicts between and among the stakeholders – local people, site managers, tour guides, tourists, local investors, etc. For example, because the residents around both Bagamoyo and

Kunduchi feel the revenue collected from the two heritage sites does not benefit them directly, contests have started to occur (see Ichumbaki, this volume). This scenario is due to lack of transparency and accountability in the management of the two heritage sites. The community members surrounding the heritage sites and in historic town face challenges such as poor road networks, especially those leading to the sites, poor school infrastructures and inadequate water services. They believe that the presence of heritage sites should have been a solution to these problems. The same perception is evident in Cabo Polonio in Uruguay (see de Souza and Dabezies, this volume), where communities face a lot of infrastructural, educational and health services problems and their perception is that the presence of heritage sites should solve these challenges. These perceptions lead to relative deprivation. Relative deprivation occurs when respective actors perceive discrepancy between their value expectations and their values' capabilities (Jeong, 2000). At several heritage sites, globally, the surrounding community perceives that their value expectations are not met and this creates discontent between them, the government and other actors.

Many conflicts in the world are resource-based. Resource-based conflicts occur when values and needs of involved actors are not mirrored in the process of sharing resources (Ibrahim et al., 2014). Faults in the resource-sharing formula often result in frustration among the actors involved and eventually conflicts. Faults in the resource-sharing formula have led to many resource-based conflicts across the world. At various heritage sites, at historic towns and in museums the resources-sharing formula between the surrounding community, entrepreneurs and tour guides is not clear, therefore creating a sense that needs and values of some of these actors are not mirrored in the distribution of revenues generated from the sites. For example, communities of Great Zimbabwe are prohibited from doing business in the sites, and they are denied the opportunity to pray and to perform rituals (see Munyaradzi, this volume). This restriction directly affects people's survival. Studies show a strong connection between the lack of basic needs for survival and conflicts (Jeong, 2000). This connection is out of the fact that the struggle to satisfy basic needs has a lot of influence on human behaviour and social interaction, thus, conflicts. In the various heritage sites presented in this volume, people's struggle to satisfy basic needs and the restriction to get these needs from the place that is near them influences the conflicts between the people in the surrounding villages and the authorities responsible to preserve the two sites.

Small-scale conflicts in the heritage sector

Small-scale conflicts among various stakeholders at heritage sites, at historic towns and in museums, are usually underreported, although very relevant for the sustainability of the respective heritage asset. Despite a growing literature on conflicts, broadly defined, little attention has been given to the systematic analysis of such conflicts (small-scale conflicts) at heritage sites. With a global view, the contributors in this volume examine the relationship between and among various heritage stakeholders with which small-scale conflicts occur. The contributors inform that these small-scale conflicts at heritage sites are frequent, therefore adversely impacting the sustainability of heritage resources. Small-scale conflicts are misunderstandings between and among various heritage stakeholders at heritage sites, in historic towns, in museums, at cultural centres and many other places of cultural legacy. There is no physical fight among the stakeholders, but their social relations and cooperation are in a dilemma. Sadly, the affected parties do not speak about it loudly; hence, there are minimal interventions to mitigate the situation. Consequently, these conflicts are increasing and will certainly expand in the near future unless relevant actions are taken.

Developing contests at heritage sites and in museums are a concern because some cultural heritage sites and museums become healing locations for societies and groups of people the conflicts and wars traumatise. Consequently, the role of cultural heritage in bringing peace among societies, including in fragile and conflict-affected countries, is broadly documented (see e.g. Bulow et al., 2023; Shilo & Collins-Kreiner, 2019). There are also pieces of literature on how wars and conflicts have destroyed archaeological sites, monuments and historic buildings besides looting museum objects (Ahmed & Oumer, 2023). Furthermore, some studies have reported the initiatives to protect cultural heritage in post-war and conflict societies, including monument restorations and cultural heritage revitalisation (Sabri et al., 2023; Munawar & Symonds, 2022). Another important contribution in the topic is Tunbridge and Ashworth's (1996) 'Dissonant heritage: the management of the past as a resource in conflict'. Tunbridge and Ashworth detail the presence of conflict at various sites in Europe and propose three approaches to solve the problem: inclusivity, minimalist and localisation. They are of the view that these three approaches will make different groups appreciate the different views about heritage values, hence, participate in their preservation initiatives. Generally, conflictual issues in the heritage sectors are among the live and hot discussions in academia. Despite the voluminous scholarships on this issue, however, very few, if any, have a global coverage.

Furthermore, among these few scholarships, many efforts have concentrated on large-scale wars and disputes with little attention to 'small-scale conflicts' at various heritage sites, worldwide. The heritage sites, commemoration monuments, displays in museums and in art galleries that face small-scale conflicts are likely to suffer on multiple scales. For example, one group is likely to destroy part of the heritage as a strategy to exemplify their anger. One example where such incidents have happened includes Domboshava in Zimbabwe (Chirikure & Pwiti, 2008) and Kunduchi ruins in Tanzania (Masele, 2012). The destruction of the former Cape Colony Prime Minister Cecil Rhodes monument in Cape Town in 2015 during the 'Rhodes Must Fall' movement (Herwitz, 2022) and taking down of the 17th-century slave trader Edward Colston monument in Bristol, UK, in 2020 (Nasar, 2020) during the 'Black Lives Matter' movement are other examples. Likewise, another group may decide to stop engaging in some of the activities that would otherwise benefit the site. For example, some research groups may decide to move to another locality, hence, limiting uncovering of other site values. Some group stopping to conduct research at Oldupai (Olduvai) Gorge in Tanzania is a good example of this scenario (Mehari & Ryano, 2016).

Because of such situations, it would be important that the 'small-scale conflicts' among heritage stakeholders at heritage sites, in museums and art galleries and in historical towns be explored alongside potential mitigation measures. The questions such as what kind(s) of misunderstandings exist at heritage sites, in historical cities and in museums in relatively peaceful countries; what the scale of these contests is and why; and what measures to take to solve the problem, hence ensuring that the sustainability of heritage sites and collections in the museums, are critical and this volume provides initial answers. The contributors are heritage researchers, practitioners and educators, each exploring answers to the previous questions.

The volume investigates contests through an analysis of the situation at a selected set of heritage sites, historic towns and museums as case studies. With diverse scholarly expertise, 13 case study chapters span multiple realms and regions to analyse past and ongoing contests among various stakeholders around heritage locales. Through these case studies, the authors provide broad factors for the contests alongside interventions that can better ensure a common desire to protect cultural heritage as per the local contexts. All the case studies are based on primary research the contibutors have conducted over several years at various heritage sites from different corners of the world. It is the first volume of its kind that brings together researchers who have first-hand information regarding the unreported misunderstandings that, on regular basis, happens at various heritage sites, in historic towns and in museums.

All the contributors inform heritage scholars, practitioners and students on the existing 'silent tensions' at various cultural heritage sites, historic towns and in museums, which endanger the initiatives to ensure heritage sustainability. A few established scholars, worldwide, investigate the history, nature and status of 'silent tensions' at heritage sites with different recognition statuses. Whereas some contributions focus on UNESCO World Heritage Sites, others focus on national monuments. There are also a few contributions looking at sites where nature and culture interplay. Other contributions focus on the historical cities and exhibitions displayed in museums. Altogether, the contributions suggest potential mitigations to ensure peace and harmony among heritage stakeholders while ensuring heritage sustainability.

For the past two to three decades, various extremist groups have continued to target and destroy cultural heritage sites and museums' collections as a strategy to express their political concerns. Although a few books on this issue exist, 'The Routledge handbook of heritage destruction' edited by José Antonio González Zarandona Emma Cunliffe and Melathi Saldin (2024) is the most recent and comprehensive resource. With contributions from around the world, the volume offers insights on why (the drivers) and how (the contexts) heritage destruction takes place. Another recent volume is 'Heritage destruction, human rights and international law' edited by Amy Strecker and Joseph Powderly (2023). The volume is framed in the context of international cultural heritage law and heritage studies to scrutinise international law and governance dealing with heritage destruction from the perspectives of human rights. With case studies from both armed conflicts and peaceful zones, the contributions examine intentional heritage destruction including those caused by large-scale infrastructural development or resource extraction. Building on a similar framework, Bülow and colleagues have edited 'Heritage and war: ethical issues' published by the Oxford Academic Press (2023). While citing different case studies where conflicts have resulted in heritage destruction, the authors provide a range of ethical perspectives to be considered as a strategy to mitigate heritage destruction and protection challenges.

Despite these publications of global nature, there are a few other books that focus on either a single country or specific region, especially in the Middle East and North Africa, as a case study to tell heritage destruction during conflicts. A selection of these includes 'The destruction of cultural heritage in Iraq' edited by Peter Stone and Joanne Bajjaly (2011) and 'The wicked problem of cultural heritage and conflict: Military involvement in the protection and devastation of cultural property' by Christopher Herndon and Joris Kila (2017). While nearly all the contributions provide a broad picture of what is happening in various parts of the world, the focus is on either the just-ended or the ongoing heritage destruction during the armed conflicts. Indeed, there is limitation of case studies where 'silent conflicts' among stakeholders exist and which would potentially result in heritage destruction, soon or later. *Contested Heritage: Global Perspectives on Stakeholder (Dis)harmony at Heritage Locales* bridges this gap.

The book will interest many academic and research institutions, as well as faculty, students, the private sector and other organisations managing heritage sites, conservation areas, museums and art galleries. There are three reasons why this volume is timely. First, heritage studies programmes are emerging quickly, but the number of reference books for academics and students is limited. Considering the initiatives to start degree programmes on various aspects of heritage, there is a potential that many universities and other research institutions will find the volume key. Second, the desire to protect heritage sites, conservation areas and museum collections for tourism, educational and scientific research has expanded significantly, especially over the past two decades. Given the growing interests to protect heritage for tourism and educational purposes, various heritage stakeholders will require this book. Third, several countries and communities are in the 'dilemma of disharmony' where cultural heritage sites and museum objects are among the threatened parts of human culture. Developing contests at heritage sites, historic towns and in museums is a concern because some cultural heritage sites and museums become healing locations for those traumatised by conflicts and wars. Given that this volume covers a wide range of disputes happening at diverse heritage sites, historic cities and cultural landscapes, worldwide, the book is a critically important resource for different institutions dealing with heritage research and practices.

The global view of contested heritage

Contested Heritage: Global Perspectives on Stakeholders' (Dis)harmony at Heritage Locales volume has 13 chapters divided into three parts, each with a certain goal. In the first part, the editor, Elgidius B. Ichumbaki of the University of Dar es Salaam (UDSM), sets the contexts for the volume. He offers the historical background on how conflicts of different scales affect heritage and the kind of existing literature documenting the issue. What the editor stresses is that several types of literature have concentrated on heritage destruction because of wars and extremism happenings, especially in the Middle East and North Africa. He also cites a few examples, mainly from recent wars between Russia and Ukraine as well as Israel and Palestine. The editor expresses concern about active and passive conflicts, which calls for intervention, for they destroy the heritage the communities need for sociocultural, political and economic growth. He also addresses how conflicts at heritage locales affect heritage sustainability which national and international heritage stakeholders' campaign to achieve inclusive growth among surrounding communities.

The second part of the volume has four chapters that present case studies from Europe, Africa and South America. The represented countries in this part are Spain, Turkey, Republic of Uruguay and the United Republic of Tanzania. The chapters connect to each other to document how some selected heritage sites and historic towns, in both developed and developing countries, worldwide, experience conflict problems at their cultural heritage sites, hence endangering the sustainability of such heritage assets.

Building on the introductory part, Chapter 2 by Colin Breen of the University of Ulster, UK, focuses on heritage, tourism and conflicts in Barcelona, Spain. The author documents the complex relationships between city residents, the government and investors struggling to establish tourism facilities to meet visitors' accommodation needs. Breen details the significant pressure mass tourism places on the social integrity, well-being and place in the Catalan capital of Barcelona. Breen's narratives utilise cultural heritage to elaborate on how the increasing number of tourists in Catalonia leaves many parts of the medieval city centre inaccessible, resulting in accommodation problems for residents. The chapter states that a few developments have emerged to solve accommodation problems in Barcelona, but residents resist something that continues to raise dilemmas among stakeholders in the city.

Focusing on the Turkish's Mediterranean southern region, in Chapter 3, Mesut Dinler of the Polytechnic University of Turin, Italy, and Özgün Özçakır of Middle East Technical University, Turkey, present the mythos of urban heritage regeneration and its aftermath. The authors document how implementing urban heritage protection efforts in Turkey encountered opposition, primarily due to their ramifications on residents and living standards within the designated zones. The chapter describes how the conservation plan's restrictions on construction activities sparked discontent among residents whose life quality was also affected. Dinler and Ozcakir's chapter confirms that the discontent presented is not unique to Antalya in Turkey. Instead, there are similar challenges in other designated conservation sites in the country and in many others in Europe. The authors argue that such instances underscored a stark disjunction between urban heritage preservation objectives and the lived realities of the communities residing in monumental structures in developed and developing cities.

The fourth chapter by Gabriel de Souza and Juan Martin Dabezies of the University of the Republic of Uruguay presents contests in cultural heritage management in Uruguay. The case study is Cabo Polonio, a charming coastal village along the south-eastern shores of Uruguay. Renowned for its captivating natural beauty and strong tourist appeal, the village represents a model in which difference, affirmed as a core value of the protected area, redefines disconnection and inaccessibility as distinctive assets. Being one of the Uruguay's most prominent protected areas in terms of symbolic and touristic significance, Cabo Polonio embodies key values of the country's natural heritage, serving as a lasting emblem of the imagery once central to its tourism branding. The contributors explore how the conflicting interests of stakeholders shape the site's management, development and interpretive frameworks. Indeed, the chapter gives some intriguing scenarios on what happens when conservation, tourism and development meet each other in relatively rural areas.

In the fifth chapter, Elgidius B. Ichumbaki focuses on two sites of the central coast of Tanzania to inform on the contest between government authorities to care heritage on one hand and members of the local community on the other hand. He elaborates on what makes various heritage stakeholders value a particular heritage site, historic town, cultural objects, etc. Is it because of historical attachment the communities have over the respective site? Is it because of the benefits the respective site(s) offer today and likely to generate in the future? Using two cultural heritage sites namely Kaole ruins and Kunduchi ruins sites as case studies, Ichumbaki documents the misunderstandings between the government authorities legally mandated to care for coastal heritage sites and the surrounding communities. The author is of the view that because coastal communities value cultural heritage differently, tensions have become common across and among various stakeholders ranging from individuals, groups of people and communities to tourists. Ichumbaki concludes that some conflicts that emerge at cultural heritage sites are not because of the communities' love and feelings for the sites. Instead, the economic benefits and expectations the respective heritage properties offer to surrounding communities are also additional reasons for the contests.

The third part has three chapters, with case studies from Australia, East Asia and Africa. The specific countries used as case studies are Australia, Zimbabwe and Tanzania. The three chapters discuss the scenario where local people – the heritage owners – lack government interventions to solve problems associated with heritage preservation and utilisation for public.

Chapter 6 focuses on Western Australia, where José Antonio González Zarandona of Newcastle University (UK) and Melathi Saldin of Deakin University (Australia) present resource diplomacy, cultural heritage and community resilience. This chapter discusses how large-scale mining in Western Australia has resulted in the dispossession of Indigenous people's lands and the destruction of cultural heritage. Zarandona and Saldin use the sites of Murujuga and Jukkan Gorge as lenses to explore the local–global entanglements of heritage, politics and power, with a particular focus on the roles played by the diverse stakeholders (i.e. government authorities, multinational mining corporations, Indigenous communities, tourists, researchers). The authors argue that these entanglements have resulted in both the protection and the destruction of heritage. They also show that interrogating the contact zones where destruction and diplomacy are entangled and blurred helps establish a nuanced approach to understand the relationship between heritage destruction, resource diplomacy and community resilience.

The seventh chapter focuses on Japan's mining heritage as either national legacy or symbol of colonial oppression. In this chapter, Ryoko Nakano examines the limited consensus on Japan's imperial legacy and the history of World War II, arguing that any unilateral efforts to designate sites and buildings as World Heritage Site (WHS) cause controversies. Using the UNESCO WHS of Meiji Industrial Revolution and the Sado Island Gold Mines, Ryoko informs that as Japan makes efforts to publicise its national culture and history, internationally, contention among stakeholders, including those from neighbouring counties such as South Korea, emerges. In this contribution, the author shows that, although the disputes do not directly threaten the physical preservation of the sites, the generated controversies between and among stakeholders have a detrimental effect on the sustainability of heritage in Japan and beyond. Ryoko proposes that establishing a plural understanding of the contentious past is key to alleviating the ongoing contention surrounding these sites.

Chapter 8 interrogates the cultural heritage stewardship and community contestations at a UNESCO WHS of Great Zimbabwe in Zimbabwe. In this chapter, Munyaradzi Elton Sagiya of the Bindura University of Science Education, Zimbabwe, documents how the four communities surrounding the Great Zimbabwe archaeological site have not been the subject of archaeology and heritage research, despite the site attracting researchers for nearly a century. Sagiya's contribution answers two questions: how do the communities around Great Zimbabwe relate to each other in the context of site valorisation, and how does each community perceive and connect with various research groups and government officials with a statutory mandate to curate the site? Through locally informed cultural diplomacy and intra-community engagement frameworks, Sagiya discusses the 'silent contests' at Great Zimbabwe and proposes ways to resolve community dilemmas, hence establishing common grounds for the sustainable management of this unique World Heritage Property.

Chapter 9 documents the misunderstandings and struggles among research teams in Tanzania's Ngorongoro Conservation Area. In this chapter, Mariam Joseph Bundala of the UDSM uses the iconic paleoanthropological site of Oldupai Gorge to tell how power struggles among the gurus of human evolution and other palaeosciences do not end at publishing their counterarguments in peer-reviewed journals. She shows that the contests caused by the desire to 'monopolise certain localities' or establish territories on certain research localities endanger the future of research in the area, including training Tanzanian students struggling to specialise in palaeosciences and cognate disciplines.

Part four is the last part of the book with four chapters covering case studies from Tanzania, Russia, German and Cuba, Mexico and Spain as one case study. The tenth chapter by Craig Ross of the University of St Andrews in Scotland focuses on what he calls 'the bronze soldiers'. He presents how some cultural objects displayed in some museums and monuments mounted in various streets in the Baltic States to communicate the struggles between Russia and North Atlantic Treaty Organization (NATO). The chapter does not explain the destruction and weaponisation of cultural property in the Baltic States. Instead, it presents how people use monuments and cultural objects in local museums to express their feelings. Using the data from semi-structured interviews held with heritage and security practitioners, as well as driving examples from previous subthreshold conflicts, and in comparison, to modern military doctrine and strategies to counter irregular warfare, Ross examines cultural heritage as a valid resistance to modern unconventional threats. He argues that the contemporary hybrid tactics of destabilisation operations which present new threats to significant cultural heritage are expressed through monuments and other cultural objects displayed in community museums.

The eleventh chapter describes the silent contests happening at a nature–culture heritage site. In this chapter, Richard Nandiga Bigambo of the UDSM, Tanzania, documents the 'dilemma of disharmony' among communities within and around Saadani National Park, a wildlife sanctuary on the East African coastline. The author presents Saadani as the only park in Eastern Africa where the Indian Ocean beachfront meets the bush. The varieties of mangroves, coral reefs, palms and savannah characterise the landscape. It is also a cultural heritage site marked by 19th-century slave trade material culture, unique traditional Swahili architecture and historic salt making. Bigambo reiterates that, although unpopular, Saadani is among a few African localities where unique nature meets unique culture. Despite this uniqueness, residents' livelihoods in the nearby six villages depend on available natural and cultural resources. Consequently, contests exist on land-use priorities, economic pressure and varying perceptions of heritage value. Bigambo's chapter informs on the contests on managing the nature and cultural resources where the state recognises and legally protects wildlife without considering the cultural part, which the surrounding communities and professionals recognise and wish to see included in the conservation priorities.

The last two chapters aim to cement on the first 11 chapters informing that the discussed (dis)harmony does not end at heritage sites and in cities. Instead, contests continue with the objects that have moved from the sites to the museums. For example, in the twelfth chapter, Lars Frühsorge focuses on the ethnographic collections of Lübecker, a museum in Germany with over 30,000 objects from around the world. Lars's chapter highlights two issues. First, the complexities of storing, exhibiting and returning sacred objects and human remains to their countries of origin. The second part of the chapter discusses the reproduction of 'stolen cultural objects' and circulating them in the European market. Lars argues that the people's attempt to make 'fake cultural objects' and circulate them to European markets is a form of cultural resistance against the economic exploitation of Indigenous heritage and a strategy to raise voices missing in the colonial records. A key lesson one learns from Lars' contribution is that heritage conflicts do not only arise at sites but also occur in archaeological and ethnographical museums that preserve objects from those cultures and communities. Henceforth, examining past and present interpretations of museum collections gives a fascinating comparative insight.

In the last chapter, a team of researchers led by Castillo Mena of the Complutense University of Madrid documents how museums and archaeological sites could innovatively and proactively create resilient and peaceful communities. The team's contribution cites specific case studies in Cuba, Mexico and Spain to inform on the methodological approach to use to make archaeological sites and museums create opportunities that contribute to community resilience and sustainability. The hypothesis team maintains is that having a heritage management network that includes various local stakeholders is likely to result in resilient communities whose heritage sites become sources of pride and generate income for the surrounding communities, hence, conflict resolution.

References

Abiodun, A. R. (2014). Organizational conflicts: Causes, effects and remedies. *International Journal of Academic Research in Economics and Management Sciences*, 3(6), 118.

Ahmed, M. J., & Oumer, A. A. (2023). The impacts of armed conflicts on the heritage tourism of Dessie and its environs, Northern Ethiopia. *Journal of Heritage Tourism*, 18(1), 101–120. https://doi.org/10.1080/1743873X.2022.2145899

Bercovitch, J., Zartman, I. W., & Kremenyuk, V. (2008). *The SAGE Handbook of Conflict Resolution* (pp. 1–704). London: SAGE Publications.

Brosius, C., & Polit, K. M. (Eds.). (2015). *Ritual, Heritage and Identity the Politics of Culture and Performance in a Globalised World*. London: Routledge.

Bülow, W., Flowe, H., Matravers, D., & Thomas, J. L. (Eds.). (2023). *Heritage and War: Ethical Issues*. New York: Oxford Academic Press.

Chirikure, S., & Pwiti, G. (2008). Community involvement in archaeology and cultural heritage management: An assessment from case studies in Southern Africa and elsewhere. *Current Anthropology*, 49(3), 467–485.

Dehghan Pour Farashah, M., & Pourzakarya, M. (2025). Reviving the past: Unveiling urban industrial heritage in Yazd, Iran. In Truong, V. D., & Knight, D. W. (Eds.), *Heritage Tourism. Global Vietnam: Across Time, Space and Community.* Singapore: Springer. https://doi.org/10.1007/978-981-96-5427-7_9

Dennen, J. M. G. (2005). Introduction: On conflict. In *The Sociobiology of Conflict* (pp. 1–19). London: Chapman & Hall.

Herndon, C., & Kila, J. (2017). *The Wicked Problem of Cultural Heritage and Conflict: Military Involvement in the Protection and Devastation of Cultural Property.* New York: Colonel Publishing.

Herwitz, D. (2022). Negotiating offence of Fallist proportion: Cecil Rhodes and the removal of university of Cape Town's statue. *Third Text*, 36(6), 631–650.

Hidalgo-Sánchez, F. M., Carrascal-Pérez, M. F., Rey-Pérez, J., Plaza, C., & Mascort-Albea, E. J. (2022). Cultural heritage, sustainability, conservation, and social welfare. A management plan for the historic municipal buildings of Seville (Andalusia, Spain). *The Historic Environment: Policy and Practice*, 13(4), 426–458. https://doi.org/10.1080/17567505.2022.2146332

Holtorf, C. (2012). The heritage of heritage. *Heritage & Society*, 5(2), 153–174. https://doi.org/10.1179/hso.2012.5.2.153

Hussein, A. F. F., & Al-Mamary, Y. H. S. (2019). Conflicts: Their types, and their negative and positive effects on organizations. *International Journal of Scientific & Technology Research*, 8(8), 10–13.

Ibrahim, S. G., Abba, S., & Bibi, F. (2014). Resource based conflicts and political instability in Africa: Major trends, challenges and prospects. *International Journal of Humanities Social Sciences and Education*, 1(9), 71–78.

Ichumbaki, E. B., & Schmidt, P. R. (2021). Shrine. In *Encyclopaedia of Ancient History: Asia and Africa.* Hoboken: John Willey & Sons. 10.1002/9781119399919.eahaa00604

Isa, A. A. (2015). Conflicts in organizations: Causes and consequences. *Journal of Educational Policy and Entrepreneurial Research*, 2(11), 54–59.

Jeong, H. W. (2000). *Peace and Conflict Studies: An Introduction.* London: Routledge.

Larsen, P. B., & Logan, W. (Eds.). (2018). *World Heritage and Sustainable Development New Directions in World Heritage Management.* London: Routledge.

Leeson, M., Giovanelli, R., Ferro, S., De Bernardin, M., & Arianna Traviglia, A. (2025). Overcoming data siloes in cultural heritage crime research: A consolidated OSINT-derived dataset on art, antiquities, and the trade in cultural goods. *Archival Science*, 25, 16. https://doi.org/10.1007/s10502-025-09485-x

Masele, F. (2012). Private business investments in heritage sites in Tanzania: Recent developments and challenges for heritage management. *Journal of African Archaeological Review*, 29(1), 51–65.

Mehari, A. G., & Ryano, K. P. (2016). Maasai people and Oldupai (Olduvai) Gorge: Looking for sustainable people—Centred approaches and practices. In Schmidt, P. R., & Pikirayi, I. (Eds.), *Community Archaeology and Heritage in Africa: Decolonizing Practice* (pp. 21–45). London: Routledge.

Munawar, N. A., & Symonds, J. (2022). Post-conflict reconstruction, forced migration & community engagement: The case of Aleppo, Syria. *International Journal of Heritage Studies*, 28(9), 1017–1035. https://doi.org/10.1080/13527258.2022.2117234

Nasar, S. (2020). Remembering Edward Colston: Histories of slavery, memory, and black globality. *Women's History Review*, 29(7), 1218–1225. https://doi.org/10.1080/09612025.2020.1812815

Pacelli, V., & Sica, E. (Eds.). (2022). *The Economics and Finance of Cultural Heritage How to Make Tourist Attractions a Regional Economic Resource.* London: Routledge.

Sabri, R., Maya, R., Dalli, A., Daghstani, W., & Mayya, S. (2023). The Syrian conflict's impact on architectural heritage: Challenges and complexities in conservation planning and practice. *Journal of Architectural Conservation*, 29(3), 258–274. https://doi.org/10.1080/13556207.2023.2185855

Shilo, S., & Collins-Kreiner, N. (2019). Tourism, heritage and politics: Conflicts at the city of David, Jerusalem. *Asia Pacific Journal of Tourism Research*, 24(6), 529–540. https://doi.org/10.1080/10941665.2019.1596959

Stone, P., & Bajjaly, J. (Eds.). (2011). *The Destruction of Cultural Heritage in Iraq*. Woodbridge: Boydell Press.

Strecker, A., & Powderly, J. (Eds.). (2023). *Heritage Destruction, Human Rights and International Law*. Brill: Schöningh.

Stubbs, M. (2004). Heritage-sustainability: Developing a methodology for the sustainable appraisal of the historic environment. *Planning Practice & Research*, 19(3), 285–305. https://doi.org/10.1080/0269745042000323229

Timothy, J. (Ed.), (2023). *Cultural Heritage and Tourism in Africa*. London: Routledge.

Tunbridge, J. E., & Ashworth, G. J. (1996). *Dissonant Heritage: The Management of the Past as a Resource in Conflict*. Chichester: Wiley.

Whitehead, C., Schofield, T., & Bozoğlu, G. (2023). *Plural Heritages and Community Co-production Designing, Walking, and Remembering*. London: Routledge.

Zarandona, A. G., Cunliffe, E., & Saldin, M. (Eds.). (2024). *The Routledge Handbook of Heritage Destruction*. London: Routledge.

Zedong, M. (1987). On contradiction. *Chinese Studies in Philosophy*, 19(2), 20–82.

2

HERITAGE, TOURISM AND SOCIAL CONFLICT IN BARCELONA, CATALONIA

Colin Breen

Introduction

Over the past two decades, Barcelona in northeast Spain has become one of Europe's most popular tourist destinations. Visitors are attracted by the city's architecture, vibrant cultural and social scene, Mediterranean climate and accessibility. More than 20 million visitors from across the globe arrive by air and sea primarily on short breaks, which bring extensive capital into the Catalan economy. Still, their presence and numbers are causing significant tensions across the region. House prices have risen dramatically, with many apartments and former homes bought by private investors with a view towards the highly lucrative tourist rental market. Many of the primary thoroughfares in the city now cater almost exclusively for external visitors. The cost of living has risen exponentially, making it difficult for the locals to maintain a reasonable standard of living. These factors are partly responsible for residents' alienation from large areas of their city and have made housing effectively unaffordable for large community sections. Underlying these developments was the deliberate reimagining and repositioning of the city from the 19th century as the cultural capital of the Western Mediterranean Sea basin and the use of cultural heritage to project the Catalan capital as one of the great European historical cities (Monclús, 2000). Cultural heritage has then become highly politicised. It has been increasingly commodified as the region's leaders seek to gain independence from the Spanish state and pivot Catalonia northwards towards the European Union and away from the centralising Madrid government. Heritage practice is not a passive actor in this process; it has been used to support separatism and tourism growth and has often excluded local voices (Breen et al., 2016).

DOI: 10.4324/9781003623724-2

A few central arguments have been forwarded in this chapter.

- Barcelona's heritagisation has been selective, conformist and often elitist. In creating an 'antique' streetscape, the architects of this change selected a European medieval ideal over more recent industrial heritage and working-class or artisan architecture and place.
- Investment in and development of numerous cultural heritage centres and initiatives have become politicised as platforms to promote Catalan separatism and contribute to the city's tourism product.
- Though this was meant to have been an inclusive transformation, the city's rebuilding has often prioritised the external visitor over those who live and work in these communities.
- The number of external visitors to the city has now exceeded a sustainable carrying capacity, placing significant pressures on housing, affordability and the general well-being of the people who live there.

What follows is more of a reflective piece than the results of a targeted survey. Over the past 20 years, I have been involved in various forms of research and educational activity across Barcelona and Catalonia. This has included leading annual university field schools in the region, researching heritage and the politicisation of identity, and filmmaking around history and the separatist movement. During this time, the city has undergone significant change, and there is clear evidence that the social contract between the government and the city's peoples is breaking down. Heritage has been manipulated and commodified throughout this process and has been used as a platform for political messaging, capital gain and social influencing. The chapter will initially examine the process of heritagisation in Barcelona and how its physical character was deliberately transformed to conform to the ideals of what a medieval European capital city should look like. It will then address the significant urban transformations across the city from the early 1990s and the subsequent explosion of tourism (see also Chapter 3, this volume). As a result, there has been an increase in the levels of social disquiet and protest as the oppressive levels of tourism impact social well-being. Cultural heritage has served as an intrinsic part of these transformations, centring on the processes of social conflict.

In terms of methodology, the scope of this study depends primarily on the observation and monitoring of both traditional and social media platforms. In the digital age, there is an increased divergence between the official governance narratives and data from conventional media, including newspapers and television. Social media will often be the primary vehicle for promoting unofficial narratives and disseminating messages of dissent. Increasingly, short films that the filmmakers produce advocate and carry essential messages about unofficial dissent, and many of these are available on platforms such as YouTube. This media analysis has been supported by qualitative surveys undertaken across Catalonia but focused on Barcelona bi-annually over 15 years. These interview-led surveys have concentrated on the contestation around Separatism and the Independence issue but have included wider social conflict and unrest issues. Overtourism has increasingly emerged as a central feature of these interviews. This study represents an overview of the current trends coming from these surveys.

Heritagisation

Heritagisation, in its broadest sense, is a process associated with transforming a place, material culture or practice into cultural heritage with values assigned to it and where it is now deliberately framed for a particular function. In earlier conceptual approaches towards the process, Kevin Walsh (1992) identified the appropriation of space as the reduction of real places to tourist space. It also involves taking buildings and everyday items and transforming them into objects for the tourist gaze, where they become exhibits for display. Harrison (2013) treats this process as more loaded, where these places and objects become vehicles of official heritage. The messaging around them promotes a narrative that supports the state, territory or grouping within that area. These assemblages then play an integral part in promoting and propagating political messaging, state-building and identity formation. 'Authorities' then decide what cultural heritage is preserved, conserved and encouraged to reflect their own perspectives and agendas. Tourists then come to these places to consume these narratives and bring a set of expectations that the public display or performance of heritage will entertain them. Authenticity is expected and presumed but rarely questioned. This form of 'Authorised Heritage Discourse' at an official level heritage can be viewed as consensual or can constitute the majority collective view of what the past looked like and how it should be remembered (Smith, 2006). However, locally, 'unofficial' heritage might present a different or alternative view of the past (Harrison, 2013). Heritage is then, by its very nature, contested. As heritage becomes selected for public display, it also becomes commodified within the context of the broader tourist product. Heritage becomes a presumed necessity for a visitor's experience, and tourist places are expected to have various such experiences through museums, visitor centres, historic buildings or public spaces. Heritagisation has occurred on multiple levels in Barcelona and originates in the emergent Catalan nationalist movement in the 19th century. This will be examined in more detail in the following section as the city was reimagined and rebuilt to conform to the accepted ideals of a medieval capital.

Recreating Barcelona

Barcelona has had an often-complicated history. Originally established during the Roman period, it later emerged as a major centre for marine communications and mercantile activity during medieval times and as the capital of the region of Catalonia. At the height of its importance, Catalan influence spread across the

Mediterranean as far east as Sicily with a thriving network of ports and merchant bases (McDonogh & Martinez-Rigol, 2019). Later in the 18th century, it became subsumed within a wider Castilian Spain. Still, it developed a problematic relationship with the centre of power in Madrid as its political fortunes ebbed and flowed. During the Spanish Civil War of 1936–39, Barcelona became a capital of the Republican government and was also the centre of leftist resistance to the Nationalist movement (Preston, 2003). Following the Nationalist victory, General Franco held a heavy grudge against the Catalans, and his government imposed extensive restrictions on the region regarding the Catalan language, economy and political aspirations.

By 1990, the city had experienced decades of neglect associated with the region's deliberate marginalisation under Franco's rule. Many of its neighbourhoods had high levels of deprivation; large areas consisted of industrial wasteland or abandoned brownfield sites, and other localities were effectively no-go areas associated with high levels of criminality. The hosting of the Olympics in the city in 1992 changed much of this as the national and regional authorities invested massively in the refurbishment and reconfiguration of the urban landscape and social fabric of the urban environment (Monclús, 2000). This essentially consisted of a significant overhaul of the city's physical morphology and social fabric and has become known as the Barcelona Model, often viewed, however, correctly as a model approach for the successful transformation of a city (Monclús, 2003). At its core, the project adopted innovative planning to create a new social city using urban space as a connector between communities, different physical spaces and core socioeconomic activities across the urban space. It would be delivered as a partnership between public administration and the private sector while theoretically engaging with communities. Regeneration aimed to develop an economically prosperous but more socially equitable city modelled on accessibility and inclusivity. This was achieved by creating new urban spaces, increasing pedestrianisation and opening the city's beaches and coastal areas. Scarnato (2016) suggested that social democratic ideals primarily inspired this urban transformation programme to create a city that functioned efficiently for its residents while also serving the needs of external tourism as a primary economic driver.

In previous centuries, the waterfront had been the centre of the city's economy with a bustling port, shipbuilding areas and industry. By the closing decades of the 20th century, most industrial areas had been abandoned, and large areas were occupied by shanty towns, densely populated by the migrant poor. Opening access to the beaches was viewed to democratise social space and open a largely unused leisure and amenity area that covered over 6 km of sandy foreshore. Developed in tandem with this process of urban change was a strategy to generate cultural capital by investing in and developing new museums, cultural centres and art. At the same time, each neighbourhood saw the development of a civic centre; in doing so, the architects of this change intended to create a new centre of economic power and effectively recreate the city as the historical and cultural capital of the Western

Mediterranean. This city stood alongside other great European capitals like Paris and Rome.

Central to this re-edification of Barcelona as a significant European historical centre was reimagining the city's centre through façadisation and creating a gothic quarter in the older parts of the city. To be recognised as a significant historical city, it had to look like one. This conversion occurred since the close of the 19th century as Catalan nationalists sought to recreate the city as the cultural and political capital that would stand alongside the other capitals of Europe. A large area of dense housing immediately before the main central 15th-century cathedral was cleared to create the illusion that a medieval square was present. The building's previously bland and largely unspectacular frontal façade was rebuilt to make it appear more impressive and medieval in the late 19th century by the Catalan architect José Oriol Mestres. Subsequently, many surrounding buildings and streets were either rebuilt or reframed during 1927–70 (Gant, 2013). In some cases, new medieval-style buildings were created using the worked stone from buildings removed during the clearance or from other areas. Facades that often contained architectural forms from multiple periods were erected to create a more antique vista for the external gaze; in more recent decades, as part of the Olympic work, sections of industrial architecture were levelled, and new residential areas developed. However, the extent to which these works were successful can be questioned. Furthermore, in several instances, the resultant outcomes negatively impacted the coherence of cultural heritage and the social well-being of communities. Was this then an unrealised vision? The next section engages on this issue.

An unrealised vision?

The Barcelona Model is often forwarded as an overwhelming success, and indeed, the project did transform the city in many positive ways. However, there are also criticisms of the approaches taken. Montaner (2010) has suggested that in some instances, heritage remains were mistreated or ignored and forwards the example of the industrial heritage of the Poble Nou. In effect, they see this as a form of amnesia that deliberately sought to remove working-class memory from this city area by removing social housing, factories and cooperative centres. Montaner forwards the analogy with the collective process of forgetting around the Civil War and suggests that this form of collective amnesia has become embedded in the Spanish mindset. De Balanzó and Rodríguez-Planas (2018) have identified further issues as to why the model was not as successful as many neoliberal commentators might claim. These included the breakdown of the consensus between the city's political elite and its citizens, with a widespread belief that developers and financial gain were being prioritised over resident needs. This intensification of development led to a dramatic increase in house prices and the subsequent emergence of urban sprawl as people seeking affordable housing were driven out of the centre.

Historic central neighbourhoods like the Ciutat Vella and the Born became gentrified, and the effectiveness of inclusive governance was lessened.

These developments have also led to social conflict between various social groups' competing needs and interests, including residents, migrants and tourists. Issues such as noise, nightlife, congestion and differing social values have all increased tension. A combination of these issues has made many of the city's historic quarters virtually unliveable as anti-social behaviour impacts the everyday lives of residents. As the region has historically supported large influxes of migrants and continues to do so, these arrivals place further pressure on the existing resources. Probably the most pressing issue is the pressure on housing. Following the global economic collapse of 2008, unemployment across Barcelona soared, and there was a significant slowdown in construction. Across the city, there is now a housing shortage as many locals cannot afford the hugely inflated prices of residential property in the metropolitan area, with investors increasingly buying up any available apartment. The vast number of properties available for short-term holiday let is placing further pressure on the limited supply. These housing pressures have directly led to the emergence of a series of advocacy groups and cooperative centres that have become increasingly visible and vocal in seeking change.

A tourism juggernaut

Even though tourism began in the 18th century with European travellers visiting Catalonia, contemporary tourism in Spain developed in the 1950s to bring much-needed capital to the struggling economy following the Civil War. From the 1970s, Catalonia emerged as Spain's leading destination for internal and external tourists, a position it still holds today over the Balearic Islands – the growth in tourist numbers and infrastructure in the decades since has been phenomenal. In the 1980s, before the Olympics, under two million visitors were recorded annually, despite the city having 118 hotels in 1990. By 2013, over 12 million people had stayed in the city's hotels, with a further 12 million visitors. By then, only London, Paris and Rome supported more significant annual tourist numbers (Goodwin, 2019). Through the 2010s, tourism was responsible for up to 12 per cent of the city's gross national product and employed nearly 17 per cent of the city's residents (Garay & Cànoves, 2011). As the provision changed, 16,951 Airbnb properties were officially recorded by 2020, and the number of hotels increased from 564 in 2005 to 893 in 2023 (López, 2024).

In 2023, 23,045 homes were available for tourists, and 9.9 million visitors stayed at least one night, a 14.8 per cent rise from the previous year as the industry recovered after the COVID-19 pandemic. Just under 16 million international visitors came to Catalonia in the same year, with just over 27 million visitors in total when Spanish visitors are included (López, 2024). These figures need consideration against the city's population. Current estimates suggest that Barcelona had 1.7 million residents in 2023, while the broader metropolitan area population is 5.7

million. In the city, residents are then outnumbered by 5:1 regularly, making many areas no-go spaces for the city's inhabitants. Of the visitors to the town, Spaniards constitute 12 per cent, and US visitors make up 11 per cent. Other tourists, such as French (9%), UK (7%), Germans and Italians (6%), represent the other primary groupings (López, 2024).

Overtourism

The sheer number of tourists visiting the city has been a concern for many decades. Attempts to address this officially began in the early 2000s. Various plans have been put in place to mitigate against the pressures, but with little success, capital gain appears to have been prioritised over social well-being. In theory, a participatory, evidence-based approach has been adopted to address these concerns, but with limited success. The 2008 Municipal Action Plan forwarded a strategic tourism plan that aimed to *strengthen the balance between residents and tourists while preserving the identity values of the city* (Goodwin, 2019, 8). In addition to addressing the city's capacity to cope with tourist pressures, it also forwarded the role of cultural heritage to promote the architectural heritage of the city, the Catalan language and cuisine, and the city's role as the Catalan capital. The subsequent 2010–15 strategy attempted to position Barcelona as the Mediterranean's most vibrant and dynamic destination supported by its culture and creativity. It was based on three principles: coherence with the city model, a synergic relationship between visitors and residents and economic, social and environmental sustainability. Further commitments were made around the protection of cultural resources and values.

In 2020, a new Strategic Plan was initiated and structured around key objectives: sustainability, responsibility, redistribution and cohesion. Still, the issues persist, and as the industry recovers after the pandemic, the problems and tensions increase. Regardless of these plans, the issues associated with overtourism continue to grow. In an extensive survey of residents' attitudes and perceptions of tourism, Elorrieta and colleagues (2022) found that people across neighbourhoods were very concerned about the direct impact associated with the levels of antisocial behaviour and the continuing congestion of public space. Additionally, the residents highlighted population displacement associated with locals being priced out of many areas and weakening social structures as investors buy out real estate and retail units and reorientate towards external visitors. Local services are likewise depleted.

Protest and social conflict

The tourism industry brings significant financial benefits to the city; however, various associated problems persist. Employment is high but precarious, often short-term, insecure and poorly paid. Increasingly, many of these service positions are also undertaken by marginalised social groups from the migrant communities who have little voice. However, protests around the industry have focused on housing, living costs, visitor behaviours and access to urban space. For years, the Raval district has had a reputation for attracting the seedier elements of tourism. Banners began to appear on balconies in the 2000s with the Catalan phrase *Volem un barri digne!* (We want a dignified district!), while traders sent 100s of Christmas cards to city officials with depictions of anti-social behaviour by visitors, including sex and drug activity. The documentary *Bye Bye Barcelona,* produced by Eduardo Chibás (2014), documented many of the tensions that existed across the city. It made a powerful argument for greater regulation of the industry. The documentary emphasised the need to ensure its historic core is not subsumed by souvenir and food shops and that its residents not to be alienated and forced to move. Geographical areas of particular concern included the city's main tourist thoroughfare, La Rambla, the Ciutat Vella, the Raval, the increasingly gentrified Born and the intensive tourist footfall around La Sagrada Familia. Barceloneta, the compacted network of grid streets by the port and home to the former fishing and artisan communities, was also addressed with property speculation in recent years, which has significantly undermined the social cohesion of this distinct community. One interviewee spoke of the need to ensure that the city's rich architectural heritage did not simply become a static *papier mâché* pastiche present solely for the tourist gaze and not developing to cater for the dual needs of the internal resident and external visitor.

A series of protests was now becoming a regular occurrence, with residents complaining about increasingly restricted public access to places like Park Güell and the lewd behaviour of tourists. In late 2015, the *Assembleia de Bairros pelo Decrescimento Turístico* was established as a social organisation to address the issues around tourism in Barcelona and act as a representative body for resident community bodies in each neighbourhood (Felix and Souza, 2023). The emergence of such a collective represented one of the first global movements of this kind and reflects the depth of feeling that exists. It also reflects Barcelona's almost unique sociopolitical environment, which encourages and promotes dissent and a deeper psyche of social justice. Subsequent events included the 2017 occupation of La Rambla by 1000s of residents carrying placards stating that *Barcelona is not for sale* and complaining about tourism-related gentrification and the shift to concentrated service-related industries in the downtown areas. Across the city, anti-tourist graffiti was painted on walls while banners calling for silence at night-time and respect for neighbourhoods. Also, protesting the expansion of Airbnb was an increasingly frequent feature on the balconies of residential buildings (Figure 2.1). Though some of this activity was coordinated by political groups, much of it was reflective of the high levels of dissatisfaction that existed across resident groups. Activist organisations like Arran also undertook high-visibility actions demonstrating against the impacts of tourism (Ramos and Mundet, 2021). Some actions have attracted much attention in the international media, such as the incident of egg throwing at hotels in 2017 or the harmless use of water pistols against restaurants

FIGURE 2.1   Montage of protest signs, banners and graffiti that have appeared across the city in recent years.

in 2024. These actions were not designed to cause harm but to draw international attention to the issues. Of particular concern was the impact of daily visitors from Cruise ships. Following their arrival in port, the vessels disembark 1000s of visitors who often only visit the city's cultural landmarks for a few hours. Most of these groups contribute little in real terms to the local economy, have a low visit spend, but leave a high environmental footprint. Short-term activities like this pose major challenges to the future development of a tourism industry built on sustainability and benefiting only a few within the local community.

The city authorities have recognised the concerns of the residents. In the summer of 2024, they moved to restrict the proliferation of short-term lets and aim to phase out tourist apartments by 2028. The socialist mayor of the city, Juame Collboni, stated that the city was in danger of becoming a tourist theme park and that *Tourism needs to serve the city's model, not the opposite*. No new hotels will be allowed to be built, and new restrictions and taxes will be placed on cruise ship visitors who stay for less than 12 hours in the city.

Cultural heritage and social conflict

Across the city, cultural heritage sites and places of historical memory are associated with social conflict. These include problems with visitor pressures, congestion and the alteration of social cohesion. Two examples are presented later, representing the issues' nature but at different scales. Probably the best-known site in Barcelona is the Basílica de la Sagrada Família. Often described as the world's largest unfinished Catholic church, an architectural masterpiece designed primarily by the

FIGURE 2.2   The west elevation of the Basílica de la Sagrada Família.

Catalan architect Antoni Gaudí (1852–1926). Construction began in 1882 on a relatively conventional neo-Gothic church before Gaudí took over the project a year
later and developed a unique design that became a signature of his work. The site,
now part of a broader UNESCO World Heritage complex, has become the primary
tourist attraction in the city and attracted 4.7 million visitors in 2023, with many
more congregating in the streets around the church (Figure 2.2). In 2022, 83 per
cent of these visitors were from countries outside of Spain. This sheer volume of
visitors has placed considerable stress on the residents of the neighbourhoods surrounding the site. Because of Barcelona's unique expansion and redevelopment in
the 19th century, the settlement pattern for much of this city consists of apartment
blocks in a grid-like pattern across the area known as the L'Eixample.

These closely clustered residential units have limited external green or social
space and often rely on public areas for leisure. The units have also developed
closed social relationships between and among the residents. Substantial visitor
numbers, hotel construction and the appropriation of apartments for short-term
let have all placed significant pressures on this cohesiveness and the ability of
the residents to lead peaceful lives. During a recent survey on the location, a resident remarked that the area had been 'transformed into a theme park' and stated
they just wanted a district for living. Several community associations have been

formed, including the Association of Neighbours of the Sagrada Familia (Associació de Veïns i Veïnes Sagrada Familia), to counter these pressures and contest the continuing expansion of the complex. The transformation of the surrounding streetscapes to cater to the tourist market is also profound, with many local businesses and food shops catering to the residents now transformed into souvenir and fast-food units geared towards the external visitor. This process has severely weakened neighbourhood cohesion and is destroying the social fabric of its communities.

In Barcelona, participatory governance and planning is a key feature of civic administration, yet these principles have rarely been applied to cultural heritage. Colomer and Pérez (2024) have argued that an emergent level of participation in cultural heritage is reflected in recent changes in practice and it is associated with the tourism pressures impacting the city. Central, top-down governance remains the norm, with investment supporting major events and large-scale tourism projects to the detriment of local communities and needs. Still, local cultural governance is beginning to effect change. Colomer and Pérez (2024) highlight an essential example of the contestation around this decision-making at the site of the Roman Wall on the Street Carrer del Sotstinent Navarro in the Current Plaça Carme Simó. Here, the parents' group of a local primary school (Àngel Baixeras school, AMPA Baixeras) asked that the vacant plot in front of the wall be set aside for use as both a playground for the children and a public park for community use. A series of community festivals and events was organised in 2014 to encourage resident decision-making and argue that the exposure of this section of the old Roman Wall for tourists would only further alienate the residents and lose one of the only remaining open-air spaces left in the area. Funding was eventually granted, and Barcelona City Council commissioned the architect Josep IIinas to create an amenity space around the archaeological excavations that had taken place after building demolition that would support both the children from the school and adults from the immediate surrounding residential area (Colomer and Pérez, 2024). This has now been closed off with a fence to preserve its integrity and support its projected use by the local children.

Ultimately, these pressures are placing considerable stress not only on access to and appreciation of cultural heritage sites and places across the city but also on the structural integrity of these places. Huge visitor numbers will always constitute one of the biggest threats to sites through footfall, accidental damage, infrastructural and access change, etc. The commodification of these sites can lead to tensions between profit and conservation. The intangible heritage of these communities is also threatened through community displacement and the dilution of local traditions and practices. This is especially evident in the Barceloneta neighbourhood on the waterfront, where property speculators are buying up property for tourism lets. In doing so, they are destroying the close-knit social fabric of this community with its own distinctive set of identities and cultural practices.

Discussion

Heritagisation has occurred in Barcelona for decades and on multiple levels across society. This process began with converting streetscapes and buildings in the city's historic core to make them appear more medieval as part of creating a structural lineage alongside the great medieval capitals of Europe. In more recent times, following the death of Franco and the re-emergence of the Catalan separatist movement, heritagisation has been associated with the development of several cultural heritage places like the Born Centre to promote a distinctly Catalan perspective on the past that aims to produce a narrative in favour of the independence of Catalonia – both official and unofficial museums and galleries across the city support this messaging with varying degrees of subtlety. The orientation of these exhibits is also important, with many projecting the image of Catalonia, which is more of an integral part of Europe than Spain. The language used in the accompanying texts is often more directed towards the external tourist than the visiting Spanish person. Similarly, a number of public spaces, buildings and monuments have also been used as platforms for the propagation of this messaging. Various squares have become part of the pageantry around memory associated with the 1714 Siege of Barcelona and the supposed consequent loss of Catalan independence to the hated Bourbons. However, in prioritising the city's pre-1714 heritage, the architects of these displays effectively chose to ignore more recent histories, including the industrial heritage of the waterfront communities and industries and the social histories of the working-class communities who lived in these areas. In doing so, an overly sanitised perspective on the urban social past was selected that chose to ignore the often tricky and uncomfortable histories of the people who lived and worked in these places.

One of the issues with this messaging is that the authorities across Barcelona pride themselves on a form of participatory governance. However, heritage work offers a singular perspective and is structured around Catalan identity and its distinctiveness from the Spanish state. Catalonia is indeed a very inclusive society, but this inclusivity is often absent from historical messaging, which prioritises a very particular interpretation of the past. The region has seen significant influxes of workers from other areas of Spain, particularly Andalucía, throughout the 20th century, but their histories tend to be marginalised. Internal responses tend to be muted but have led to exclusion among specific groups favouring a single Spanish state. Similarly, planning in Barcelona is predicated on a participatory and inclusive approach. However, given the pressures that now face residents from price inflation, investor activity, congestion and changes in retail patterns, it seems inescapable that the Barcelona model has instead failed. The original ethos of the project was admirable. Still, the city's success as a tourist destination and as an international centre for digital industry and commerce is rapidly making the city unliveable and rapidly morphing into a theme park.

More recently, the burgeoning levels of tourism have placed significant strains on social cohesion across the city. The vast number of tourists visiting the city has seriously strained its ability to cope with the numbers as residents are pushed away from the centre in increasingly unaffordable and unliveable areas. Its population is responding in various ways. While most accept that the tourism industry is a vital component of the city's economy, the majority also accept that it has exceeded its carrying capacity. Uncontrolled growth in pursuit of profit undermines social cohesion and effective local governance and reduces the sustainability of the city's communities. Despite being relatively small, widespread protests have attracted widespread media attention, with images of the simple harmless act of aiming water pistols at visitors dining in a kerbstone-side restaurant appearing in print and digital media worldwide. More direct action has been limited to young activist groups, but dissent is growing, and there is an urgent need to introduce more significant regulations around the industry. The city's residents have always had a long history of collective organisation. This issue has led to new community and neighbourhood groups that have come together to campaign and advocate for better change and protect their areas. As with many aspects of governance in Barcelona, bottom-up pressure often leads to change rather than some form of aspirant top-down participatory mechanisms.

Conclusion

As the numbers visiting the city continue to rise, the pressures on housing, affordability and the well-being of the people there will worsen. Anti-social behaviour, marginalisation and the Disneyfication of the city's medieval streetscapes will lead to rising social conflict and protest levels. Episodic violence erupted across the streets of Barcelona in the months and years after the 2017 referendum on independence directed towards the heavy-handed actions of the Spanish state. The tensions around that issue have dissipated, but a new wave of anger has emerged regarding overtourism. While there are no easy solutions to these issues, several immediate steps could be taken to lessen their impact. Caps need to be considered on visitor numbers, and new taxes could be imposed, the proceeds of which could be used to support community and cultural heritage initiatives. New efforts must be made to establish genuine participatory decision-making bodies primarily guided by community voice, informed by best heritage conservation practices. Unless this is urgently and effectively addressed, violent conflict in a city under pressure maybe inevitable. Barcelona is, in many ways, broken.

Acknowledgements

I would like to thank the editor, Prof. Elgidius B. Ichumbaki, for inviting me to contribute to this volume and for his valuable insights and comments on how the text could be improved.

References

Breen, C., McDowell, S., Reid, G., and Forsythe, W. 2016. Heritage and separatism in Barcelona: The case of El born cultural centre. *International Journal of Heritage Studies* 22(6): 434–445.

Chibás, E. 2014. Online Documentary. *Bye Bye Barcelona,* available at https://www.youtube.com/watch?v=kdXcFChRpmI, accessed June 2024.

Colomer, L., and Pastor Pérez, A. 2024. City governance, participatory democracy and cultural heritage in Barcelona, 1986–2022. *The Historic Environment: Policy and Practice* 15(1): 81–100. DOI:10.1080/17567505.2023.2298546.

De Balanzó, R., and Rodríguez-Planas, N. 2018. Crisis and reorganization in urban dynamics: The Barcelona, Spain, case study. *Ecology and Society* 23(4): 6. https://doi.org/10.5751/ES-10396-230406

Elorrieta, B., Cerdan Schwitzguébel, A., and Torres-Delgado, A. 2022. From success to unrest: The social impacts of tourism in Barcelona. *International Journal of Tourism Cities* 8(3): 675–702. https://doi.org/10.1108/IJTC-05-2021-0076

Felix, F. G., and Souza, M. J. N. D. 2023. Narratives of a conflict: Discursive disputes about tourism in Barcelona. *Intercom: Revista Brasileira de Ciências da Comunicação* 46: e2023138. DOI: https://doi.org/10.1590/1809-58442023138en

Gant, A. C. 2013. The invention of the Barcelona gothic quarter. *Journal of Heritage Tourism* 9(1): 18–34. https://doi.org/10.1080/1743873X.2013.815760

Garay, L., & Cànoves, G. 2011. Life cycles, stages and tourism history: The Catalonia (Spain) experience. *Annals of Tourism Research* 38(2): 651–671.

Goodwin, H. 2019. *Managing Tourism in Barcelona.* Responsible Tourism Partnership Working Paper 1 (3rd edition). https://www.responsibletourismpartnership.org/wp-content/uploads/2019/11/Managing-tourism-in-Barcelona.pdf

Harrison, R. 2013. *Heritage: Critical Approaches.* Milton Park, Abingdon: Routledge.

López, A. M. 2024. Tourism numbers in Catalonia. *Statista Online Digital Report.* Online resource visited July 2024: https://www.statista.com/statistics/447823/yearly-number-of-international-tourists-visiting-catalonia/

McDonogh, G., and Martinez-Rigol, S. 2019. *Barcelona.* Hoboken: John Wiley & Sons.

Monclús, F. J. 2000. Barcelona's planning strategies: From 'paris of the South' to the 'Capital of West Mediterranean'. *Geo Journal* 51: 57–63.

Monclús, F. J. 2003. The Barcelona model: And an original formula? From 'reconstruction' to strategic urban projects (1979–2004). *Planning Perspectives* 18(4): 399–421.

Montaner, J. M. 2010. The Barcelona model reviewed. *Transfer* 7: 49–53.

Preston, P. 2003. *Coming of the Spanish Civil War.* London: Routledge.

Ramos, P., and Mundet, L. 2021. Tourism-phobia in Barcelona: Dismantling discursive strategies and power games in the construction of a sustainable tourist city. *Journal of Tourism and Cultural Change* 19(1): 113–131. https://doi.org/10.1080/14766825.2020.1752224

Scarnato, A. 2016. *Barcelona supermodelo. La complejidad de una transformación social y urbana (1979–2011).* Editorial Comanegra and Barcelona City Council.

Smith, L. J. 2006. *Uses of Heritage.* New York: Routledge.

Walsh, K. 1992. *Representation of the Past: Museums and Heritage in the Post-Modern World.* London: Routledge.

3

MYTHOS OF URBAN HERITAGE REGENERATION AND ITS AFTERMATH IN TURKEY

Mesut Dinler and Özgün Özçakır

Heritage and development

The contest between development and heritage preservation in urban contexts has been ongoing for over a century. The emergence of the contests in urban heritage preservation, especially in the European context, resulted from industrialisation's social, economic, political and ideological transformation (see Breen, this volume). The 19th-century recognition of the historic city (ancient city and medieval city) as an object to reflect on is simultaneous with the emergence of urbanisation in different European contexts. Some examples of this phenomenon can be seen, for instance, in the contemporary reactions against Baron Haussmann's Paris operations, Juskin's and Morris' writings and works, Cerda's study of Barcelona and his use of the term *urbanism,* and Camillo Sitte's *Städtebau* (Choay, 2001; Bandarin & Oers, 2012). Among these historical figures representing different approaches towards dealing with the historic city, the Italian architect Gustavo Giovannoni's (1873–1947) writings should be particularly mentioned as they highlight the issue as an urban and territorial planning problem (Giovannoni et al. 2024).

To resolve contests, in the early 2010s, the UNESCO World Heritage Centre conceptualised, developed, advocated and promoted the Historic Urban Landscape approach (Bandarin & van Oers, 2012; UNESCO World Heritage Centre, 2011) to manage change within historic urban landscapes. Developing strategies to manage contests was more advantageous than opposing change or development for preserving the tangible urban fabric. In the current 'sustainable development' discourse, international attention increasingly goes to underlining the pivotal role that heritage can play in achieving sustainable growth despite its marginalisation in development discussions (Labadi, 2022). This global attention to preserving urban heritage can be seen, for instance, in UNESCO's efforts to highlight the role

DOI: 10.4324/9781003623724-3

of World Heritage Sites in achieving the UN's Sustainable Development Goals (UNESCO World Heritage Centre, 2019) and the European Commission's commitment on the role of culture in sustainable development (European Commission, 2022a; 2022b).

Despite acknowledging urban heritage as a vital component of sustainable development, achieving this goal presents a challenge due to the inherent conflicts related to the diverse interests of a vast network of stakeholders who have a role in managing cultural heritage. These conflicts become even more complex in urban heritage sites, where the scale issue demands a multilevel approach. Overcoming the conflicts surrounding urban heritage sites requires not only technical expertise but also diplomatic and political skills, given the involvement of a wide range of multiple stakeholders, each with their agendas, ambitions and objectives and each with diverse interests in the management of a site (Bandarin & van Oers, 2012). Thus, fostering consensus and framing shared objectives among multiple stakeholders remains an obstacle. This chapter aims to provide insights into these conflicts, arguing that they emerge not only because of the varying needs of diverse stakeholders but also because of the historical context generated by national and international politics and power games.

The notion of 'development' is historically linked to the power dynamics of colonialism and industrialisation. In post–World War II, the idea of development gained a new specific connotation related to the Cold War and the geopolitical struggles of that time (Goldsmith, 2002; Scott, 2020; Escobar, 1995). During this period, 'Developing countries' were often portrayed as being on a developmental trajectory that 'Western' nations had already achieved for decades, if not centuries, ago (Unger, 2018). This developmental discourse suggested that the so-called 'underdeveloped' countries could achieve similar success by adopting Western strategies and the infusion of Western expertise (Escobar, 1995). Within this framework, tourism emerged as a key sector, particularly in the Global South, where it was often positioned as the engine and primary investment area for spurring economic growth.

In Turkey, where Cold War dynamics had operated as a political background in forming an authorised heritage discourse (Dinler, 2022), urban conservation projects' designs and implementation processes exemplify how tourism was framed as an engine of development. Moreover, it illustrates the conflicts among different actors, including users and inhabitants whose lives experience irreversible change in the post-implementation phase. Antalya, as the current chapter shows, represents one of the earliest examples of urban heritage management geared towards tourism-driven economic development. Such an understanding of development was not without its conflicts and challenges. Even though tourism has brought financial benefits to some, it has also generated social tensions and environmental degradation. In Antalya, the transformation of the historic city did not respond to the needs of local communities. It resulted in multiple challenges, such as displacement and social inequality, and triggered broad discussions about the capitalist uses of Turkish Mediterranean coasts.

Research strategies

In this chapter, we analyse the Antalya Yacht Harbour Project (*Antalya Yat Limanı Projesi*) of the 1970s using a multi-faceted research approach, drawing from various local, national and international sources. Our analysis relies heavily on the Conservation Development Plan (*Koruma İmar Planı*) for the harbour, a primary document that offered critical insights into the project's planning and implementation stages. Moreover, the archives of the World Bank were instrumental in understanding the broader context, as the project was an integral part of the more significant South Antalya Tourism Development Project supported by the World Bank. These archives provided information on the financial, logistical and developmental frameworks surrounding the initiative.

To better capture the local perspectives and contextualise the contestations surrounding the project, we consulted a range of national newspapers from the era. These sources illuminate the voices of residents and stakeholders, revealing the diverse reactions to the project's implementation and its impact on the community. Additionally, we explored professional viewpoints through an analysis of architectural and urban accounts, which documented the reactions of planners, architects and other experts to the transformation of the harbour. Furthermore, we critically evaluated these developments within the politically and economically turbulent atmosphere of the 1970s in Turkey, since the project initiated debates on using coastal areas.

To contextualise this project within the heritage governance framework, we reviewed relevant national laws, policy frameworks and development plans, offering a comprehensive understanding of the institutional environment that shaped contests in the heritage sector in Turkey. While some of these sources came from the digitised archives, we consulted the local archives. By combining these diverse materials, this chapter unravels the technical- and policy-related aspects of urban heritage and the human and social dimensions, particularly the local voices of those affected by the tourism-driven development initiatives.

Tourism as an agent of development in the Cold War context

Though the role of heritage in the development discourse has been a prominent theme since post–World War II (Labadi, 2022), Arturo Escobar's influential critique of the notion of 'development' provides a valuable political backdrop for critical insight. Escobar critiques how a specific understanding of 'development', shaped by Europe and the United States, was implemented in the Global South (or the so-called developing nations or 'Third World') during the Cold War in a top-down, ethnocentric and technocratic fashion. Escobar's critique of development in exploring how the Global South was constructed as 'underdeveloped' through Western discourses mirrors Edward Said's framing of *Orientalism* (Said, 1978). Whereas Said focuses on the cultural representations of the 'Other', Escobar emphasises the direct interventions and material implementation of development policies. Escobar acknowledges Said's influence in analysing how power and knowledge create conditions that legitimise Western dominance. Still, in the development context, this manifests through concrete projects and economic models imposed on the Global South (Escobar, 1995: 6–7). Escobar is of the view that this development model resulted in various interconnected issues, including economic inequality, environmental degradation, social dislocation and increased dependency on developed nations. Rather than resolving poverty, this developmental strategy often exacerbated it, making local populations more vulnerable to external economic and political forces.

Even as the Cold War power dynamics shaped the Third World, capitalist and socialist blocs recognised tourism's potential to stimulate economic growth and extend political influence over developing nations. Indeed, these countries were often rich in cultural and natural assets; however, they lacked industrial infrastructure, and tourism was promoted as a strategy to attract foreign investment, foster international cooperation and enhance political ties (Bozdoğan, Pyla, & Phokaides, 2022: xxxi–xxxiii). The Marshall Plan was launched in 1948 to help European countries rebuild their economies, industries and physical infrastructures. In the Marshall Plan, countries in Southern Europe, including Turkey, were encouraged to focus on tourism as an alternative to industrialisation, which was deemed too costly or politically risky. With its promise of job creation and infrastructure development, tourism became a way to integrate these nations into the Western-led global order (Bozdoğan et al., 2022: xxxii). The Cold War era facilitated economic modernisation and social transformation by constructing infrastructure, particularly highways, hotels and resorts. It also embedded countries more deeply into the global political order, fostering closer ties with the United States through the infusion of foreign capital and expertise (Adalet, 2018).

Furthermore, Bozdoğan and colleagues (2022) contend that leisure – understood as a form of tourism centred around relaxation, recreation and enjoyment, often associated with sunny beaches, coastal resorts and other vacation-oriented destinations – was developed as a means of income generation. The European and American visitors were primarily embraced as a mechanism to provide financial resources for fostering social, cultural and economic development. This thrust involved the construction of new hotels, building highways to facilitate access to these sites and capacity-building initiatives aimed at training skilled workers to serve in the hospitality sector and transforming coastal landscapes into 'leisurescapes'. Another dimension of the Cold War's transformative impact in Turkey includes the industrialisation of agriculture and the consequent migration wave from rural to urban areas, as people's work was replaced by tractors. Though the image of the tractor became associated with modernisation, this form of development profoundly impacted the characteristics of both rural and urban areas and the conflicts and power imbalances related to the urban–rural dichotomy (Iplikci & Aykaç, 2024). Regarding transforming from a rural to an urban society, see Chapters VI–VII in

Keyder (1987). For an extensive understanding of the Cold War's impact on the higher education field, see Erdim (2020). This model promoted economic growth and aligned Western countries with a shared understanding of development led by American geopolitical interests. Consequently, a new approach emerged within this context, especially in urban heritage sites, where urban heritage conservation was intertwined with touristic and economic objectives.

This intertwined relationship between urban heritage conservation and economic objectives formed the basis for state-led development strategies that became central to Turkey's modernisation efforts in the mid-20th century. These strategies were implemented through legislative and policy instruments, including key urban planning tools like the Five-Year Development Plans discussed in the next section. These plans outlined economic development strategies across various sectors, ranging from agriculture and industrialisation to transportation and the public sector. Tourism was one of the main pillars of economic development model for Turkey's Mediterranean coasts.

Realising post-war ideals through state instruments and development plans

The transition to a new economic development model in the 1960s was, in part, a reaction to the government policies of the 1950s. The post-war plans in Europe during the 1950s introduced a reimagined approach to development, with Turkey experiencing a distinct shift during the same decade. This period marked a move from orthodox, state-led modernisation towards a development model heavily influenced by the United States. During the late 1950s, Turkey had shifted to increasing political repression under a populist government that employed polarising religious rhetoric. The 1960 coup d'état completely transformed the state structure by designing and implementing a new constitution, which provided a relatively liberal political space. Although there were already foreign expert reports for establishing a state-led development scheme even before the coup d'état, the pre-coup government dismissed these reports. Although the groundwork for a technocratic system to foster development had already been laid, the political context necessary to implement these ideas emerged after the 1960 coup d'état. Like the transformation in state-led economic development approaches in other countries, such as the New Deal in the United States or the Monnet Plan in France, Turkey also embraced a planned development strategy in the 1960s (Keyder, 1987: 143).

The State Planning Office (SPO), staffed with skilled technocrats holding privileged positions, organised the economy-related ministries that emerged in the aftermath of the coup. The SPO began developing five-year development plans to centrally coordinate investment decisions (Keyder, 1987: 148). This central management scheme, however, created a conflicting situation. On the one hand, the new constitution encouraged autonomous and powerful local authorities; on the other hand, the process was never fully formulated in law and was left to future governments. Moreover, the SPO and its centralised decision-making mechanism became an obstacle to achieving a decentralised management scheme (Tekeli, 2009: 177–79).

The Five-Year Development Plans reflected the approach of instrumentalising tourism-related projects for economic development. The monetary value of urban heritage and its potential to drive economic growth were also recognised in these plans, which emphasised that the conservation of deteriorating structures could benefit tourism (Madran & Özgönül, 1982). These plans called for repurposing of the historical monuments, such as madrasas, caravanserais and mansions as tourist accommodations managed by either the private sector or the Director General of Foundations. Accordingly, the Directorate received a budget for restoring its properties (Altınyıldız, 1997: 108–9). The 1973 Old Artefacts Law, the first law on cultural heritage in the Turkish Republic, was an extensive formulation of such economic motivations to valorise cultural heritage in Turkey (Madran & Özgönül, 1982). Before 1973, cultural heritage regulation consisted of a series of Ottoman decrees (*Asar-ı Atika Nizamnameleri*), the last of which was enacted in 1906 and remained active until a new law was passed in 1973.

Tourism was a key factor in these plans alongside restoration efforts. The designated tourism investments in the initial two plans (1963–72) attracted a significant budget. This investment encompassed hotel construction, infrastructure development (including airports and roads), language training for staff, international advertising campaigns and various additional initiatives (Anon, 1963, 1968). These developments and the state's control over urban heritage in historic cities through tourism and touristic investments continued until another coup d'état that reshaped the state structure again in 1980. While this new coup d'état facilitated the neoliberal transformation of Turkey, it also shifted state policies in the management of urban heritage to favour private investments (Çalışkan, 2021). Regarding Antalya, which will be discussed as a case study later, it is noteworthy that before its touristic potential was highlighted in the 1963–72 plans, the leading investment sectors were forestry, agriculture and industry (Alpan, 2014).

The concept of 'sit': urban heritage and planning as an engine of economic development

While the Five-Year Development Plans were designed to outline investment areas for using the economic potential of heritage in achieving development, implementations were orchestrated by state-led programmes that collaborated with international agencies such as UNESCO and the United Nations Development Programme (UNDP). By then, Turkey and international organisations (UNESCO and UNDP) viewed tourism as a mechanism to foster economic development and global influence. The projects these international organisations initiated aimed to enhance rural tourism by restoring historic sites and promoting cultural events (Luke & Leeson,

2022). While internationally backed investment programmes in the tourism sector were a common feature in Third World countries, a push for internationalisation led to the rise of a global conservation movement (Meskell, 2018; Glendinning, 2013). Along with this internationalisation, conservation shifted from protecting individual monuments and their surroundings to preserving urban heritage on a larger city-wide scale. With the introduction of the 1973 Old Monuments Law in Turkey, it became possible to designate historic areas as conservation zones or 'sit areas' extending beyond single buildings to encompass entire historic urban centres (Dinler, 2021). This shift, which reflected European standards in historic preservation, was overseen by expert committees with decision-making power over Turkey's cultural heritage.

Between 1973 and 1982, over 417 sites became conservation areas, including Antalya's inner castle, one of the earliest designations (Dinler, 2022). A similar and earlier approach to urban conservation is evident in creating *secteurs sauvegardés* under France's 1962 *loi Malraux*. Similar to *secteurs sauvegardés,* the *sit area* designations and subsequent implementations encompassed entire urban sites and framed a frozen approach to these areas. This approach, adopted in the 1973 law, triggered several conflicts among different actors. *Sit* designations had the authority to override existing master plans. The High Council, the primary preservation authority with the immense central power in Turkey from 1951 to 1983, was tasked with creating 'temporary development conditions' for these *sit* areas until a new Conservation Master Plan (CMP) could be established. These temporary conditions primarily involved a ban on construction activities within *sit* boundaries. However, until 1975, no temporary conditions were outlined, leaving local authorities powerless to act since their master plans were effectively nullified (Dinler, 2022).

This situation shifted when local authorities appealed to the Court of State to challenge the *sit* designations. The High Council's initial intent in cancelling the master plans without providing guidance was to compel authorities to develop CMPs. Unfortunately, many local authorities lacked the expertise and budget to formulate a CMP, which led to growing frustration among local authorities and the public. From the High Council's perspective, this approach was a reasonable way to prevent further damage caused by master plans to historic environments. At the very least, until a CMP was prepared, no new construction, false restorations or demolitions could harm landmark towns. This decision, however, faced significant backlash (Dinler, 2022).

The 1973 law and subsequent *sit* designations can still be considered as a positive step towards integrated conservation despite the drawbacks in enforcing the law. One of the initial site designations was in 1973 for the inner castle of Antalya, including the city's Yacht Harbour. To understand the contestations triggered by this project, it is necessary to look at the country's political situation. Since the 1970s, Turkey has experienced political instability and social unrest, beginning with the military's 1971 intervention and violent political clashes. The global Cold

War dynamics, such as the Islamic Revolution in Iran, fuelled domestic tensions. The 1974 Cyprus conflict added to the already complex and volatile situation. In addition, within the bipolar global power dynamics of the Cold War context, the tension between right- and left-wing sympathisers accelerated in Turkey to the limit of armed conflicts between the two wings. Amid this turmoil, urban planning became a key issue in coastal areas like Antalya where debates arose whether the areas be privatised or preserved for public use.

Tourism in the Turkish Mediterranean

The sustainable management, conservation and potential transformation of Turkish Mediterranean coasts are regulated under the legal frameworks. For the first time in 1972, Turkey introduced its first coastal regulation by adding Articles 7 and 8 to the Construction Law. These articles provided overall guidelines for planning and construction along coastlines, rivers and lakes. The regulation established minimum coastal strip widths, requiring at least 10 metres in areas with construction plans, 30 metres in unplanned residential areas and 100 metres in other areas. These regulations paved the path towards the designation of a specific law dedicated to using the coast. In 1984, the Coastal Law was enacted, followed by the regulations for its implementation in 1985. This law further standardised the coastal strip requirements, setting a minimum of 10 metres in planned areas and 30 metres in unplanned ones. Significant changes were in 1990 with the passage of the 3621 Coastal Law, which introduced stricter controls on coastal zones. The minimum width of coastal strips increased to 20 metres in areas with development plans. For the unplanned areas, it was extended to between 50 and 100 metres (Turoğlu, 2009). Further amendments were made in 1992 through Law No. 3830, which prohibited construction within 50 metres from the shoreline, except for public utilities. This law aimed to ensure that coastal areas serve public interest. Beyond the initial 50 metres, the law allowed for the construction of specific facilities, including recreation areas and certain tourism-related structures, while continuing to protect public access and environmental integrity.

Several other coastal management laws were introduced throughout the 1970s and 1980s. The 1982 Tourism Encouragement Law empowered the Ministry of Tourism to designate certain coastal areas for tourism development, providing incentives for private investment in these regions. Similarly, the 1983 Environmental Law aims to protect natural resources, including coastal areas, by regulating land use and development to prevent environmental degradation. The 1982 Constitution of Turkey played a crucial role in shaping coastal management policies. It established that coastal areas were under state control and must prioritise public interest, ensuring that these zones remain accessible to the public. Over time, coastal regulations became more focused on balancing protection with public use, permitting carefully regulated development for recreational and tourism purposes while safeguarding these regions' natural and cultural heritage (Sesli & Akyol, 1999).

Turkish coastal laws have evolved to address the challenges of managing and protecting coastal areas. The increasing complexity of regulations, coupled with overlapping responsibilities among various governmental agencies, has created challenges in enforcement. To ensure the long-term protection of coastal areas, better coordination and enforcement of laws are needed, emphasising the importance of prioritising public interest and environmental sustainability (Ferudun, 2009). However, as diverse stakeholders have conflicting interests, achieving public benefit and environmental sustainability is increasingly becoming complex, especially considering the high real estate value of the coastal areas. We further highlight this issue in the next section.

Conflicting interests among different actors in heritage planning and conservation

As mentioned earlier, for the *sit* designated areas, CMPs are essential for planning conservation areas, which often include urban heritage. Due to Turkey's development strategies, CMPs were also requested to plan coastal conservation areas primarily urbanised. However, preparing CMP for such coastal heritage sites involves multiple stakeholders with differing objectives, leading to conflicts that can hinder practical conservation efforts (Eceral & Taciroğlu, 2017). CMPs outline the regulations for any heritage-related activity (i.e. restoration, preservation and permissible developments) within the designated conservation zones. The preparation of these plans is governed by Law No. 2863 on the *Protection of Cultural and Natural Assets.* The preparation process also involves a complex administrative procedure involving various actors, including the Ministry of Culture and Tourism, local municipalities and regional conservation councils. While the Ministry oversees cultural heritage preservation at the national level, local municipalities are tasked with implementing conservation plans and managing local urban development. Regional conservation councils provide expert opinions and approvals for conservation projects (Özçakır et al., 2018). On the other hand, urban planners and architects are tasked with drafting conservation master plans, striving to protect heritage sites while accommodating modern demands. Local communities, consisting of residents and local business owners directly affected by the conservation regulations, are also key stakeholders.

The lack of coordination and communication among different government bodies within such a complex governance scheme, coupled with the involvement of a broad-based stakeholder network, can lead to inter-agency conflicts. Similarly, excluding local communities and NGOs from planning processes often results in opposition. Numerous cases in Turkey, particularly in coastal areas, illustrate these conflicts. Although this situation is pertinent for almost all historic sites, including in Istanbul and its surroundings, it gains a historical layer in the southern

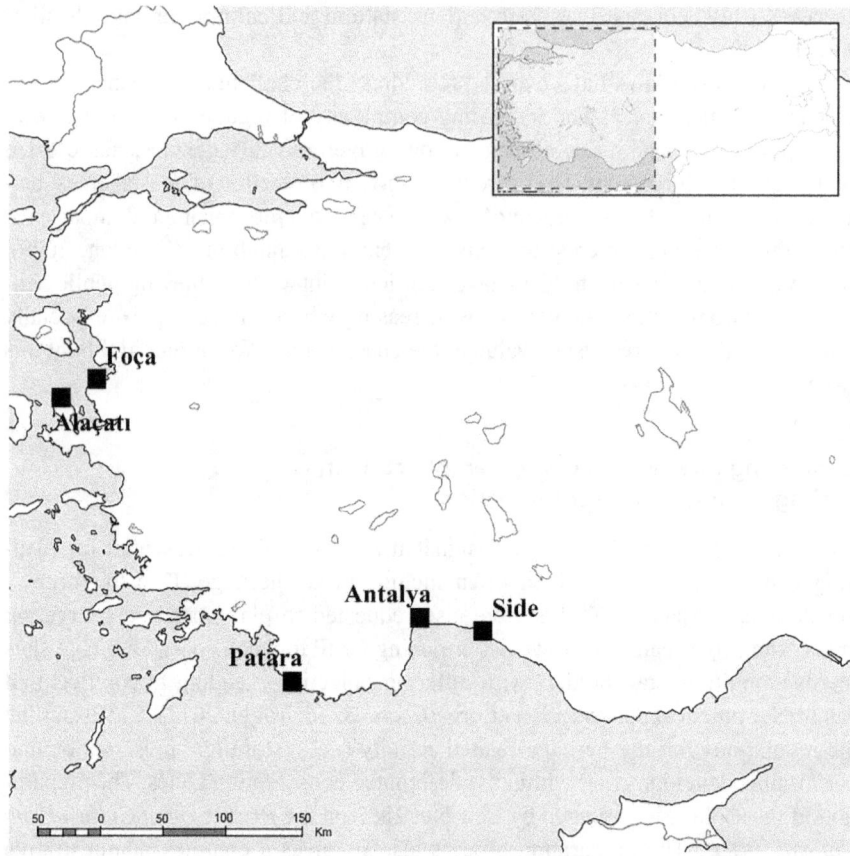

FIGURE 3.1   A map of Turkey indicating Antalya, Alaçatı, Patara, Side and Foça locations.

Source: Map by Özçakır, 2024

Mediterranean coasts because of historical dynamics that targeted economic development highlighted in this chapter. Historic sites such as Alaçatı, Patara, Side or Foça have been the focus of contestation in recent years (Figure 3.1).

Alaçatı, a coastal town renowned for its traditional stone architecture and windsurfing attractions, has been at the centre of a contentious debate over the development of a new port and related tourism infrastructure. The transformation of Alaçatı, initiated in the late 1990s and early 2000s, was part of the *Çeşme Tourism Development Region* and aimed to turn the hitherto agricultural town into a high-value tourism destination. The project focused on boutique tourism, leveraging Alaçatı's historic architecture, windsurfing potential and natural landscapes. The proposed initiative, spearheaded by developers looking to enhance the town's tourism offerings, features a marina and upscale accommodations. Key stakeholders comprise local entrepreneurs aiming to establish boutique hotels, the local government promoting investment, NGOs championing conservation and residents frequently sidelining in decision-making. Both national and international investors have been crucial in financing and developing the area's tourism prospects. Nonetheless, this venture has encountered considerable backlash from heritage conservationists and sectors of the local community who contend that the project jeopardises the integrity of historical sites and presents serious environmental threats to the coastal ecosystem. By the late 2000s, Alaçatı had become a boutique tourism hub. However, the development increased property values, gentrification and social inequalities, with many locals displaced or excluded from economic benefits. While the project boosted the area's economy and international recognition, it highlighted tensions between cultural preservation, tourism development and local community interests (Gürkan, 2008).

Another example of conflict surrounding the conservation of coastal areas is Patara, situated in Antalya on the Mediterranean coast. Patara serves as a critical nesting site for endangered loggerhead sea turtles and a location of archaeological remains from the Lycian civilisation. As an Archaeological Site, a Natural Heritage Site and a Special Environmental Protection Area, Patara is protected under multiple designations. However, the area has faced significant challenges due to controversial master plans that foresaw new constructions. When the Ministry of Environment, Urbanism, and Climate proposed a master plan change for the Special Environmental Protection Area, different NGOs and professional organisations (including the Chamber of Architects and Chapter of Landscape Architects) filed a court case for an injunction to stop the execution of the decision as the master plan enabled the construction of new villas and tourist accommodations (Doğan, 2019). The contestations surrounding this master plan change are noteworthy for this volume's scope. Reports in national newspapers have highlighted how such projects threaten the fragile ecosystem and ancient ruins, with prominent archaeologists pointing to irreparable damage to the Nekropolis and surrounding archaeological areas (Acar, 2023). Environmental advocates emphasised the need to protect the fragile ecosystem, while archaeologists underscored the importance of preserving the ancient ruins. In contrast, developers and specific local business interests support tourism expansion to stimulate economic growth in the region. This debate highlights the complex intersection of environmental conservation, heritage preservation and economic development in the coastal areas (Çınar, 2024).

The transformation of Side's Ancient Harbour (Antalya) into a modern yacht marina also presents a complex case study in the ongoing tension between heritage preservation and economic development. Historically recognised for its archaeological significance, Side's harbour has long been a site with multiple heritage values, from historical to architectural and technical. In 1969, a master plan was introduced proposing to preserve the harbour as a traditional fisherman's port. However, recent governmental bodies have shifted focus towards expanding the harbour into a yacht marina to accommodate the rising demand for tourism. This proposal has raised significant concerns among preservationists and environmentalists who argue that the expansion threatens the site's archaeological integrity and the surrounding ecosystem. They contend that converting the ancient harbour into a large-capacity marina would diminish Side's historical significance, as increased tourist activity and yacht traffic risk causing irreparable damage to the ancient structures and marine environment (Çubuk, 2013).

Foça Club Méditerranée (Club Med), established in 1966, is one of Turkey's earliest examples of international tourism development. The resort's development, in partnership with the Turkish government, highlighted the strategic role of tourism in strengthening the national economy during the 1960s. The land for the resort was acquired through the privatisation of public lands, with involvement from the Turkish Pension Fund (Emekli Sandığı) and donations of municipal land. While Foça Club Med was anticipated to bring economic benefits and employment opportunities to the local community, it also symbolised the broader shift towards privatisation in Turkey's tourism sector, with foreign investment playing a critical role in developing the country's tourism infrastructure. A significant aspect of Foça Club Med is its location within a protected area. The resort lies within a 2nd Degree Natural Conservation Site and partly within a 1st Degree Archaeological Site. Under the law, 1st Degree Archaeological Sites permit no interventions other than preservation, while 2nd Degree Archaeological Sites allow interventions subject to the approval of a conservation board. In contrast, 3rd Degree Archaeological Sites permit new constructions, provided prior studies and permissions are completed. A similar classification applies to Natural Conservation Sites: 1st Degree sites prohibit any intervention, 2nd Degree sites allow limited use with official permission and 3rd Degree sites permit new constructions with the necessary approvals. Over time, the Foça Club Méditerranée site was also registered as a cultural property, further complicating its conservation status. Despite its success, the resort was abandoned in 2005, leading to significant deterioration. Since its closure, the complex has suffered from physical decay, with buildings and the surrounding landscape falling into disrepair. Overgrown vegetation, structural damage and illegal dumping have further contributed to its decline (Saf, 2019). In 2021, the rights to operate Foça Club Med were privatised again, with the site transferred to a private enterprise for 49 years under Turkey's 'restore–operate–transfer' model (İlhan & Tanrıvermiş, 2023). Currently, there are plans to reuse the area for touristic purposes.

The conflicts observed in coastal heritage sites such as Alaçatı, Patara, Side and Foça, where economic development projects often clash with environmental and cultural conservation efforts, highlight key stakeholders' lack of coordination and exclusion. These situations frequently result in opposition and inter-agency conflicts, exemplifying the tension between heritage preservation and economic growth. This challenge is further intensified by the historical and environmental significance of Turkey's southern Mediterranean coast, and this ongoing conflict is examined in greater detail through the case of Antalya in the next chapter.

Antalya Yacht Harbour as an urban heritage landscape

Antalya Yacht Harbour (also known as Kaleiçi, meaning 'inner citadel' – Yacht Harbour), located in the historic core of Antalya, represents a crucial component of the city's architectural and urban heritage. Situated along the Mediterranean coastline and adjacent to significant urban elements and memory places from various historical layers, covering the Roman era to the Ottoman and Republican periods (Anon, 2003), the harbour area has undergone dynamic transformations shaped by economic, political and social factors.

The Roman city of Attaleia (modern-day Antalya) was strategically located to support economic and military expansion into the Eastern Mediterranean due to its suitability for maritime trade and defence. Complementing these advantages, the natural topography of the harbour, characterised by limestone and travertine cliffs, played a role in ensuring its functional continuity. Although the area's steep elevation and limited accessibility posed challenges, its strategic position enabled sustained habitation and economic activity (Büyükyıldırım, 2017, cited in Uyar, 2018). Throughout the Byzantine era, Antalya maintained its role as an important naval base and customs centre, facilitating economic exchanges with other Mediterranean towns. The strengthening of defensive infrastructure during this time highlights the harbour's geopolitical significance, especially as a reaction to growing maritime threats. The Seljuk conquest in the 11th century increased Antalya's commercial importance, linking the port to vast trade networks that joined Europe and Anatolia with Africa and the Middle East. Urban development initiatives, including constructing caravanserais, fostered economic growth and regional connectivity (Kurt, 2010).

The architectural transformation of the harbour reflects the successive layers of cultural influence that have shaped Antalya's urban morphology. Roman-period grid planning remains discernible within the contemporary urban fabric, while Seljuk fortifications and Ottoman commercial structures illustrate the city's adaptation to shifting economic and political contexts (Süer, 2006; Argın, 2012). By the 19th century, travellers documented the spatial organisation of the harbour, emphasising its role as a focal point of trade and administrative activity (Değerli, 2022). The Ottoman period marked a significant phase in Kaleiçi's architectural and spatial transformation, integrating traditional Anatolian residential typologies with functions tied to maritime trade. The urban fabric of this period is characterised by timber-framed dwellings with projecting upper stories and enclosed courtyards. At the same time, Ottoman-era hans, mosques and caravanserais near the harbour played a crucial role in sustaining its economic and sociocultural continuity (Figure 3.2). As can be noted from this figure, the photograph captures a view of Antalya's old harbour from an elevated perspective, showcasing its original morphological features and the area's low-density use. This was before significant redevelopment efforts began in the 1970s. The harbour, with its small wooden fishing boats and traditional coastal structures, reflects the town's pre-tourism economy. The

FIGURE 3.2 Aerial View of the old harbour before the transformation in the mid-20th century.

surrounding landscape is characterised by modest dwellings and unaltered natural cliffs, highlighting the intimate scale of the settlement before state-led tourism initiatives reshaped the urban fabric (Madran, 2001).

By the 20th century, the harbour underwent significant changes as its role shifted from a commercial hub to a touristic and recreational space. The restoration and transformation efforts initiated in the 1970s aimed to introduce new functions to traditional dwellings, such as boutique hotels, restaurants and cultural venues, and to implement urban design projects for specific open areas in the district. While these processes have driven the tourism-oriented transformation of the harbour area and its surroundings, as the next section illustrates, stakeholder reactions have differed based on their priorities and motivations (Figure 3.3). Learning from this photograph showing a post-transformation view of Antalya's old harbour, one

FIGURE 3.3 View of the old harbour above after the area's transformation during the 1980s.

notes the significant changes brought about by redevelopment efforts during the 1980s. The densification of the urban fabric, with high-rise buildings dominated the skyline, and intensified use of the marina expanded to accommodate many boats. The contrast with earlier periods reflects the shift from a modest fishing harbour to a bustling tourism and leisure hub, aligning with broader state-led initiatives to position Antalya as a key Mediterranean tourism destination. The waterfront's physical restructuring and the addition of new infrastructure showcase the long-term impact of conservation and tourism-driven urban planning on historic coastal areas (Saim n.d).

Transformation of Antalya Yacht Harbour for tourism-led development since the 1970s

Antalya was strategically targeted to generate a tourism-oriented development strategy within the context of instrumentalising tourism as a means of economic development. Although Antalya was a small tourist attraction centre even during the 1950s, in line with the national economic development programmes mentioned earlier, the first steps of a World Bank-supported project were taken during the 1970s. As elaborated later, these first steps would have decades-long repercussions that reach today.

The South Antalya Tourism Development Project, backed by a US$46.2 million loan from the World Bank in 1976, was carried out by the Tourism Bank – a state bank under the Ministry of Tourism created to support local administrations' tourism investments. The project transformed an 80-km stretch of coastline with a depth of 3 km into a significant destination for international tourists. The project included increasing the bed capacity of the region, creating specific cleaning plans, constructing new marinas and investing in infrastructure such as roads, airlines, hotels, holiday villages and other tourism-related facilities. This development highlighted how international financial support was closely tied to Turkey's broader Cold War strategies (Luke & Leeson, 2022).

The South Antalya Tourism Development Project also transformed the old Hacht Harbour and the inner castle area. In 1973, the High Council designated the area as a *sit* (protected site), annulled any existing master plans and required the preparation of a Conservation Master Plan (CMP). The CMP for Antalya was assigned to the Middle East Technical University. Moreover, the CMP for Antalya was assigned to the Middle East Technical University; however, its final approval by the High Council was not granted until 1979. Meanwhile, already in 1973, following the *sit* designation decision, a formal agreement was established between the Ministry of Culture and Tourism, the Antalya Municipality, the Ministry of Development and Housing, and the High Council. The deal concerned the transformation of the old harbour together with its close surroundings of the harbour, excluding the inner castle area. This first phase foresaw expropriation of 39 buildings from small shops (24 m²) to large industrial complexes (1,200 m²) (Uyar, 2018: 73). The main objective was to construct a marina complex in the old commercial harbour while transforming its surroundings into a tourism and recreation area, including restoring larger houses along the town walls for tourist accommodations (Alpin, 2014: 142–4). Once expropriation was completed, the Ministry of Culture became the area's official owner, with the Bank of Tourism taking responsibility for its management (Anon 1984a). The project was also showcased in Amsterdam in 1975 as part of the European Architectural Heritage Year campaign (Özgönül, 2017).

In 1979, new regulations were introduced for the conservation site, establishing a revised approach that treated the Walled Town and the old harbour area as distinct entities. Under this framework, the planning authority for the inner castle was assigned to the municipality. In contrast, the Ministry of Tourism and Promotion was responsible for planning the old harbour area. It was planned that the inhabitants of the inner castle would restore their own houses, following the successful examples implemented in the expropriated houses surrounding the harbour (Alpan, 2014: 142).

The old town consisted of four districts, and as of 1975, it had 4,300 people living in 974 low-rise, one- or two-story dwellings (Alpin, 2014: 149–150). Following the conservation decisions, wealthier residents were the first to leave, as the dwellings no longer met modern living standards, and conservation restrictions prevented architectural modifications. Consequently, the primary inhabitants became low- and middle-income citizens with limited resources to maintain their buildings. Additionally, the Romani community was among these residents, introducing ethnic dynamics to the site's management. Over time, a new group of buyers emerged, acquiring these deteriorated houses, which gradually led to the displacement of Romani residents as well. As the inhabitants moved out, many of the buildings quickly deteriorated, and most became ruins quickly (Alpan, 2014: 150–157). The Mayor of the Antalya Municipality also acknowledged this problem as a 'blockage/obstacle' for the inner castle. He argued that the *sit* designation needed to be revisited to solve this blockage since 633 dwellings had various problems due to the limitations imposed by the *sit*. In addition, the CMP failed to answer these problems (Anon, 1984b). Furthermore, with the delays in installing underground infrastructure, the project's completion continued until the late 1980s. Meanwhile, the old harbour was eventually restored and equipped with new tourist facilities. The harbour becomes a tourist attraction. By 1987, German, English, French, Australian, Swedish and Greek yachts frequented the harbour (Anon, 1987). The goal of boosting tourism was achieved; however, strict conservation regulations worsened locals' living conditions. Moreover, as Emre Madran (2001) argues, these efforts led to the homogenisation of historic architecture, diminishing the unique identities of towns like Antalya.

Within the sociopolitical context of Turkey, the transformation of Antalya also triggered intense debates about the use of coastal zones and the touristic development of historic cities. Much of the discussion focused on opposing the privatisation of coastal areas, advocating for their preservation for public use. During the 1976 conference, The Use of Coasts for Public Benefit, co-hosted by the Antalya Municipality and the local Chamber of Architects, concerns were raised about how capitalist structures not only exploited labour but also led to unchecked and speculative urbanisation of coastal areas (Anon, 1976). Renowned planning professor İlhan Tekeli emphasised that coastal areas presented conflicting interests among stakeholders, forcing planning professionals to make politically and ideologically charged decisions favouring some groups. Tekeli also criticised how the Tourism Bank and the Ministry of Tourism framed tourism as a public good, arguing that this notion primarily served the interests of specific social classes. He called for a more precise definition of 'public benefit', a sentiment echoed by other speakers, who also pointed out the term's inherent ambiguity and subjective interpretation (Tekeli, 1976). The use of Turkish coasts is still an ongoing debate, evolving around different stakeholder interests.

In line with these discussions, a new Coastal Law was enacted in 1984, but the Constitutional Court overturned it in 1987, permitting unrestricted construction along coastal strips without clearly defining the public benefit of such use. During the three-year gap, legal uncertainties arose under the management of the Ministry of Development. A revised law was introduced in 1990, allowing private investments in coastal zones while specifying permissible constructions (Uysal, 1991). In the 2000s, further legal amendments permitted private investments and authorised construction of infrastructures such as airports, railways and train stations in coastal areas. Further constitutional changes in 2007 facilitated investments by enabling the privatisation of coastal zones. By the 2010s, this expansionist approach extended to 1st Degree Natural Conservation Areas designated for biodiversity preservation, with scientific research being the only permitted intervention.

Conclusion: heritage for a sustainable development

The contemporary discourse on tourism development underscores the necessity of a holistic approach (see Bigambo, this volume) that establishes common ground between the conservation of cultural heritage and economic growth for sustainable development (Creaco & Querini, 2003; Landorf, 2009; Coccossis, 2016; Rössler, 2023; Zhao et al., 2023). Coastal settlements, including harbours, confront mounting pressures from climate change and tourism-related challenges, necessitating policies that integrate local priorities with global sustainability objectives. Addressing these concerns is essential for the long-term resilience of historic coastal towns and for safeguarding their cultural heritage (Rowberry, 2022; Nocca, 2017; Dangi & Jamal, 2016).

To balance tourism expansion and conservation presents significant challenges for harbours as urban heritage landscapes. Managing urban growth and increasing visitor numbers while mitigating environmental and cultural degradation demands adaptive strategies. Sustainable infrastructure development and public awareness campaigns promoting responsible tourism practices may be proposed as important steps in this direction (Brooks et al., 2023). Cultural heritage risks being commodified without effective management frameworks, diminishing its intrinsic social and cultural values (Smith et al., 2023). However, urban heritage management is often fraught with tensions stemming from the competing interests of diverse stakeholders across multiple sectors.

The conflicts within urban heritage management are mainly associated with the diverse interests of various stakeholders from different sectors. However, as in the case of Antalya in the Turkish Mediterranean, costs demonstrate that these conflicts have a historical and sociopolitical context linked to national and international power dynamics. This complexity is rooted in the Cold War period, in which the US-induced notion of development required a planned control of entire landscapes and historic urban areas. The case of Antalya occupies a significant place in this narrative in Turkey because it illustrates how urban heritage became a battleground for conflicting interests, with the development of tourism as the primary economic strategy. While the preservation of historic sites was a key component of this strategy, it often clashed with the needs and realities of residents. These tensions highlight the challenge of balancing heritage conservation with modernisation in a rapidly changing sociopolitical environment. Like Antalya, also in other Turkish sites, expropriation and privatisation have become the main tools for implementing development. These tools accelerate the transformation process but exacerbate existing conflicts among different stakeholders.

The push for development in Turkey, primarily influenced by Western-led models during the Cold War, prioritised economic growth at the expense of more nuanced, community-oriented approaches to urban conservation. Though intended to preserve history, the designation of sites and the imposition of rigid conservation laws frequently led to the deterioration of living conditions and the homogenisation of historic architecture. As seen in Antalya, these conservation efforts were often more aligned with capitalist interests than with the well-being of local communities.

The ongoing contestation between heritage preservation and economic development reflects deeper historical and geopolitical forces. The legacy of Cold War-era development strategies continues to shape how urban heritage is managed in Turkey today. The need for a more integrated approach that values heritage and development as inseparable components of sustainable growth is recognised at the policy-making level, even though the mythos of development still prevails, overshadowing a mind shift to frame heritage as an integral component of sustainable development.

Acknowledgements

We thank the Editor for their comments, which provided insightful modifications in the chapter's development phase. We also thank Hamed Arnaut for sharing his research when the idea of investigating Antalya first emerged.

References

Acar, C. (2023). Patara'da arazi satışı: ÖÇKB de tanınmadı caretta carettalar da. *yeşil gazete,* 20 November. https://yesilgazete.org/patarada-arazi-satisi-ockb-de-taninmadi-caretta-carettalar-da/.

Adalet, B. (2018). *Hotels and Highways: The Construction of Modernization Theory in Cold War Turkey.* Stanford University Press.

Alpan, A. (2014). *Urban Restructuring Process of Antalya Walled-Town and The Roles of Stakeholders.* PhD Thesis, Middle East Technical University.

Altınyıldız, N. (1997). *Tarihsel Çevreyi Korumanın Türkiye'ye Özgü Koşulları (İstanbul 1923–1973).* PhD Thesis, Istanbul Technical University.

Anon. (1963). Kalkinma Plâni (Birinci Beş Yil) 1963–1967. *Ankara: T. C. Başbakanlik Devlet Plânlama Teşkilâti.* https://www.sbb.gov.tr/wp-content/uploads/2022/07/Kalkinma_Plani_Birinci_Bes_Yillik_1963–1967.pdf.

Anon. (1968). İkinci Beş Yillik Kalkinma Plani 1968–1972. *Ankara: T. C. Başbakanlik Devlet Plânlama Teşkilâti.* https://www.sbb.gov.tr/wp-content/uploads/2022/07/Kalkinma_Plani_Birinci_Bes_Yillik_1963–1967.pdf.

Anon. (1976). Kıyılar Halk Yararına Kullanılmalıdır. *Mimarlık* 147: 33–40.

Anon. (1984a). Tek Yapıdan Çevre Korumasına. *Mimarlık* 201: 3–4.

Anon. (1984b). Antalya Kaleici Ele Aliniyor, *Cumhuriyet Gazetesi.* 17 July

Anon. (1987). Yat limaninda hareket. *Cumhuriyet Gazetesi.* 23 June.

Anon. (2003). Antalya Kültür Envanteri. https://antalya.ktb.gov.tr/TR-293913/antalya-kultur-envanteri.html.

Argin, G. (2012). *Changing Sense of Place in Historic City Centers: The Case of Antalya, Kaleiçi*. Master's Thesis, Middle East Technical University.

Bandarin, F., & van Oers R. (2012). *The Historic Urban Landscape: Managing Heritage in an Urban Century*. Wiley Blackwell.

Bozdoğan, S., Panayiota, P., & Phokaides, P. eds. (2022). *Coastal Architectures and Politics of Tourism: Leisurescapes in the Global Sunbelt*. Routledge. https://doi.org/10.4324/9781003240716.

Brooks, C., Waterton, E., Saul, H., & Renzaho, A. (2023). Exploring the relationships between heritage tourism, sustainable community development and host communities' health and wellbeing: A systematic review. *PLoS One* 18(3).

Büyükyıldırım, G. (2017). 20. *Yüzyılda Su İşleri ve Antalya*. Devlet Su İşleri.

Çalışkan, U. (2021). Critical review of the tourism planning history of Turkey. In *Tourism in Turkey*. Apple Academic Press.

Choay, F. (2001). *The Invention of the Historic Monument*. Cambridge University Press.

Çınar, M. (2024). Patara'da imar planı iptal edilsin' çağrısı. *DHA Demirören Haber Ajansı*, 15 March. https://www.dha.com.tr/gundem/patarada-imar-plani-iptal-edilsin-cagrisi-2404687.

Coccossis, H. (2016). Sustainable development and tourism: Opportunities and threats to cultural heritage from tourism. In *Cultural Tourism and Sustainable Local Development* (pp. 65–74). Routledge.

Creaco, S., & Querini, G. (2003). The role of tourism in sustainable economic development, 43rd Congress of the European Regional Science Association: "Peripheries, Centres, and Spatial Development in the New Europe", 27th–30th August 2003, Jyväskylä, Finland, European Regional Science Association (ERSA), Louvain-la-Neuve.

Çubuk, M. (2013). Turizmin Rehin Aldığı Antik Kent ve Side Antik Limanının Yat Limanına Dönüşümü Üzerine. *Journal of Planning* 23(1): 6–11.

Dangi, T. B., & Jamal, T. (2016). An integrated approach to "sustainable community-based tourism". *Sustainability* 8(5): 475.

Değerli, A. (2022). Seyahatnamelerin İzinde On Dokuzuncu Yüzyıl Antalyası. In Taşbaş, E. (ed.), *Antalya'nın Sosyal ve İktisadi Tarihi (Osmanlı Dönemi)*. Gazi Kitapevi.

Dinler, M. (2021). Scale matters: Political dynamics of urban conservation. In Ess, J., Froschauer, E. M., Richter, E., and Schulte, C. J. (eds.), *Werte Wandel* (pp. 135–46). De Gruyter.

Dinler, M. (2022). A political framework for understanding heritage dynamics in turkey (1950–1980). *Urban History* 49(2): 364–82.

Doğan, R. (2019). Kaş'ın Patara ve Fırnaz Koyu'nu yapılaşmaya açan karara yargıdan fren. *Artı Gerçek*, 6 December.

Eceral, T. Ö., & Afra, T. (2017). Doğal ve tarihi/arkeolojik değerlere sahip kentsel kıyı yerleşimlerinin planlama sorunu: Foça örneği. *Meltem İzmir Akdeniz Akademisi Dergisi* 2: 68–84.

Erdim, B. (2020). *Landed Internationals: Planning Cultures, the Academy, and the Making of the Modern Middle East*. University of Texas Press.

Escobar, A. (1995). *Encountering Development: The Making and Unmaking of the Third World*. Princeton University Press.

European Commission. (2022a). *Strengthening Cultural Heritage Resilience for Climate Change: Where the European Green Deal Meets Cultural Heritage*. Publications Office. https://data.europa.eu/doi/10.2766/44688.

European Commission. (2022b). Report from the Commission to the European Parliament, the Council, the European Economic and Social Committee and the Committee of the Regions on the Cultural Dimension of Sustainable Development in EU Actions. https://eur-lex.europa.eu/legal-content/EN/TXT/?uri=COM:2022:709:FIN.

Ferudun, A. (2009). Kıyı Alanlarının Hukuki Statüsü. *Journal of Naval Sciences and Engineering* 5(1): 76–93.

Giovannoni, G., Semes, S., Siravo, F., & Cody J. W. (2024). *New Building in Old Cities: Writings by Gustavo Giovannoni on Architectural and Urban Conservation*. Getty Conservation Institute.

Glendinning, M. (2013). *The Conservation Movement: A History of Architectural Preservation: Antiquity to Modernity*. Routledge.

Goldsmith, E. (2002). Development as colonialism. *World Affairs: The Journal of International Issues* 6(2): 18–36.

Gürkan, İ. (2008). *Tourism as an Agent of Change, Lzmir-Alaçatı Case in Turkey.* M.S.– Master of Science Thesis, Middle East Technical University.

İlhan, A. T., & Tanrıvermiş, Y. (2023). Koruma Alanlarında Özelleştirme Yaklaşımı ve Uygulamaları. *Eurasian Business & Economics Journal* (34): 61–74.

Iplikci, M., & Aykaç, G. (2024). The establishment process of Türk Traktör between 1948 and 1963: A Critique of "modernization" as development in early cold war Turkey. *Planning Perspectives* 39(4): 853–80.

Keyder, Ç. (1987). *State and Class in Turkey: A Study in Capitalist Development*. Verso.

Kurt, Ö. (2010). *Kaleiçi'nin (Antalya) Kuruluşundan 16. Yüzyıla Kadar Mekânsal Değişimi*, Master Thesis, Istanbul University.

Labadi, S. (2022). *Rethinking Heritage for Sustainable Development*. UCL Press. https://doi.org/10.14324/111.9781800081925.

Landorf, C. (2009). Managing for sustainable tourism: A review of six cultural world heritage sites. *Journal of Sustainable Tourism* 17(1): 53–70.

Luke, C., & Leeson, M. (2022). UNESCO-UNDP tourism and security in cold war Turkey and Iran. *Journal of Heritage Tourism* 17 (6): 669–84.

Madran, E. (2001). Koruma İmar Planlari ve Antalya Kaleiçi Örneği. *Mimarlik* 297: 32–24.

Madran, E., & Özgönül, N. (1982). Planlı Dönemde (1963–1981) Tarihsel Çevre'nin Korunması ve Degerlendirilmesinde Kamu'nun Yakalaşımı. In *Türkiye Birinci Şehircilik Kongresi*, 2. Kitap: 283–301. Ankara: ODTÜ Şehir ve Bölge Planlama Bölümü.

Meskell, L. (2018). *A Future in Ruins: UNESCO, World Heritage, and the Dream of Peace*. Oxford University Press.

Nocca, F. (2017). The role of cultural heritage in sustainable development: Multidimensional indicators as decision-making tool. *Sustainability* 9(10): 1882.

Özçakir, Ö., Altinöz G. B., & Mignosa, A. (2018). Political economy of renewal of heritage places in Turkey. *METU Journal of the Faculty of Architecture* 35(2).

Özgönül, N. (2017). The Turkish involvement in the 1975 European architectural heritage year and its impact on heritage conservation in Turkey. *Monumenta Bd* 3: 332–45.

Rössler, M. (2023). Balancing tourism and heritage conservation: A world heritage context. In Cameron, C. (ed.), *Evolving Heritage Conservation Practice in the 21st Century. Creativity, Heritage and the City*. Vol. 5. Springer.

Rowberry, R. (2022). Climate change, coastal built heritage, and critical challenges facing the heritage law frameworks of the United States, United Kingdom, and France. *Built Heritage* 6: 1.

Saf, H. O. (2019). Sürdürülebilir Tasarımdan Terk Edilmişliğe: Foça Club Méditerranée. *Mimarlık* (406): 67–73.

Said, E. (1978). *Orientalism*. New York, NY: Vintage Press.

Scott, J. C. (2020). *Seeing Like a State: How Certain Schemes to Improve the Human Condition Have Failed*. Yale University Press.

Sesli, F. A., & Akyol, N. (1999). Türkiye'de Kıyı Alanları Konusunda Geçmişten Günümüze Ulusal Mevzuat. *Harita ve Kadastro Mühendisliği* (86): 101–11.

Smith, T. F., Elrick-Barr, C. E., Thomsen, D. C., Celliers, L., & Le Tissier, M. (2023). Impacts of tourism on coastal areas. *Cambridge Prisms: Coastal Futures* 1.

Süer, A. (2006). *The Analysis of Historical/Cultural Pattern Development and Conservation Plans of Antalya Kaleiçi*. Master's Thesis, İzmir Institute of Technology.

Tekeli, İ. (1976). Kıyı Planlamasının Değişik Boyutları. *Mimarlik* 147: 41–47.

Tekeli, İ. (2009). *Cumhuriyetin Belediyecilik Öyküsü, 1923–1990*. Vol. 4. Tarih Vakfı Yurt Yayınları.

Turoğlu, H. (2009). 3621 Sayılı Kıyı Kanunu ve Onun Uygulama Problemleri. *Türk Coğrafya Dergisi* (53): 31–40.

UNESCO World Heritage Centre. (2011). Recommendation on the historic urban landscape. https://whc.unesco.org/en/hul/.

UNESCO World Heritage Centre. (2019). 'UNESCO thematic indicators for culture in the 2030 agenda for sustainable development'. https://whc.unesco.org/en/culture2030indicators/.

Unger, C. R. (2018). *International Development: A Postwar History*. Bloomsbury Academic. https://cadmus.eui.eu/handle/1814/58724.

Uyar, C. (2018). *The Sustainability of Public Spaces in the Urban Conservation Field: The Sample of Antalya Kaleici Marina*. Master's Thesis, Mimar Sinan Fine Arts University.

Uysal, Y. (1991). 'Kiyi Yasasi'nda Bakanlik "Yorumu"'. *Cumhuriyet Newspaper*, 9 June.

Zhao, L., Li, Y., Zhang, N., & Zhang, Z. (2023). Public policies and conservation plans of historic urban landscapes under the sustainable heritage tourism milieu: Discussions on the equilibrium model on Kulangsu Island, UNESCO world heritage site. *Built Heritage* 7(1): 6.

4

TRANSFORMING A PLACE THROUGH HERITAGIZATION AND CONSERVATION IN AN ICONIC COASTAL DESTINATION IN URUGUAY

Gabriel de Souza and Juan Martin Dabezies

Introduction

In recent years, the Atlantic coast of Uruguay has experienced a remarkable surge in sun-and-beach tourism, expanding from west to east. The most notable tourism growth occurred along the Rocha Department's coastal stretch, one of Uruguay's 19 political–administrative divisions. This region covers about 170 km of coastline, where largely untouched and sparsely populated areas persist. The departmental stretch shares its south-eastern border with Brazil (Figure 4.1); it is one of the last areas in the country to undergo urbanization. Colonial border disputes and the challenging terrain – poor grazing lands, dunes, and flood-prone lowlands – hindered modern development for decades. Since the late 20th century, seaside towns and villages like La Paloma, La Pedrera, Valizas, and Punta del Diablo have emerged, driven by tourism pursuit at pristine and unspoiled beaches.

The overcrowding of seaside towns like Punta del Este and Piriápolis in the Maldonado Department, which are near the Río de la Plata capitals of Montevideo and Buenos Aires (Argentinian capital), with improved access to the eastern region, has fuelled the subdivision and sale of rural coastal lands in Rocha. Although infrastructure and services have developed gradually, the tourism image of Rocha's coast has remained rooted in its natural beauty and slower pace of growth, setting it apart from the busier seaside towns in the Maldonado Department. This unique positioning has been key in promoting the Uruguay natural brand, a government initiative designed to elevate the country's green image.

DOI: 10.4324/9781003623724-4

FIGURE 4.1   The Uruguayan coast highlights the main seaside tourist towns of the Rocha Department and Cabo Polonio, which are about Montevideo and Buenos Aires.

Source: Author: Leticia Georgalis

The acceleration of tourism modernization along the coast has, however, generated multiple tensions, summarized in the statements of then President José Mujica in a public speech in 2011:

> Some dunes along the Atlantic coast have been under the Ministry of Agriculture and Livestock for years, and that land is useless for farming or livestock. For lazing around in the summer. It's a beautiful Atlantic coast that we need to auction off in pieces. It's worth a lot, tourists will build houses, and the local poor will tend their gardens and take care of their homes. . . . We talked about selling it, and suddenly an environmental movement appears [laughter from the audience], an environmental movement that says: How can you privatise this?'

And of course, we're going to privatise it so that those with money pay, pay, and pay, and with that money, we'll buy land for settlers [applause].

(Telemundo 12, President José Mujica's public presentation in 2011. Retrieved in December 2023 from https://www.youtube.com/watch?v=JRl7V3XusNs)

Simultaneously, the Rocha coastal region has become a central focus of public policies aimed at nature conservation, leading to the establishment of numerous protected areas (PAs). In Uruguay, these protected areas are integrated into the National System of Protected Areas (SNAPs) established in 2000 (Law 17.234) and formally regulated in 2005 (Decree No. 52/005). As Latin America's youngest natural heritage system, SNAP comprises 17 protected areas, four of which are in the Rocha Department, collectively covering less than 1 percent of the national territory. According to the Uruguayan government, SNAP is "a tool that harmonises environmental protection, particularly biodiversity conservation, with the country's economic and social development."

The tension between Mujica's remarks and the conservation policies underscores the divergent approaches to one of the most contentious and debated protected areas: Cabo Polonio. Tourism is the primary socioeconomic activity in this area. Since its inclusion in SNAP, Cabo Polonio has received the most significant public investments in infrastructure, tourism facilities, and human resource development (MVOTMA, 2009, 2019).

Several geophysical characteristics have greatly enhanced Cabo Polonio's appeal. Situated on a rocky peninsula that juts into the Atlantic Ocean, it forms a protected bay highly prized for sun-and-beach activities. For years, it has served as the iconic representation of the Uruguay Natural brand, thanks to attributes that reflect its wild, untamed character and a sure promise of quality of life. However, the area is designated as a National Park, one of the most restrictive categories regarding human activity. The fiscal lands were transferred from the Ministry of Livestock, Agriculture, and Fisheries to the Ministry of Environment to enforce public conservation policies. This classification is based on recognizing Cabo Polonio as the most authentic remnant of the original Atlantic ecosystem, preserving fragile and exceptional ecosystems. To sustain this natural authenticity, the Ministry of Environment highlights the uniqueness of its dune system and emphasizes significant heterogeneity of environmental units across its territory (MVOTMA, 2009).

The National Decree 337/009, establishing the area's inclusion in the SNAP and the Management Plan, is a key reference that outlines the permitted and prohibited tourist uses within the protected area (MVOTMA, 2019). These documents reflect a radical change in how tourists, whether day trippers or vacationers, are conceived and treated. The thousands of visitors who enter year after year during the summer, once seen as a sign of economic growth, job creation, and foreign exchange generation, are now considered a threat to the area's environmental conservation values. A review of press news could give us an overview of the social productivity of the conflicts (Merlinsky, 2013) that have unfolded there and the assumption of these tensions as a public problem with various repercussions. Cabo Polonio's unique characteristics allow for exploring the contradictions inherent in local and international conservation and development agendas, which debate the values and criteria of what should be protected and sustained in this seaside village.

Research and data contexts

To analyze the tensions between tourism development and conservation policies, this chapter adopts the perspective of frame analysis (Goffman, 2006) as models or orientations that guide actions, delimit collective experience, and shape the ways of conceiving and producing a National Park or a seaside village as a tourist destination. The frameworks allow individuals to interpret or "locate, perceive, identify, and label" what is "happening here" (Goffman, 2006: 21) within living spaces, giving meaning and guiding action. Sometimes, the reference framework is explicitly and articulated through postulates and rules. Other times implicitly and disorganized through latent structures, these systems allow us to interpret and label events within their terms, even when users are unaware of them "nor able to describe them in detail if asked about them, but that does not prevent them from easily applying them in their entirety" (Goffman, 2006: 23).

From this perspective, frameworks are not merely shared interpretation schemes, affinities, and attachments between individuals based on their interaction and transmission in specific contexts. They also represent the outcomes of negotiations that shape and structure social interaction. They provide habitual and available ways to understand and anticipate how to position ourselves about exploiting, producing, and conserving protected areas intertwined with sun-and-beach touristic practices and configurations. These divergent frames or reference frameworks imply the problematic coexistence of principles guiding practices and discourses that generate opposing ordinary senses, establishing coordinates or references that provide value orientations for specific audiences. In our case, on the one hand, they orient the growth model of sun-and-beach tourism, and on the other hand, they guide the conservation of the National Park as an ecotourism destination.

To understand these different perspectives, we conducted ethnographic fieldwork consisting of 3–7 days in Cabo Polonio every 3–4 months over three years. Between 2020 and 2023, we interviewed 80 people (32 women and 48 men) with a wide range of profiles: residents, entrepreneurs, and providers of various tourist services, political and technical government teams, representatives of NGOs, and various visitors. During the research, the interviewees were selected based on their involvement, knowledge, and positions of reference and representation for the other actors in Cabo Polonio. In several cases, the interviews led to participant observation, particularly focused on spaces where social actors negotiate, dialogue, and influence (or not) the management of the protected area and their daily spaces and ways of living there. One of us participated in the Specific Advisory Commission (CAE), a consultation forum for public institutions and private actors, residents, property owners, and organizations. This space is led by the institutions that manage the protected area – the Ministry of Environment (MA) and the Municipality of Rocha (IR) – and is tasked with advising, promoting, monitoring, and controlling the protected areas. CAE acts as a participation forum for local communities in the area's management, as Decree 52/2005 stipulates for implementing Law 17.234.

To understand the framework of environmental conservation policies, we structured our inquiry around the following questions: What are the different actors' assessments of Cabo Polonio's inclusion in the SNAP? Which issues and values are being protected, and which are not, depending on the perspective? How have conservation policies generated benefits or harms for the actors involved? On the other hand, to understand references regarding tourism development, we posed the following questions: What are the tourism values in Cabo Polonio? What elements constitute its main tourism differentiators? What are the links between the different values and conservation? Why is tourism in the protected area a source of tension and conflict?

The answers to these questions revealed trajectories that envision the future differently. However, they overlap in defining the meaning of Cabo Polonio, how to protect it, exploit it for tourism, and the transformations that will shape its future. To address these contradictions and the intersections between conservation and tourism, we grouped the orientations guiding the ways of conceiving, treating, and inhabiting the place into two significant frames. On one side, the sun-and-beach tourist destination (the seaside village), and on the other, the protected natural area, to understand the disputes between the administration of the protected area and its residents, regular visitors, and property owners.

Seaside village as a valuation framework

For thousands of years, fishing and hunting sea lions were the primary activities in the area now known as Cabo Polonio (Villamarzo, 2018). During the colonial period (16th–19centuries), seasonal sea lion harvesting, known as "zafra," was the dominant activity. In the 1920s, some sea lion hunters built huts in the area, and the settlement gradually expanded, giving shape to the village (Chouhy, 2013, 2008). From the second half of the 20th century onward, new visitors and seasonal residents from urban areas began to arrive in Cabo Polonio to spend their vacations. The 1954 Tourism Guide was one of the first publications to highlight the area's unique features for tourism:

> the most spectacular point along the Uruguayan coast of the South Atlantic. On the numerous islets, one can often see sea lions, and . . . it can only be visited on horseback or by jeep through spectacular dunes, making it an unforgettable excursion.
>
> (Da Cunha et al., 2012: 203)

From a historical perspective, we address the emerging tourism image of Rocha during these early stages, where representations of the area began to focus on the benefits of sun, beach, sea baths, and vacations. The spread of these images in the main urban centers from which visitors originated spurred significant changes along Uruguay's coastline. In this context, identity representations began to differentiate the tourism image of the Maldonado coast from that of Rocha through dichotomous archetypes such as modern/traditional, connected/isolated, urbanized/untouched, fast-paced/slow, sophisticated/bohemian, and conventional/alternative. As a result, the development of Rocha's seaside villages diverged from the urban order of its neighboring department in a subversive way.

Previous research informs how, during the 1980s, people began to build huts "on extensive, unproductive dunes . . . on their initiative or outside the market value . . . in a chaotic occupation that, over time, became an attractive feature" (Da Cunha et al., 2012: 211). This "spontaneous" development of the village, without fences or boundaries, without public services such as electricity or potable water, and with limited connectivity and access, has become a valued attribute for the area's residents and visitors, giving the place a peculiar and distinctive character that persists to this day. Chouhy (2013) contends that the expansion of summer huts accelerated due to the lack of administrative controls and the improved connectivity options provided by new access routes to the area. A key milestone in these transformations was the replacement of the traditional horse-drawn carts, which used to bring in summer visitors, with 4WD vehicles capable of transporting between 20 and 40 passengers per trip in much less time, enabling other forms of connection with the place, such as day trips. Geographically, the model of territorial occupation expanded from the rocky point where the sea lions and the lighthouse are located toward the South and La Calavera beaches, in the direction of Oceanía del Polonio and Valizas, respectively (see Figures 4.2 and 4.3). The epicenter of the seaside village's social life revolves around the beach shelters, which are partially protected from the strong winds and waves of the sea. The first constructions of summer huts in the areas identified as the tombolo and dome prompted the expansion of services by permanent residents and waves of hut construction along the coastline.

During the last decades of the 20th century, recreational and tourism practices coexisted with fishing and sea lion harvesting until it was outlawed in 1992. Like in other seaside villages in the region, this led to the gradual domestication of nature by stabilizing the dunes through planting pines and acacias (Benseny, 2011: 87). Beginning in the 1990s, a tourism boom impacted land use, and in some cases, led fishing families to shift their focus to construction and tourism services progressively. According to Uruguayan national population censuses, there were 106 dwellings in the area in 1985, increasing to 178 in 1996 and 403 in 2004. Most of these homes remained unoccupied outside the tourism season. For example, in 2004, 94 percent of the total dwellings were only used during the summer. Additionally, the resident population during the winter dropped to fewer than 100 people by the end of the 20th century (MVOTMA, 2019). The proximity and coexistence

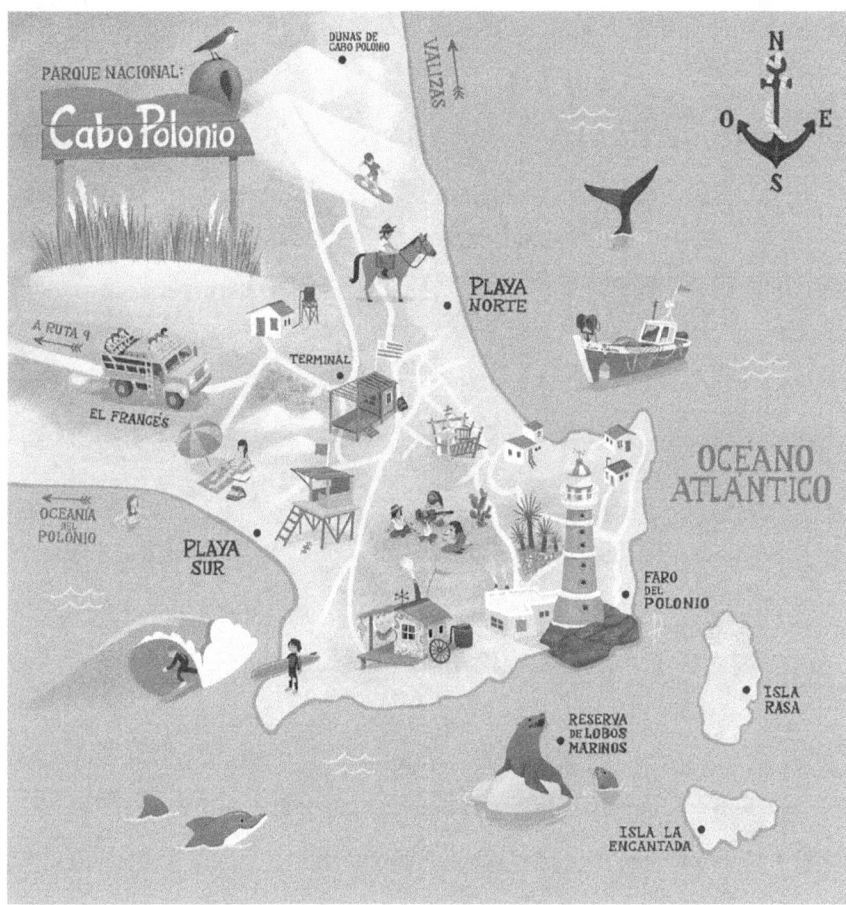

FIGURE 4.2 Representation of summer vacation imaginations in Cabo Polonio.

Source: Alfonso Rosso. Retrieved from https://alfonsorosso.com/cabo-polonio, April 2023

of fishing families, sea lion hunters, and pioneer vacationers gradually encouraged them to occupy public and private lands along the coastal strip.

The local residents we interviewed informed us how they occupied common lands in the past. They emphasized neither the livestock nor the businesspeople had interest on the land due to its low productivity. This is no longer the case today. The area has become modern with several tourism facilities around the attributes that guide the tourist valuation but with no proper planning. This irregular and informal land tenure, outside of state control, contributed to the territorial image of the tourist destination. These conditions influence ways of living together, giving the village specific characteristics of austerity, simplicity, rusticity, and precariousness. At the same time, the absence of facilities and infrastructures such as promenades, luxury

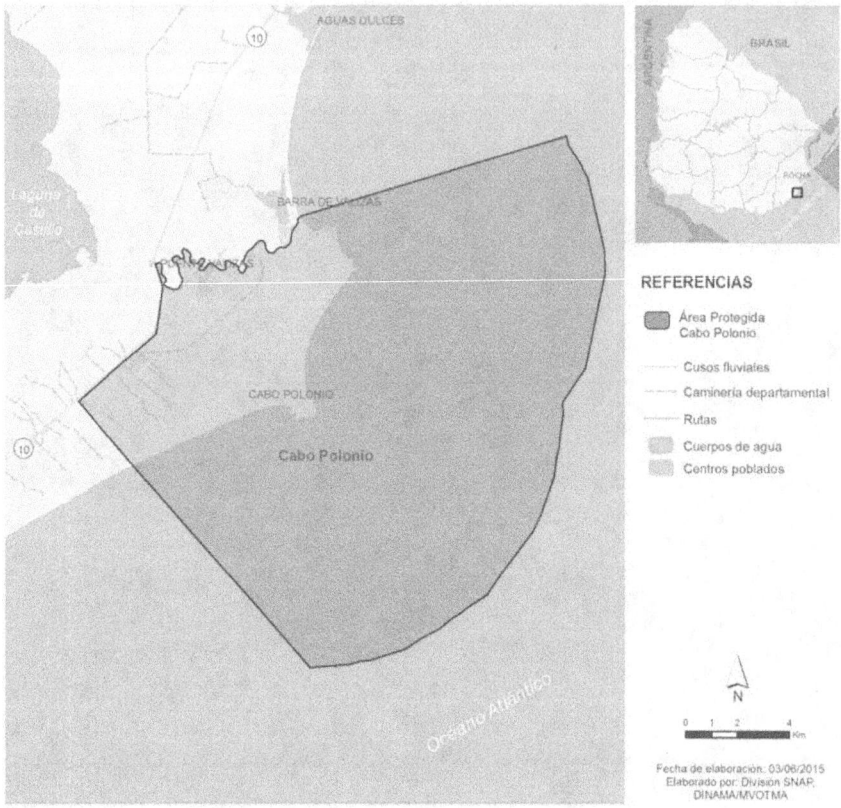

FIGURE 4.3 Location of the Cabo Polonio National Park.

Source: MVOTMA 2019: 8

hotels, casinos, swimming pools, sports facilities, and other amenities is defended by local service providers, who sometimes present Cabo Polonio as a trip back in time to a traditional village grappling with the modernization pressures of neighboring seaside towns and villages.

To this day, the village remains without electricity from state power plants as well as running water. The absence of these state services has contributed to the perception of the area as a place outside the state's influence, attracting new residents from various backgrounds. The topographical conditions also play a role in this perception, as only off-road vehicles, pedestrians, and horses can access the area. Consequently, this spatial isolation and the regulations in place impose an entry and exit schedule that reinforces the sense of remoteness from the urbanization processes that characterize Uruguay's Atlantic coast towns (Santos &Chouhy, 2018: 41). This uniqueness is widely publicized and defended by the residents and visitors, who criticize government efforts to "turn Polonio into just another link in a chain of seaside touristic villages. Why should they all be the same? We could have something different that attracts so many European tourists"[1].

The identity representations that invoke the village's past are forged in interaction with the limitations in infrastructure and services, which make Cabo Polonio a unique space–time somewhat removed from the influences of the state and modern life. The debates surrounding local resistance to electricity and public lighting services illustrate this point. A 2013 study in Cabo Polonio shows that about 85 percent of the community opposed the extension of the electrical grid to homes. Whereas 63.4 percent were against any possibility of extension, 19.5 percent supported bringing electricity only to the cold chain or the school, but not to individual homes (Machado, 2013: 26). This people's awareness of Polonio's uniqueness has improved, limiting public lighting to the light beam from the lighthouse, which flashes every 12 seconds. Moreover, discourses and actions related to the night sky's serialization (Smith, 2006) is an exceptional value that distinguishes the area from other Rocha touristic towns.

This territorial image is also supported by the geography of the area, described as an island welded to the coast due to the force of the winds and sand (Moreno, 2010), the lighthouse, stories of shipwrecks, and the presence of sea lions and fur seals. These exceptional conditions exemplify the representations that build the promise of uniqueness, promoting lifestyles perceived as traditional, slow, alternative, or isolated, in contrast to contemporary trends and modernizing services.

Distance and disconnection are key elements of tourism, sacralizing attractions by creating "a world of hope, promise, and salvation" that maintains differences from "this world" (Graburn, 1985; Urry, 2004; MacCannell, 2017). The allure is built on the representation of contrast between the village, which clings to the past, and its tension with the present. This discrepancy is often expressed as a critique of the present, commonly framed in terms of authenticity, heritage, and primitivism, or as an incredible, wonderful, mind-blowing, "out-of-this-world" experience. It is seen as a survival of earlier times that must be protected from misguided modern developments (Bissell, 2005: 228).

Tourist actors celebrate a past transformed into dune landscapes as a source of nostalgic contemplation, recreation, and pleasure. They are not concerned with potential conservation and reconstruction challenges including unplanned coastal urbanization. As Lowenthal (1985) proffers, "the past is a foreign country." It is inaccessible, provoking attraction and repulsion, much like the future. Although out of physical reach, they are part of our imaginations, "their memory and expectation cover every present moment" (Lowenthal, 1985: 27). In Cabo Polonio, returning to "that foreign country" involves, among other things, slowing down the degradation of the dune dynamics affected by the domestication practices along the Atlantic coast. These changes played a key role in accelerating the establishment of coastal seaside touristic towns. At the same time, several local inhabitants feel trapped by the representation of differences that often limit them in a maze of complex solutions. An example of this is the Machado siblings, who manage one of the first and most well-known restaurants in Cabo Polonio called "Mariemar." Located at the tip of the north beach, the place evokes much of the history of the early days of the resort. Hunged on the walls of tourism facilities are some photos of Toto Machado, one of the most beloved and respected people in the village. Our conversations with Toto's son and daughter informed us about the families' views:

> Those of us who are here didn't choose it, but we have family attachment. It's hard to leave because I work from here and earn income. From the little house and the shack here, we get some benefits. No fridge, no light, no vehicles but are happy with it. They [the migrants] already had that, which is why they settled here. Whoever has lived here is different. You don't see the beach; you don't touch the water. Living here has its qualities; I am used to the silence and solitude, and I miss it when I am away.[2]

The presentations of Cabo Polonio as a simple place, far from urban standards of comfort and consumption, where nature imposes its own pace and spatial–temporal rhythm (Santos & Chouhy, 2018: 41), reflect the limitations, motivations, and desires of residents from urban centers who seek out natural spaces that offer a connection to the past and engagement with the wild environment. These discourses and practices contribute to the area's tourist appeal by emphasizing the production of difference (Urry, 2004) as a key element that reinforces the framework of the National Park as a natural testimony to the past. Cabo Polonio is a tourist destination capable of evoking the conquest of "another time" and moving toward the past by preserving certain traditions and exceptional landscapes. At the same time, it grapples with the tension of not being left behind by the teleology of capitalist modernization, which is perceived as the only valid condition for maintaining relationships with the present.

National park as a valuation framework

The surface area of the current protected natural area, incorporated into SNAP in 2009, covers 25,820 hectares bounded by National Route No. 10 to the west; the Valizas stream to the north; the Atlantic Ocean to the east; and cadastral lot No. 1577 to the south in the 10th Cadastral Section of the Rocha Department (MVOTMA, 2019). The area's designation as a National Park implied a specific concept of nature and culture conservation strategies with numerous socio-territorial impacts. This protective designation is defined by the International Union for Conservation of Nature (IUCN) as "large areas of natural or nearly natural landscapes established to protect large-scale ecological processes, along with the complement of species and ecosystems characteristic of the area, which also provide a basis for spiritual, scientific, educational, recreational, and visitor opportunities" (Dudley, 2008: 19).

The designation process is based on an international categorization that emphasizes attention to ecosystems, aiming to protect natural biodiversity, preserve the underlying ecological structure, and maintain the environmental processes that support these ecosystems. This focus often overlooks the valuation of cultural aspects. It has led to an approach oriented towards valuing the dune system designated as a natural monument by Decree No. 266/966 of June 2, 1966 (MVOTMA, 2019: 12), and revalidated in 2009 with its inclusion in SNAP, despite human interventions that have shaped the area over decades. The analysis of technical and political documents related to the process of incorporating Cabo Polonio into SNAP (de Álava et al., 1992; MVOTMA, 2009, 2019) highlights the characteristics of Cabo Polonio that were emphasized as arguments for conservation policies and heritage valuation efforts. These include its geomorphological uniqueness, diversity of ecosystems and environments, and, to a lesser extent, its prehistoric, historical, and sociocultural heritage. The preliminary studies that led to the Management Plan describe Cabo Polonio as:

> one of the few territories in Uruguay that retains characteristics representative of the landscape before the colonisation and modern urbanisation of the Uruguayan coast. . . . Such a landscape has attributes that make it highly valuable for conservation. . . . . This Park constitutes the central area of SNAP for conserving representative samples of mobile transverse dunes.
>
> (Sprechmann & Capandeguy, 2011: 24)

This condition of being a representative environmental relic is highlighted as evidence of a remnant of a dune field that was once much more extensive (Chouhy, 2008, 2013). During the colonial occupation between the 16th and 19th centuries, the coastal zone held little economic value for livestock farming, which was the primary measure of productivity. As a backdrop to large estates, landowning families occasionally used it as a recreational spot during the summer, but without generating income (Bertoncello, 1993). From the 20th century onward, development policies began to view the geography of the Atlantic coast as a resource to colonize and exploit, with tourism being the main alternative to livestock farming.

These conquests have been driven by narratives of "dune tamers" (Noel, 2020) and their epic stories, often centered around themes such as the conquest of nature, the adventure of establishing coastal seaside tourist towns, bravery, struggle, sacrifice, and a superhuman work ethic. In these narratives, studied in Argentina in the case of the Buenos Aires coastline (Bertoncello, 1993; Noel, 2011, 2020), resistance is represented by impenetrable and unproductive dune fields, while the heroes are those who manage to immobilize and condition them for settlement and the subdivision of land for sale.

The primary strategy for domestication along the Uruguayan coast was planting vast areas of pine and acacia in the mid-20th century to control dune movement and facilitate the creation of roads, highways, more fertile soil, and valuable pastures. The incorporation of Cabo Polonio into SNAP can be interpreted as an initiative by the protected area's administrators (Ministry of Environment and the Municipality of Rocha) to break with reference frameworks of coastal seaside touristic development and coastal afforestation in Eastern Rocha. This decision did set the pace and common sense of tourism development since the 1950s. This challenge to coastal expansion is framed by a counter-current of valuing the transverse dune system in Cabo Polonio as the primary argument for conservation. In the 1990s, the government implemented actions to "restore the coast" and "contain urbanization" through a program that included the demolition of houses. Paradoxically, during the same period and despite these public actions, the number of constructions on public land and the occupation of private land doubled between 1996 and 2004. In an atmosphere of uncertainty regarding land ownership, new tensions arose between residents who either embraced or rejected Cabo Polonio's inclusion in SNAP.

The institutionalized settings altered the traditional seaside village's traditions and practices. Some installations including the park ranger corps and control posts, the interpretation center, the visitors' management post, and waste management were completely new to the area. The offering of sanitary and nursing services, environmental education courses, and the promotion of tourism trail changed the area's original look. All these interventions became detrimental to heritage despite their contribution to entrepreneurs (Becker, 2018). To mitigate the situation, a set of rules was introduced and instituted within the National Park (Smith, 2006; Dabezies, 2018). Also, the protagonists of the seaside village, with varying levels of legitimacy, because of their length of stay, land ownership status, or other attributes, felt uncomfortable due to disturbances, pressures, and tourism impacts.

As Valcuende and colleagues (2011) argue, in protected areas, the adoption of new ways of conceiving, treating, and interacting with nature is associated with the valuation and reinvention of traditions, balances, and immutability, proclaimed as new guiding thread of history and supported by heritage categories. This new teleology selects socio-environmental aspects to recover from constructing a primeval nature and a culture that can adapt with transformed environment (Valcuende et al., 2011: 50). This history generates legitimizing discourses where some become worthy of paradise, while others are accused of disturbing an original ideal situation that serves as a model. Since no "balance point" in space–time can be anchored as a reference to follow, this task becomes utopian in a changing context, such as the acceleration of capitalism. Even from a natural perspective, the coastal dynamics is a disputed issue where the legitimacy of residents and visitors in Cabo Polonio is at stake, in shaping the touristic value of the created paradise.

The tourism activities control and directives as well as the land-use planning protocols cause some tensions between the government and residents. Partly, the tensions were also caused by limiting residents from building new houses and extending their original homes. A good testimony is that of Gonzalo Nuñez, a delegate of the residents in the CAE and who regarded himself as a protagonist of the value and charm of the seaside village. He worked as a dentist in Montevideo and migrated to Cabo Polonio about 30 years ago to make music, engage in cultural production and management, and work in a bar and a store. For more than ten years, Gonzalo Nuñez run a hostel in his home. As a moral entrepreneur, going against the current of official heritage preservation, he has advocated for the place to remain isolated, without light and circulating vehicles. He was against homogenizing controls that the state championed but later changed. Narrating new construction in Cabo Polonio, during the face-to-face interview in 2021, he said those who did not want to enter [Cabo Polonio to join SNAP] were the ones owning buildings. The remaining people supported the initiative.

For other residents, the heritage designation as a national park could be a hopeful regulation to define and legitimize those who have already been successful. For example, landowners began to extend an agreement with tour operators officials mandated to care for the National Park. In other words, tourism growth was a blessing to the haves than the have-nots. For the government, creating a national park was key for environmental conservation and the well-being of socio-ecosystems. Consequently, in the 1990s, a Directorate of the Environment, Ministry of Housing, Land Planning, and Environment implemented a "coast recovery" and "urbanization containment" program in Cabo Polonio, which included the demolition of 98 houses (MVOTMA, 2019). Then, new constructions happened, and these were expected to produce income to the locals. Constructions on public land and occupations of other private properties doubled between 1996 and 2004. The waves of housing construction and their counter demolitions resulted in conflicts among residents and government officials over the control of public and private land.

Except for the more organized private landowners, there is no general agreement among the residents and different groups in the CAE. Several groups of both permanent and seasonal residents have mobilized to resist the official land-use proposals deployed by the State. In the early years after entering the SNAP, this anti-heritage movement was organized under the slogan "Let Polonio Be." Years later, another group of temporary residents organized new banners under the slogan "Polonio is Protected." The latter group opposed new demolition proposals in the Management Plan for the rocky area near the lighthouse. Other groups supported the National Park. The diversity of ideas among different groups caused uncertainties in the distribution of resources and tourism opportunities in the coastal areas. Different private actors mobilized using various strategies including legal actions, press demonstrations, and other forms of resistance, to claim their legitimacy and underline their fundamental role in the tourism attributes of the seaside village. A 20-year resident in Cabo Polonio refers to the protected area in the following way:

> We understand that National Parks do not allow settlement. However, the situation is different because people have been here before the national park was established. It is therefore impossible to make a town disappear to create a National Park. Moreover, there is nothing to protect in the so-called protected area and it is us who clean the beach most of the time. The government officials

are not here to protect anything apart from stopping expansion. The protected area was created with the idea of making money from it and not otherwise. During Pepe Mujica's time, I remember they wanted to sell the Buena Vista part of the public lands there. I cried. I could not believe what was happening.[3]

The ambiguity in the valuation of the inclusion in SNAP has been marked by waves of disillusionment throughout, often associated with the forms of local participation and the implementation of transformations linked to the national park. Although national conservation policies prescribe that the PAs within SNAP must have developed consultation tools such as public hearings and maintain the CAE, these social participation spaces have been devalued and disintegrated. Since its foundation, the CAE of Cabo Polonio has been marked by a climate of hostility between different groups of residents and the managers in charge. However, participation is even more unlikely now, given that the conflicts have become judicialized, and building spaces for encounter and negotiation no longer seems feasible.

In the same way, there is no unanimous agreement among the public administrators of the protected area. Although between 2009 and 2013, they were more organized through what was called "The Contact Group," in recent years, they have disbanded as a block in their opposition proposals to the seaside village. Initially, public actors conceived the National Park as a form of restoration that would bring benefits. They even aspired to place tourism growth at the forefront of residents' well-being as well as the sustainability of the environmental ecosystems for the benefits of all Uruguayans (MVOTMA 2009, 2019). For example, Óscar Calimares lived in Cabo Polonio throughout his life and has been a sea lion hunter as well as one of the most recognized fishermen in Rocha. For several decades, he also dedicated himself to repairing, painting, and maintaining the homes inhabited and rented only during the summer. His account offers a different perspective on the factors that led to the disintegration of the CAE, questioning the residents who speak on behalf of others in meetings:

> They all speak for us but what do they know about Polonio apart from nailing boards to add another bed. To me, they are people who were nobody until they came to Polonio. The majority are desperate people who come here for summer and leave the place without giving something in return.[4]

This testimony also sheds light on some emotional and subjective transformations that shape socialization in the seaside village. It also informs about the inevitable tensions that led to accusations among neighbors, limiting interpersonal relationships due to limiting building houses. Critical studies have addressed these types of tensions, particularly the political opportunities of heritage use by social movements (Valcuende et al., 2011; Roura, 2023). For example, Roura (2023: 222) explains that, in Casa Pumarejo in Seville, Spain, some neighbors were not interested in heritage, as they saw it as something abstract, elitist, and reserved for experts, incapable of condensing their experience of the world. However, as negotiations progressed, it became a mobilization that embraced heritage. It eventually transformed into a struggle identified with an alternative, anti-establishment, and subaltern heritage as a strategic discursive decision adopted for pragmatic and instrumental purposes. This strategy resulted in affective, emotional, and subjective transformations. In their case, the heritage declaration served as a connective platform or interface for mediation with heterogeneous agents (public officials, technical specialists, universities, etc.) and as an emotional device for the subjectification and political recoding of the social movement (Roura, 2023: 230–231).

Similarly, in Cabo Polonio, various actors have expressed their opposition or reorientation of conservation policies through challenges to the regulatory proposals in the Management Plan (MVOTMA, 2019). Involved in the socioeconomic transformations of living or vacationing in a protected area, they have claimed alternative heritage protection figures in participation instances. These mobilizations have not only had repercussions among the interested and affected parties but also reached people involved in the conflict. Public controversies have persisted since the first public hearings in 2007 and set the tone for local conversations, expanding concerns about the meaning of the transformations of a valuable and symbolically expressive place. For example, global public figures, such as artists Manu Chao or Jorge Drexler, have been spokespersons for far-reaching statements about demolishing houses on the rocks and the transformations associated with joining SNAP.

The national park and the sun-and-seaside village

The heritage process of the National Park involved distinguishing Cabo Polonio from the rest of the fishing villages that had become touristic attractions in Rocha coastal seaside (de Álava et al., 1992; Sprechmann & Capandeguy, 2011). The respective places symbolize a shared history among local stakeholders and, according to the SNAP Director, "a gateway of tourism" in the rest of the Uruguayan coast. The coastal seaside tourist towns allow us to expand our interpretation to account for the negotiations and struggle to define the area's shared history, identity, interaction dynamics, and transformations. They serve as starting points for our analysis and but not sources of value in themselves. These tourism spots are not strictly guided by institutional codifications, rules, or stable terms, nor are they closely aligned with preordained structures. However, they help us understand the experiences, purposes, and desires related to how tourism should be organized in areas considered valuable naturally and historically. As Graeber (2001: 47) advises, if the Navajo community in Rimrock places great value on "harmony" and Texans value "success," it is key to understand the meaning and social context of these concepts. Indeed, this is what is needed at Cabo Polonio.

The testimonies of President Mujica from 2011 resonate with the desire to develop spots for tourism activities. Such spaces are worthy of the exclusivity of life in the summer paradise. This sparks new waves of conflict about certain ecological risks that bring dimensions of what is valuable and socially productive. Defining who is responsible for environmental damage becomes a complex political issue, as social actors use beliefs about risks to assign responsibility and demand accountability (Merlinsky, 2013: 18). A few residents who have lived in Polonio for over 30 years have not met their expectations regarding the protection of the place. In conveying the message about this issue, one of the respondents had the following to say:

> Politicians come with promises and reforms regarding what would happen after the establishment of a National Park or Protected Area. For those with money, everything is protected, but for us, it is getting worse and worse. I don't know if protected areas are made for that. What I know is that these places benefit the elites that dictate how a protected area should be used. The elites discourage Valizas or Punta del Diablo; they want seaside farms for people with money who invest.[5]

The residents connect tourism growth with the trajectories of elitization, whitening, standardization, and gentrification to denounce homogenization of differences in capital accumulation (Harvey, 2018). Paradoxically, the tourists who have become residents align conservation policies with territorial transformations and the development of services and tourist attractions. This growth is accompanied by public and private investment in tourism infrastructures and other supporting facilities. One of the fishermen in Cabo Polonio describes the migrants "those who parachuted in to tell them what Cabo Polonio is and what we need to do."[6] For Óscar, the evolution of the seaside tourism village is synonymous with the town's destruction in what was thought to be development. The other tourist destinations, which underwent modernization, are experiencing an irreparable decline due to poor human management that tends to neglect local knowledges. This implies that tourism development and conservation initiatives that prioritize state apparatuses and without consideration of local people's knowledge are likely to fail (Gadino et al., 2022). However, this does not imply that the future is predetermined as public and private actors are willing to forgo lucrative opportunities in favor of conservation.

These representations are common in village conversations and sometimes transform into accusations and conflicts, bringing to light dimensions of values some of which are wrong. Notably, the contestations vary depending on tourists' seasonal flows, capital, and ideas from the tourist-sending centers. In this context, defining who is responsible for the degradation of what is valuable is a political issue due to fluctuations in the annual tourism cycle. At the local level, a widespread consensus blames the summer visitors, whether entrepreneurs or tourists, who burden the place with different opportunities. In this scenario, certain private and public actors demand actions and seek justifications. Because of the annual climatic conditions, the tourism practices of seaside villages and national parks coexist in space but not in time, projecting different connections with the place driven by seasonality. The annual variations in weather and the structured leisure periods of the middle classes cause significant price fluctuations, which can double or triple between December and March. Even during the summer, this tourism trend allows different profiles of socioeconomic sectors to visit Cabo Polonio beyond the peak demand in January, creating an income difference. The income differences cause tensions between interests to traditionally preserve the place and initiatives to develop and enhance the destination's value to attract more tourists.

These discussions reflect some clues to address the difficulty of assembling the coastal seaside touristic village project developed by the seasonal or permanent population and the national park as a valuation framework led by the institutions of a complex public network. This means that, for some people, protecting the place's unique characteristics radically contradicts what other actors prioritize, highlight, and consecrate as having heritage value. Until his death in February 2024, Joselo Calimares was one of the most respected residents in the area. He and his family lived through the transformation of a village of sea lion hunters and fishermen into one centered on providing tourism services.

> We already know, you see, the money issue; they envy us a lot. Everyone wants to have a place here. They have 3 or 4 houses elsewhere, buildings, mansions, but they want their little shack here. What do they do? They throw money to pressure these corrupt governments . . ., and the speculation is crazy. Whether it is the private sector or the government, we must leave en masse . . . Of course, because we are poor. However, now that it is filling up with rich people, they will be happy because wealthy people are buying in. Of course, I like to do business, go to hostels, and do other crazy things. It is all a lie. Do you think a private neighbourhood[7] Does a protected area make sense? For God's sake! Does money make everything beautiful?[8]

Like Joselo, some residents have propagated the interpretation of Cabo Polonio's entry into the SNAP as a conspiracy. Cabo Polonio's conservation project is viewed as a land-use strategy between the State and private landowners to concentrate power and influence over its development. From there, taking control would imply a calculated distribution of increasingly higher taxes implemented to consolidate the National Park and promote new actions and strategies. Thus, new coalitions encourage agreements with landowners to maximize rents and boost real estate speculation. This interpretation aligns with some critical studies linked to political ecology that have pointed out how conservation strategies have been used as more or less "failed actions that later favour the neoliberal market order" (Fletcher, 2023) and have been integrated into capitalist dynamics, focusing on selling nature to save it (McAfee, 1999; Dempsey & Suarez, 2016). According to testimonies, the populations that positioned this destination in the tourism market feel displaced, hence, oppose the initiative. At the same time, the utilization process is tied to official heritage preservation. It is accompanied by local actors who can collaborate and align with these environmental conservation policies. Emerging from this, the actors involved in conservation policies need to recognize the shame of not having achieved alternatives to the mechanisms of nature commodification.

Final remarks

Implementing the national park designation in Cabo Polonio is challenging to frame theoretically. Partly, because a broader valuation process already marked the initiation of the PA project into the territory. Such a progression was linked with the transformation of the Rocha coastline into seaside towns and villages. In this context, the models do not correspond with the reality and the valuation frameworks merge, confront, or mutually support each other in the context of tourism development. Within the framework of the National Park, the primacy of the place is claimed as a testimony of a coastal dynamic lost in the rest of the country. These dynamics are at the heart of conservation initiatives. The Management Plan suggests precautionary measures to mitigate the risks of degradation of the coastal areas. Some of these measures, however, prevent various stakeholders from framing Cabo Polonio within a set of premises and coalitions for economic growth. The anticipated development impulses including employment, investment, and other favorable conditions associated with the prosperity that José Mujica advocated has not been fully realized.

According to Milton Santos (2002), each period carries a meaning that articulates and represents how history materializes the promises of technology. Based on this assertion, at least two relatively autonomous frames can be identified, which nonetheless mutually influence one another. In this converging intersection, tourism differentiation becomes a knot that ties the logic of exploitation and conservation in a village with a fishing tradition. These knots shift and reassemble as the social productivity of evolving conflicts. As the national park transforms the sun-and-beach seaside village and vice versa, the resistances from one or the other reference framework determine the perception of legitimacy or desecration of the actors who manage, inhabit, vacation, or visit Cabo Polonio. The tourism specialization of this territory contrasts with the urban development frameworks of neighboring coastal seaside tourist towns. In the same context, Cabo Polonio seems to turn its back as part of the production of difference in a dialogical relationship. The references oriented toward anti-conventional development are marked by the absence of services such as electricity, running water, and road connectivity. The other challenges include poor dispersion of huts, low density, and the promotion of traditional, slow, bohemian, disconnected, and alternative lifestyles. This disconnection promotes tourism in Cabo Polonio. The affirmation of difference as the supreme value of the PA turns disconnection and disorder into virtues, praising inaccessibility as a source of wealth. Such differences are evaluated by the degree of isolation, distance, or remoteness from the rest of the world. Accordingly, the production of this promise of uniqueness goes hand in hand with the recreation of this isolation, which aims to slow down and postpone both the development and conservation agendas. From this perspective, the unproductive dunes that evoke a lost past in the slogan "let Polonio be" express grace and virtue that project the Uruguay Natural brand, reinforcing attributes associated with naturalness and quality of life.

These discussions can help us understand the meaning of protected areas when tourism activities shape relationships, heritage valuation exercises, and public policy efforts. At the same time, this discussion invites heritage, conservation, and tourism scholars and practitioners to reflect on the tensions of development and conservation. This problem invites us to reflect on how far we are willing to sacrifice the primary testimony of what the Uruguayan Atlantic coast once was for tourism development. In times when "we are ashamed" of the future, and the representations of what lies ahead seem to dictate a conservative order guided by "every man for himself," we still have an opportunity to slow down and, collectively, protect what we consider transcendent. Transformations that challenge us to reconnect with specific geographies and valuable cultural expressions, values that have been maintained despite the expansion of seaside towns and villages along the coastal strip. Subversively, we must remain vigilant to the loss of meaning and guard against the degradation of our living conditions, while actively sustaining the possibility of a shared world.

Acknowledgements

We want to express our sincere gratitude to all the participants who generously opened the doors of their homes, businesses, and public institutions to discuss Cabo Polonio. Your dedication and commitment to sharing your experiences and insights have been invaluable to this research. Thank you for your time and for contributing to a deeper understanding of this unique place.

Notes

1 Interview with an anonymous Polonio resident in 2022.
2 Interview with an anonymous Cabo Polonio resident in 2021.
3 Interview with an anonymous Cabo Polonio resident in 2023.
4 Interview with an anonymous Cabo Polonio resident in 2021.
5 Interview with an anonymous Cabo Polonio resident in 2022.
6 Interview with Oscar Calimeres, 2021.
7 Joselo Calimares refers to the real estate project Arenas del Cabo – see at https://balsayasociados.uy/portfolio-item/progra-ma-arenas-del-cabo/ – which announces the sale of a large part of the northern beach of Cabo Polonio. Retrieved December 2023.
8 Interview with an anonymous Cabo Polonio resident in 2021.

References

Becker, H. S. (2018). Outsiders: Studies in the sociology of deviance. Free Press.
Benseny, G. (2011). La valorización turística de la costa atlántica. El surgimiento de Villa Gesell, Argentina. Aportes y transferencias, 2, 79–102.

Bertoncello, R. (1993). Configuración socio-espacial de los balnearios del Partido de la Costa (Provincia de Buenos Aires). Buenos Aires: Universidad de Buenos Aires.

Bissell, W. C. (2005). Engaging colonial nostalgia. Cultural Anthropology, 20(2), 215–248.

Chouhy, M. (2008). Cabo Polonio: Representaciones sociales en diálogo en un área protegida. Montevideo: Universidad de la República.

Chouhy, M. (2013). Cabo Polonio, área protegida: Conservacionismo en diálogo con cosmovisiones salvajes. Anuario de Antropología Social y Cultural en Uruguay, 11, 87–102.

Da Cunha, N., Campodónico, R., Maronna, M., Duffau, N., & Buere, G. (2012). Visite Uruguay: Del balneario al país turístico, 1930–1955. Montevideo: Banda Oriental.

Dabezies, J. M. (2018). Heritagization of nature and its influence on local ecological knowledge in Uruguay. International Journal of Heritage Studies, 24(8), 1–15. https://doi.org/10.1080/13527258.2018.1428663

de Álava, D., Fernández, G., Panario, D., Céspedes, C., & Gutiérrez, O. (1992). Propuesta de manejo para el área protegida Cabo Polonio. Montevideo: Intendencia Municipal de Rocha & Facultad de Ciencias, Universidad de la República.

Dempsey, J., & Suarez, D. C. (2016). Arrested development? The promises and paradoxes of selling nature to save it. Annals of the American Association of Geographers, 106(3), 653–671. https://doi.org/10.1080/24694452.2016.1140018

Dudley, N. (Ed.). (2008). Directrices para la aplicación de las categorías de gestión de áreas protegidas. Gland: Unión Internacional para la Conservación de la Naturaleza (UICN).

Fletcher, R. (2023). Failing forward: The rise and fall of neoliberal conservation. Los Angeles: University of California Press.

Gadino, I., Sciandro, J., Taveira, G., & Goldberg, N. (2022). Tendencias y efectos socioambientales del desarrollo inmobiliario turístico en zonas costeras de Sudamérica: El caso de Región Este, Uruguay. EURE, 48(145), 1–23. https://doi.org/10.7764/EURE.48.145.05

Goffman, E. (2006). Frame analysis: Los marcos de la experiencia. Madrid: Centro de Investigaciones Sociológicas.

Graburn, N. H. H. (1985). The anthropology of tourism. Annals of Tourism Research, 12(1), 1–28.

Graeber, D. (2001). Toward an anthropological theory of value: The false coin of our dreams. London: Palgrave.

Harvey, D. (2018). Justicia, naturaleza y geografía de la diferencia. Instituto de Altos Estudios Nacionales de Ecuador. Quito: Traficantes de Sueños.

Lowenthal, D. (1985). The past is a foreign country. London: Cambridge University Press.

MacCannell, D. (2017). The tourist: A new theory of the leisure class. Los Angeles: University of California Press.

Machado, F. (2013). Energía y desarrollo: El caso del Cabo Polonio (Licenciatura thesis). Facultad de Ciencias Sociales, Universidad de la República.

McAfee, K. (1999). Selling nature to save it? Biodiversity and green developmentalism. Environment and Planning D: Society and Space, 17(2), 133–154.

Merlinsky, G. (Ed.). (2013). Cartografías del conflicto ambiental en Argentina (Vol. 1). Buenos Aires: Ediciones CICCUS.

Moreno, M. (2010). Cabo Polonio: Vidas sin tregua entre el cielo y el mar. Montevideo: Ediciones de la Banda Oriental.

MVOTMA. (2009). Proyecto de ingreso de Cabo Polonio al SNAP. Montevideo: Ministerio de Vivienda Ordenamiento Territorial y Medio Ambiente.

MVOTMA. (2019). Plan de manejo Parque Nacional. Montevideo: Ministerio de Vivienda Ordenamiento Territorial y Medio Ambiente.

Noel, G. (2011). Guardianes del paraíso: Génesis y genealogía de una identidad colectiva en Mar de las Pampas, Provincia de Buenos Aires. Revista del Museo de Antropología, 4(1), 211–226. https://doi.org/10.31048/1852.4826.v4.n1.5487

Noel, G. (2020). A la sombra de los bárbaros: Transformaciones sociales y procesos de delimitación moral en una ciudad de la Costa Atlántica bonaerense (Villa Gesell, 2007–2014). Buenos Aires: Teseo.

Roura Expósito, J. (2023). A rampant heritage? Problematising heritage activism through the Casa del Pumarejo social movement. International Journal of Heritage Studies, 29(3), 220–238. https://doi.org/10.1080/13527258.2023.2179099

Santos, C., & Chouhy, M. (2018). Los enclaves del Uruguay Natural en los márgenes del neodesarrollismo. In F. Suárez & C. Ruggerio (Eds.), Los Conflictos Ambientales En América Latina I: Áreas de reservación, conflictos mineros e hidrocarburíferos, conflictos forestales, agronegocios (pp. 37–56). Buenos Aires: Universidad Nacional de General Sarmiento.

Santos, M. (2002). Por uma geografia nova: Da crítica da geografia a uma geografia crítica (Coleçao Milton Santos). São Paulo: Editora da Universidade de São Paulo (Edusp).

Smith, L. (2006). Uses of Heritage. London: Routledge.

Sprechmann, T., & Capandeguy, D. (2011). Plan parcial de ordenamiento territorial para la denominada zona del Cabo y Tómbolo: Propuesta tentativa. Montevideo: Ministerio de Vivienda Ordenamiento Territorial y Medio Ambiente.

Urry, J. (2004). La mirada del turista. Lima: Universidad de San Martín de Porres.

Valcuende, J. M., Quintero Morón, V., & Cortés Vázquez, J. A. (2011). Naturalezas discursivas en espacios protegidos. AIBR. Revista de Antropología Iberoamericana, 6(1), 27–56. https://doi.org/10.11156/39

Villamarzo, E. (2018). Gestión integral del patrimonio arqueológico costero: Investigación y extensión en dos casos de estudio: Parque Nacional Cabo Polonio y Paisaje Protegido Laguna de Rocha [Doctoral dissertation, Universidad Nacional del Centro de la Provincia de Buenos Aires].

5

CONTESTS ON THE DEVELOPMENT AND USE OF COASTAL MONUMENTS IN TANZANIA

Elgidius B. Ichumbaki

Introduction

Several cultural heritage sites in Africa and their surrounding landscapes have multiple values ranging from historical, aesthetic, scientific, technological to spiritual uses. Although some of the heritage sites such as monumental structures are in a dilapidated state, people living near these assets value and use them to meet their livelihoods. On the other hand, the Government departments and commissions such as National Museums and Monuments have packaged these sites as touristic attractions for income generation. Because of these multiple values and uses, the assets and their surrounding landscapes have resulted in contestations among different stakeholders (Sabri, 2024).[1] This chapter presents a disposition of these conflicts, their causes, and highlights possible mitigation measures. Two heritage sites on the Swahili coast in Tanzania, namely Kunduchi and Kaole ruins are used as case studies. The data obtained from in-depth interviews and group discussions are analysed to explore tensions and misunderstandings among stakeholders.

Conflict on the use of Kunduchi ruins site

The Tanzanian coast is part of the Swahili coast, a coastline of about 3,000 km stretching from Mogadishu in Somalia in the north to Inbuane in Mozambique in the South (Ichumbaki & Pollard, 2021). The area has several cultural heritage sites mainly in the form of stone town built as part of the Indian Ocean maritime trade that happened between the 10th and 18th centuries AD (Horton & Middleton, 2000). One example is built heritage site of Kunduchi, famously known as 'Kunduchi Ruins site' with multiple settlement histories dated between the first and second century AD and

DOI: 10.4324/9781003623724-5

FIGURE 5.1   A section of Kaole ruins site with stone-built tombs.

with stone-built tombs of the 18th century (see Figures 5.1 and 5.2). Because of its cultural significance, in the 1960s, Kunduchi was gazetted and proclaimed a national monument by Government Notice No. 411. At that time, the monument covered an area of approximately 25 acres. Twenty years later, the area was reduced to about 12 acres, and the remaining 13 were given to a religious institution to build an Islamic school, Kunduchi Girls High School (Masele, 2012). For unknown reasons, the Government body legally charged with responsibilities of protecting cultural heritage assets did not intervene in denouncing and stopping the action.

Despite the reduced area being culturally important, before the study presented in this chapter, no records of strong conflict that resulted from this decision. Lack of such knowledge resulted in the conclusion that both the local people at Kunduchi and the Government had welcomed the project (Schmidt, 1996). Recall that the Department of Antiquities nominated the site as a national monument and is responsible for its protection. Schmidt (1996) postulates two reasons for what he considered a lack of both Government's and local people's intervention. The first is the fear that opposition to the Islamic community over the project was politically dangerous, and the second is a belief that construction of an Islamic structure on a traditional Islamic site was an acceptable historical process (Schmidt, 1996: 23).

Most likely Schmidt's first assumption relates to the fact that, at the time when the site obstruction was done, the president who is also commander-in-chief was a Muslim. Besides, it is possible that Schmidt's (1996) second supposition regarding Kunduchi as an Islamic site could have emanated from two issues. These relate

FIGURE 5.2 A pillard tomb decorated with Chinese porcelains at Kunduchi ruins site.

to the fact that ruins of tombs and a mosque both have Islamic affiliations and continued use of the site as a graveyard by the Muslim community. For the current chapter, there was a key question to address. For instance, did the local people of Kunduchi-Mtongani village really allow the construction of an Islamic school or not? With a view to exploring and grasping the local people's perceptions of built heritage assets and subsequent protection, I explore answers to this question in the next paragraphs.

Oral data collected through both in-depth interviews and group discussions refute Schmidt's (1996) assumption that the local people welcomed the project during the 1980s. As it will become apparent, there were local people who strongly opposed such site interference but were silenced with both religious and political propaganda. Should they have not changed within the timeframe between Schmidt's and my research,[2] the local people informed me that they never welcomed any use of the site apart from their day-to-day interactions. The local people recount that an individual and a certain group requested to use a part of the area to build an Islamic school. Some informants revealed that two camps emerged. On the one hand, some local people received a request of using the land and establishing a school positively and, on the other hand, other members rejected the then-proposed project.

Attempts by the first camp to deny leasing the land for the then-proposed establishments were due to two main reasons. Some local people at Kunduchi maintained that the area was for the Muslim community to bury their deceased and their other religious activities such as *ziara,* and not otherwise.[3] They further argued that the school would benefit people from afar instead of their children. In this regard, this camp maintained that unless reasonably convinced, they were not ready to see 13 ha piece of land being used for building an Islamic school. The camp that supported leasing the land thought that because the area belonged to Muslims, the school would serve their children as well. They thus saw no reason to oppose the establishment; instead, they look for alternatives to benefit local people.

Both interviews and group discussions revealed that, compared to the one that supported the project, the camp that opposed establishing the school was too weak to win. Its initiatives bore no fruits and two reasons contributed to this. The first one is that, according to participants, there were strong campaigns in mosques and other unofficial gatherings to make sure that people support the proposal to build the school. Many members of the village were informed that because the Muslim community has lagged in terms of education, they had to glorify and support such opportunity. The second relates to the contemplation that the president supported the project. The local people were therefore requested to bless it.

The local people were being informed that opposing a project that had blessings from their fellow Muslim (the president) would not only mean to oppose the opportunity to educate Muslim youths but also continue promoting Christianity. Although I did not find concrete evidence to prove this, my participants alleged that the president of that time, that is, the late Ali Hassan Mwinyi provided a 'memo' to the group that was requesting the area. If this was the case, it is likely that the 'memo' was presented to the relevant authorities[4] that suggested allocating the land as requested.

The two camps remained in opposition for quite some time, although they later agreed. In fact, this was after the village elders and religious leaders had reached a compromise. This compromise, however, was after the two camps and an investor reached a verbal agreement. The agreement was that the investor would sponsor a certain number of students from the community. Consequently, the investor was permitted using about 13 ha of the site for constructing a school.[5] The school was built in the northern part of the site, and although it continues to function, its fence encroaches on the site very rudely. Because of this rude encroachment, students at the school have made the northern part of the site a rubbish dumping place. Although the school continues to operate, it seems that sponsoring students from the community ceased after few years. Lack of records on this issue from both the school and the Kunduchi ward executive officer's office supports this assumption. Additionally, some respondents from the Kunduchi-Mtongani community informed me that supporting the students from community had ended several years ago.

The second interference of the Kunduchi Ruins site is that of the early 2000s, about 20 years after the first interruption. In the 2000s, the Department of Antiquities, which according to the Antiquities' Act No. 10 of 1964 (United Republic of Tanzania–URT 1964) and its Amendment Act No. 22 of 1979 (URT 1979) is responsible for the site's protection, in collaboration with 2050 Konsult AB Limited, agreed to develop the site for tourism purposes. A key aim of this Government-initiated project was to use three acres of the site to establish tourist facilities that included developing a tourist campsite. The two parties signed a memorandum of understanding ready to implement the project. However, the project did not materialise as it faced very strong opposition from the local people, which involved demolishing initial undertakings (a constructed permanent toilet; Masele, 2012). Most of the local people condemned the Government's desire to develop the site without their consent. Incidentally, in contrast to the previous scenario, this second intervention was done when the president was a Christian.

Following this incident, a few questions are critical: (a) Why did the local people oppose the construction of touristic facilities including developing a campsite (a form of investment but site intervention)? (b) Assuming the president (commander-in-chief) was, during this time of site obstruction, a Muslim, would the local people have opposed or supported the proposed project to develop a campsite? (c) What if either the Department of Antiquities and 2050 Konsult AB Limited or any other investor changed the nature of investment (say towards a non-tourism project like an Islamic school again), would the people of Kunduchi-Mtongani area accept or reject such an initiative? I explore answers to these questions.

Frank Masele did a study and came out with the reasons as to why the local people had opposed the project (Masele, 2012). After interviewing some people and reading various reports housed in the Department of Antiquities resource room, he provides two reasons: first, he found that the local people believe that the site is theirs. It is because of this belief that they continue using it as a cemetery. Second, they claim that they were not involved in all the processes of privatising it and constructing touristic facilities. This is what he says:

> The Kunduchi-Mtongani community strongly believes that the archaeological and historic site is theirs, as evidenced by their ongoing use of it as a cemetery. ... During and after the 2004 conflict, the local community alleged that they had not been consulted and had not been informed of the different development

and promotional plans for the site. They stated that they were against the hand-ing over, privatization, and commercialization of the site. Furthermore, they alleged that the implementation of the development and promotional plans at the site were secret, and did not offer any opportunity for Kunduchi-Mtongani residents' views to be taken into consideration.

(Masele, 2012: 59–60)

Both documentary evidence and oral information from the local participants indicate that, soon after the conflict, there were strong initiatives to make the community participate so that they would condone the project thereafter. Among the methods used in resolving the 2004 conflict was the Department of Antiqui-ties holding several meetings with the local people. It was envisaged that these meetings would create good grounds for the implementation of future projects. The aim was to make the community aware of the investments, thereby being ready to support them. In due course, the two parties agreed to form a commit-tee comprising five people, all from the local community. This step was thought important as the committee would mediate between the Government and the local community.

With support from the Government, the formed committee got an opportunity to visit other coastal sites, including the ruins at Kilwa Kisiwani, Songo Mnara, Bagamoyo and Zanzibar all of which with touristic investments experience. The aim of these visits was to expose the Kunduchi team to the commercial use of cultural sites and their importance. After the visit, the team was supposed to come back and educate their fellows about what they had learned from the other sites that they had visited (Maro, 2004).

Nevertheless, having listened to the local people's views and concerns, I noted that although the local community appreciated the developments made at other sites, they were not ready to see both private investors and the Government develop touristic establishments at Kunduchi. Instead, they insisted that the Government continue to take care of the site, and that whenever anything other than visiting the ruins emerged, they be informed through a local committee. The local people accepted that the site belongs to the Government, but believed that they were the custodians, and that they be allowed to continue using it. This is what they rely on for legitimising their demands.

On the basis of the data being presented in the foregoing discussion, I want to argue against the conclusion that local people opposed the project simply because they had not been informed right from the beginning. This counteraction stems from the fact that the local community continued to oppose the project. This pursuit by the local people progressed even after they had been informed and had partici-pated at some point in time. Had they not been involved or informed of the main reason from the beginning, one would expect that the local community would have given such projects a go-ahead after being informed accordingly. On the contrary, they continued to oppose the endeavours, and there are possibilities that future attempts, or any developmental investment at the site, will be rejected. Also, my experience at the site (presented later in this chapter) supports this perspective.

One thing which I once again bring to the fore is that, before this research, the cultural sequence and general history of the Kunduchi Ruins site remained almost non-existence in the literature of the Swahili coast. To better reconstruct the site's history, I conducted archaeological excavations (see Ichumbaki, 2015). My excavation works received visits from a few local people who came to the cemetery for their spiritual practices. They were passing by the excavation units and asked what my research team was doing. I explained the details regarding the research and its relevance towards reconstructing the site's history to whoever visited, and they showed interest and listened. Nevertheless, many of them seemed to remain with more questions than answers and suspected the explanations I provided them.

My dilemma regarding their response was their perception of the ongoing excavations and the reasons behind them. There could be various and numerous answers to this dilemma, but the most plausible one comes from the existing but silent antagonism between them and the Government (see also Masele, 2012). The local people perceived my excavation as a gateway to privatising their land, including the ruins. When I interrogated one of the community members regarding the matter, I was informed that most local people, especially the Muslims, are not ready to see their land being taken and utilised by anybody. They are of the view that without interfering, especially at the initial stages, their cemetery area that belongs to Muslims would be privatised and used contrary to Islamic customs.

A cited example to verify their claim is the intervention they made in 2004. They maintained that had they not demolished the establishment of the 2004 project, their heritage site would have been gone.[6] For the local people, it is important to doubt and question whatever activity, which in one way or another, involves obstruction to their cultural heritage site. One issue that surprised me was to learn later that the doubts by few members who got the opportunity to visit earlier test trenches are also shared by many members of the local community. The doubts were apparent on the morning of 22 January 2014 when I was excavating.

As excavation continued, groups of men with hoes, shovel and *panga* (matchet) passed heading towards the cemetery. I later on learnt that someone in the village had died, and the groups headed to making a grave. My excavation crew and I did also note that the burial ceremony was to take place that morning (22 January 2014). The ceremony took place at around 10.30 am and about 200 men attended the event. Noticeably, the groups which attended the funeral were not happy about our work, and their faces looked probing. Their curiousness was stimulated not only by the ongoing land disturbance but also by the fact that the trench was located close to the previously demolished establishment.

After about half an hour or so, a few people ($n = 10$) came and informed me about the deliberations reached by the whole group attending the burial ceremony. They informed me that the group was shocked to see the land being disturbed without their consent. Additionally, they angrily discussed the issue and called the chairman to come[7] and either provide satisfactory explanation on what we were doing or otherwise allow them to destroy my research initiatives at the site. These people asked me to be prepared to provide satisfactory answers when the entire group arrives and asks me to do so. They emphasised that I prepare myself to explain to them what the work was about, and why I was working near the developer's targeted area. Short of that they were going to destroy everything we had, including harming the research team.

After about 15–20 minutes, the big group came directly to where I had established the trench. Incidentally, I had backfilled it. They only saw the disturbed area, materials recovered and the equipment used. When they noticed that most of them had arrived, one member requested citizens to pay attention to him. The person introduced himself as one of the religious leaders and a member of the ruins committee formed to oversee the ruins and negotiate with the Government whenever any problem regarding the site arose. He first lamented not being informed of our activity and called the chairman to explain to the people about the matter in question.

The whole group shouted in support of the speaker, some raising their voices uttering 'umeongea maneno pilau[8] hayo' loosely meaning he had spoken it correctly. When the chair stood up to speak, he first accused the people of reacting negatively on an issue instead of asking for clarification amicably. He further informed the crowd that the group (my research team) was at the site legally and that whoever would disturb them was going to suffer the consequences. This statement was not well received. While many of the members shouted angrily, some even claimed that I had bribed the chairman.[9] Due to this chair's comment, the situation became even worse, and everyone started arguing their own way. After some few minutes, I requested their attention to explaining the matter to them. I intervened both politically and diplomatically asking them to become silent and listen to one another.

I first informed them that their doubts were genuine, and wherever you go especially at the sacred sites such as Kunduchi, custodians of the land should question whatever activity is taking place on their land. Such a comment was followed by claps of hands and utterances such as 'maneno pilau hayo' meaning that I had spoken correctly. After that, I explained to them that my research followed all the relevant procedures and that the presence of the team at the site was also blessed by both the ward and village authorities. Furthermore, I explained to them the importance of this research on their side, and that other researchers and I had done the same elsewhere along the coast of East Africa.

Many of the people accepted and believed what I explained to them.[10] Some of them wished they had been informed of the work before it started and blamed the chairperson for not informing them in due course. A good number of them therefore allowed me to continue and requested me to inform them about the research results. More importantly, they seriously warned me not to dare erect any form of construction at the site, and that such an action would result in an endless fight. They further advised me that, next time I come to the site for a similar work, I should not trust the ward and village authorities. Instead, I should consult religious leaders who would spread the information through the mosque.

However, there were some voices of a few people who were totally against the research. They raised their voice, commenting that Kunduchi is an Islamic land and that it should not be disturbed anyhow. One of the members of the groups was quoted saying:

> I do not accept you being here. This is a holy Islamic land that belongs to Muslims and not anybody else. Today you pretend to be doing research and tomorrow you will establish touristic facilities. This will happen because Muslims have become so relaxed. Slowly things will change, and we will not be able to intervene. Today we allow them to do research, tomorrow they will come and build a church in a holy Islamic land. After that, they will be stopping us from burying the deceased simply because they call it a protected area. Because we have failed to recognize these issues now, we will notice in the end, and it will be too late. I feel sorry for my fellow Muslims because they will have nowhere to be buried and bury their children. My personal land is large enough to accommodate me and my family.

This worry from some members did not end at uttering their feelings publicly but continued some days after excavations. I noticed this when I visited the site on 27 August 2014. While at the site, surprisingly, I noted that one of the established and backfilled test trenches was uncovered, and there was other two pits nearby. When I inquired from the site security personnel on what had happened, he said that about two months after I finished the excavations, a group of people came to the site and started digging up the area looking for beacons my team installed. They did this because they were not sure of the exact location they tried at two points without success and managed to get the point at their third trial. Obviously, they did not find what they had expected. I wish I could manage to locate at least some of these people and get their opinion; unfortunately, my efforts failed.

While local communities' reaction towards anybody's interference with the ruins and the general landscape is like that, the Government had proposed to build a wall surrounding the site.[11] With my experience, one can imagine the intensity of the conflict that would emerge in case the Government continues with the planned project. To get some insights into this issue, I interviewed some members of the local community as well as Antiquities officers. Surprisingly, the oral data collected from both parts support the construction of a wall around the site. While the officers are of the view that the constructed wall will result in smooth management of the site, the local people think that the presence of a wall will keep Christians and other people away from burying their deceased at the site.[12] Yet the wall has not been built up to date, October 2025.

A key question that needed addressing was why the local people allowed the construction of a school but later resisted the establishment of touristic facilities that would result in providing employment opportunities to the community sons and daughters. A critical analysis of the oral data collected and discussions between some community members and I revealed that it is not because of the cemetery that local people rejected the projects. This is because Muslims do not give much care to tombs and especially when they are sure that the deceased has decayed. Some participants narrated stories related to several incidents in which bones of dead people are dug up while making new graves. When they find them, they just put them aside and continue making the new grave. In fact, for Muslims, a grave becomes a normal land after 40 years.

What make local people reject any further development are the spiritual uses and economic gains obtained from these sites. Although they do not want to be labelled so publicly, in addition to some local people, influential figures including politicians and successful businesspersons visit the Kunduchi site for spiritual practices. Because of such visitors, practitioners obtain income that they use to meet their livelihoods. Conversely, few local people have a strong belief that these ruins resolve their social problems. An example of such a belief goes that, if the devil attacks someone, or someone has been cursed, or has any other related problem, they will receive treatment from the spiritual site, in this case, Kunduchi.

The participants revealed that they finally accepted the school project because it was relocated away from the point of spiritual practices. However, because the then-proposed campsite and permanent toilet were to be located close to one of the important spiritual areas, local people could not accept the initiatives. The same reasons should explain why they re-excavated my backfilled test trench that I also located close to the same location.

A few members of the community who are spiritual practitioners make money for taking their customers to those places. They are of a view that, if the Government or independent business companies invest in these sites, they will jeopardise opportunities to use the assets for generating income. Of paramount importance is that some of these practitioners such as Muslim leaders are greatly respected by a big number of community members. They thus have a greater opportunity to influence local people to oppose proposed projects.

Conflict over the use and protection of the Kaole ruins site

Kaole, a 13th–18th-century ruined heritage site (see Figures 5.3 and 5.4), has been experiencing a conflict between its management and one of the neighbouring families, that of Omar Sherdel. The conflict is over an area of about one acre containing archaeological artefacts, including a house foundation, local and imported ceramics as well as glass beads. The neighbouring family wants to own the area as much as the Government of Tanzania does, through the Department of Antiquities. This conflict over the site started in the mid-1980s and has

FIGURE 5.3   A section of Kaole ruins viewed from the south.

FIGURE 5.4   A section of Kaole ruins viewed from south-western corner.

until today not been resolved. The reasons for the continuing demand by the neighbouring family, a Government order notwithstanding, are presented in the next sections. However, before that, it is important to know the historical background of the conflict.

The family of the deceased Omary Sherdel claims ownership of the land since the late 19th century. The written documents that the family provided to me to verify the ownership, some of which are in the German language, indicate that the farm is a combination of pieces bought from different neighbours at different times. For instance, a part of the claimed farm was bought by Mr. Omar Sherdel from Dinward Mumbi, Dinan Gangura and Haji Ali bin Dad Rahim in 1895. Another part of the farm was bought from Mwenemkuu bin Diwan Sigeura in 1900. An additional part of the farm was bought from Beha Mwinyimkuu in 1914. Although these documents mention neither the farm size and contents nor boundaries for each bought part, a document of 1936 indicates that the whole farm had 2,060 fully grown and 576 small coconut trees. It is further documented that, on the north, the farm was bordered by that of Yahya Mohabat and the Sea, on the south by a farm owned by Din Mohamed Delmurad, on the west by the farm of Mtwana Hassan and on the east by the sea.[13]

Between 1936 and the mid-1980, there are no documents that indicate what was happening on this farm. In other words, there are no written documents in which this family describes what was taking place on the farm despite various excavations and conservations that took place in the late 1950s, 1960s and 1970s. A document linking the family to the farm is dated back to the eighth day of July 1985 from Bagamoyo District Council addressed to the members of the family.[14] The document is a response to the family's application to register the coconut farm found at Pumbuji – Kaole. It is clear in this document that the registrar in consultation with the Director of Land Development Services and, in terms of the then leaseholds conversion to Rights of Occupancy Act of 1969, the Government granted a right of occupancy of the said land for 99 years starting from the first day of July 1985. However, it should be noted that my aim is not to discuss matters pertaining to land occupancy and ownership. Instead, I provide a background to the discussion of the conflicts surrounding built heritage assets and nearby cultural landscapes.

Documentary evidence indicates that the Kaole Ruins were declared a national monument in 1937, and this was based on the Monument Preservation Ordinance of the same year. The area in which the declared monument is located was part of somebody's farm, and it is not documented anywhere whether the Government compensated the owner of the farm. Oral information from one of the members of the family[15] claiming ownership of the farm indicates that the owner did generously grant the ruins and the surrounding area to the Government. Unfortunately, it is not documented. The available document is the one that defines Kaole as a conservation area and dates to 1937. The ruins conserved area is said to be demarcated by four concrete blocks and sisal plants placed in four corners of the area. Former antiquities officer at Kaole who has been involved in the conflict resolution had the following to say:

> It is true that the Sherdel's family owns the area around *magofu* (the ruins); however, no verification documents were presented to the land officers in 2010 when the District was in the process of resolving the conflict. From their family, there was also a contradiction of when their family started to live here. Some family members said that before the colonial time, others mentioned the 1880's and some mentioned 1900's. They were also asked to produce evidence of ownership, and the only evidence they could produce was a map claimed to be drawn in 1986. Unfortunately, the land officers in Bagamoyo failed to locate evidence for the claimed ownership. What I know is that the British Colonial Government declared Kaole ruins the national monument in 1937. Unfortunately, there is no record if the Government made any compensation to whoever owned the area during that time, despite demarcating it with four concrete blocks.

This boundary, however, is not clear as it does not mention the buffer zone to indicate where the conserved area begins and where it ends. Consequently, according to a former Antiquities' officer at Kaole, lacking a well-defined buffer zone gave neighbours a loophole to shift these markers and made a fake map of the area in 1986. Since then, the conflict had not been settled there. It gained momentum in January 1987 when this neighbour filed a case in the court of law. Mr. Samahani Kejeli, who was a site guard at that time, was accused of entering the farm, disturbing employees who were taking care of the farm, and hunting wild animals without the owner's permission. A criminal case number 166 of 26 January 1987, against the accused, was filed at Mwambao Primary Court in Bagamoyo. Unfortunately, I could not find the documents explaining how the matter was handled and what the judgement was. However, my informal interactions with the accused person, the late Kejeli, revealed that the case was dismissed as there was no evidence to prove their claim.[16]

It seems that between the 1990s and mid-2000s this conflict ceased, and there are no documents detailing the issue. Most likely this must have been due to a lack of a family member to pursue it further as they had moved from Bagamoyo to Kibaha and others to Mbeya, in the south-east Tanzania.[17] During this time, the local people took up the opportunity and started to undertake farming in the farm. They grew fruits and vegetables, but when the family came back, they asked the villagers who were undertaking such farming activities to vacate. Members of the late Omar's family did not even allow the local people time to at least harvest whatever they had grown, and whoever asked for permission to do that was responded to with brutality. It is further reported that the family has a reputation of using excessive force to trespassers on their property. Since then, the conflict continues, and it is between the family members and some local people on the one hand, and the Kaole Ruins management on the other hand.

It followed that, in 2010, the matter was reported to the Land Department of Bagamoyo District Council (LDBDC) for arbitration. After receiving the complaints, the LDBDC ordered the two parties to submit evidence verifying each one's claims. Based on the evidence submitted, and Government Notes No. 186 of 1937, on 6 August 2010, LDBDC wrote a formal letter to Omar's family informing them that the claimed area belongs to the Department of Antiquities. In other words, the area is protected as per the Antiquities Act No. 10 of 1964 and its Amendment Act No. 22 of 1979. However, irrespective of the provided order from such a Government official body, Omar's family continued to claim the right to the area. I managed to talk to the representative of the family, Madam Kuruthum, the eldest sister who has been struggling to make sure that the land remains in the family's hands.

I was also lucky to have a group discussion with other members of the family. These participants told me that before their father died, he advised on the uses of the land in question. According to these respondents, the father asked the family to use that land to build a mosque and an Islamic college that would benefit the Muslims of Bagamoyo and beyond. They further narrated that many Muslims in Bagamoyo are aware of the late Omar's promise to build a mosque and college on his land, and that the majority are waiting to see it happen. Moreover, Ms Kuruthmu informed me that the family has obtained funds that could be used to erect both a mosque and a college but because of this conflict, the project cannot begin. According to Ms Kuruthmu, the family's current desire is to involve BAKWATA (Tanzania's Muslims' Council) and ask them to help on the matter. She insisted that she will not give up until her late father's instructions are realised, and the family seems to be committed to that.

I noticed the family's commitment to this issue on 12 November 2014 when I received a call from the eldest sister. She wanted to talk to me, and unfortunately, I had left Bagamoyo. Surprisingly, she insisted that if I agree, she would come to Dar es Salaam and talk to me. So, she came to Dar es Salaam and was accompanied by one of his sons. When she saw me, she gave a deep sigh and thanked me for accepting her request to meet, despite the very short notice. She ordered food and a drink for me and after that requested that I listen very carefully to what she was going to say. This is part of what she said:

I am sorry my son. I called you because I want to tell you what happened yesterday and request you to advise me on this issue. Yesterday I was on my duties, and someone called me to go back home immediately, saying that there was a problem. So, I immediately went home and waited to see what was going to happen. A few minutes later, a group of about ten people came and started to move around the 'alleged *magofu* area'. They were just doing their discussions within the family farm but never talked to me. I asked why they were surveying our farm without our consent. One of them replied that they had no power to speak to me and that I wait for the group leader or top management that was coming.

After about twenty minutes later, three other people came to the same area, showing one another the *magofu* area part, which is part of our farm. They saw me, but nobody greeted me. I just went close to them, greeted them, and then asked them why they were trespassing our farm. They went on showing one another, and discussing even without informing me about what was going on. One member of the group members arrogantly replied, asking me what my problem was. They told me not to disturb them as they were implementing a government project. I asked her if that project was proposed to take place on our farm without our consent, let alone informing us. She insisted not to be disturbed and that I had no right to ask and disturb them. This woman advised me that if there was a problem I should report to the relevant authority, and not to shout at them. They went on moving around what they considered to be 'the *magofu* area', a part of which is our farm.

When they left, our family held a meeting to discuss this problem, and look for a way forward. As a family, we agreed to report the matter to the relevant authority and seek advice from friends and colleagues. I reported the matter to the village chairman, and he gave us a go-ahead (she showed me a letter from the chairman). Since this morning, we have been struggling to meet relevant people and authority and report the problem. My mother went to the District Commissioner's (DC) office to report this problem. Unfortunately, she could not manage to talk to him because he was away in one of the wards in the district. However, she set an appointment, and the DC promised to call for a meeting when he comes back in office. My son went to the office of Bagamoyo's head of Muslims. Similarly, I am meeting you here and will be going to talk with the head of BAKWATA about this matter after here. I am meeting and narrating this story to you because you are a teacher. Therefore, I request you to advise me on what to do, to make sure that our father's desire is fulfilled. Besides, you may know some '*magofu* people' particularly those from the Ministry. I request you to talk to them so that they allow us to use this family land as our father directed.

Later, after two weeks, I noticed that her effort to involve the Muslim community was accepted by the BAKWATA and other Muslim leaders in Bagamoyo and Dar es Salaam. This is because they started to make a follow-up on the matter including visiting the area in question to see how they could step in. I came to know their visitation to the site from the head of the Kaole Ruins station, Ms. Siyawezi Hungo. She informed me that BAKWATA leaders from Bagamoyo and Dar es Salaam visited and toured the ruins and were showing one another and discussing land in conflict. Generally, waqf endowment attached to this land is the basis of support for the Omar's family claim to the area. They argue that constructing a mosque and an Islamic college were the wills of the original farm owner, and that if not fulfilled the family's day-to-day activities will always face problems.

However, while the Omar family claims that the land is a waqf property as their father had wanted it to be used for building a mosque and Islamic college, some of the local people and former Antiquities' officer shared different views. They are of the view that because the land in Bagamoyo, and especially near the Kaole ruins, has become a highly demanded resource, the family wants to capitalise on the site's neighbourhood to acquire even the one that belongs to the Government. The key participant, who sees members of this family as opportunistic, is Samahani Kejeli.[18] He knew a lot about the site, and before the mid-1980s he used to be a friend of the late Omar Sherdel. Mr. Kejeli claims to know the real boundary of the conserved area, and during our discussion he even drew its map on the ground. He is of the view that increases in tourists at Kaole and the benefits that accrue from the industry trigger Omar's children to fight to grab the land in question. The following quotation summarises his thinking:

> The Kaole ruins are not like those of the 1970s and 1980s when stone-built tombs were tombs. Now the tombs have changed to become resources and many people in Bagamoyo have understood this. They have become sources of income, and Omar's children want to use the opportunity. Their ambition to claim ownership of the land started even before their father died. They convinced him to file a case against me, that I had entered their land to disturb their workers. Nevertheless, the case was dismissed because they lacked evidence to prove the allegations. I think these children have noticed that visitors at Kaole have increased, and they think that if they acquire the land very close to the ruins, they will use it for investment and, therefore, make a fortune for their survival.
>
> (Field notes, Sept. 2014)

Mr. Simon Materu, a former Antiquities' officer, likewise, was of the same thinking as Mr. Samahani Kejeli, regarding causes for the conflict:

> On the one hand, the economic factor is a major cause of the Omar's family to continue claiming ownership of the conserved area. In recent years, Bagamoyo and particularly the area surrounding the ruins, has become so expensive due to an increase in tourism activities as well as various proposed Government projects, particularly the Mbegni Port and the Bagamoyo Special Economic Zone project. This has caused the land value to appreciate and affluent businesspeople from Dar es Salaam are now intensifying their interests in Bagamoyo, and particularly the area between the Kaole Ruins and the Mbegni estuary.
>
> On the other hand, the Government has never shown commitment on the issue in question since problems arose during the 1980s. The Department of Antiquities especially at the headquarters has done virtually nothing to resolve the problem. Former site managers, including myself, have written several reports to address the issue and requested funds that could be used to fence the area. Unfortunately, no support was given until recently when funding for such an activity was allocated. It was in 2012, during a meeting in Morogoro when

it was brought to the Ministry's lawyer's attention. Practically nothing has been done, and this shows that, there is poor coordination between the head office and its stations to resolving important issues, land conflicts being one of them. Consequently, because local people in Kaole and especially the claimant family are aware of this weakness, and also because they have been witnessing in and outflow of tourists at the site; they want to use this Government's weaknesses to acquire the land and operate tourism business.

(Email correspondence with Simon Materu, Nov. 2014)

This comment from a former Antiquities staff indicates that the Government, and especially through the Department of Antiquities, is not firm in resolving outstanding problems happening on cultural heritage sites. If the problem has existed for over 30 years and yet there have not been strategies on how to harmonise these two parties, it is more likely that there will be more difficulties in the future.

Conclusion

There could be several explanations for these conflicts happening at Kaole and Kunduchi ruins on the coast of Tanzania. However, the failure of the state in its capacity to mobilise resources for improving the communities' livelihoods seems to hold true for these conflicts. Communities living along the central coast of Tanzania are faced with social problems including extreme poverty. Because of these hardships and failure of the state to offer relevant social services, the means of survival have become so limited. Consequently, the people are struggling to find means of survival, including resolving social problems and improving their livelihoods. Accordingly, trying to commercialise built heritage assets and surrounding landscapes has become one of the strategies to solve life hardships. In the process to harness these locally created opportunities, the local people have conflicted with the Government that has forgotten them.

For the past two decades, there has been a significant increase in interest by the Tanzanian Government and independent business companies and individuals to use the shore areas for building tourist hotels, diving centers and recreational places. The most targeted areas are those considered to be historically important, and especially those with ancient ruins such as mosques, stone-built tombs and historic buildings. These places with built heritage are preferred because of their complimentary advantage. They are located very close to aesthetic white sandy beaches needed by many tourists for recreational activities. The strategy is to create environments where tourists will be able to enjoy the sea and the beach, and at the same time visit these cultural heritage attractions (Ichumbaki, 2013).

On the other hand, historically, local people have been using the same landscapes for holding spiritual practices and meet their socioeconomic needs. Coastal areas, and especially those with built heritage assets such as ruined mosques and stone-built tombs (mostly surrounded by baobab trees), not only provide spiritual comfort to poor coastal people but also act as sources of income to meet their liveli-hoods. The income comes from several people including politicians, businessmen, women with fertility problems and other people with social problems who visit the 'fundi' (traditional healer) seeking help (see Alex & Ichumbaki, 2024; Said & Ichumbaki, 2022). While the Government and business companies are of the view that such investment, as the previously proposed one at Kunduchi, would benefit the local people by providing them with employment and other related opportuni-ties, the local people have a different view. They are of the view that such invest-ment will not only jeopardise their spiritual practices, especially after kicking them away from their cultural land, but also close their sources of income to sustain livelihoods.

The contested perceptions over investments in built heritage assets have resulted in conflicts among the involved stakeholders, hence threatening the sustainability of these heritage assets. The ongoing conflicts at Kunduchi and Kaole ruins are testimony to this. At some other sites on the coast where investment has not yet started (but there is unverified information that such plans are underway), local people have started to solicit strategies to use in the future to defend their interests. An initiative to renovate a stone-built tomb of an unknown deceased at Mkadini (Alex & Ichumbaki, 2024) presents a good example of this scenario. It is argued in this chapter that, unless the ideological constructs of built heritage from the local people's perspective is thought of, conflicts over these assets will intensify and cause more problems. The conflicts between the local people and Government officials and heritage professionals are becoming social and humanistic problems that need further analysis.

Notes

1 J. Chevalier defines stakeholders as groups, constituencies, social actors or institutions of any size or aggregation that act at various levels (domestic, local, regional, national, international, public or private), and that have a significant and specific stake in each set of resources and can affect or be affected by resource (for this case-built heritage) man-agement problems or interventions (Chevalier, 2001). In a summarised manner, Chiri-kure & Pwiti (2008) describe these stakeholders as communities of interest. As used in this case, stakeholders include local people, Government officials and professionals all with stake in built heritage.
2 Between Peter's publication and time of this research, there is a gap of about 20 years. Because a lot has changed within this timeframe, there could be a possibility that local people have changed their mind and perceptions towards the school. However, this is not the case because several participants interacted with who during the time incidences were living in the area indicate opposition to the project. Similarly, the school management supports oral information and confirmed that the school used to support some students from the community. Such assistance, however, is no longer provided.
3 Interview with Mzee Mtihani 26/3/2014. Mzee Mtihani is a site guide and resident of Kunduchi village. He has been guiding the site since the mid-1980s and well conversant with its history.

4 These authorities included the Ministry of Land titled to allocate the land to developers as well as the Department of Antiquities which is titled by the law to protect the cultural heritage assets of Tanzania.

5 Interview with an anonymous participant at Kunduchi 28/2/2014.

6 These answers resulted from the discussions I made with a group of Muslim men who were coming from the Mosque on the afternoon of Friday, 14 March 2014.

7 The chairman had not attended the burial ceremony although he was not far away from the site. Fortunately, because he was aware of our presence, he arrived at our trench before the arrival of this big group.

8 Pilau is a spiced rice, eaten by many East African people and commonly prepared whenever there are official events to celebrate.

9 Field notes recorded on 22 April 2014. Writing down the notice for this matter was done after the group had gone and after discussing the matter with my research assistants.

10 All people referred to in this case are males only. Women attended the ceremony but remained very far from the cemetery. Similarly, they did not come at the test pits as they are not around to join men's gathering. However, few of the women from the community that I managed to interview share similar opinions with the men presented in the text.

11 According to the antiquities' officers stationed at Kunduchi, the Government had set aside some money for constructing the wall surrounding the site. Both the Government and officials at the site believe that a wall will be the only means to protect the site from local communities destroying the ruins through grazing cattle in the site (26/3/2014).

12 Interview and discussions with a group of elders at a tea shop at Kunduchi (2/3/2014).

13 All this information was obtained from Omar's family's file and managed to access this file through Kuruthmu (Mama Duzu) who is a family member and responsible for taking care of the family farm.

14 The letter from the District Council is addressed to Omar Sherdel, Abdallah Sherdel, Abdulrahman Haji Gandust, Mariam Sherdel, Ganjahatum Sherdel, and Fatuma Sherdel.

15 Interview with Kuruthum Omary Sherdel 24/8/2014.

16 Interview with Mzee Samahani Kejeli, 7 September 2014.

17 Email correspondence with Simon Materu, a former Antiquities officer who was stationed at Kaole.

18 Samahani Kejeli (famously known as Prof. Kejeli – 65 years old, by then) is a resident of Bagamoyo and retired employee of the Department of Antiquities, Ministry of Natural Resources and Tourism. He was involved in excavations that were conducted by N. Chittick and H. Sassoon during the 1950s, 1960s and 1970s. He also participated in other archaeological excavations that took place at different coastal sites including Tongoni, Kilwa and Manda. He worked as a site guard and tourist guide and stayed at Kaole between the 1970s and late 1990s. Currently, he is retired but works as a freelance guide and has trained many young tour guides in Bagamoyo.

References

Alex, M., & Ichumbaki, E. B. 2024. Unless we Value the Intangible Heritage, the Tangible Will Never be Safe! Linking the Tangible and Intangible Aspects of Heritage Sites in Africa. *Journal of Heritage and Society,* 17(2), 219–238. https://doi.org/10.1080/21590 32X.2023.2230752

Horton, M. C., & Middleton, J. 2000. *The Swahili: The Social Landscape of a Mercantile Society.* Oxford: Blackwell.

Ichumbaki, E., & Pollard, E. 2021, March 25. The Swahili Civilization in Eastern Africa. *Oxford Research Encyclopedia of Anthropology.* Retrieved 3 October 2025, from https://oxfordre.com/anthropology/view/10.1093/acrefore/9780190854584.001.0001/acrefore-9780190854584-e-267.

Ichumbaki, E. B. 2013. Linking Cultural Heritage and Eco-Tourism in Tanzania: Reflections from a New Cultural Heritage Policy of 2008. *The Eastern African Journal of Hospitality, Leisure and Tourism*, 1(1), 34–44.

Ichumbaki, E. B. 2015. Monumental Ruins, Baobab Trees and Spirituality: Perception of Value and Uses of Built Heritage Assets of the East African Coast. (PhD. Dissertation). University of Dar es Salaam.

Maro, E. E. 2004a. Mkakati wa Uanzishaji wa Miradi na Ushirikishwaji wa Wananchi katika Uhifadhi na Uendelezaji wa Vituo vya Mambo ya Kale. Paper presented at the Antiquities Department Annual General Meeting-Tanga. 3–5 November 2004.

Masele, F. 2012. Private Business Investments in Heritage Sites in Tanzania: Recent Developments and Challenges for Heritage Management. *Journal of African Archaeological Review*, 29(1), 51–65.

Sabri, R. 2024. A Future Beyond the Impasse? Exploring Post-Conflict Religious Heritage. *The Historic Environment: Policy & Practice*, 15(3), 302–327. https://doi.org/10.1080/17567505.2024.2386640

Said, C., & Ichumbaki, E. B. 2022. Ours or Yours? Localizing the 'Mixed Sites' Concept for the Sustainable Preservation of Heritage in Africa: The Case of Chongoleani Peninsular, Tanzania. *International Journal of Cultural Policy*, 29(3), 299–313. https://doi.org/10.1080/10286632.2022.2049769

Schmidt, P. R., 1996. The Human Right to a Cultural Heritage: African Applications. In: P. R. Schmidt & R. McIntosh, eds. *Plundering Africa's Past*. Bloomington: University of Indiana Press, pp. 18–28.

United Republic of Tanzania–(URT). 1964. *An Act to Provide for the Preservation and Protection of Sites and Articles of Paleontological, Archaeological, Historical or Natural Interest and for Matters Connected Therewith and Incidental Thereto*. Dar es Salaam: Government Printer.

United Republic of Tanzania–(URT). 1979. *Antiquities Amendment Act No. 22 of 1979*. Dar es Salaam: Government Printer.

6

RESOURCE DIPLOMACY, CULTURAL HERITAGE AND COMMUNITY RESILIENCE IN THE PILBARA, WESTERN AUSTRALIA

Melathi Saldin and
José Antonio González Zarandona

Introduction

> Indigenous peoples have suffered from historic injustices as a result of, inter alia, their colonization and dispossession of their lands, territories and resources, thus preventing them from exercising, in particular, their right to development in accordance with their own needs and interests.
>
> United Nations Declaration on the Rights of
> Indigenous Peoples (United Nations, 2007: 3)

This chapter uses the Murujuga Cultural Landscape as a lens to explore the nexus between the protection and the destruction of heritage in Australia. Murujuga is the largest rock art site in the world with continued significance to present-day Indigenous communities, which coincidentally also host some of the most extractive industries that process and transport natural gas, iron ore and salt (González Zarandona, 2020a). The Murujuga Cultural Landscape was included in Australia's World Heritage Tentative List in 2020. The Australian Government nominated this property for inclusion in the UNESCO World Heritage List in January 2023 (Murujuga Aboriginal Corporation, 2023). The nomination was formally accepted by the UNESCO World Heritage Centre in March 2024, with an evaluation of the property by the International Council for Monuments and Sites (ICOMOS) – a UNESCO Advisory Body – taking place later that year (Murujuga Aboriginal Corporation, 2024). Murujuga was listed by the World Heritage Committee in 2025 (Department of Climate Change, Energy, the Environment and Water, 2024).

The nomination of Murujuga to Australia's UNESCO World Heritage List is a result of decades of activism by the Indigenous Ngarda-Ngarli people to safeguard

DOI: 10.4324/9781003623724-6

what is considered the world's 'largest, densest and most diverse' collection of rock art (Government of Western Australia & Murujuga Aboriginal Corporation, 2019a) from periods of damage and destruction from extractive industries. The Murujuga Cultural Landscape was accepted under three criteria: (i) a masterpiece of human creative genius; (ii) a unique cultural tradition that is living; and (iii) an outstanding example of human settlement, land or sea representative of a culture, or human interaction with the environment (Murujuga Aboriginal Corporation, 2024). As a result, Murujuga Cultural Landscape is the second Australian property to be nominated solely for its Indigenous values, following the World Heritage listing of the Budj Bim Cultural Landscape in 2019.

Heritage as resource diplomacy

This chapter establishes the intellectual framework to advance work on the relationship between heritage destruction, protection and diplomacy by looking into contact zones where destruction and diplomacy are entangled and blurred. We refer to these blurry spaces as cracks. Indeed, much of the academic and popular debates on heritage's political and economic entanglements are framed through the lenses of dissonance, conflict or contestation (Winter, 2015, p. 997). These lenses of problematising the complexities of heritage and preservation have inadvertently resulted in the subsuming of other equally productive modes of heritage analysis. Given this context, scholars such as Winter (2015, p. 998) advocate the importance of achieving a sense of analytical balance to illustrate the complexities emerging from the politicisation of heritage and bring to focus hitherto under-theorised means of heritage analysis. Thus, scholars have increasingly begun to demonstrate the importance of diplomacy for understanding the matrix of cultural heritage politics and have focused on exploring and analysing the role of heritage and culture as a resource for international cooperation and aid (Akagawa, 2016; Clarke, 2014; Luke & Kersel, 2012; Winter, 2016). The increasing importance of cultural cooperation and aid within the broader diplomatic ties of the Asia-Pacific region is also reflected in the increasing academic interest in 'heritage diplomacy' (Luke & Kersel, 2012; Winter, 2016) and 'cultural diplomacy' (Akagawa, 2016; Clarke, 2014) in the sphere of 'Heritage Studies' – broadly defined.

However, not all diplomatic antics are the same. In this chapter, we are concerned about resource diplomacy coined in the 1970s. According to Arndt (1974, p. 6), the term designates the 'use of economic power for political purposes . . . or the use of political power for economic purposes'. In the Australian context, this translates into a foreign policy that exploits natural resources to maximise Australia's profits from trade with other countries. It also minimises foreign ownership and control of Australia's resources while safeguarding Australia's future needs for these resources. Other perceived benefits include encouraging domestic processing for export thus minimising Australia's dependence on foreign supplies of resources as a matter of security, while safeguarding the interests of Australian Indigenous people in developing these resources (Arndt, 1974, p. 8). Partially based on Australian Prime Minister Gough Whitlam's desire to, on the one hand, encourage the extraction and processing of minerals in Australia and, on the other hand, to take responsibility for the effects of mining on the lands of the Indigenous people, this policy introduced in the 1970s (a few decades after the discovery of rich deposits of mineral resources in the Pilbara) would have secured the preservation and conservation of Indigenous heritage sites. The policy, unfortunately, took a different turn, and today, foreign and domestic companies dominate the market and hold ownership of the Indigenous lands, sometimes in conjunction with Indigenous groups. As a result, Indigenous heritage sites in Australia exist in a contact zone where protection and destruction constantly overlap. Perhaps, there is no better example to illustrate this overlap than the visit of the former Minister of Foreign Affairs, Julie Bishop, organised in 2014, when she took more than 80 ambassadors and heads of state to Western Australia to tour 'mine sites, Aboriginal sites and a port and in the resource-rich Pilbara' (Minister for Foreign Affairs, 2014).

The Murujuga cultural landscape: a case study

Located in the Pilbara district in Western Australia, about 1,650 km from Perth, Murujuga (meaning hip bone sticking out in the Yaburara language, one of the many Ngayarda languages that are closely related in the Pilbara) is an Indigenous name for an island that forms part of the Dampier Archipelago. It is also known by its colonial name, the Burrup Peninsula (Figure 6.1).

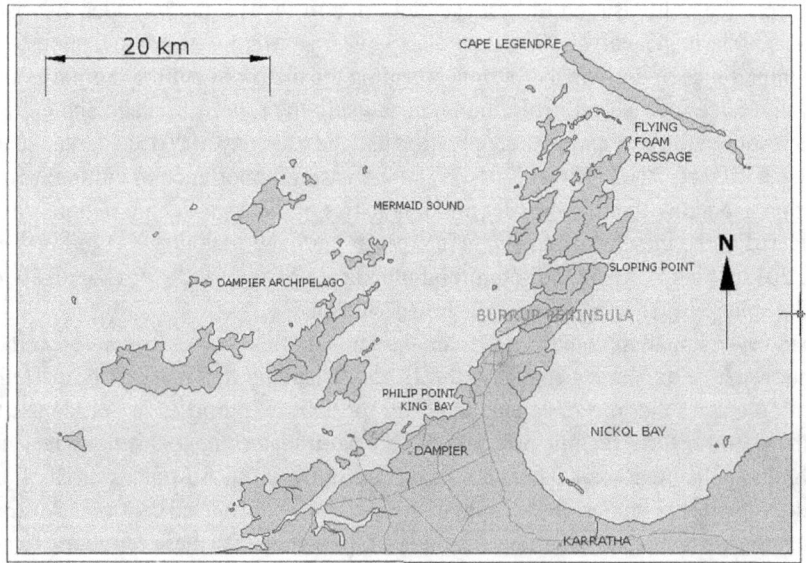

FIGURE 6.1 The Dampier Archipelago and Burrup Peninsula, Western Australia, 2008.

Source: Wikimedia Commons

Archaeological evidence indicates that human occupation of the area dates to the late Pleistocene era, with important evidence of shifting land use in response to environmental and landscape changes (McDonald et al., 2018). The area received its European name from William Dampier, an English explorer, seaman and adventurer who first sailed to the area in 1699 but did not mention the petroglyphs that dot the landscape. Jefferson Stow was the first European explorer to indicate its existence; he was shown 'drawings' on the rocks by the area's Indigenous inhabitants (Figures 6.2 and 6.3). Stow recorded sketches of 'fishes, turtles, lizards, and

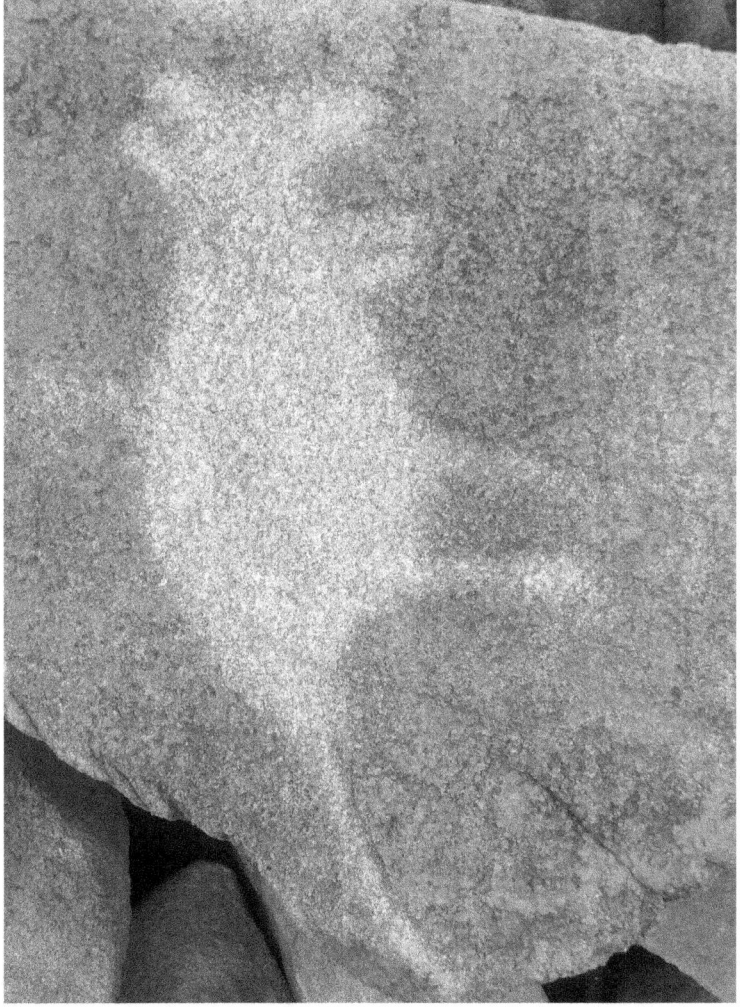

FIGURE 6.2   Carving of native species (marsupial) from the Burrup Peninsula, 2012.

Source: Photograph by Jussarian, Wikimedia Commons

FIGURE 6.3   Carving of a hunting scene in the Burrup Peninsula, 2012.

Source: Photograph by Tradimus, Wikimedia Commons

different kinds of birds, including emus' among the rocks (Stow, 1981, p. 66). The local Indigenous people believe that the *Marrga,* or Creator Spirits, made these drawings to show people how to live on the land (Government of Western Australia and Murujuga Aboriginal Corporation, 2019b). The petroglyphs embody the laws of the local Indigenous people. As such, they are didactic images that teach the young generations about the guidelines to follow when caring for the country[1] (González Zarandona, 2020a). In a sense, the petroglyphs are the literal materialisation of *heritage*, as the concept is nowadays understood: celebrating the past in the present for the future.

Early colonial accounts named the area's original inhabitants the Yaburara people, whose numbers were decimated following European contact. The Flying Foam Massacre of 1868 was a particularly violent encounter in sustained efforts by European settlers to eliminate the Indigenous inhabitants of Murujuga (Bednarik, 2022; Paterson et al., 2023), and some scholars contend that up to 100 Yaburara men, women and children were killed in this attack (Bednarik, 2022). Diseases such as smallpox introduced by European settlers further devastated Indigenous populations in the region (Paterson et al., 2023, p. 23). By the 19th century, a nearby whaling station and a pearling industry were established, and the Yaburara people were enslaved to obtain the pearls, with many of them living in pastoral stations after a process of acculturation. Following colonisation, the knowledge about the petroglyphs and their meanings remained secret and scarcely communicated to the younger generations (González Zarandona, 2020a, p. 23). Owing to the small number of Yaburara people in the present day, there are five Traditional Owner groups – Ngarluma, Yindjibarndi, Yaburara, Mardudhunera and Wong-Goo-Tt-Oo – collectively known as the Ngarda-Ngarli who care for the country. They are represented by the Murujuga Aboriginal Corporation (MAC) in matters relating to the present-day use of this land (Government of Western Australia and Murujuga Aboriginal Corporation, 2019b). MAC comprises two members of the following Indigenous groups (two members each from the Ngarluma, Yindjibarndi, Yaburara and Mardudhunera groups). In comparison, four Wong-Goo-Tt-Oo members are represented on the MAC Board of Directors. Though the Yaburara people tradition-ally inhabited Murujuga in the past, today, all five groups are interested in taking care of the land as a collective. Their perceptions about rock art are all similar as they treat the petroglyphs as didactic images that Elders use to teach the younger generations about the Law (the guidelines) to take care of the Country.

National politics and World Heritage listing: diplomacy and destruction

The destruction of heritage sites in Murujuga dates to the discovery of extensive deposits of natural resources such as iron ore and natural gas in the 1960s (Bed-narik, 2006; González Zarandona, 2020a; Mulvaney, 2011). When the Australian government lifted the embargo on exporting iron ore in 1961, the Pilbara became an industrial hub for excavating, processing and exporting the much-sought-after minerals. By mid-1965, several companies had already been established, and the town of Dampier had been founded (González Zarandona, 2020a, p. 144). Although the extraction of minerals and liquefied natural gas is performed far away from Murujuga, the processing and transport of the minerals to the ships in the port have damaged the site in many places. This increased commodification of land resulted in the controversial deregistering of Murujuga from the Western Australian Herit-age Register in 2015 (McQuire, 2015; Parke, 2015; Zaunmayr, 2015). Other stud-ies have established that industrial pollution caused by companies operating on the island has damaged the petroglyphs in many ways (Smith et al., 2021, 2022).

The destruction of rock art sites in Murujuga in the 1960s was not systematically recorded. Therefore, it is unknown how many sites were destroyed, or petroglyphs removed owing to the construction of roads and belt conveyors for mining opera-tions or through pollution from the mining process. Regardless of the destruction type, the mining impacts on Murujuga cannot be overstated. Following decades of damage and destruction to the site, Murujuga was included on the Austral-ian National Heritage Register in July 2007 as the Dampier Archipelago (includ-ing the Burrup Peninsula). This was owing to it containing one of the world's

FIGURE 6.4   Murujuga National Park, 2017.

Source: Photograph by Marius Fenger, Wikimedia Commons

largest and densest collections of rock art, complex stone arrangements and other archaeologically significant features, as well as its ongoing significance to the Indigenous Ngarda-Ngarli people (Department of Climate Change, Energy, the Environment and Water, 2021). Another important form of protection came in the form of the declaration of the Murujuga National Park in January 2013, with the park co-managed by MAC and the Western Australian Department of Biodiversity, Conservation and Attractions (Mulvaney, 2022, p. 156) (Figure 6.4).

The primary legislation in place to manage Aboriginal heritage sites in Western Australia is the Western Australian (WA) Aboriginal Heritage Act (1972), which was, in theory, one of the most advanced heritage protection legislations when it was created. However, throughout the years, the Act has become a tool that governments (pressured by mining companies and other interest groups) have used to facilitate development, resulting in the legal destruction of Indigenous heritage sites (Dortch, 2024, p. 25; Mulvaney, 2022, p. 161). As Maramanindji scholar Sonia Smallacombe (2005, p. 9) contends, much of the early Australian heritage legislation drafted in the 1960s and 1970s, including the WA Aboriginal Heritage Act (1972) (Government of Western Australia, 1972), was formulated with the support of academics and heritage professionals but with little to no input from the Indigenous peoples themselves. The WA Aboriginal Heritage Act is, arguably, one of the more problematic heritage legislations of all Australian states and territories. The Act is over half a century old and has only undergone minor amendments over the last few decades. A moment of change in this largely impotent legislation was evident in 2021 when mining giant Rio Tinto destroyed another significant Indigenous rock art site in nearby Juukan Gorge in its bid to extend the Brockman 4 iron ore mine (Huntley & Wallis, 2023, p. 386). The destruction of this site resulted in a global outcry, and the Australian government also launched a Federal Parliamentary Inquiry into its destruction (González Zarandona, 2020b; Huntley & Wallis, 2023). These events ultimately pressured the WA government to review the Act in 2021, with the most significant amendments requiring a more robust consultation with Traditional Owners. Despite this seeming progress, the amended Act was repealed less than a month after coming into force in 2023, owing to sustained pressure from opposition political parties and farming/pastoralist organisations (Carmody, 2023; Wallace & Pollock, 2024). Moreover, using political power to influence economic purposes through resource diplomacy is evident here. The protection of Indigenous sites in WA occurs *after* the resources are extracted, commodified and sold.

In this respect, the push for World Heritage status by Indigenous activists and other stakeholders of Murujuga appears to be a last resort to ensure its preservation,[2] following the repeated failures of state- and national-level legislation to protect it sufficiently. From the viewpoint of Traditional Owners, World Heritage status will bring many benefits. These include global visibility, increased tourism and, most importantly, the 'obligation' of the Australian and WA Governments to protect Murujuga's World Heritage values. Achieving World Heritage status also require to develop proposals that constitute a significant threat to World Heritage values to be referred to the Australian Government for a decision on the need for a heritage impact assessment (HIA) (Government of Western Australia & Murujuga Aboriginal Corporation, 2019a).

Though World Heritage status can, among other benefits, go a long way in creating greater global visibility for the ongoing conservation and protection efforts at Murujuga, these also come with some limitations. First, the high thresholds of the concept of Outstanding Universal Value (OUV) mean that many values at the local/community level are not readily recognised or protected and, hence, more vulnerable to destruction (Buckley, 2018; Cameron, 2015). Second, like with many other parts of the world, Australian legislation, at both state and national levels, is weak in recognising and protecting the intangible dimensions of heritage. Indeed, even conservation best practice guidance documents, such as the 2013 Australia ICOMOS Charter for Places of Cultural Significance (the Burra Charter), are limited to offering guidance on safeguarding intangible heritage that is only associated with the place (Australia ICOMOS, 2017; Buckley & Sullivan, 2014, p. 39). Such a narrow scope precludes important intangible elements such as language, cultural practices and beliefs about the natural environment and contradicts the Country's more holistic Indigenous worldview (Buckley & Sullivan, 2014, p. 39).

Third, heritage sites in the Pilbara, including Murujuga, must contend with the irony and conflict of interest of mining companies employing archaeologists and other heritage consultants. Indeed, what we know about these heritage sites is based on archaeological assessments and other forms of research carried out by archaeologists and other heritage professionals who are either employed or funded by the same companies that destroy them. Moreover, most of this knowledge is not made public and remains unavailable (Morse & White, 2009). In archaeological impact assessments that must be undertaken before any development activities, the resource diplomacy in play is also responsible for creating knowledge that is often discarded once the permits to operate on Indigenous heritage sites are received. Indeed, any HIA must be conducted by objective third parties. Therefore, while the quest for World Heritage status can improve the current status quo, valuable lessons from other World Heritage Sites, including those within Australia, can be a caution for Murujuga.

Implications of World Heritage listing

Most state Parties treat achieving World Heritage status as the 'most desirable and prestigious badge for nation-states to secure' (Meskell, 2013, p. 157). Purported benefits include comprehensive protection and conservation of the respective cultural and natural heritage, marketing of the respective sites to the global community and development of cooperation between the host country of the inscribed site and other nations. Moreover, World Heritage Sites attract tourists, which may be a catalyst for preserving the heritage of humanity, increasing the participation of local communities in safeguarding heritage, and bringing economic benefits from tourism and other economic activities (Galla, 2012; UNESCO World Heritage Centre, 2008, p. 3). Despite such broad claims, some scholars are more circumspect about these claimed benefits and argue that the World Heritage Program's increasing focus is on adding properties to an already burgeoning list, with less concern for safeguarding those already inscribed (Caust & Vecco, 2017; Meskell & Liuzza, 2022, p. 392; Vecco & Caust, 2019).

Meskell and Liuzza (2022) observed that the focus on listing results from the increased politicisation of the World Heritage system in recent decades. This scenario is evident in the growing divergence between the Advisory Body's recommendations on nominations (i.e. Referral, Deferral and Not to Inscribe) and subsequent World Heritage Committee decisions. This disparity, some scholars argue, is particularly evident when the nominating State Party has a mandate to the World Heritage Committee (Liuzza & Meskell, 2023; Meskell, 2014). Other critiques are the undue influence some World Heritage Committee members (particularly those who are BRICS members) wield to guarantee the inscription of properties nominated by their States Parties (Bertacchini & Saccone, 2012; Meskell, 2012, 2014). There is also a push by some Committee Members to ensure threatened World Heritage properties from within their (and allies') state borders remain off the World Heritage in Danger List (Hølleland et al., 2019; Meskell, 2014).

What about Australia? An early signatory to the World Heritage Convention, Australia had 21 properties on the World Heritage List by 2026. Despite having several mandates to the World Heritage Committee, with its most recent term being between 2017 and 2021, Australia has shown a restrained approach to nominating properties to the World Heritage List. This is notable given the contention of some scholars of the eagerness of certain States Parties who have mandates to the World Heritage Committee to use their influence to guarantee the inscription of their nominated sites to the World Heritage List (Bertacchini & Saccone, 2012; Liuzza & Meskell, 2023; Meskell, 2012). Other scholars, however, are more critical of Australia's role in the global heritage stage, particularly concerning its approach to Indigenous heritage (Boer, 2020; Boer & Gruber, 2017; Lilley & Pocock, 2018; Logan, 2007, 2013). The clash between heritage values and the value of mineral resources for the Australian economy is most evident in the type of World Heritage Sites listed in Australia.

Murujuga are the only Australian World Heritage properties listed solely for its Indigenous cultural values. However, as scholars such as Lennon argue, 60,000 years of Indigenous intervention in the land have meant that the whole of Australia is a cultural landscape (Lennon, 2016, p. 272). Despite this assertion, colonial processes and their institutionalisation in the present day have rendered Indigenous presence on the land largely invisible (Byrne, 2003; Head, 2012). Indeed, Indigenous people remain poorly represented in Australia's 21 World Heritage-listed properties (Lilley & Pocock, 2018). Many of the early World Heritage inscriptions from Australia were inscribed solely for 'natural' heritage values, while Indigenous places and ongoing cultural and spiritual connections therein were often not recognised in the original listing, nor were Traditional Owners meaningfully engaged in the nomination process or the management and conservation initiatives for these sites (Aplin, 2004; Boer, 2020; Lilley & Pocock, 2018). As will be described in detail shortly, those sites that were recognised as mixed properties,[3] such as the Kakadu National Park, laid bare the issues stemming from the tensions between developmental policies and the rights of Traditional Owners (Aplin, 2004; Logan, 2013; O'Brien, 2014). Indeed, as Lilley and Pocock (2018) argue, 'none of Australia's three sites inscribed purely for cultural reasons [Sydney Opera House, Royal Exhibition Building and the Australian Convict Sites[4]] recognises Aboriginal people'. An extreme example of this can be seen in the context of the original 1982 listing of the Tasmanian Wilderness World Heritage Area (TWWHA), which only recognised the archaeological records of Indigenous people but failed to recognise the ongoing association that present-day Indigenous people might have to the area (IUCN, 1989, pp. 6–7). The 1982 International Union for Conservation of Nature (IUCN) technical evaluation referred to the Tasmanian Indigenous people as 'extinct' – echoing the 19th-century narratives of colonial settlers and explorers. Though this statement was removed from official UNESCO documentation in 2023 (Dumas, 2023), it is symptomatic of the broader issues stemming from the permeation of colonial memory into heritage legislation (and practice) in Australia (Davis, 2007).

Several scholars (e.g. see Aplin, 2004; Charlesworth et al., 2006; Logan, 2007, 2013) argue that Australia has an inconsistent approach to managing and conserving its World Heritage properties. How it applies management and conservation principles in World Heritage settings that intersect with Indigenous values. For example, Logan (2007, 2013) argues that managing World Heritage properties with Indigenous values has created human rights conundrums. This is evident in how Traditional Ownership is questioned, and Indigenous communities are restricted in their access to traditional lands (Logan, 2007, 2013). Other scholars, such as Aplin, astutely observe that Australia 'picks and chooses out of all the agreements to which it is a signatory the ones it will apply and adhere to in spirit, as well as to the letter' (Aplin, 2004, p. 172). Furthermore, Charlesworth and colleagues (2006, p. 65) label Australia as 'Janus-faced' in its upholding of (or lack thereof) human rights, particularly in the context of World Heritage properties with Indigenous values. Indeed, there are numerous examples of Australia's inconsistent approach to protecting and safeguarding properties of Indigenous value, World Heritage or otherwise, especially those of Indigenous heritage value located in resource-rich areas.

These tensions are best illustrated in the long-standing issues around Indigenous ownership, resource extraction and politics at the World Heritage Listed Kakadu National Park. As many scholars have argued, at the core level, the issue at Kakadu stemmed from a lack of engagement with the Indigenous Mirarr people (Aplin, 2004; Logan, 2013; O'Brien, 2014). The issues centred on the impact on cultural sites from the uranium mines within the Kakadu National Park, which are located outside the World Heritage boundary area (Aplin, 2004; Logan, 2013; O'Brien, 2014). The exacerbation of these issues resulted in the Mirarr passing the Australian government and taking their grievances directly to the World Heritage Committee, calling for an expert mission to be sent to assess the damage to their sites and to inscribe Kakadu on the List of World Heritage Sites in Danger (Aplin, 2004; Logan, 2007, 2013). As a result, the World Heritage Committee held a single Extraordinary Session on Kakadu in July 1999 (Logan, 2013; O'Brien, 2014). This scenario likely raised global attention to the issues the Mirarr people faced; however, the in-danger inscription that the Traditional Owners had hoped for did not eventuate. There are many possible reasons for this outcome. For example, there was intense Australian government lobbying and other diplomatic manoeuvres to keep Kakadu off the List of World Heritage in Danger. Australia also held a mandate to the World Heritage Committee during the height of discussions around the possible Danger listing of Kakadu, which may also have influenced the decision to keep this property off the List of World Heritage Sites in Danger. Another Australian World Heritage property – the Great Barrier Reef – has also evaded Danger listing on numerous occasions despite growing scientific evidence indicating otherwise (Pocock, 2021), pointing to other more recent examples of the 'diplomatic' machinations some State Parties resort to in evading Danger listing.

For Logan, the Kakadu issues tarnished Australia's good standing on the global heritage stage, resulting in a 'bad boy' reputation in World Heritage circles (Logan, 2013). After more than three decades of inaction, the Australian Labour government has finally ended uncertainty for the Mirarr people. The government's refusal to renew the Jabiluka mineral extraction lease with the majority Rio Tinto-owned Energy Resources Australia mining conglomerate attests to its resolve. Moreover, the Australian government plans to absorb the site into the Kakadu National Park permanently (Greber & Houlbrook-Walk, 2024). Despite this move, Australia has a long way to go to fully repair its standing in the global heritage arena. Indeed, as observed elsewhere (Logan, 2013), heritage professionals still grapple with the Kakadu legacy. The challenge lies in transitioning from the concept of heritage

sites to a more restricted emphasis on the preservation of OUV, where high standards frequently lead to overlooking more localised values (Logan, 2013, p. 163).

Similarly, Disko and Dorough (2022, p. 495) observe that, narrowly, the OUV
has made it almost impossible to recognise Indigenous values without assessing
them to be 'outstanding' in their own right. The additional requirement of being
'unique' or 'exceptional' also stands in contrast to Indigenous worldviews, which
do not claim 'exceptionality' of their heritage over those of other Indigenous communities (Cameron, 2020, p. 849; Disko & Dorough, 2022, p. 495). Whereas
the heritage discourses embodied by international organisations privilege human
genius and individual ownership of the land, Indigenous worldviews emphasise
that they are not the owners of the land but caretakers, and that no one can own
it. The clash of values resulting from these tensions is ever more present in Western Australia (González Zarandona, 2020a). Moreover, the re-spatialisation of the
sacred Indigenous landscape through World Heritage listing, in particular, the rede-
ployment of tools such as boundaries, buffer zones and other forms of control to
contain and tame Indigenous heritage places, may also contribute to weakening
Indigenous claims to the land and interfere with the holistic management of heritage. As Manno Ramutsindela (2020, p. 219) argues, the delineation of 'National
Parks' is premised on the hierarchical ordering of beings and is representative of
the colonisation of nature and people. He further argues that the essence of these
colonial ideologies is perpetuated in present-day international conventions and
protocols, resulting in the sustained alienation of Indigenous people from their
lands (Ramutsindela, 2020). The delineation and division of Indigenous heritage
sites using Western frameworks is also an apt reflection of how companies operating in those protected areas can extract the resources within those sites without
severe legal consequences. However, recent shifts, such as the move towards a
more holistic understanding of heritage as a 'place' in the global heritage management and conservation discourse, present promising possibilities for overcoming
these limitations (Ishizawa & Jo, 2024).

Other challenges facing current and potential Indigenous World Heritage properties in Australia include the Australian government's reticence to ratify the 2003
Convention for the Safeguarding of the Intangible Cultural Heritage (hereafter
referred to as the 2003 ICH Convention). Indeed, as many scholars have argued
in the context of World Heritage and otherwise, the primary focus on the physical fabric of sites has resulted in less attention being paid to the equally important
intangible elements, impeding its holistic management and conservation (Chapagain, 2017; Saldin et al., 2025; Silva, 2022; Sinha, 2017). This reticence to assent
to the ICH Convention is even more problematic in places like Australia because,
unlike the 2003 ICH Convention, the 1972 World Heritage Convention makes no
explicit reference to either human rights or international human rights instruments
(Boer & Gruber, 2017, p. 13; Disko & Dorough, 2022, p. 490). The 2019 revisions to the Operational Guidelines for the Implementation of the World Heritage Convention made progress in adopting human rights in the implementation

of the Convention. However, no concrete mechanism ensures that human rights processes are upheld. Instead, the revisions only 'encourage' States Parties to adopt rights-based approaches when implementing the Convention (Vrdoljak et al., 2021, p. 4). This issue is further compounded in Australia, which does not have a Bill of Rights to ensure the rights of all citizens, particularly Indigenous people, the most disadvantaged communities in the country (Australian Government, 2020; Boer & Gruber, 2017, p. 13).

Further complications also arise because heritage (and related) laws span three tiers of government (Federal/Commonwealth, State and Local), with different laws operating across Australia's nine states and territories. How heritage laws are applied in Australia (particularly at the State and Local government level) has resulted in mixed outcomes. Though there are certainly some common approaches, there is much inconsistency in the definitions, the scope of legislation, governmental policy and administrative arrangements (Aplin, 2007, p. 9; Boer & Gruber, 2017, p. 1). Although there is legislation to protect Indigenous heritage, the reality is that this legislation, especially in mineral resource-rich states, was created with extraction in mind in the first place. In other words, past and existing legislation to protect Indigenous heritage in Australia was born out of the necessity to start extracting natural resources, creating a veneer of legality for these industrial operations. Loopholes in weak heritage legislation have repeatedly been co-opted to avoid any legal ramifications for the destruction of the cultural landscape. The resource diplomacy between Australia and its international trade partners also characterises the relationship between the Australian State and its Indigenous citizens concerning the protection of their heritage: one that privileges political power for economic gain. This scenario is of great concern because all Australian World Heritage properties are on lands significant to local Indigenous communities. As Disko and Sambo Dorough observe:

> many World Heritage Sites are managed in ways that are harmful to Indigenous people and the protection of their heritage, and highly inconsistent with the standards affirmed in the UNDRIP [United Nations Declaration on the Rights of Indigenous Peoples].
>
> (Disko & Dorough, 2022, p. 491)

These challenges notwithstanding, there have also been some positive shifts, particularly a conscious effort to blur tangible–intangible (nature–culture) boundaries and adopt a more holistic management and conservation approach to places of cultural significance. This is evident in the re-inscription of Uluru-Kata Tjuta as a cultural landscape in 1993, the inscription of the Budj Bim Cultural Landscape solely for its Indigenous cultural values in 2019, as well as the retrospective mapping of Indigenous cultural values in several Australian World Heritage properties (see, e.g. the recognition of Indigenous cultural values at the Royal Exhibition Building and Carlton Gardens World Heritage property (GML Heritage, 2022)).

However, such retrospective changes are often not smooth and do not always result in equitable outcomes. The re-inscription of Uluru-Kata Tjuta as a cultural landscape in 1993, for example, enabled Anangu elders to reclaim their role as Traditional Owners of the site and to officially refer to the site by their traditional place names: Uluru and Kata Tjuta (Taylor & Lennon, 2011, p. 550). However, other changes, such as banning tourists from climbing up to Uluru's summit – a sacred Anangu site – was only achieved in 2019, and this was preceded by a rush of tourists wanting to climb the summit one last time. These indicate unequal partnerships between conventional and Indigenous management mechanisms (see also Everingham et al., 2021). Similarly, the claim of extinction of Indigenous Tasmanians in the context of the TWWHA obstructed the recognition of the ongoing/living connection of Tasmanian Indigenous people to that site and, more broadly, has also resulted in structural barriers to their inclusion in heritage and related institutions (Dumas, 2023).

Even though adopting the cultural landscape category, particularly that of associative cultural landscapes, has helped to encourage recognition of intangible values in the context of the 1972 World Heritage Convention, some scholars are more circumspect about what this has achieved. Disko and Dorough (2022) argue that the cultural landscape approach has created a further divide between nature and culture. After all, the World Heritage Committee removed any references to human agency from the World Heritage natural criteria, further impeding the formal recognition of Indigenous peoples' connection to their lands in statements of OUV (Disko and Dorough, 2022, p. 495). In this respect, ratifying the 2003 ICH Convention and the conscious harmonisation of the World Heritage and Intangible Cultural Heritage Conventions at relevant properties can have numerous merits for places like Australia (Connolly, 2007, p. 199; Lixinski, 2020, p. 116). Indeed, as Isabelle Connolly argues, the 1972 World Heritage Convention cannot be fully and meaningfully implemented in Australia and elsewhere (see Ichumbaki, this volume) without ratifying the 2003 ICH Convention (Connolly, 2007, p. 199). This argument is especially pertinent owing to the numerous management and conservation issues evident in Indigenous heritage properties in Australia, particularly those stemming from the artificial separation of nature and culture and tangible and intangible heritage. Developing comprehensive management and conservation strategies that can holistically deal with properties of Indigenous heritage value, such as Murujuga and others, can significantly help recognise their ongoing significance to Indigenous communities, which is crucial to ensuring the well-being of these heritage places and associated communities.

Conclusion

We reflect now on the opening UN quotation of our chapter on the enduring injustices impacting Indigenous peoples globally. As Logan astutely observes in the context of the Kakadu issue, 'Heritage protection has always been about resource management and resource allocation and, therefore, has always had a powerful political dimension and governance context' (Logan, 2013, p. 158). As the Australian examples of Kakadu and Murujuga indicate, Indigenous groups can only expect their heritage to be protected if governments and mineral extraction industries exhaust the natural resources first. The impacts of colonisation, even in so-called postcolonial nations, are perpetuated in diverse ways owing to the institutionalisation of colonial memory in current heritage governance structures, evident in many of the examples discussed in this chapter. This is particularly true of those that binary approaches to heritage affect, such as the nature–culture and tangible–intangible divides.

Despite efforts to address them, such issues remain deeply embedded in international frameworks such as the UNESCO World Heritage and Intangible Cultural Heritage instruments. These issues are compounded by the diverse ways such instruments are operationalised in national/local heritage settings. This includes how state parties comply with World Heritage requirements, such as boundaries, buffer zones and others, to protect heritage. Protection (in the Western legal sense) almost always destroys heritage. In Australia, in particular, such neatly contained notions of heritage stand in contrast to the Indigenous worldviews of the Country, which speak not only to Indigenous people's connections to place (the lands, waterways and sky) but also to a connection that transcends the bounds of physical space (AIATSIS, 2022). Examples worldwide have shown us that developmental needs often trump those of communities, and the impacts are even more significant on the more vulnerable sections of society. There is no easy solution to these issues. However, recognising communities as equal stakeholders and collaborators rather than consultants will be a key first step. Governments will need to listen to the communities they claim to represent. More effort must be made to make space for truth-telling and reparation in complex settler colonial spaces such as Australia. Academics and practitioners, as the interface between the state and the public, have a key role to play, and as we have seen with Murujuga, academic/practitioner activism has gone a long way in calling focus to long-standing conservation issues and ultimately gaining the support needed for World Heritage nomination (Mulvaney, 2022). However, we must also acknowledge the implications of these mining corporations with recourse to archaeology/heritage professionals and funding HIA work, and thus play a part in heritage knowledge creation. Moreover, the recent 'silver sponsorship' of the Australia ICOMOS National Symposium and Annual General Meeting in Perth in October 2024 by the Woodside Energy company (whose operations in the Pilbara have destroyed Indigenous heritage) is a further example of the concerning shifts and conflicts of interest that emerge when such entities also have a stake in knowledge dissemination. Equally troubling are heritage organisations whose mandate is to safeguard heritage and seek and accept their support (see, e.g. Mazza, 2024).

Some may further contend that Australia's record with the treatment of Indigenous people associated with World Heritage Sites paints a rather dismal picture for the future, with only the Indigenous-led nomination of Budj Bim standing as an anomaly. Budj Bim is widely celebrated as an Australian success story. It is the first Indigenous-led and Indigenous-owned World Heritage Site co-managed by Traditional Owners and state heritage authorities (Parks Victoria). The site is primarily managed according to the customary frameworks of the Gunditjmara people (Parks Victoria, 2025). While the Budj Bim example reminds us that achieving just futures is not always an impossibility, we must also be mindful that Budj Bim, unlike Kakadu or Murujuga, does not contain mineral resources such as uranium, iron ore and natural gas, which host multi-billion-dollar extractive industries. In this regard, the inclusion of Murujuga into the World Heritage List is a litmus test for the Australian government's ability to respectfully deal with Indigenous communities, especially where significant economic interests are at stake.

Notes

1 Country is the term used to describe the connection Australia's Indigenous people have to the lands, seas and waterways (AIATSIS, 2022).
2 For a detailed account of the more than 40-decade-long activist work that made the Murujuga World Heritage nomination possible, see (Mulvaney, 2022).
3 The mixed property category recognises both natural and cultural values but not those values that emphasise the interaction between the two.
4 All these properties however have commenced or are in the processes of retrospectively mapping the Indigenous cultural values of these sites but these do not form part of the OUV (see, e.g. GML Heritage, 2022).

References

AIATSIS. (25 May 2022). "Welcome to Country", available at: https://aiatsis.gov.au/explore/welcome-country#toc-what-is-country- (accessed 3 March 2025).

Akagawa, N. (2016). "Japan and the Rise of Heritage in Cultural Diplomacy: Where Are We Heading?", *Future Anterior*, University of Minnesota Press, Vol. 13 No. 1, pp. 124–139.

Aplin, G. (2004). "Kakadu National Park World Heritage Site: Deconstructing the Debate, 1997–2003", *Australian Geographical Studies*, Blackwell Publishing Ltd, Vol. 42 No. 2, pp. 152–174, https://doi.org/10.1111/j.1467-8470.2004.00258.x.

Aplin, G. (2007). "Heritage Protection in Australia: The Legislative and Bureaucratic Framework", in Jones, R., and Shaw, B.J. (Eds.), *Geographies of Australian Heritage: Loving a Sunburnt Country?*, Ashgate, Hampshire, pp. 9–23.

Arndt, H.W. (1974). "Australian Resource Diplomacy", *Advance Australia Where? Foreign Policy in the 1970s. Australian Institute of International Affairs Fourth National Conference*, Australian Institute of International Affairs (AIIA), Adelaide.

Australia ICOMOS. (2017). *Practice Note on Intangible Cultural Heritage and Place*, Australia ICOMOS, Australia.

Australian Government. (2020). *Closing the Gap Report 2020: The Annual Report to Parliament on Progress in Closing the Gap*, Canberra.

Bednarik, R. (2006). "Australian Apocalypse–Petroglyphs Under Threat", *Teaching History*, Vol. 40 No. 3, pp. 36–41, https://doi.org/10.3316/ielapa.200701728.

Bednarik, R.G. (2022). "The Killing Fields of Murujuga", *Sovereign Union – First Nations Asserting Sovereignty*, available at: http://nationalunitygovernment.org/content/flying-foam-massacre-killing-fields-murujuga (accessed 16 April 2024).

Bertacchini, E.E., and Saccone, D. (2012). "Toward a Political Economy of World Heritage", *Journal of Cultural Economics*, Vol. 36 No. 4, pp. 327–352, https://doi.org/10.1007/s.

Boer, B. (2020). "The Destruction and Revival of Indigenous Heritage in Australia", *Sydney Law School–Legal Studies Research Paper*, Vol. 20/10 No. July, https://doi.org/10.2139/ssrn.3548333.

Boer, B., and Gruber, S. (2017). "Legal Frameworks for World Heritage and Human Rights in Australia", *Sydney Law School–Legal Studies Research Paper*, Vol. 17/28 No. March, pp. 29–30.

Buckley, K., and Sullivan, S. (2014). "Issues in Values-Based Management for Indigenous Cultural Heritage in Australia", *APT Bulletin*, Vol. 45 No. 4, pp. 35–42.

Buckley, K. (2018). "World Heritage Sites Designation," in *The Encyclopedia of Archaeological Sciences*, John Wiley & Sons, Inc., https://doi.org/10.1002/9781119188230. saseas0610.

Byrne, D. (2003). "Nervous Landscapes: Race and Space in Australia", *Journal of Social Archaeology*, Vol. 3 No. 2, pp. 169–193.

Cameron, C. (2015). "Entre Chien et Loup: World Heritage Cultural Landscapes on the Fortieth Anniversary of the World Heritage Convention," 4 in Taylor, K., St Clair, A., and Mitchell, N.J. (Eds.), *Conserving Cultural Landscapes: Challenges and New Directions*, Routledge.

Cameron, C. (2020). "The UNESCO Imprimatur: Creating Global (in)Significance", *International Journal of Heritage Studies*, Routledge, Vol. 26 No. 9, pp. 845–856, https://doi.org/10.1080/13527258.2020.1746923.

Carmody, J. (2023). "Cook Government to Scrap Aboriginal Cultural Heritage Act After Months of Controversy", *ABC News*, 4 August, available at: https://www.abc.net.au/news/2023-08-04/wa-government-scrap-aboriginal-cultural-heritage-act-/102692282 (accessed 20 February 2025).

Caust, J., and Vecco, M. (2017). "Is UNESCO World Heritage Recognition a Blessing or a Burden? Evidence from Developing Asian Countries", *Journal of Cultural Heritage*, Elsevier Masson SAS, Vol. 27, pp. 1–9, https://doi.org/10.1016/j.culher.2017.02.004.

Chapagain, N.K. (2017). "Blurring Boundaries and Moving Beyond the Tangible/Intangible and the Natural/Cultural Classifications of Heritage: Cases from Nepal", in Silva, K.D., and Sinha, A. (Eds.), *Cultural Landscapes of South Asia: Studies in Heritage Conservation and Management*, Routledge, Abingdon & New York, pp. 24–38.

Charlesworth, H., Chiam, M., Hovell, D., and Williams, G. (2006). *No Country Is an Island: Australia and International Law*, UNSW Press, Sydney.

Clarke, A. (2014). "Scotland in Kolkata: Transnational Heritage, Cultural Diplomacy and City Image", *Historic Environment*, Vol. 26 No. 3, pp. 87–97.

Connolly, I. (2007). "Can the World Heritage Convention be Adequately Implemented in Australia Without Australia Becoming a Party to the Intangible Heritage Convention?", Vol. 24, pp. 198–209.

Davis, M. (2007). "Legislation for Preservation", *Writing Heritage: The Depiction of Indigenous Heritage in European-Australian Writings*, Australian Scholarly Publishing, Kew, Vic.

Department of Climate Change, Energy, the Environment and Water. (2021). "National Heritage Places–Dampier Archipelago (including Burrup Peninsula)", available at: https://www.dcceew.gov.au/parks-heritage/heritage/places/national/dampier-archipelago (accessed 14 February 2025).

Department of Climate Change, Energy, the Environment and Water. (2024). "Joint Media Release: Next Step in Murujuga World Heritage Nomination", available at: https://minister.dcceew.gov.au/plibersek/media-releases/joint-media-release-next-step-murujuga-world-heritage-nomination (accessed 7 March 2025).

Disko, S., and Dorough, D.S. (2022). "We Are not in Geneva on the Human Rights Council: Indigenous Peoples' Experiences with the World Heritage Convention", *International*

Journal of Cultural Property, Cambridge University Press, Vol. 29 No. 4, pp. 487–530, https://doi.org/10.1017/S0940739122000418.

Dortch, J. (2024). "The Shifting Sands of Aboriginal Cultural Heritage Management in Western Australia", *Australian Archaeology*, Taylor and Francis Ltd., https://doi.org/10.1080/03122417.2024.2317524.

Dumas, D. (2023). "UNESCO Removes 'Hurtful' Document Claiming Tasmanian Aboriginal People 'Extinct'", *The Guardian*, 23 August, available at: https://www.theguardian.com/australia-news/2023/aug/28/unesco-removes-hurtful-document-claiming-tasmanian-aboriginal-people-extinct (accessed 25 November 2024).

Everingham, P., Peters, A., and Higgins-Desbiolles, F. (2021). "The (im)possibilities of Doing Tourism Otherwise: The Case of Settler Colonial Australia and the Closure of the Climb at Uluru", *Annals of Tourism Research*, Elsevier Ltd, Vol. 88, https://doi.org/10.1016/j.annals.2021.103178.

Galla, A. (2012). "Introduction", in Galla, A. (Ed.), *World Heritage: Benefits Beyond Borders*, Cambridge University Press, Cambridge, pp. 1–3.

GML Heritage. (2022). *Traditional Owner and First Peoples' Cultural Values for the Royal Exhibition Building and Carlton Gardens Final Report with Addendum*, Sydney, Canberra, Melbourne.

González Zarandona, J.A. (2020a). *Murujuga: Rock Art, Heritage, and Landscape Iconoclasm*, University of Pennsylvania Press, Philadelphia.

González Zarandona, J.A. (2020b). "The History of Indigenous Australia is not Written in Books but it is Engraved on the Rocks in the Landscape; that is why Indigenous Heritage is Obliterated in Australia.", *Alfred Deakin Institute for Globalisation*, available at: https://adi.deakin.edu.au/news/the-history-of-indigenous-australia-is-not-written-in-books-but-it-is-engraved-on-the-rocks-in-the-landscape (accessed 22 June 2023).

Government of Western Australia. (1972). "Aboriginal Heritage Act 1972 Government of Western Australia".

Government of Western Australia and Murujuga Aboriginal Corporation. (2019a). "Why Nominate Murujuga and What Will it Mean?", available at: https://www.dbca.wa.gov.au/management/world-heritage-areas/murujuga-world-heritage-nomination (accessed 11 January 2024).

Government of Western Australia and Murujuga Aboriginal Corporation. (2019b). "Traditional Owners of Murujuga", available at: https://www.dbca.wa.gov.au/management/world-heritage-areas/murujuga-world-heritage-nomination (accessed 11 January 2024).

Greber, J., and Houlbrook-Walk, M. (2024). "Jabiluka Uranium Mine to Become Part of Kakadu National Park in Historic win for Mirarr Traditional Owners", *ABC News*, 26 July, available at: https://amp.abc.net.au/article/104148912 (accessed 25 November 2024).

Head, L. (2012). "Cultural Landscapes", in Hicks, D., and Beaudry, M.C. (Eds.), *The Oxford Handbook of Material Culture Studies*, Oxford University Press, Oxford, pp. 1–13, https://doi.org/10.1093/oxfordhb/9780199218714.013.0018.

Hølleland, H., Hamman, E., and Phelps, J. (2019). "Naming, Shaming and Fire Alarms: The Compilation, Development and Use of the List of World Heritage in Danger", *Transnational Environmental Law*, Cambridge University Press, Vol. 8 No. 1, pp. 35–57, https://doi.org/10.1017/S2047102518000225.

Huntley, J., and Wallis, L.A. (2023). "Case Study: The Destruction of Australian Aboriginal Heritage and its Implications for Indigenous Peoples Globally", in González Zarandona, J.A., Cunliffe, E., and Saldin, M. (Eds.), *The Routledge Handbook of Heritage Destruction*, Routledge, London and New York, pp. 384–394.

Ishizawa, M., and Jo, E. (2024). In Ishizawa, M., and Jo, E. (Eds.), *Heritage Place Lab: A Model for Research-Practice Collaboration in the Context of World Heritage – Report of the Pilot Phase 2021–2022*. ICCROM, Rome.

IUCN. (1989). "507: Tasmanian Wilderness (Australia)–World Heritage Nomination IUCN Summary", *IUCN, Gland*, available at: https://whc.unesco.org/en/list/181/documents/ (accessed 26 November 2024).

Lennon, J. (2016). "Sustaining Australia's Cultural Landscapes", *Landscape Journal: Design, Planning and Management of Land*, Vol. 35 No. 2, pp. 271–286.

Lilley, I., and Pocock, C. (2018). "Australia's Problem with Aboriginal World Heritage", *The Conversation*, https://theconversation.com/australias-problem-with-aboriginal-world-heritage-82912 (accessed 7 November 2023).

Liuzza, C., and Meskell, L. (2023). "Power, Persuasion and Preservation: Exacting Times in the World Heritage Committee", *Territory, Politics, Governance*, Routledge, Vol. 11 No. 7, pp. 1265–1280, https://doi.org/10.1080/21622671.2021.1924851.

Lixinski, L. (2020). "Article 3(a). Relationship to Other International Heritage Instruments", in Lixinski, L., and Blake, J. (Eds.), *The 2003 UNESCO Intangible Heritage Convention: A Commentary*, Routledge, London.

Logan, W.S. (2007). "Closing Pandora's Box: Human Rights Conundrums in Cultural Heritage Protection", *Cultural Heritage and Human Rights*, Springer, New York, pp. 33–52.

Logan, W.S. (2013). "Australia, Indigenous Peoples and World Heritage from Kakadu to Cape York: State Party Behaviour under the World Heritage Convention", *Journal of Social Archaeology*, Vol. 13 No. 2, pp. 153–176, https://doi.org/10.1177/1469605313476783.

Luke, C., and Kersel, M.M. (2012). *U.S. Cultural Diplomacy and Archaeology: Soft Power, Hard Heritage*, Routledge, New York.

Mazza, G. (2024). " 'Highly offensive': Cultural Heritage Conference Sponsored by Woodside", *The Last Place on Earth*, available at: https://www.lastplaceonearth.com.au/heritage-preservation-group-accepts-sponsorship-from-woodside-despite-murujuga-rock-art-threat/ (accessed 22 March 2025).

McDonald, J., Reynen, W., Ditchfield, K., Dortch, J., Leopold, M., Stephenson, B., Whitley, T., Ward, I., and Veth, P. (2018). "Murujuga Rockshelter: First Evidence for Pleistocene Occupation on the Burrup Peninsula", *Quaternary Science Reviews*, Elsevier Ltd, Vol. 193, pp. 266–287, https://doi.org/10.1016/j.quascirev.2018.06.002.

McQuire, A. (2015). "WA Government Deregisters World's Oldest Rock Art Collection as Sacred Site", *Newmatilda.Com*, available at: https://newmatilda.com/2015/04/29/wa-government-deregisters-worlds-oldest-rock-art-collection-sacred-site/ (accessed 22 November 2017).

Meskell, L. (2012). "The Rush to Inscribe: Reflections on the 35th Session of the World Heritage Committee, UNESCO Paris, 2011", *Journal of Field Archaeology*, Vol. 37 No. 2, pp. 145–151, https://doi.org/10.1179/0093469012Z.00000000014.

Meskell, L. (2013). "UNESCO and the Fate of the World Heritage Indigenous Peoples Council of Experts (WHIPCOE)", *International Journal of Cultural Property*, Vol. 20 No. 2, pp. 155–174, https://doi.org/10.1017/S0940739113000039.

Meskell, L. (2014). *States of Conservation: Protection, Politics, and Pacting within UNESCO's World Heritage Committee, Source: Anthropological Quarterly*, Vol. 87.

Meskell, L., and Liuzza, C. (2022). "The World is not Enough: New Diplomacy and Dilemmas for the World Heritage Convention at 50", in *International Journal of Cultural Property*, Cambridge University Press (CUP), Cambridge, pp. 1–17, https://doi.org/10.1017/s0940739122000030.

Minister for Foreign Affairs. (2014). "Diplomatic Corps Visit to Western Australia", *Minister for Foreign Affairs, The Hon Julie Bishop MP*, available at: https://www.foreignminister.gov.au/minister/julie-bishop/media-release/diplomatic-corps-visit-western-australia (accessed 22 March 2025).

Morse, K., and White, J.P. (Eds.). (2009). "Pilbara Archaeology", Western Australian Museum, Perth.

Mulvaney, K. (2011). *Murujuga Marni – Dampier Petroglyphs: Shadows in the Landscape, Echoes Across Time*, University of New England, Armidale.

Mulvaney, K. (2022). "Without Them, What then? People, Petroglyphs and Murujuga", in Tacon, P.S.C., May, S.K., Frederick, U.K., and McDonald, J. (Eds.), *Histories of Australian Rock Art Research*, Australian National University, Canberra, pp. 155–172.

Murujuga Aboriginal Corporation. (2023). "World Heritage Nomination Places Ngarda-Ngarli at the Heart of Decision-Making for Murujuga", *Murujuga Aboriginal Corporation*, 10 February, available at: https://murujuga.org.au/world-heritage-nomination-submitted/ (accessed 8 August 2024).

Murujuga Aboriginal Corporation. (2024). "World Heritage Listing", *Murujuga Aboriginal Corporation*, available at: https://murujuga.org.au/world-heritage/world-heritage-listing/ (accessed 11 January 2024).

O'Brien, J. (2014). "No Straight Thing: Experiences of the Mirarr Traditional Owners of Kakadu National Park with the World Heritage Convention", in Disko, S., and Tugendhat, H. (Eds.), *World Heritage Sites and Indigenous Peoples' Rights, IWGIA. Forest Peoples Programme and the Gundjeihmi Aboriginal Corporation, Copenhagen*, IWGA, Copenhagen, pp. 313–338.

Parke, E. (2015). "World Heritage Hopes Pinned on Archaeological Dig in Burrup Peninsula Industrial Heartland", *ABC News*, 19 July, available at: https://www.abc.net.au/news/2015-07-19/burrup-peninsula-archaeological-dig-world-heritage-hopes/6631322 (accessed 7 November 2024).

Parks Victoria. (2025). "Co-Operative Management", available at: https://www.parks.vic.gov.au/managing-country-together/traditional-owner-partnerships/cooperative-management (accessed 22 March 2025).

Paterson, A., McDonald, J., and Gara, T. (2023). "Lifeways to Massacre: A History of Encounter Across Dampier Archipelago", in McDonald, J., and Mulvaney, K. (Eds.), *Murujuga: Dynamics of the Dreaming*, UWA Publishing, Perth, pp. 3–45.

Pocock, C. (2021). "Great Barrier Reef World Heritage: Nature in Danger", *Queensland Review*, Cambridge University Press, Vol. 28 No. 2, pp. 118–129, https://doi.org/10.1017/qre.2022.8.

Ramutsindela, M. (2020). "National Parks and (Neo)Colonialisms", in Legun, K., Keller, J.C., Carolan, M., and Bell, M.M. (Eds.), *The Cambridge Handbook of Environmental Sociology: Volume 1*, Vol. 1, Cambridge University Press, Cambridge, pp. 206–222, https://doi.org/10.1017/9781108554510.015.

Saldin, M., Buckley, K., Tantinipankul, W., Teraparbwang, K., and Sweet, J. (2025). "Applying the UNESCO Competence Framework for Cultural Heritage Management at Chiang Mai, Thailand", *Journal of Cultural Heritage Management and Sustainable Development*, Vol. forthcoming.

Silva, K.D. (2022). "Mapping Intangible Cultural Heritage in Asian Historic Urban Landscapes", *The Routledge Handbook of Cultural Landscape Heritage in The Asia-Pacific*, Routledge, Abingdon, pp. 356–370.

Sinha, A. (2017). "Introduction", in Silva, K.D., and Sinha, A. (Eds.), *Cultural Landscapes of South Asia: Studies in Heritage Conservation and Management*, Routledge, Abingdon and New York, pp. 1–9.

Smallacombe, S. (2005). "Protecting Indigenous People's Knowledge Systems", *Ngoonjook*, Vol. 26, pp. 7–14, https://doi.org/10.3316/ielapa.912302833702213.

Smith, B.W., Black, J.L., Mulvaney, K.J., and Hoerlé, S. (2021). "Monitoring Rock Art Decay: Archival Image Analysis of Petroglyphs on Murujuga, Western Australia", *Conservation and Management of Archaeological Sites*, Vol. 23 No. 5–6, pp. 198–220.

Smith, B.W., Black, J.L., Hoerle, S., Ferland, M.A., Diffey, S.M., Neumann, J.T., and Geisler, T. (2022). "The Impact of Industrial Pollution on the Rock Art of Murujuga, Western Australia", *Rock Art Research: The Journal of the Australian Rock Art Research Association (AURA)*, Vol. 39 No. (1), pp. 3–14.

Stow, J.P. (1981). *The Voyage of the Forlorn Hope from Escape Cliffs to Champion Bay 1865*, Adelaide, Sullivans Cove.

Taylor, K., and Lennon, J. (2011). "Cultural Landscapes: A Bridge Between Culture and Nature?" *International Journal of Heritage Studies*, Vol. 17 No. 6, pp. 537–554, https://doi.org/10.1080/13527258.2011.618246.

UNESCO World Heritage Centre. (2008). *World Heritage Information Kit*, UNESCO, Paris.

United Nations. (2007). *United Nations Declaration on the Rights of Indigenous Peoples*, United Nations, Paris.

Vecco, M., and Caust, J. (2019). "UNESCO, Cultural Heritage Sites and Tourism: A Paradoxical Relationship", *Overtourism*, Routledge, New York, pp. 67–78.

Vrdoljak, A.F., Liuzza, C., and Meskell, L. (2021). *UNESCO, World Heritage, and Human Rights Compliance*, Duke Centre for International & Global Studies, Durham.

Wallace, C., and Pollock, J. (2024). "An Update on the Aboriginal Heritage Act Regime", *Lavan*, available at: https://www.lavan.com.au/advice/planning_environment_land_compensation/An_Update_On_The_Aboriginal_Heritage_Act_Regime (accessed 9 March 2025).

Winter, T. (2015). "Heritage Diplomacy", *International Journal of Heritage Studies*, Vol. 21 No. 10, pp. 1–19.

Winter, T. (2016). "Heritage Diplomacy: Entangled Materialities of International Relations", *Future Anterior*, Vol. 13 No. 1, pp. 16–34.

Zaunmayr, T. (2015). "Burrup Peninsula 'Deregistered' as Sacred Site", *The West Australian*, Seven West Media, Perth.

7

JAPAN'S MINING HERITAGE IN DISPUTE

Plural understanding for heritage sustainability

Ryoko Nakano

Introduction

Japanese historical sites related to World War II (WWII) remain controversial and contested in East Asia. On 19 August 2024, the Yasukuni shrine was targeted for vandalism, by which three Chinese men spray-painted the word 'toilet' on the stone pillar on the site and recorded the gesture of urination against the pillar (Jiji, 2024). The act was done presumably because this Shinto shrine has been regarded as a symbol of Japanese military aggression. The shrine has honoured the Japanese war dead, including class A war criminals in the Tokyo Tribunal; its museum on the site exhibited the belongings of Japanese soldiers and remnants of the imperial military force, praising the loyal spirits of Japanese soldiers. While Japanese supporters of the Yasukuni shrine suggest that it is dedicated to remembering the war dead, including those nameless people who lost their lives for the country, Asians whose ancestors' death and suffering is linked to the Japanese army perceive visits to the Yasukuni shrine as a lack of repentance for Japanese wartime aggressions. After the graffiti and video footage of vandalism against the Yasukuni shrine were noticed, the Japanese police obtained an arrest warrant for three Chinese men, two of whom had already left Japan.

This episode symbolically highlights the lack of consensus in East Asia regarding Japan's imperial legacy, encompassing its industrialisation, modernisation and militarisation processes leading up to WWII. Accordingly, interpreting Japan's modern history remains a highly contested issue in East Asia. Was Japan's modernisation a successful legacy of sociopolitical transformation, adapting to the changing international climate, or a history of injustice marked by the suppression of autonomy and dignity among the subjects of Japanese rule? Though the Meiji period (1868–1912) is often viewed favourably compared to the wartime era within

DOI: 10.4324/9781003623724-7

Japan, Chinese and Korean nations threatened by Japan's military expansion often perceive the entire modernisation process as a prelude to wartime aggression. This sentiment is particularly pronounced in South Korea, the southern half of the Korean peninsula, where Japanese control was imposed well before the outbreak of WWII.

The lack of consensus on the remembrance of WWII in East Asia has become evident in the post–Cold War era's changing geopolitical and socioeconomic contexts (Jager & Mitter, 2007). The increasing global interconnectedness, deepening economic interdependence and shifting power dynamics in East Asia have empowered countries like China and South Korea to challenge Japan's dominant WWII narrative. The rise of human rights and historical justice movements has also heightened awareness of linking memory issues to contemporary human rights concerns, especially in countries like South Korea that had undergone democratisation in 1987 (Kim & Schwartz, 2010; Shin, Park, & Yang, 2007). Japan maintains that WWII issues were resolved legally and politically when and after the (re) opening of diplomatic relationships with other Asian countries; nevertheless, the memories of war victims' experiences are uncovered and shared beyond national borders (Frost et al., 2019). As a result, Japan faces criticism from governments and civil society groups, mainly in South Korea and China, who remember themselves as victims.

Without much improvement in nurturing a mutual understanding of memories, Japan sought to promote its historical narrative in constructing and promoting its industrial heritage in the 2010s. Under the leadership of Abe Shinzo, widely regarded as a historical revisionist who refused to accept the view of Japan solely as a perpetrator of WWII. Japan nominated two historical sites related to the mining industry: the Sites of Japan's Meiji Industrial Revolution and the Sado Gold Mine. While Japan views those sites as something disassociated with WWII historical memories, South Korea regard them as the iconic symbols of Korea's national humiliation under Japanese rule. Because of this perception gap, nominating and declaring the WWII memory sites as World Heritage Sites in 2015 and 2024 created controversies within and beyond East Asia. The contestation continues today. This chapter documents the contests at the sites of Japanese mining history, focusing on genesis, nature, evolution and current status. It also presents the stakeholders' perceptions of the site and potential mitigation measures.

Specifically, I seek to answer the following questions: Why did Japan nominate the former mining sites in Hashima and Sado Island to become a UNESCO World Heritage Site (WHS) despite many Koreans deeply associating them with memories of forced labour under Japanese colonial rule? How did the Koreans perceive the nomination and subsequent listing in the UNESCO WHS? In answering these two questions, the chapter has six sections. The first section outlines the history of the Japanese mining industry and its controversial nature in the regional context of East Asia. The second section examines Japan's international efforts to promote its Meiji industrial heritage and South Korea's reaction to these efforts.

The third section discusses Japan's lack of action for plural remembrance following the inscription of the Meiji industrial sites on the World Heritage List (WHL).
The fourth section explores the Sado Island Gold Mines case as another significant
example of Japanese legacy promotion. The fifth section provides insights into the
heritage sustainability in the context of the Japan–South Korea relationship. The
chapter's concluding section proposes strategies for overcoming the current challenges to heritage sustainability.

Mining industrial heritage in Japan: national legacy or the symbol of colonial oppression?

The concept of preserving old industrial sites was adopted during Japan's rapid
economic development in the 1960s and 1970s. Japan's preservation system for
'cultural property' (bunkazai) was firmly established after the Act on Protection
of Cultural Properties was enacted in 1950. However, the concept of designating
industrial sites and properties as 'heritage' is relatively new and has been influenced
by European practices. Inspired by the British and German eagerness to study and
preserve old mining properties, Japanese industrial archaeologists established the
Industrial Archaeology Society of Japan in 1977 to promote the study and active
usage of industrial heritage (Komatsu, 1980). As UNESCO recognised industrial
heritage, especially with sites such as the Iron Bridge in the UK and the Zollverein
Coal Mine Industrial Complex in Germany being inscribed on the World Heritage
List, Japan became optimistic that these industrial sites could also be nominated for
international recognition, hence, contribute to the boosting of the country's tourism
and regional revitalisation.

The history of Japan's mining industry is rich and dense. Initially, Japan
depended on imports of iron, copper and gold from China and domestic resources
gathered from its mountains, rivers and oceans. However, by the mid-16th century,
Japanese feudal warlords concentrated on mining and metal production to bolster
and sustain their territorial power. After the Tokugawa Shogunate consolidated its
power in Japan in 1603, the industrial systems within each domain were strictly
regulated and closely monitored. Under the direct control of the Shogunate, Sado
Island (located in present-day Niigata Prefecture) became a significant site of gold
mining in this era (Figure 7.1). Iwami silver mine (in Shimane Prefecture) also
became a centre of Japan's economy and trade in East Asia (Takeda, 2010). The
production of copper in seventeenth- and eighteenth-century Japan increased due
to international trade, which was later followed by a rise in domestic consumption
(Shimada, 2006, pp. 24–33).

After the Meiji Restoration of 1868, modern mining technologies were substantially introduced from Western countries, such as Britain and Germany, to
Japan. To catch up with Western powers, the newly established Meiji government
focused on adopting Western technologies, introduced new mining techniques and
invested in infrastructure to support the rapid industrialisation of Japan. Primary

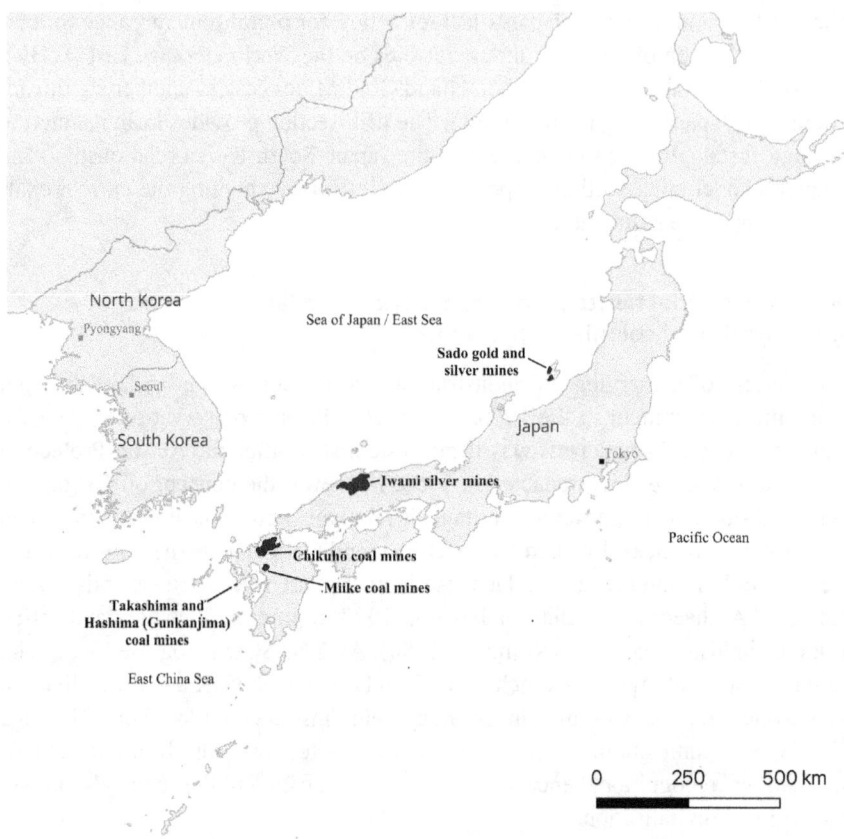

FIGURE 7.1 Major historic mining sites in Japan.

mining operations were privatised as part of the broader effort to transform Japan's economy, with large conglomerates, or *zaibatsu*, such as Mitsubishi and Mitsui, becoming central players. These conglomerates introduced mechanised drilling and smelting technologies that increased efficiency and output (Shibagaki, 1966). Key coal mining operations were centred in Miike, Chikuho and the islands of Takashima and Hashima, commonly known as Gunkanjima (Battleship Island; Figure 7.2) due to the battleship (*gunkan*)-like shape of the island, located off the coast of Nagasaki, all in the Kyushu region. In addition to coal, other mining ventures, such as the Sado Island Mines, produced the most significant quantities of gold and silver under Mitsubishi's operation, further contributing to the nation's industrial progress. By the early 20th century, mining had evolved from a localised activity to a national industry integrated into Japan's rapidly expanding industrial economy.

FIGURE 7.2 Hashima, known as the Battleship Island.

Although the mining sector was crucial for Japan's industrialisation and modernisation, it also had troubling aspects, such as labour exploitation and a lack of regulation, which resulted in environmental harm. A key example is the Ashio copper mine, located in what is now Tochigi Prefecture, which released toxic substances into adjacent rivers, causing severe environmental damage (Takahashi & Sagisaka, 2023). The contamination of water sources resulted in the poisoning of local citizens throughout the late 19th century, sparking public protests. This environmental disaster became a focal point for social activism, marking Japan's first environmental movements and underscoring the ongoing tension between industrial progress and ecological sustainability. Another issue is the working conditions and low wages of mining labourers. Mining jobs have long been associated with severe risks, including deaths and life-threatening environments, particularly due to the spread of metal dust during the mining process. For example, the 1914 disaster at Mitsubishi's Hojo coal mine is claimed to have caused over 600 deaths (Shimanishi, 2024). Due to the lack of strong labour unions among miners, workers faced harsh working conditions but were forced to take risks due to a lack of other means to earn an income.

Non-Japanese migrant workers from the Korean peninsula and China faced difficult situations. Other workers were prisoners captured during the Russo-Japanese War (1904–05) and WWII. After Japan annexed Korea in 1910, many impoverished Korean peasants were recruited for mining and relocated to Japanese companies in Fukuoka prefecture's Miike and Chikuho regions (Arents & Tsuneishi, 2015). Workers from Korea and China were considered 'cheap labour' compared to those from Japan. As Japan entered a full-scale war with China in 1937 and then the US in 1941, labour shortage became a serious issue. The Miike coal mine in

Omuta, under Mitsui Kozan, part of Mitsui Zaibatsu (business conglomerate), used many war prisoners and Korean and Chinese workers (Palmer, 2021). Following the introduction of the National Mobilisation Law in 1938, Korean men began to be conscripted into the Japanese military. Additionally, many were forcibly recruited as labourers for Japanese industries, particularly in coal mining. While the exact number of Korean labourers remains uncertain and disputed, estimates suggest it ranges between 720,000 and one million (Park, 2007, p. 56). Some were sent to the Kyushu region and worked under harsh conditions in Miike, Takashima and Hashima mining sites under the operation of Mitsui and Mitsubishi (Johnsen, 2021; Palmer, 2023).

After WWII, Korean labourers were released from Japanese rule. Some returned to the Korean peninsula, while others continued to stay in Japan. Coal mining remained a critical industry for Japan's economic recovery, but gradually, Japan's energy landscape changed as oil and other imported energy sources emerged as more cost-effective options. The downturn in mining became particularly pronounced in the 1970s when numerous mines were abandoned. Mitsubishi ceased operations of many of its mines during this time, and by 1974, sites like Hashima (Gunkanjima) were left deserted, symbolising the broader collapse of Japan's mining sector (Johnsen, 2021). Those old, abandoned sites were rediscovered as industrial heritage tourism and education sites in the 1980s and 1990s. Iwami Ginzan Silver Mine, which acquired the World Heritage designation in 2007, gained considerable publicity as the first industrial heritage of Japan recognised internationally. This historic site in Shimane Prefecture, where silver mining was conducted from the early 16th century to the 1920s, did not invite any criticism as the site has no historical record of labour exploitation or forced labour issues. That is, the site has no industrial narratives that present a dark history.

In contrast to Iwami Ginzan Silver Mine, modern mining sites are more contentious, as they carry the diverse memories of mining workers, including non-Japanese labourers. If the focus is solely on the economic impact of industrialisation, these workers are mainly contributors to Japanese economic development. The Tomioka Silk Mill, inscribed on the UNESCO World Heritage List in 2014, gave such an interpretation. Japan's nomination of this site hardly discussed the exploitation of female workers in the silk mill and focused on the formation of a selective, glorifying narrative (Kimura, 2023). In contrast, the local consortium that promoted the former Ashio copper mine for World Heritage designation included the dark element of mining history. This memory of pollution is vivid and well taught in Japanese schools. It incorporated the stories of collective efforts for pollution control and soil and water conservation in its heritage interpretation (Education Committee of Nikko City, 2019).

Besides the preservation and interpretation issues of the mining sites, many lawsuits have been filed in Japan, South Korea and the United States since the 1990s, demanding individual compensation for those who were forced to serve in the Japanese military as 'comfort women' and 'forced labourers' (Park, 2007). The

Japanese government and the companies that operated the mining sites were sued to compensate these labourers and their bereaved families. Alongside the comfort women activism, the civil society groups seeking justice for forced labour issues challenged the conventional legal viewpoint that the 1965 (Japan–South Korea Claims Settlement Agreement) resolved war-related compensation issues. Although the Korean group never won in Japanese courts, they succeeded in Korean courts. For example, the Korean Supreme Court's 2012 decision on the legitimacy of individual compensation claims and the 2018 decision ordered Japanese companies to pay compensation. The campaigns to acquire forced labour recognition and compensation garnered significant international support, even though the Japanese government and private companies have not complied.

With little consensus on the status and conditions of Korean labourers under Japanese rule during WWII, it may be easy for Hashima (Gunkanjima) and Sado mining sites to gain a critical spotlight. This is because they have been promoted as positive legacies of Japan's modernisation and industrialisation, a perspective that Koreans contest. In the following sections, I explore the process of converting Japanese memories into UNESCO WHS and how this initiative created controversy and contestation among heritage stakeholders in East Asia and beyond. I will also discuss the impact of these contests on the sustainability of Japan's abandoned mining sites, which are included in the UNESCO World Heritage List.

Promoting Japan's mining site as part of Japanese industrial heritage

The Sites of Japan's Meiji Industrial Revolution: Iron and Steel, Shipbuilding and Coal Mining (SJMIR), inscribed in the WHL in 2015, was a product of an unconventional revitalisation initiative. In 2008, Japan's Cultural Agency (JCA) decided to include the significant industrial heritage in the Kyushu and Yamaguchi regions on Japan's World Heritage Tentative List. Due to the sites and properties being spread across different parts of southwest Japan, they prepared 'serial nominations' to connect all properties with a single storyline. Eventually, the nominated sites were reorganised to include 23 components of industrial complexes in 11 sites within eight areas. Hashima (Gunkanjima) is a focal point of controversy between Japan and South Korea.

The principal architect of SJMIR was Kato Koko, a Harvard graduate in town planning and the author of *Sangyo Isan* [Industrial Heritage] (1999). Kato's father was Kato Mustuki, one of the prominent politicians of Japan's long-dominant Liberal Democratic Party (LDP). This connection gave her strong ties to LDP members and senior bureaucrats, including Abe Shinzo, who served as Japan's Prime Minister from 2006 to 2007 and again from 2012 to 2020. Local governors and corporate stakeholders in the Kyushu and Yamaguchi prefectures sought to leverage the rich historical value of Meiji-era sites for tourism and regional revitalisation. In 2006, Kato gained Abe's support and successfully united the interests of local governments, business corporations and the central government into a cohesive effort to promote SJMIR. Under her initiative, the relevant locations were incorporated into a success story of modern Japan under the unified theme of 'industrial heritage'. Following extensive negotiations and consensus-building led by Kato in collaboration with local government agencies, the Japanese government nominated the site in 2013.

The SJMIR narrative aligns with the views of historical revisionist politicians such as Prime Minister Abe Shinzo. The Meiji Restoration, marking the end of the Tokugawa Shogunate and the restoration of imperial rule under Emperor Meiji, was one of the significant power transformations in Japanese history. The arrival of Western industrial powers on Japanese soil in the mid-19th century catalysed this power change. Since then, Japan started a nationwide campaign for modernisation and industrialisation based on the knowledge and skills learned from the Western examples. For Japanese historical revisionists, this incredible legacy should not be overshadowed by the Japanese acts in WWII (Nakano, 2021). Japan's nomination document for SJMIR prominently featured this narrative, deliberately narrowing its focus to the period between the 1850s and 1910 (UNESCO, 2015). In this regard, Palmer (2021) asserts that this selective periodisation does not match the actual period of 'industrialisation' if this term means the shift from manual to mechanised labour. Presumably, the intention behind this periodisation is to exclude Japan's colonial rule over the Korean peninsula, not to mention the events of WWII.

Promoting the SJMIR for World Heritage designation followed an unusual path in Japan. Conventionally, Japan's engagement in UNESCO's World Heritage is under the provision of JCA in the Ministry of Education, Culture, Sports, Science, and Technology (MEXT). However, their role was substantially limited in the case of the SJMIR, as a new committee on industrial heritage was established in 2012 under the Office for the Promotion of Regional Revitalisation in the Cabinet Secretariat. The committee aimed to guide the selection of industrial heritage sites, including properties in operation, to be proposed for inclusion in the WHL (Prime Minister's Office of Japan, 2012). The examination of SJMIR as World Heritage was explicitly assigned to this committee, even though the one in JCA is usually in charge of World Heritage matters. The committee included Japanese and non-Japanese heritage experts who had already served as advisors for the regional consortium under Kato's initiative for the SJMIR's World Heritage nomination. Esteemed professionals such as Sir Neil Cossons (former chairman of English Heritage), Michael Pearson (Heritage Planning Consultant in Australia) and Dinu Bumbaru (ICOMOS Canada) were invited to provide their expertise and endorse the significance of SJMIR. With strong support from these external authorities, the Japanese government ultimately submitted SJMIR for nomination in 2014.

Creating a new route for Japan's heritage nomination was deemed political. From the outset, MEXT officials and academic members of the World Heritage Committee in JCA expressed their concern over the practical challenges in terms of management of the nominated properties in operation, such as Mitsubishi No. 3

Dry Dock and Mitsubishi Giant Cantilever Crane in Nagasaki Shipyards (Japan Cultural Agency, 2012, pp. 30–33). Japanese officials in the Ministry of Foreign Affairs (MOFA) were also reluctant to promote SJMIR, including Gunkanjima, fearing a potential conflict with China and South Korea because the narrative of industrialisation in some sites is related to 'forced labour' issues. Those voices in MEXT and MOFA that preferred to take a cautious approach to the nomination of SJMIR could be an obstacle to the nomination of SJMIR; the World Heritage Committee in JCA indeed prioritised another heritage site for the 2014 nomination. However, the new committee's suggestion overrode the recommendation by the JCA under the Abe administration.

South Korea outrightly criticised Japan's nomination of SJMIR because of the inclusion of Gunkanjima and the property of Mitsubishi Shipyard in Nagasaki, which were relevant to the forced labour history. Korean activists regarded the Japanese promotion of SJMIR, whose stories did not include the history of forced labour, as another confirmation of Japanese unrepentance over its colonial oppression and wartime aggression. Then, Korean President Park Geun-hye expressed her concerns directly to the UNESCO Director General in 2014. Together with the issues of 'comfort women', who were forced into sexual slavery by the Japanese military forces, it was difficult for the South Korean government to ignore the issue publicly. Without much dialogue between the Japanese and South Korean governments, the Japanese nomination went to the table of the World Heritage Committee session in 2015.

World Heritage inscription and afterwards

SJMIR marked a significant conflict point during the session. Because of the difficulty in solving the disagreement in public, Japan and South Korea were invited to have a closed meeting. In the end, Japanese ambassador Sato Kuni acknowledged at the meeting that civilians from the Korean peninsula were brought to the island and 'forced to work' and promised to take measures to inform visitors of the history of Korean victims (Ministry of Foreign Affairs of Japan, 2015a). South Korea endorsed Japan's nomination of SJMIR, regarding this as the official acknowledgement of forced labour. However, a day after the inscription, Japan's Minister of Foreign Affairs, Kishida Fumio, stated that the expression 'forced to work' did not mean the historical acknowledgement of 'forced labour'. Japan did not change its position that the Claims Settlement and Economic Co-operation Agreement of 1965 settled the matter of workers from the Korean Peninsula (Ministry of Foreign Affairs of Japan, 2015b). This statement also denied Japan's breach of the 1930 Forced Labour Convention of the International Labour Organisation. In contrast, the South Korean media reported the Japanese Ambassador's remark of 'forced to work' as another deception that caused anger among the Korean public (Gil, 2015).

After the inscription of SJMIR in the World Heritage List, the issues surrounding Gunkanjima occasionally resurfaced. South Korea's two major labour groups, the Federation of Korean Trade Unions and the Korean Confederation of Trade Unions, erected statues/monuments of Korean forced labourers in 2017. The first statue was placed in Bupyeong Park, the former site of a Mitsubishi Heavy Industry factory in Incheon, and the second in front of Yongsan Station in central Seoul (Korea.net, 2017). In the same year, CJ Entertainment, a leading Korean entertainment company, released the film Gunhamdo [Gunkanjima]. This fictional film depicted the escape of Korean coal miners from the forced labour system in Gunkanjima, organised by the Japanese military. Gunkanjima was presented as the 'Island of Hell' where South Koreans endured inhumane working conditions. This portrayal was disseminated in South Korea and internationally through an advertising campaign in Times Square and a special pre-screening in Paris for UNESCO headquarters officials and Korean diplomats. These efforts further intensified the tensions and frustrations, fueling Japanese revisionist memory activism (Choi & Sakamoto, 2021).

In June 2020, the dispute intensified again due to the action taken by the Japanese government. Having promised to exhibit information about forced labour, Japan opened the Industrial Heritage Information Centre in Tokyo amid the COVID-19 pandemic. However, this move did not meet Korean expectations, as they had anticipated the information would be displayed on Gunkanjima itself. Primarily, the exhibition featured Japanese testimonies denying the presence of forced labour rather than including Korean accounts (Boyle, 2022). Although visits to the centre were restricted due to the global pandemic, the South Korean Ministry of Foreign Affairs and the media criticised the centre, describing it as a failure of Japan to acknowledge the forced labour issues. The South Korean government also wrote to UNESCO about Japan's failure to keep a promise at the World Heritage Committee in 2015.

Kato continued to serve as a special advisor to the Abe cabinet (2015–19) and as the managing director of the Information Centre (2019–present [2025]), playing a key role in shaping the centre's interpretation of Gunkanjima's miners' history. She has actively gathered testimonies from Japanese individuals asserting the absence of forced labour in collaboration with a civil society group that seeks to refute claims of forced labour. The testimonies, some of which were exhibited at the centre, are highly selective. One testimony from a Korean man discerned his pride in his father for being a hard worker in Gunkanjima, but the father did not live on the site during WWII (Takeuchi, 2024). The centre used testimonies from those who described a positive image of Gunkanjima as the authentic voice of the island's WWII history. When the author visited the centre in December 2021, there was also an elderly guide who mentioned that he lived in Gunkanjima. He denied the existence of forced labour issues, describing a Korean claim as a lie. His self-description of 'being local' was intended to lend credibility to his statement, even though he may have lacked comprehensive knowledge of the site then.

To assess the interpretation and presentation of SJMIR after the WHS inscription, the UNESCO/ICOMOS mission visited the Industrial Heritage Information

Centre in 2021. Its report suggested that Japan failed to keep a promise made in the 2015 session, that is, to provide sufficient information to 'acknowledge that Koreans and others, including prisoners of war, were brought against their will to work at some of the Meiji Industrial sites after 1910' (UNESCO, 2021). The mission urged Japan to take appropriate measures to remember the victims and keep Japan's promise at the World Heritage Committee in 2015. However, there is no sign of change on the Japanese side.

Japan's promotion of the Sado Island gold mines

While the discourse regarding the SJMIR remains a topic of vigorous debate. In 2022 and 2023, the Japanese government proposed another contentious mining site called Sado Island Gold Mines (see Figure 7.3) for inclusion in the World Heritage List. Following extensive discussions and considerations surrounding the historical and cultural significance of the site, the World Heritage Committee ultimately approved the nomination. Consequently, the Sado Island Gold Mines were officially inscribed on the UNESCO World Heritage List in 2024, marking a significant development in preserving and recognising Japan's industrial heritage. Japan's nomination form submitted to UNESCO indicates that the property consists of two areas on Sado Island that exhibit the concrete gold production system, including the mining technology, production processes, administration, town planning and mining culture. They showcase Japan's largest and most important national gold mining operation that contributed to the stability of the Edo period (1603–1868) under the rule of the Tokugawa Shogunate (UNESCO, 2023). The preserved

FIGURE 7.3   Aikawa gold and silver mine, part of the Sado Island Gold Mines.

properties and landscape, including mining facilities, settlements and infrastructure, are deemed valuable to illustrate the societal and technological transformations over the centuries.

A coalition of local and national Japanese stakeholders drove the nomination of the Sado gold mines as a UNESCO World Heritage Site. For example, a civil society group initiated a local campaign to achieve World Heritage status for the site as early as 1996.[1] This campaign aimed to boost the tourism industry, which was crucial for an area suffering from depopulation and lacking industry. Niigata Prefecture and Sado City supported the idea, the latter of which had experienced significant economic decline and a reduction in tourism since the 1990s. They saw the nomination as a chance for regional revitalisation, with local officials highlighting the mines as a significant cultural asset that could bring economic benefits to the remote island, far from the mainland.[2]

The gold mining continued to operate even after the Meiji Restoration, up to WWII. Despite this history, Japan's nomination emphasised the significance of traditional mining technologies and the system of gold production and strategic management in the Edo period. The mechanisation and technological development enhanced by the government and business corporation Mitsubishi in the later period were not given the deserved recognition. This tactical decision avoided forced labour issues, like the periodisation of Meiji's industrial heritage. Nevertheless, Japan's nomination of the Sado Gold Mine with a specifically periodised explanation once again raised questions about the integrity of Japan's historical narratives and accountability. For this reason, the Japanese government was hesitant about whether to nominate Sado Goldmine as a World Heritage in 2022. Known as a moderate politician, Prime Minister Kishida was cautious in going ahead with the nomination. Having experienced the uproar of the historical dispute when he served as Foreign Minister in the Abe administration, he presumably aimed to avoid another damaging act on the Japan–South Korea relationship. Thus, the Japanese government under Kishida initially showed an attitude to delay the nomination in 2022 (Kyodo News, 2022).

However, there was a push from former Prime Minister Abe and his faction's politicians, including Takaichi Sanae (then the Political Research Council Chairman of the LDP), Takatori Shuichi (LDP's Diet member from Niigata) and Hanazumi Hideyo (LDP-supported Niigata governor). In particular, the former two expressed their determination not to compromise on South Korea's claim about forced labour. Historical revisionist groups, including the Japan Institute for National Fundamentals, orchestrated the promotion of Sado goldmine, like the case of Gunkanjima, the group members strongly criticised South Korea's claims and the international media such as the New York Times that described the Sado Island Gold Mines as emblematic of Japan's reluctance to confront its wartime atrocities (Nishioka, 2022). Abe was no longer the Prime Minister; yet the Kishida administration relied on the various factions, including the Abe faction in the LDP, to sustain the party's solidarity. In the end, the Kishida administration decided to nominate the site. Although the nomination was rejected in this round because part of the recommendation documents submitted for the nomination were 'insufficient' (Asahi Shimbun, 2022), Japan resubmitted the nomination documents in 2023.

Members of the South Korean government and civil society groups expressed their strong opposition to the Sado Mines' nomination, primarily due to the explicit narratives dismissing the forced labour issues during WWII. Then President Moon Jae-in, expressing deep regret over Japan's decision to pursue the nomination, stated that 'to find a solution that victims can accept and promote true reconciliation, a sincere attitude and mindset toward history matter the most' (Lee, 2022). Moon framed the issue as one of historical justice and human rights, advocating for Japan to include the experiences of Korean forced labourers in its portrayal of the site. His administration pursued diplomatic protests and emphasised dialogue to resolve historical grievances. Along with this argument, the South Korean Ministry of Foreign Affairs urged Japan to stop its nomination attempt (Republic of Korea Ministry of Foreign Affairs, 2022).

Despite South Korea's official criticism of Japan's nomination and inclusion of the site on the World Heritage List, a shift in its leadership in May 2022 resulted in a more lenient stance. With Yoon Suk-yeol now in the Presidential office, enhancing diplomatic relations with Japan became a priority, emphasising the significance of collaboration with the neighbouring country (Lee & Lim, 2023). His administration conditionally supported the nomination, requesting that Japan acknowledge forced labour in its interpretive materials. Japan's refusal to do so prompted Yoon's administration to avoid escalating the issue further. Yoon's conciliatory stance sparked domestic controversy. In February 2023, the South Korean National Assembly passed a resolution urging Japan to withdraw its bid to list the Sado gold mine as a UNESCO World Heritage Site (Kim, 2023). The Northeast Asian History Foundation in Seoul also released a report on the issues of Sado forced labour and human rights (Jeong, 2022). The South Korean media, *Hankyoreh* and *Yonhap News,* continued to criticise Japan's approach, framing the nomination as a deliberate attempt to erase exploitation of Korean labourers from historical memory.

Against this backdrop, the governments of Japan and South Korea agreed to have a shared moment to commemorate all miners, including Korean labourers, on Sado Island in 2024. The intention was presumably to demonstrate a cooperative mood towards reconciliation and progress in pursuing historical justice (Mainichi, 2024). To pay tribute, representatives from South Korea, including the Korean Ambassador to Japan, were invited to participate in the ceremony. However, this attempt did not work out well, primarily because the commemoration was not to acknowledge the mistreatment of Korean labourers, and Japan's selection of Ikuina Akiko, Parliamentary Vice-Minister for Foreign Affairs, as the top Japanese representative at the ceremony drew criticism from South Korea. Her status was not equivalent to Korea's expected representative, and she has a record of visiting the Yasukuni Shrine (Ji, 2024). Koreans demanding social justice considered Japan's decision an insult, leading the South Korean government to send no one to the ceremony.

Japan's intention to invite South Koreans to a commemoration ceremony on Sado Island was initially seen as a significant step towards reconciliation. However, it proved to be a superficial gesture that failed to acknowledge the site's complex historical narratives. The insensitivity demonstrated by the Japanese side undermined the original purpose, exacerbating existing political and social tensions. As a result, the location remains a symbol of fractured memory, poignantly illustrating the fragile and unsustainable relationship between Japan and South Korea.

Heritage sustainability in the context of Japan–South Korea industrial history tensions

In the serialisation process of making World Heritage, the Gunkanjima and Sado Island mining sites embody the deep-seated conflict between Japan and South Korea. The tensions discussed in this chapter have significantly impacted and continue to influence initiatives related to the protection, funding, research and associated issues of Japanese mining heritage in dispute. The Japanese central and local governments look after the physical sustainability of the sites and properties. Repairing the breakwater seawalls surrounding Gunkanjima is challenging and costly, but it can be done as part of the historic site protection.[3] In contrast, the relationship between Japan and South Korea in sustaining these sites' value is broken and not as easily repairable. The Japanese and South Korean governments have spent more resources collecting evidence to support their respective narratives of the Japanese mining industry's history. This funding distribution has created a zero-sum game, where researchers are pressured to validate one side's perspective while discrediting the other.

Japan's inability to incorporate diverse historical perspectives on modern mining sites arises from the conventional belief that sustainability should be viewed strictly within national limits. The Japanese portrayal of these mining locations during the World Heritage Site nomination was shaped by the prevalent idea that Japan's indigenous technology and innovative thinkers underpin its economy and prosperity. After these sites were recognised for their historical and cultural significance as WHS, the perception of their heritage value within the Japanese narrative seemed increasingly valid to the public. Residents and visitors to the sites are encouraged to view them as part of Japan's national legacy, which is linked to the vitality of future generations in Japan.

However, Japan's current approach will not benefit present and future generations who need a peaceful international environment where an amicable Japan–South Korea relationship is strategically crucial. It is a missed opportunity for collaborative research and joint education in which both nations could explore and appreciate these heritage sites from diverse and inclusive viewpoints. This also means that the sustainability of the sites is in question. Harrison (2012, 2013) argues that contemporary cultural heritage sustainability requires management to consider its relevance to present and future societies. In his case studies, the heritage in question has lost its value in the present context. Instead of leaving the accumulation of heritage untouched, he suggests that making active decisions to delist or prune heritage is essential for the sustainable production of social memory. This approach acknowledges that heritage sustainability encompasses many environmental, economic, social and political concerns. In the case of Japanese mining sites included in the WHS lists, their social value can be strengthened and endurable in the regional and global contexts only if the interpretation of those sites is pluralistic. The sustainability of Japanese mining heritage depends on Japan's commitment to remembering the memories of non-Japanese individuals associated with these sites.

Looking ahead

So far, there has been little indication of a significant shift in Japan's stance regarding the interpretations surrounding the two abandoned mining sites that have become focal points of historical contention. The long-standing dispute between Japan and South Korea, once a simmering source of tension, appears to have eased somewhat. This change can largely be attributed to the recent transformation in South Korea's political leadership, particularly under President Yoon, who has underscored the importance of fostering amicable relations with Japan, often prioritising diplomatic engagement over historical grievances. However, beneath the surface of this tentative rapprochement lies a fragile veneer. The precarious nature of their relationship is evident; a shift in South Korea's leadership could swiftly alter the current dynamics. Should a new administration emerge favouring a more confrontational approach to historical issues, the prospect of cooperative engagement could quickly unravel, thrusting the debate over the heritage interpretation back into the limelight. Such a scenario could reignite public discourse and diplomatic tensions, transforming these historical sites from mere points of contention into deeply polarising symbols in the broader narrative of Japan–South Korea relations.

The strategy towards resolving the contests alongside ensuring heritage well-being is to move beyond the national narrative and adopt a broader perspective to make the heritage serve as a vehicle for reconciliation. Japan should recognise a moral obligation to negotiate with other nations as equal stakeholders rather than outsiders. To make contested heritage sustainable, sustainability must be considered beyond national borders, and a more pluralistic narrative must be adopted in the regional context. To that end, Japan should bring the heritage issues into the hands of a diverse group of stakeholders. Heritage matters should not be dealt with by a handful of individuals who focus only on forming a monolithic national narrative, even though it was initially sufficient for the WHS requirement. The Industrial Information Centre's exhibition content needs to be scrutinised by a third-party academic group and modified in a dialogue with civil society groups in and outside Japan to make the serialisation process more inclusive and accountable.

Acknowledging the Korean labourers in the history of Japanese mining sites is a fundamental ethical issue. Supporting the focus on plural remembrance requires separating historical remembrance from the agenda of individual compensation. As long as the agendas of remembering the past and compensation are connected and pursued, the Japanese government and civil society become overly defensive and view the monolithic historical narrative as safeguarding their legal claim. In this sense, the South Korean government must approach this issue with caution to ensure that the act of remembrance is not reduced to merely a legal compensation claim. Furthermore, the Governments' tentative measures to avoid conflict fall short of fostering sustainable heritage in a large regional community. Addressing conflict openly and treating it as a fundamental issue in sustainability efforts is crucial. Heritage sites hold the potential to serve as platforms for creative opportunities to discuss and question their meanings and enable dialogue across diverse perspectives and positions. By rethinking heritage, these sites can facilitate broader, inclusive discussions to build a sustainable heritage for future generations.

Notes

1 Interview with Nakano Ko, the chairman of the civil society group that promotes Sado as the World Heritage. March 17, 2022.
2 Interview with Kawanabe Hiroya, the chief of the World Heritage section in Sado City. March 16, 2022.
3 Interview with Hayashida Tsubasa, the chief of the World Heritage section in Nagasaki Prefecture. August 28, 2019.

References

Arents, T., & Tsuneishi, N. (2015). The uneven recruitment of Korean miners in Japan in the 1910s and 1920s: Employment strategies of the Miike and Chikuhō coalmining companies. *International Review of Social History, 60*(S1), 121–143. https://doi.org/10.1017/S0020859015000437

Asahi Shimbun (2022, July 28). Including the Sado gold mine site on the World Heritage list is 'difficult'. *The Asahi Shimbun.* https://www.asahi.com/ajw/articles/14681778

Boyle, E. (2022). Shifting borders of memory: Japan's industrial heritage information centre. *Journal of Cultural Heritage Management and Sustainable Development, 12*(1), 19–31. https://doi.org/10.1108/JCHMSD-05-2021-0088

Choi, Y., & Sakamoto, R. (2021). Battleship Island and the transnational dynamics of cultural memory between South Korea and Japan. *Inter-Asia Cultural Studies, 22*(3), 298–315. https://doi.org/10.1080/14649373.2021.1962092

Education Committee of Nikko City. (2019). Ashio Dozan no Kogai Bojo Isangun [Pollution Control Heritage Site of Ashio Copper Mine]. *Nikko City.* https://www.city.nikko.lg.jp/material/files/group/42/kougaiboujoisangun_68593172.pdf

Frost, M.R., Schumacher, D., & Vickers, E. (Eds.). (2019). *Remembering Asia's World War Two.* New York: Routledge.

Gil, Y. (2015, July 7). S. Korea and Japan debate comments about being 'forced to work'. *Hankyoreh.* http://english.hani.co.kr/arti/english_edition/e_international/699205.html

Harrison, R. (2012). Forgetting to remember, remembering to forget: Late modern heritage practices, sustainability and the 'crisis' of accumulation of the past. *International Journal of Heritage Studies, 19*(6), 579–595. https://doi.org/10.1080/13527258.2012.678371

Harrison, R. (2013). *Heritage: Critical Approaches.* London: Routledge.

Jager, S.M., & Mitter, R. (Eds.). (2007). *Ruptured Histories: War, Memory and the Post-Cold War in Asia.* Cambridge: Harvard University Press.

Japan Cultural Agency. (2012). The minutes of the special committee on world cultural heritage. https://www.bunka.go.jp/seisaku/bunkashingikai/isanbukai/sekaitokubetsu/1_01/pdf/gijiroku.pdf.

Jeong, H. (2022). *The Sado Complex of Heritage Mines. A Site for Testing the Full History and Common Sense of Human Rights.* Seoul: Northeast Asia History Foundation.

Ji, D. (2024, November 20). Japan to hold the first memorial for Korean forced labour victims at the Sado Mine. *The Korean Herald.* https://asianews.network/japan-to-hold-1st-memorial-for-korean-forced-labour-victims-at-sado-mine/

Jiji. (2024, August 19). Pillar at entrance to war-linked Yasukuni Shrine vandalised again. *The Japan Times.* https://www.japantimes.co.jp/news/2024/08/19/japan/crime-legal/yasukuni-shrine-vandalism/

Johnsen, N. (2021). Katō Kōko's Meiji industrial revolution: Forgetting forced labour to celebrate Japan's World Heritage Sites-part 1. *The Asia-Pacific Journal: Japan Focus,* 19(1).

Kato, K. (1999). *Sangyo Isan* [Industrial Heritage]. Tokyo: Nihon Keizai Shimbunsha.

Kim, M., & Schwartz, B. (Eds.). (2010). *Northeast Asia's Difficult Past: Essays in Collective Memory.* London: Palgrave McMillan.

Kim, N. (2023, February 27). Nat'l Assembly adopts resolution urging Japan to withdraw UNESCO bid for Sado Mine. *Yonhap.* https://en.yna.co.kr/view/AEN20230227008700315

Kimura, T. (2023). Memories and displays of Japan's early industrialisation through the production of silk, the Tomioka Silk Mill, Nomugi Pass and WWII propaganda. In Burrett, T., & Kingston, J. (Eds.), *Routledge Handbook of Trauma in East Asia* (pp. 158–168). London: Routledge.

Komatsu, Y. (1980). The industrial heritage in Japan. *Industrial Archaeology Review,* 4(3), 234–244. https://doi.org/10.1179/iar.1980.4.3.234

Korea.net. (2017, September 14). Statue goes up to honor colonial forced labor. https://www.korea.net/NewsFocus/Society/view?articleId=149282

Kyodo News. (2022, January 20). Japan mulls delaying controversial Sado Mine list for World Heritage. https://english.kyodonews.net/news/2022/01/aa547ec27203-japan-mulls-delaying-controversial-sado-mine-list-for-world-heritage.html?phrase=88&words=

Lee, H. (2022, February 10). Moon expresses regret over Japan's push for UNESCO recognition of mine linked to forced labor. *Yonhap News.* https://en.yna.co.kr/view/AEN20220210003700315

Lee, J.Y., & Lim, A. (2023). Japan-Korea relations: The return of shuttle diplomacy. *Comparative Connections,* 25(1), 147–160.

Mainichi, The. (2024, November 25) Japan holds first memorial for 'all workers' at Sado gold mines but blurs WWII atrocity. Why? https://mainichi.jp/english/articles/20241125/p2g/00m/0na/028000c

Ministry of Foreign Affairs of Japan. (2015a, 14 July). Decision to record the Heritage of Japan's Meiji industrial revolution: Iron and steel, shipbuilding and coal mining in the UNESCO World Heritage list. http://www.mofa.go.jp/mofaj/pr_pd/mcc/page3_001285.html

Ministry of Foreign Affairs of Japan. (2015b, July 5). Extraordinary press conference by Foreign Minister Fumio Kishida. https://www.mofa.go.jp/press/kaiken/kaiken4e_000181.html

Nakano, R. (2021). Mobilising Meiji nostalgia and intentional forgetting in Japan's World Heritage promotion. *International Journal of Asian Studies,* 18(1), 27–44. https://doi.org/10.1017/S1479591420000467

Nishioka, T. (2022, March 3). Criticising biased NYT article on Sado Gold Mines. *Japan Institute for National Fundamentals.* https://en.jinf.jp/weekly/archives/9184

Palmer, D. (2021). Japan's World Heritage Miike coal mine – Where prisoners-of-war worked 'like slaves'. *Asia-Pacific Journal: Japan Focus,* 19, 13(1), 1–27.

Palmer, D. (2023). Ignoring the history of foreign forced labour at Japan's 'sites of the Meiji industrial revolution'. In Burrett, T., & Kingston, J. (Eds.), *Routledge Handbook of Trauma in East Asia* (pp. 143–157). London: Routledge.

Park, S.W. (2007). The politics of remembrance: the case of Korean forced laborers in the Second World War. In Shin, G.W., Park, S.W., & Yang, D. (Eds.), *Rethinking Historical Injustice and Reconciliation in Northeast Asia: The Korean Experience* (pp. 55–74). London: Routledge.

Prime Minister's Office of Japan (2012, June 26). Establishment of the expert committee on the industrial heritage including operative properties. https://www.cas.go.jp/jp/sangy-ousekaiisan/sangyouisan/yuushikisya/kadouisan01/siryou_e02.pdf

Republic of Korea Ministry of Foreign Affairs. (2022, January 28). MOFA spokesperson's statement on Japan's decision to nominate the Sado Island Gold Mines for inscription on the World Heritage List. https://www.mofa.go.kr/eng/brd/m_5676/view.do?seq=321987

Shibagaki, K. (1966). The early history of the Zaibatsu. *The Developing Economies*, 4(4), 535–566.

Shimada, R. (2006). *The Intra-Asian Trade in Japanese Copper by the Dutch East India Company during the Eighteenth Century.* Leiden: Brill.

Shimanishi, T. (2024). Coal in modern Japanese history. In *Japanese Society and Culture* (vol. 6, pp. 149–158). Bunkyo: Tokyo University.

Shin, G.W., Park, S.W., & Yang, D. (Eds.). (2007). *Rethinking Historical Injustice and Reconciliation in Northeast Asia: The Korean Experience.* London: Routledge.

Takahashi, W., & Sagisaka, H. (2023). Ashio copper mine mineral pollution incident: The starting point of environmental pollution history in Japan. In Yokemoto, M., Hayashi, M., Shimizu, M., & Fujiyoshi, K. (Eds.), *Environmental Pollution and Community Rebuilding in Modern Japan* (pp. 17–35). Singapore: Springer.

Takeda, T. (2010). Sado no sangyo isan to sangyo hakubutsukan [Industrial heritage and museums in Sado]. *Nihon Kansei Kogakukai Ronbunshi,* 9(2), 465–474.

Takeuchi, Y. (2024). *Chosenjin Kyosei Rodo no Rekishi Hitei wo Tou* [Questioning the Denial of History of Korean Forced Labor]. Tokyo: Shakai Hyoronsha.

UNESCO. (2015). Nomination file, 1484. https://whc.unesco.org/uploads/nominations/1484.pdf

UNESCO. (2021). Report on the UNESCO/ICOMOS mission to the industrial heritage information centre related to the world heritage property 'sites of Japan's Meiji industrial revolution: Iron and steel, ship-building and coal mining' (Japan) (c1484). *WHC.21/44.COM/.* https://whc.unesco.org/en/documents/188249/

UNESCO. (2023). Nomination text: Sado Island gold mines. https://whc.unesco.org/document/199046

8

CULTURAL HERITAGE STEWARDSHIP AND COMMUNITY CONTESTATIONS AT THE GREAT ZIMBABWE WORLD HERITAGE SITE

Munyaradzi Elton Sagiya

Introduction

Cultural heritage is inherently local, rooted in the worldviews of specific communities (Ndoro & Wijesuriya, 2015; Baillie & Sørensen, 2021). Increasingly, the involvement of local communities in the conservation and management of cultural heritage places has gained significant scholarly attention in Africa and globally (Waterton, 2005; Chirikure et al., 2010; Jopela, 2018; Colecchia, 2019; Pirkovic, 2020; Jang & Mennis, 2021). Central to these ongoing discussions is the recognition that local communities have been the long-standing but often sidelined custodians of heritage places for centuries (Jopela, 2018; 2022; Loza, 2023). Meanwhile, conflicts and contestations among local communities living within or near heritage sites remain an understudied but increasingly important subject in cultural heritage management. In extreme cases, invaluable heritage sites have been vandalised or destroyed due to conflicts and disagreements among the immediate communities (Lambert & Rockwell, 2012; Ndoro, 2021; Singh, 2022; Isakhan & Meskell, 2024). In countries such as Sri Lanka and Kosovo, the long-term local conflicts have negatively impacted their rich cultural heritage (see Spencer, 1990; Hoxha, 2012). However, local and Indigenous communities remain the key actors in managing and conserving heritage sites, and their participation is critical for the effective and sustainable stewardship of cultural heritage.

In Zimbabwe, the Great Zimbabwe World Heritage Site presents an intriguing case study that illuminates the complexities of local communities' relationships and contestations over the stewardship of cultural heritage. Great Zimbabwe is an ancient Iron Age settlement whose occupation dates between 1200 AD and 1600 AD (these dates vary among the archaeologists who have researched and published about the site) (Huffman, 2011; Chirikure, 2020). This cultural heritage site is,

DOI: 10.4324/9781003623724-8

arguably, one of the most popular archaeological sites in the world. What remains today are the skeletal archaeological remnants, mainly in the form of dry-stone structures. Archaeologists have categorised these dry-stone walls and structures into four major zones: Hill Complex, Valley Enclosures, Great Enclosure and the Peripheral sites (Chenga, Nemanwa and Mtero; see Figures 8.1 and 8.2). Today, Great Zimbabwe remains one of the most contested and multi-layered heritage sites in southern Africa (Pwiti, 1996; Ndoro, 2005; Fontein, 2006; Basinyi & Sagiya, 2019; Sinamai, 2020). It is conceptualised and imbued with diverse meanings by various stakeholders and communities. To some, the Great Zimbabwe is an archae-ological site, a monument, a World Heritage Site, a shrine or an ancestral cultural landscape (Pwiti, 1996; Ndoro, 2005; Fontein, 2006; Sinamai, 2020). Regardless of the diverse valorisations, understandings and interpretations, Great Zimbabwe is one of the most extensively excavated, researched, published, photographed, filmed and televised heritage sites in Africa (Fontein, 2006; Pikirayi, 2001; Huff-man, 2011; Chirikure, 2020). For over a century, the processes and practices of conserving and managing Great Zimbabwe have been intricately intertwined with the expectations and voices of the four historic communities of Nemanwa, Mugabe, Murinye and Charumbira (Hall, 1905; Fontein, 2006). This chapter addresses how these four local communities relate to each other in the context of Great Zimba-bwe's valorisation and how they perceive and engage with research groups and government officials in managing this heritage site.

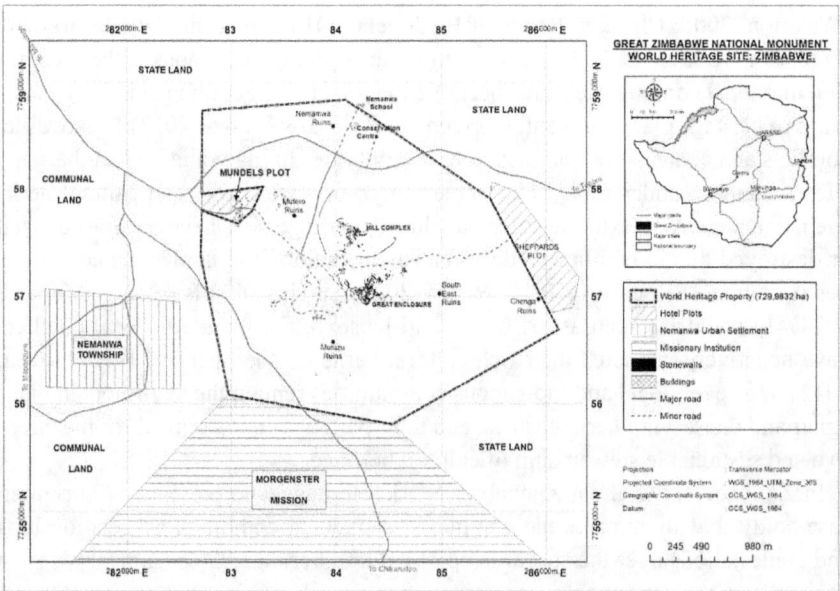

FIGURE 8.1 Great Zimbabwe boundaries and the archaeological zones.

Source: Great Zimbabwe Integrated Management Plan, 2024–2028, p. 18

FIGURE 8.2 Aerial view of the great enclosure.

Source: Author (2021)

The chapter addresses five key issues. First, it presents the various datasets and methods used to examine local communities' contestations over the stewardship of the Great Zimbabwe. Second, it discusses the concept of contact zones as a theoretical lens for understanding the complex relationships and conflicts among the local communities. Third, the chapter provides a historical context for the four local communities of Nemanwa, Mugabe, Murinye and Charumbira, which have shared the same cultural landscape for over a century. Fourth, it explores the nature and intricacies of the contestations among these communities. Finally, the fifth section offers a discussion and conclusions regarding the community contestations over the stewardship and ownership of the Great Zimbabwe World Heritage Site.

Materials and methods

The issues I present and discuss in this chapter come from four primary sources. The data stem from personal experiences from childhood, pursuing studies, working in the heritage sector and academia in the same specialisation. I was born and grew up in the Nemanwa community. Growing up, I listened to the elders during social gatherings where oral traditions and narratives about the Great Zimbabwe often evoked ancestral stories, leading to lengthy discussions and debates. This background motivated and influenced me to pursue a degree in heritage studies. This qualification enhanced my understanding of the Great Zimbabwe by combining local and academic knowledge of the site and its surrounding communities.

Upon completion of the degree programme, between December 2010 and April 2021, the National Museums and Monuments of Zimbabwe (NMMZ – the statutory body responsible for taking care of heritage in the country) employed me as a curator of archaeology based at the Great Zimbabwe. As a curator, my duties included being a community engagement liaison.

Document analysis also informs this chapter, which reviews the archival materials at the Great Zimbabwe Research and Conservation Centre. I extensively consulted NMMZ files which contain reports, memoranda and other correspondence between the management of Great Zimbabwe, conservation professionals, local chiefs and spirit mediums. I constructed a biography of the contemporary local communities' conflicts and contestations discussed in this chapter. Additionally, the chapter draws on several recorded interviews conducted over ten years with various members of the local communities, including the elders, women and the youth.

Great Zimbabwe as local communities' contact zone

To synthesise the different data sources and situate them in the context of this chapter, I deployed the concept of 'contact zones'. In this case, Great Zimbabwe is conceptualised as a contact zone, a space where the four different communities of Nemanwa, Mugabe, Murinye and Charumbira and their historical narratives intersect. Mary Louise Pratt developed the concept of the contact zone, which she defined as areas where diverse perspectives and narratives converge, influencing how cultural heritage is understood and perceived (Pratt, 1991, 2007). This concept provides a valuable lens through which to understand and analyse the contestations and conflicts that often arise over the use of shared cultural spaces. The concept of contact zones has been mainly used in museum studies (see Clifford, 1997; Chipangura & Chipangura, 2019; Clifford-Napoleone, 2013). In this chapter, the concept of contact zones is helpful in unravelling community contestations over the Great Zimbabwe World Heritage Site. Here, this cultural heritage site is regarded as a contact zone. In this power-laden heritage space, four local clans and their competing narratives collide and interact, often in conflict.

Historiographical overview of Great Zimbabwe's local communities

Great Zimbabwe is in south-eastern Zimbabwe, near the city of Masvingo. From the 1890s to the present, the curation of the Great Zimbabwe has been a government and professional-led practice guided by successive legal frameworks. The site was designated a national monument in 1937, during the colonial era from 1890 to 1980. In 1986, the 720-hectare estate of Great Zimbabwe was incorporated on the UNESCO World Heritage List. Currently, the site is administered by the NMMZ, a parastatal organisation under the Ministry of Home Affairs and Cultural Heritage.

Due to its importance, size and other archaeological characteristics, Great Zimbabwe remains central in the narratives of the pre-, during and postcolonial periods. It is an archaeological site used to recreate the past and remember certain aspects by local communities and state governing regimes (Garlake, 1982; Ranger, 2004; Pikirayi, 2001, 2013). As a result, a large corpus of academic and even fictional literature has been published on Great Zimbabwe. Reviewing such voluminous literature lies beyond the scope of this chapter. It is worth noting that the focus of many writers has been and continues to centre on the site's origins and its use over time (Garlake, 1982; Pikirayi, 2001; Huffman, 2011; Chirikure, 2020). Consequently, less scholarly attention has been paid to research about the local communities whose association with the site goes back to the 18th century AD. Scholars such as Aquina (1965), Mtetwa (1976), Fontein (2006) and Ndoro (2005) have explored the historical and contemporary relationships between local communities and Great Zimbabwe. Ndoro (2001, 2005) has analysed the tensions between the state, as represented by NMMZ, and the selected local communities regarding the meaning and preservation of Great Zimbabwe. In this chapter, I discuss the inter- and intra-community contestations over the stewardship of the Great Zimbabwe among the four surrounding local communities and other stakeholders.

Of what has been published about the local communities, many of the intricacies of their relationships, conflicts and claims remain oral and undocumented, yet essential for the sustainable management of Great Zimbabwe. The current population of the people living around Great Zimbabwe is between 15,000 and 30,000 (Great Zimbabwe National Monument World Heritage Site Integrated Management Plan, 2024–2028, p. 11). Of this population, the majority, if not all, are *VaKaranga*, a branch of Shona speakers who speak a dialect commonly found in south-central Zimbabwe (Mazarire, 2013). The four clans of Nemanwa, Mugabe, Murinye and Charumbira descended from two totemic clusters of *Shumba* (lion) and *Moyo* (ox-heart). Relying on a review of literature, personal experiences and oral tradition, the following sections present abridged historical versions of each of the four local communities without following a specific order.

Nemanwa clan

The Nemanwa clan refers to themselves as *VaMera*. This praise name emanates from the claim that the Nemanwa people 'germinated' at Great Zimbabwe. They argue that they have always been there, unlike other local clans who migrated to the Great Zimbabwe area. The claim of being the first in the area is supported by other clans such as Charumbira and even academics, but the narrative of germination has always been treated with scepticism. Aquina (1965) and Mtetwa (1976) found it difficult to accept the germination claims and instead attributed the Nemanwa to Mutoko in northern Zimbabwe. Aquina and Mtetwa argue that Nemanwa broke away from the Budya Shumba Nyamuzihwa dynasty in the late 17th century and found the Great Zimbabwe uninhabited. In other literature sources, the Nemanwa people have also been recorded as the earliest custodians of Great Zimbabwe (Aquina, 1965; Burke, 1969; Mtetwa, 1976; Fontein, 2006). Their monopoly over the stewardship of Great Zimbabwe ended around the early 1800s with the arrival of Murinye, who came with his sons (in some sources, they are referred to as brothers), Mugabe and Shumba-Chekai. It is from this period that Great Zimbabwe became a contact zone.

Ever since the 1890s, the Nemanwa and Mugabe clans have been entangled in long-standing contestations and conflicts over the custodianship of Great Zimbabwe, which they recognise as a shrine as opposed to a national monument or archaeological site (Ndoro, 2001; 2005; Fontein, 2006; Basinyi & Sagiya, 2019). Aquina (1965) mentions that the Mugabe people liked the territory they found Nemanwa occupying, leading to fierce fighting and disputes. The 1890s battles fought between the Nemanwa and Mugabe clans have been recorded by a few historians and other writers (Aquina, 1965; Mtetwa, 1976; Fontein, 2006). In addition to such references in literature and oral histories, there is a plaque that was erected during the early years of colonisation, supposedly memorialising the position where Sir John Willoughby, one of the early Europeans to excavate Great Zimbabwe in 1892, witnessed one of the battles. This plaque is a few metres west of the museum's site. Although it is not far from the designated pathway, it is often left out of the routes used by tour guides during their tours, reflecting the dominance of archaeology in interpreting and presenting the Great Zimbabwe. Indeed, the histories and struggles of local clans over the stewardship of Great Zimbabwe remain at the margin. The plaque (Figure 8.3) has inscriptions in capital letters indicating that

FIGURE 8.3 Plaque erected at the position where John Willoughby watched a battle between the Mugabe and Nemanwa clans in 1892.

Source: Author (2021)

the place is where Sir John Willoughby watched the battle between the Nemanwa and Mugabe clans in 1892.

The end of what Fontein (2006: 19) refers to as the pre-colonial Nemanwa/ Mugabe wars was orchestrated by John Willoughby. In his bid to source labour for his excavation, he arranged for a 'peace conference' between the two warring clans in 1892 (Fontein, 2006). This led to the alienation of the local clans from Great Zimbabwe and the surrounding lands. In these new developments, Nemanwa was left worse off, losing the Great Zimbabwe territory and the title of Chief (Aquina, 1965; Fontein, 2006). Since then, Nemanwa became a sub-chief (renamed Headman in postcolonial Zimbabwe) under Charumbira. The Nemanwa chieftainship was only resuscitated in 2022 after more than a century of lobbying with the colonial and postcolonial governing authorities.

Like the histories of the other three clans, there are multiple and sometimes diverging accounts and oral traditions of the Nemanwa clan. The popular version, however, points to them as the first to arrive or rule in the Great Zimbabwe area before they were forced out of the monument area to resist colonialism, with the Mugabe clan elevated in their stead. Thus, for centuries, the history of the Nemanwa clan has always been entangled and intertwined with that of the Mugabe, Charumbira and, more recently, the Murinye clans. However, there seems to be a 'hereditary' dispute between the Nemanwa and Mugabe clans over Great Zimbabwe. Today, it is uncommon for intermarriages between these two clans, something that often happens with other local clans.

Mugabe clan

Regarding origins, the Mugabe and Murinye clans are part of what Mtetwa (1976) refers to as the Duma confederacy, which declined at the end of the 19th century. This Duma confederacy traces its ancestry back to a Pfupajena, whose descendant, Chief Masungunye (area of jurisdiction is about 150 km south-east of Great Zimbabwe), is still often recognised as the most senior of all the Duma clans (Fontein, 2006, p. 30). This group is believed to have migrated from Uteve (now part of Mozambique) around the 1700s (Aquina, 1965). The first Europeans to visit Great Zimbabwe in the early 19th century found the Mugabe clan occupying part of the Hill Complex. The Mugabe clan controlled the site when it colonised the region (Aquina, 1965; Mtetwa, 1976; Fontein, 2006). With colonisation, Great Zimbabwe became a state property with new boundaries and all the local clans were removed from the estate. Unlike the Nemanwa, the Mugabe clan retained part of their territory and chieftaincy. Today, the Mugabe community maintains a strong claim on Great Zimbabwe because both have been the site's last pre-colonial residents, and some of their ancestors were buried there (Fontein, 2006).

During the research for this chapter, the Chief of the Mugabe clan was Matubede Mhute Mudavanhu. His ascendancy to power was a subject of intra-community contestations. In 2021, Chief Mugabe graduated with a Bachelor of Arts in

Archaeology, Museums and Heritage Studies from the Great Zimbabwe University. In an informal discussion, he revealed that he was inspired to pursue this degree programme to better relate to and articulate the site's archaeological (Western) and local knowledge (Great Zimbabwe). Chief Mugabe's academic, professional and traditional standing is not the only one. Other local chiefs, such as Chief Murinye, a trained lawyer, and Chief Charumbira, the former president of the Chiefs' Council of Zimbabwe and the current president of the Pan-African Parliament, also possess similar educational and leadership credentials. The Pan-African Parliament is one of the organs of the African Union, providing a platform for people from all African states to be involved in discussions and decision-making on the problems and challenges facing the continent. The calibre of the chiefs leading the four local communities at Great Zimbabwe adds a layer of complexity to the conversations around stewardship and management. These leaders are educated and informed in Western and Indigenous epistemologies, often resulting in a lack of compromise and common ground on issues relating to Great Zimbabwe.

Charumbira clan

Different sources have a consensus that the Charumbira people arrived at Great Zimbabwe after the Mugabe and Murinye clans. It is alleged that the ancestors of the Charumbira people were great elephant hunters who migrated from the Mbire dynasty in northern Zimbabwe (Aquina, 1965; Mtetwa, 1976; Mazarire, 2013). The name Charumbira is attributable to the fame acquired by Mudavanhu, an ancestor of the present community. It is claimed that after arriving at Great Zimbabwe, Mudavanhu consolidated power and political supremacy from his uncle Bika. His *mukurumbira* (fame) spread far and wide, earning him the nickname Charumbira – derived from *Chakurumbira* (Aquina, 1965).

Bika, one of the founders of the Charumbira clan, assisted the Nemanwa people in fighting the Mugabe clan over the control of Great Zimbabwe (Aquina, 1965; Fontein, 2006). Due to this assistance, Bika emerged with a larger territory than his host, the Nemanwa clan (Mazarire, 2013, p. 10). During the colonial era, the Charumbira clan enhanced its political powers such that the Nemanwa people came under the authority of the Charumbira chiefdom. This fostered a long-standing friendship between the two clans, strengthened by frequent inter-marriages. However, this friendship has been negatively affected by the recent resurrection of the Nemanwa chieftainship. The Charumbira community has disputed this development as illegitimate and unfounded. For several reasons, the Charumbira people do not receive recognition for Nemanwa as a chief. One key factor is that the Charumbira clan's long-standing claim of the Great Zimbabwe site was due to their historical superiority as the Chief over the Nemanwa, whom they acknowledge as the first inhabitants. The Charumbira see the revival of the Nemanwa chieftainship as a challenge to their traditional authority and control over Great Zimbabwe.

Murinye clan

Until recently, the history and claims of the Murinye local community over Great Zimbabwe have been subsumed under the broader banner of the vaDuma group. This has been the case despite the recognition of Murinye as the founding ancestor of other influential Duma clans living around Great Zimbabwe, such as the Mugabe, Chikwanda and Shumba-Chekai (Mazarire, 2013). Even in the ethnographic research of Joost Fontein, who studied the communities around Great Zimbabwe, the Murinye community was presented and discussed under the 'Mugabe–Matake and the VaDuma clans' subheading (Fontein, 2006, pp. 30–34). This is because, over the years, the traditional leaders of the Murinye clan had not been actively involved in the contestations over Great Zimbabwe until 2009, when Ephias Munodawafa was installed as Chief of Murinye. Since then, the community has become active and continues to engage in the ongoing conversations over Great Zimbabwe's custodianship, ownership and other related issues. The Murinye's activeness to claim their stake in Great Zimbabwe has led to recognising their distinct identity and role rather than being subsumed under the broader vaDuma banner, as was previously the case. Historically, the Murinye clan appears in Carl Mauch's ethnographic research as the father of the Mugabe clan. Mauch, who claimed to have 'discovered' Great Zimbabwe in 1871, was instrumental in popularising this archaeological site for the outside world through his diaries and writings (Burke, 1969). While Mauch's and Richard Hall's (1905) writings were often imbued with racial and Eurocentric interpretations of Great Zimbabwe, they also recorded the histories of encountered communities, including the Murinye.

Historical accounts and oral traditions recognise that the Murinye clan arrived in Great Zimbabwe before the Mugabe clan but did not occupy the site. However, the prominence and influence of Mugabe have overshadowed that of the Murinye in the literature, likely due to Mugabe's centrality to the conflicts over the control of Great Zimbabwe since the 1800s (Aquina, 1965; Mtetwa, 1976 Mazarire, 2013; Sinamai, 2020). Today, the Murinye and Mugabe communities remain engaged in boundary disputes that have resulted in clashes during funerals and other community gatherings. In June 2023, for instance, Chief Murinye was assaulted by an angry mob in Boroma, a village located a few kilometres east of the Great Zimbabwe site. While the assault is reportedly a row over a burial site (Maponga, 2023), it is essentially a manifestation of the ongoing chiefdom boundary disputes between the Murinye and Mugabe communities.

The histories of the Nemanwa, Mugabe, Murinye and Charumbira communities are deeply intertwined. Each clan has created and continues to shape its historical narratives to position itself as Great Zimbabwe's rightful custodian and even owner (Fontein, 2006; Basinyi & Sagiya, 2019). Over time, some local communities' oral histories have become mythologised, inflated, factual and even fictitious. Community historical accounts' fluidity and ever-evolving nature should not be considered problematic. Every society has its myths about its origins, which researchers need to interpret to establish the 'truth'. Regardless of their diverging historical claims, the Nemanwa, Mugabe, Murinye and Charumbira communities have a strong attachment to Great Zimbabwe through descent and proximity to the site. For these communities, Great Zimbabwe is a shared space (a contact zone) where their diverging histories, narratives, interests and perspectives constantly interact and influence one another. The following section details the nature of community contestations in the stewardship and management of the Great Zimbabwe World Heritage Site.

Community contestations at Great Zimbabwe

The Nemanwa, Mugabe, Charumbira and Murinye have coexisted for over a century. Due to localised migrations, intermarriages and other relationships forged over time, the different clans are not exclusively settled under their respective chiefdoms. Each clan resides under the jurisdiction of its respective chief. Over the centuries, stewardship, ownership and benefits issues have caused inter-community and intra-community contestations. Disagreements exist among and between the Nemanwa, Mugabe, Murinye and Charumbira clans over Great Zimbabwe. There are also disagreements among individuals within a single clan. Individuals, families and clans' varying interests and expectations cause intra- and inter-community contestations over the site. The inter-community and intra-community contestations have hurt the effective and sustainable management of the Great Zimbabwe World Heritage Site, as I show in the four sections.

The country name 'Zimbabwe' was derived from the site of Great Zimbabwe. The prefix 'Great' was added by the early European visitors and writers in the early 19th century to distinguish this site from the many other similar, but smaller, sites found within the plateau and the neighbouring countries of Botswana, South Africa and Mozambique. To the four local communities, especially that of the elderly, the site is known as 'Zimbabwe' or simply 'Dzimbahwe', an indigenous Shona word meaning a 'house of stones', a locale of aura, power and authority. One of the longstanding and unresolved issues among Great Zimbabwe's local communities is the question of ownership. Who owns Great Zimbabwe? This question is crucial for a heritage site from which the country derives its name. The local communities do not subscribe to the notion that heritage belongs to the state. Godfrey Mahachi, the former Executive Director of the NMMZ, remarks:

> The law states that all heritage belongs to the state. However, the state acknowledges the critical importance of the communities with an interest, which can be cultural, spiritual, or through association with whoever put up that monument. There can be confusion regarding how people interpret a monument's existence in different places, but that does not negate a state being the owner of all heritage sites, of course, on behalf of the people.
>
> (Interview with Godfrey Mahachi, 1 March 2018)

Zimbabwean heritage practitioners and scholars recognise the clarity of heritage law; however, local communities are asserting their rights to participate in the stewardship and management of Great Zimbabwe. Great Zimbabwe is not considered state property among these communities, particularly the chiefs. They view it as a shrine that belonged to their ancestors, which was taken during the colonial era. Despite this shared sentiment, the four chiefs disagree on the rightful ownership of Great Zimbabwe. During an interview on 16 May 2020, Paul Mavhima, the acting Headman of the Nemanwa community, believes Great Zimbabwe belongs to them (Nemanwa), emphasising that the Mugabe community are newcomers who were just welcomed and given land to settle. On the other hand, Chief Murinye has been recorded at different local forums and meetings, noting that Great Zimbabwe belongs to the Duma clan. He claims his Murinye forefathers had allowed the Mugabe clan to occupy the Great Zimbabwe site when they first arrived in the region before colonisation. The differing claims and contestations over the ownership and control of Great Zimbabwe among the local chiefs and communities highlight this issue's complex and unresolved nature. The lack of consensus and the competing narratives demonstrate the deep-seated disagreements over Great Zimbabwe.

The Charumbira people do not claim to have built Great Zimbabwe. Historically, they strongly supported the traditional authority of the Nemanwa Headman over the site, but this relationship has changed recently. In October 2022, the Government of Zimbabwe reinstated the Nemanwa chieftainship, which had been abolished during the early years of colonial rule. This development has led to a feud and power struggle between the Charumbira and Nemanwa clans, with the Charumbira considering the elevation of Nemanwa's traditional leadership to a full chieftaincy as illegitimate. These disputes between the two clans are often marked by fist fighting during village gatherings, funerals and other community events. The tension over the control of Great Zimbabwe remains a source of ongoing conflict between the Charumbira and Nemanwa communities. This antagonistic community relationship makes it complicated to involve the local communities in the conservation and management of the site; it is a significant challenge.

The Masvingo Rural District Council, the local authority overseeing all administrative affairs in the area where Great Zimbabwe is located, has previously attempted to delineate the site's boundaries in the context of local chiefdoms. In 2012, the councillors wanted to gazette a resolution to determine which chiefdom the monument falls in among the four chiefdoms of Nemanwa, Mugabe, Murinye and Charumbira (The Herald, 2012). The councillors and the chiefs, ex-official Masvingo Rural District Council members, could not reach a consensus. As a result of this impasse, the council declared the area a 'no man's land' or, instead, a state land. This decision highlights the inability of the local authorities and the traditional leadership to resolve the competing claims and jurisdictions over the site. The lack of consensus and the failure to delineate the site's boundaries among the local chiefdoms have led to the area being designated as state land by default, which complicates the local people's involvement in the conservation and management of the site.

Meanwhile, the ownership claims of the Great Zimbabwe by the four surrounding communities have been dismissed by some historians, such as Aeneas Chigwedere. Chigwedere, a controversial Zimbabwean historian and former Minister of Education, argued in an interview with *The Herald*, one of the country's newspapers, that none of the local chieftainships should claim ownership and control of the Great Zimbabwe World Heritage Site (The Herald, 2012). Chigwedere further postulated that Chief Nemanwa and his people found the Great Zimbabwe site already built. The Mugabe and other clans arrived around the 1840s, resulting in these long-standing contestations over the site's control and stewardship. The contestations have existed for years because, as Mazarire (2013) observes, the region around the Great Zimbabwe was a theatre of considerable human traffic between c. 1750 and 1850. The views of some historians have challenged the ownership claims made by the surrounding communities, suggesting that the site's history and occupancy predate the current local chieftainships, which have fuelled ongoing debates and disputes over the rightful custodianship and authority over Great Zimbabwe, a site of immense cultural and historical significance. These differing historical perspectives have further complicated the local communities' contestations over the control and management of the site. The lack of consensus among historians and the local traditional leadership continues to be a significant challenge in resolving the ownership and governance issues surrounding the site.

The question of the rightful traditional stewards of the Great Zimbabwe is a sensitive and emotive matter that has been causing disputes and contestations both within and between the local communities (Fontein, 2006). Each of the four chiefs and their subjects explains the history of Great Zimbabwe, pointing to their clan and legitimising claims of traditional custodianship. The Nemanwa people emphasise that they are the original custodians of the Great Zimbabwe, who gave the Duma (Murinye and Mugabe) and Charumbira descendants a place to stay. In contrast, the Mugabe community claims that when Carl Mauch visited the Great Zimbabwe in 1871, he found Haruzivishe, the great Mugabe ancestor, at the site and ruling. This suggests that the Mugabe were the last occupants of the Great Zimbabwe and that their ancestors are buried on the Hill complex. These varying historical narratives and claims of traditional stewardship have fuelled ongoing contestations among the local communities. Each group attempts to legitimise its ownership and control of Great Zimbabwe by invoking its clan's historical connection and presence there.

Over the years, the Great Zimbabwe has also become a resource. With its World Heritage status and other archaeological and historical considerations, the site has become an economic resource through cultural tourism. There is a tug-of-war over who can benefit from the economic spinoffs among the four local communities (Nemanwa, Murinye, Mugabe and Charumbira). Such contestations often arise while recruiting local labour for conservation and restoration projects, both short and long terms. The traditional leaders of each community lodge complaints to the NMMZ if they feel that the people from their clans have not been considered. Each clan has been manoeuvring to control the site for over a century, leading Great Zimbabwe into a contact zone. It has become a shared space that evokes tension and debate over 'who is the rightful custodian'. The claims over the economic benefits and employment opportunities associated with the management and conservation of Great Zimbabwe have further exacerbated the tensions among the local communities. The lack of a transparent and inclusive governance framework has allowed these competing interests to dominate the discourse around the site's custodianship, hindering collaborative efforts for sustainable management and preservation.

There are also intra-community contestations among different branches within a clan, especially when the incumbent chief dies. No elaborate criteria regarding heirship to the throne exist in all four communities surrounding Great Zimbabwe. Within the VaKaranga tradition, succession is supposed to occur within the royal houses (families) within a particular clan. The clan's founding ancestors usually constitute such families. However, due to political connections and other related factors, traditional successions are not always abided by, resulting in serious disputes and conflicts within the clans. Most intra-community contestations are unknown to outsiders, including researchers and heritage practitioners at Great Zimbabwe. This situation creates challenges in effectively engaging the local communities in research and site management. To collaborate successfully with the local communities at Great Zimbabwe, one must develop a more complex understanding of the local communities' internal politics and dynamics. The intricate power structures and succession disputes within the clans are another layer of complexity to the already sensitive issue of traditional custodianship of Great Zimbabwe. Addressing these intra-community power dynamics is crucial for establishing inclusive and effective governance frameworks that facilitate meaningful engagement and collaboration among heritage stakeholders at Great Zimbabwe.

Until the late 1990s (see Matenga 2000; Ndoro, 2005; Fontein, 2006; Chirikure, 2020), the value of local claims to Great Zimbabwe and its past have been overlooked by archaeologists on the basis that all local communities are latecomers. As Fontein (2006: 22) puts it, this assumption forgets that researchers and NMMZ officials are more recent despite their activities being backed by the law. Great Zimbabwe is not only about the spectacular dry-stone walls or famous archaeological objects such as the soapstone carved birds (popularly known as the Zimbabwe birds). The site also contains other cultural and natural heritage features that have not been of interest to many writers. One such feature is the Mujejeje, a linear intrusive vein of quartz exposed on a granite outcrop (*ruware* in the local Shona language), located about 200 m east of the Hill Complex (see Figure 8.4). Mujejeje features in the local communities' oral histories and beliefs, particularly among the Nemanwa clan. According to oral tradition, Mujejeje is the sacred entrance to Great Zimbabwe. It is believed that during its occupation by the original builders and later custodial clans, upon reaching this point, individuals would pick a pebble

FIGURE 8.4 Mujejeje, showing the quartz line.

Source: Author (2023)

and tap along the line, murmuring a prayer to the ancestral spirits. This ritual was performed when entering and exiting the stone-built centre. The practice entailed tapping along the granite outcrop for about 20 m with a stone thrown at the end of the line.

According to the Nemanwa elders interviewed in the context of this work, Muje-jeje is an integral part of their clan praise name (*chidawo*). One of the lines of the clan praise chanting goes like this: 'Vajejeje, vagara dombo, vamera, vagara Dzimbabwe', which means, 'Those of Mujejeje, the ones who can sit on a rock, those who germinated, and those who reside in the (great) Zimbabwe'. For the Nemanwa, Mujejeje symbolises their ancestral connection to Great Zimbabwe. Meanwhile, the Mugabe clan has a similar narrative but does not associate it with the Nemanwa clan. In August 2012, Mujejeje was vandalised, but it was unclear who had vandalised it. A month later, a delegation of elders from the Nemanwa clan tabled their concerns to the management of Great Zimbabwe, including assessing the extent of the damage.

During further inquiries, the site management team learned that a local community member searching for his cattle within the Great Zimbabwe estate had witnessed an act of vandalism. He reported the incident to Nemanwa, a headman under Chief Charumbira. The Nemanwa elders were upset that site management had not informed them of the incident. Following a tense meeting, the author, other site curators and the director accompanied the Nemanwa elders to the Mujejeje site, where rituals were performed to address the situation and assess the damage. On that visit, we found that two heaps of stones beside the quartz bar were damaged, and the area was smeared with snuff and salt. This vandalism sparked speculation within the local communities about the perpetrators and their motivations, with the Nemanwa clan suspecting members of the rival Mugabe clan. Despite the heritage management team's efforts to unite the communities for the physical and spiritual restoration of the Mujejeje feature, disagreements over leadership and which clan's protocols to follow led to a stalemate. As a result, the Mujejeje feature remains unrestored, a situation that has persisted since 2012.

Discussion and conclusion

The local communities are at the heart of World Heritage Site management and are crucial for the sustainable conservation of these properties (Chirikure & Pwiti, 2008; Brown & Hay-Edie, 2014; Basinyi Sagiya, 2019). Including local communities is one of the five strategic objectives in implementing the World Heritage Convention of 1972. The centrality of local communities in the future of World Heritage Sites is unquestionable. The best practices for engaging local communities in the stewardship of heritage sites, such as Great Zimbabwe, where rival communities remain vague. Issues around the ownership, access and custodianship of Great Zimbabwe are sources of conflicts and contestations among the local communities, and these have continued for a very long time. These contestations have not been given due attention in the ever-increasing literature about the site, except for Fontein's (2006: 13) remark on the ethnographic and historical accounts of the issue.

The current chapter has focused on the historic and ongoing intra- and inter-community conflicts in Great Zimbabwe. Hopefully, this contribution will awaken the government authorities in Zimbabwe, including policymakers, heritage practitioners and researchers, to take the initiative to solve this problem. Conflict, by its very nature, leads to the destruction and disruption of cultural heritage assets and associated events (Ndoro, 2021). The local community's contestations over Great Zimbabwe negatively impact its long-term conservation and management. As a result, these contestations should be resolved. Developing effective diplomatic frameworks for conflict resolution and community engagement is key to heritage management at Great Zimbabwe.

The community contestations over the Great Zimbabwe require no externally formulated solutions. Instead, they require local and tailor-made diplomacy and conflict resolution mechanisms. The NMMZ has been trying to implement this since 1980, but with limited success. As Matenga (2000) informs, in 1984, a bira (traditional ceremony) was held at the site but ended in a fiasco with elders trading blows and heated words – the question of 'who is who' among the communities was at the heart of the conflict. After the fracas, it was deemed practical not to hold such ceremonies, for it was not the best course of action but a form of *modus vivendi* (Matenga, 2000, p. 13). After the 1984 incident, the NMMZ remained almost two decades without seriously engaging and involving the local communities in the preservation and management of the site. In 2000, the NMMZ held a traditional ritual to reopen the sacred fountain, known as Chisikana, within the Great Zimbabwe estate. Matenga (2000) reports that the ceremony proceeded smoothly, with consensus among local community delegates that Great Zimbabwe belonged to them and not to outsiders.

Ten years later, NMMZ facilitated the creation of a local community management committee with representatives from all the communities around the site. Unfortunately, this committee has not effectively resolved the historical contestations over Great Zimbabwe. Their respective leaders have disowned some of the members of the committee. Most local people see the Great Zimbabwe Local Management Committee as a 'toothless dog'. Despite weaknesses, the local community committee working with the site management was ideal for harmonious cooperation among various stakeholders. In 2021, NMMZ established a contentious onsite spiritual centre. The political dynamics and complexities surrounding this new initiative require thorough scholarly examination. The four local communities presented earlier express divergent perspectives concerning the centre's functions and purpose. Consequently, NMMZ must prioritise the development of effective diplomatic frameworks for conflict resolution and community engagement as it navigates the intricate cultural politics and competing claims associated with this World Heritage Site.

Despite these few cases of community cooperation and collaboration, the four communities continue to be embroiled in what can be described as 'inherited contestations and conflicts' over the site. The prevailing situation demonstrates that the involvement of local communities in heritage management is frequently called for, but not necessarily easy or without its challenges (Chirikure & Pwiti, 2008; Chirikure et al., 2010; Jopela, 2018; Sinamai, 2020; Baille & Sørensen, 2021). Regardless of the complexities and challenges of dealing with local communities in heritage management, these communities bestow value on heritage sites. Therefore, creating a harmonious environment that allows for cooperation and collaboration between and among various stakeholders (local communities, researchers and heritage managers) is critical. There is a need for a collective redress of the custodianship legitimacy debate and contestations, which are also entangled within the politics of chieftainship.

Drawing from the VaKaranga epistemologies of peace and conflict resolution, as a neutral actor in the local clan politics, NMMZ should facilitate intra-community dialogue and conversations. Meanwhile, the ability of the NMMZ to initiate this process relies on cultural diplomacy and conflict resolution expertise, which is currently lacking within the organisation's workforce. Overcoming persistent conflicts and contestations over the Great Zimbabwe site will require the NMMZ to bolster its community engagement and conflict resolution capacity. Establishing effective frameworks for collaborative heritage management, where the diverse local communities' voices and perspectives are meaningfully incorporated, is crucial for this World Heritage Site's long-term preservation and sustainable stewardship.

The conflicts and contestations among local communities are a topic that has often been neglected in heritage studies. As a result, there is a limited availability of research-based cultural diplomacy and conflict resolution toolkits or models that have been published so far. Consequently, heritage managers at sites such as Great Zimbabwe often find it very difficult to engage and involve the local communities locked in a historic tug-of-war over the ownership and custodianship of the place. Dealing with the Great Zimbabwe local communities and other similar contexts elsewhere as heritage practitioners requires cultural diplomacy and conflict resolution skills, which are not necessarily part of the country's archaeology and heritage studies curricula.

Taking into cognisance that the existence of conflictual aspects within local communities is prevalent in different heritage sites (Gould, 2018), it is imperative for archaeology and heritage management training to also consider cultural diplomacy and conflict resolution as key areas of study. Equipping heritage professionals with these specialised skills would significantly enhance their ability to navigate the complex sociopolitical dynamics at heritage sites and foster more effective community engagement and collaborative management approaches. Addressing this gap in heritage studies curricula and professional development is crucial, as it would enable heritage managers to better understand and respond to the nuanced community contestations that often underlie the stewardship and preservation of significant cultural sites like Great Zimbabwe. Integrating cultural diplomacy and conflict resolution as core components of heritage education and training would be a valuable investment in preparing the next generation of heritage practitioners to tackle these critical challenges.

Disputes among local communities surrounding the Great Zimbabwe stem from various issues, including stewardship rights, ownership and the legitimacy of one another's claims to the site. These deep-rooted and complex conflicts pose significant challenges for heritage management and preservation, as stakeholders' diverse interests and power dynamics must be navigated thoughtfully. A nuanced, collaborative approach is essential to effectively address the intricate web of community conflicts and claims regarding Great Zimbabwe. This strategy should actively engage local clans and work towards harmonising their differing interests and perspectives. For heritage managers and researchers, developing effective cultural diplomacy and conflict resolution strategies is crucial for preserving this important archaeological site while fostering a more inclusive and equitable stewardship model.

At the Great Zimbabwe World Heritage Site, there are many different community interests and competing valorisation processes at work, transforming the site into a veritable 'contact zone' where local cultures meet, clash and grapple with one another, often in highly contentious and conflictual contexts (Zukas, 2022). This situation has starkly demonstrated the significant implications that can emerge when multiple communities claim the same heritage place. Even though it may be challenging, there is a clear need to transform Great Zimbabwe from being a 'battleground' for rival community attachments into a space of meaningful dialogue, empowerment and shared prosperity for all, regardless of clan affiliations. Achieving this will require developing and implementing locally tailored cultural diplomacy and conflict resolution strategies. Investing in such localised conflict resolution approaches is essential, as it can potentially shift Great Zimbabwe from being a site of ongoing contestation to one that fosters mutual understanding, shared ownership and collective prosperity among the surrounding communities. This shift would benefit the local populations and contribute to the more effective conservation and transmission of Great Zimbabwe's invaluable cultural heritage to future generations. This case study highlights the need for heritage professionals to engage sensitively and equitably with all stakeholders to safeguard the multi-layered cultural significance of cultural heritage sites.

Acknowledgements

This chapter was revised and completed during a nine-month (October 2024–June 2025) research fellowship at the Käte Hamburger Kolleg, *inherit* – Heritage in Transformation at the Humboldt-Universität zu Berlin, which the Federal Ministry of Research, Technology and Space (formerly the Ministry of Education and Research) funds.

References

Aquina, S.M. (1965). Tribes in Victoria Reserve. *NADA*, 9(2): 6–15.

Baillie, B., and Sørensen, M.L.S. (2021). Heritage Challenges in Africa: Contestations and Expectations. In Baillie, B., and Sørensen, M.L.S. (Eds.), *African Heritage Challenges: Communities and Sustainable Development* (pp. 1–43). Singapore: Palgrave Macmillan.

Basinyi, S., and Sagiya, M.E. (2019). World Heritage Communities, Anchors and Values for Safeguarding Intangible Cultural Heritage in Southern Africa: Zimbabwe and Botswana. In Akagawa, N., and Smith, L. (Eds.), *Safeguarding Intangible Heritage: Practices and Politics.* London and New York: Routledge.

Brown, J., and Hay-Edie, T. (2014). *Engaging Local Communities in Stewardship of World Heritage: A Methodology-Based on the COMPACT Experience.* Paris: UNESCO.

Burke, E. (1969). *The Journal of Carl Maunch: His Travels in the Transvaal and Rhodesia.* Salisbury: Archives of Rhodesia.

Chipangura, N., and Chipangura, P. (2019). Community Museums and Rethinking the Colonial Frame of National Museums in Zimbabwe. *Museum Management and Curatorship*, 35(1): 35–56.

Chirikure, S. (2020). *Great Zimbabwe: Reclaiming a 'Confiscated' Past.* London: Routledge.

Chirikure, S.C., Manyanga, M., Ndoro, W., and Pwiti, G. (2010). "Unfulfilled Promises? Heritage Management and Community Participation at Some of Africa's Cultural Heritage Sites." *International Journal of Heritage Studies,* 16(1–2): 30–44. https://doi.org/10.1080/13527250903441739.

Chirikure, S., and Pwiti, G. (2008). Community Involvement in Archaeology and Cultural Heritage Management: An Assessment from Case Studies in Southern Africa and Elsewhere. *Current Anthropology,* 40(5): 843–849.

Clifford, J. (1997). "Museums as Contact Zones". In *Routes: Travel and Translation in the Late 20th Century.* Cambridge: Harvard University Press.

Clifford-Napoleone, A.R. (2013). A New Tradition: A Reflection on Collaboration and Contact Zones. *The Journal of Museum Education,* 38(2): 187–192.

Colecchia, A. (2019). Community Heritage and Heritage Community. Participatory Models of Cultural and Natural Heritage Management in some Inner Areas of the Abruzzo Region (Italy). In Cerquetti, M., Sánchez-Mesa Martínez, L.J., and Vitale, C.(Eds.), *The Management of Cultural Heritage and Landscape in Inner Areas. Il capitale culturale* (p. 19). Studies on the Value of Cultural Heritage.

Fontein, J. (2006). *The Silence of Great Zimbabwe: Contested Landscapes and the Power of Heritage.* Harare: Weaver Press.

Garlake, P. (1982). *Great Zimbabwe: Described and Explained.* Harare: Zimbabwe Publishing House.

Gould, P.G. (2018). *Empowering Communities through Archaeology and Heritage. The Role of Local Governance in Economic Development.* London and New York: Bloomsbury.

Great Zimbabwe National Monument and World Heritage Site Integrated Management Plan, 2024–2028. Harare: NMMZ.

Hall, R.N. (1905). *Great Zimbabwe, Mashonaland, Rhodesia. An Account of Two Years' Examination Work in 1902–4 on Behalf of the Government of Rhodesia.* London; Methuen.

Hoxha, G. (2012). The Impact of Conflict on Cultural Heritage in Kosovo. In *Protecting Cultural Heritage in Times of Conflict: Contributions from the Participants of the International Course on First Aid to Cultural Heritage in Times of Conflict* (pp. 39–46). Rome: ICCROM.

Huffman, T.N. (2011). Debating Great Zimbabwe. *South African Archaeological Bulletin,* 66(193): 27–40

Isakhan, B., and Meskell, L. (2024). Local Perspectives on Heritage Reconstruction after Conflict: A Public Opinion Survey of Aleppo. *International Journal of Heritage Studies,* https://doi.org/10.1080/13527258.2024.2342288

Jang, H., and Mennis, J. (2021). The Role of Local Communities and Well-Being in UNESCO World Heritage Site Conservation: An Analysis of the Operational Guidelines, 1994–2019. *Sustainability,* 13(13): 1–14.

Jopela, A. (2018). Reorienting Heritage Management in Southern Africa: Lessons from Traditional Custodianship of Rock Art Sites in Central Mozambique. In Ndoro, W., Chirikure, S., and Deacon, J. (Eds.), *Managing Heritage in Africa: Who Cares?* (pp. 55–71). London and New York: Routledge.

Jopela, A. (2022). The Trouble with Participation: Heritage Places, Politics and Communities in Africa. In Abungu, G.O., and Ndoro, W. (Eds.), *Cultural Heritage Management in Africa: The Heritage of the Colonised.* London: Routledge.

Lambert, S., and Rockwell, C. (2012). *Protecting Cultural Heritage in Times of Conflict: Contributions from the Participants of the International Course on First Aid to Cultural Heritage in Times of Conflict.* Rome: ICCROM.

Loza, R. (2023). Local Communities as Custodians of Cultural Heritage: Perspectives from Africa. *International Journal of Heritage Studies,* 29(2): 123–135.

Maponga, G. (2023). Chiefs' Council Condemns Attack on Chief Murinye. *The Herald, 11 July 2023.* Available at: https://www.bing.com/search?pglt=41&q=Maponga%2C+G.+ (2023).+Chiefs%E2%80%99+Council+Condemns+Attack+on+Chief+Murinye.+The+ Herald%2C+11+July+2023+.&cvid=495bf002ef0b4189b8b2eb23788dc650&gs_lcrp= EgRlZGdlKgYIABBFGDkyBggAEEUYOTIHCAEQ6wcYQNIBCDExMDZqMGoxq AIIsAIB&FORM=ANNTA1&PC=HCTS

Matenga, E. (2000). Traditional Ritual Ceremony Held at Great Zimbabwe. *NAMMO Bulletin Official Magazine of NMMZ,* 1(9): 14–15.

Mazarire, G. (2013). Carl Mauch and Some Karanga Chiefs Around Great Zimbabwe 1871–1872: Re-Considering the Evidence. *South African Historical Journal.* https://doi.org/10.1080 /02582473.2013.768290.

Mtetwa, R.M.G. (1976). 'The "Political" and Economic History of the Duma people of South-Eastern Rhodesia from the Early 18th Century to 1945'. PhD thesis, University of Rhodesia.

Ndoro, W. (2001). *Your Monument Our Shrine: The Preservation of Great Zimbabwe*. Studies in African Archaeology 19. Department of Archaeology and Ancient History, Uppsala University.

Ndoro, W. (2005). *The Preservation of Great Zimbabwe: Your Monument, Our Shrine*. Rome: ICCROM.

Ndoro, W. (2021). Cultural Heritage and Conflicts in Africa. *Oxford Research Encyclopedia Anthropology* (pp. 1–18). https://doi.org/10.1093/ACREFORE/9780190854584.013.270

Ndoro, W., and Wijesuriya, G. (2015). Heritage Management and Conservation: From Colonization to Globalization. In Meskell, L. (Ed.), *Global Heritage: A Reader* (pp. 131–149). Wiley Blackwell.

Pikirayi, I. (2001). *The Zimbabwe Culture: Origins and Decline of Southern Zambezian States*. Lanham: Alta Mira Press.

Pikirayi, I. (2013). Stone Architecture and Development of Power in the Zimbabwe tradition AD 1270–1830. *Azania: Archaeological Research in Africa*, 48(2): 282–300.

Pirkovic, J. (2020). Heritage Management at Local Levels: Heritage Communities and Role of Local Authorities. *Issues in Ethnology and Anthropology*, 15(3): 829–840.

Pratt, M. (1991). Arts of the Contact Zone. *Profession*, 33–40.

Pratt, M.L. (2007). *Imperial Eyes: Travel Writing and Transculturation*. London: Routledge.

Pwiti, G. (1996). Let the Ancestors Rest in Peace? New Challenges for Heritage Management in Zimbabwe. *Conservation and Management of Archaeological Sites*, 1(3): 151–160.

Ranger, T. (2004). Nationalist Historiography, Patriotic History and the History of the Nation: The Struggle over the Past in Zimbabwe. *Journal of Southern African Studies*, 30(2): 215–234.

Sinamai, A. (2020). "We are Still Here": African Heritage, Diversity and the Global Heritage Knowledge Templates. *Archaeologies*, 16: 57–71.

Singh, K. (2022). When Peace is Defeat, Reconstruction is Damage: "Rebuilding" Heritage in Post-Conflict Sri Lanka and Afghanistan. In James, C., and Weiss, T.G. (Eds.), *Cultural Heritage and Mass Atrocities*. Los Angeles: Getty Publications.

Spencer, J. ed. (1990). *Sri Lanka: History and the Roots of Conflict*. London: Routledge.

The Herald. (22 June 2012). *Three Chiefs Fight Over Great Zimbabwe Control*. Available at: https://www.bing.com/search?q=The+Herald.+(22+June+2012).+Three+Chiefs+Fight+Over+Great+Zimbabwe+Control.&cvid=186385de24034196ae373d6d062b3b18&gs_lcrp=EgRlZGdlKgYIABBFGDkyBggAEEUYOTIHCAEQ6wcYQNIBBzQwNmowajSoAgiwAgE&FORM=ANAB01&PC=HCTS

Waterton, E. (2005). Whose Sense of Place? Reconciling Archaeological Perspectives with Community Values: Cultural Landscapes in England. *International Journal of Heritage Studies*, 11: 309–320.

Zukas, L.L. (2022). Zimbabwe's National Museums and Monuments: Constructing Culture and Making Money. *Economic Anthropology*, 9: 22–34.

9

FIGHTING FOR MULTI-MILLION-YEAR FOSSILS AND LOCALITIES

Exploring contests among research groups at Oldupai (Olduvai) Gorge in Northern Tanzania

Mariam Joseph Bundala

Introduction

The primary objective of this chapter is to conduct a comprehensive examination of the complex social dynamics that exist among scientists working on research projects at Oldupai Gorge (OG), an essential site for paleoanthropological studies. This chapter aims to clarify how contentious disputes – disagreements or arguments – affect critical research aspects including collaborative efforts, training opportunities, and academic publishing among scientists. Historically, conflicts at OG, which is globally recognized as a significant site for paleoanthropology, have often arisen from competition over which locality to conduct excavation as well as limited resources. These resources include access to fossil sites, camping facilities, and the management of collections of studied samples that are typically controlled by specific research teams or government heritage institutions.

The relevance of this investigation is underscored by the increasing number of active Tanzanian paleoanthropologists, whose growing presence is anticipated to profoundly enhance our collective understanding of human origins. Their work is imperative not only for advancing scientific knowledge but also for establishing Tanzania as a leading nation in Africa in the field of paleoanthropology. For this chapter, I cite the University of Dar es Salaam (UDSM) as a case study due to its significant contributions to paleoanthropology and archaeology. UDSM has a rich history of engagement in collaborative research projects and training initiatives that promote academic growth and knowledge sharing among researchers. This institution is notably the primary hub where researchers have conducted extensive fieldwork at OG over the years. Through these efforts, valuable global partnerships have been forged, allowing for the exchange of ideas and resources.

DOI: 10.4324/9781003623724-9

In providing insights into the root causes of conflicts among researchers in Paleoanthropology at OG, the data presented in this chapter come from both primary and secondary sources. Primary data were gathered through in-depth interviews with Tanzanian academicians who are actively engaged in research at OG. These interviews provided a wealth of first-hand information, which was further enhanced by personal experiences and observational notes accumulated from my own research work at the site. For secondary data, I reviewed various published articles examining the nature of conflicts at OG alongside institutional reports and pertinent newspaper articles. The Internet, as a vital repository of information, played a crucial role in facilitating comprehensive secondary data, offering critical perspectives and insights into the complexities of contests at OG. Importantly, the study primarily relied on narratives gathered from a carefully selected group of willing academicians who were open to sharing their perspectives and experiences candidly.

Paleoanthropological inquiry

Palaeoanthropology is a scientific study of human evolution. It is a subfield of anthropology that encompasses studies of human culture through prehistoric archaeology and biology using physical anthropology (Campbell & Loy, 2000; Jurmain et al., 2014; Kottak, 2011). It focuses on the study of fossilized human ancestors, cultural remnants, and other evidence of extinct human life forms (Delisle, 2018; Kovarovic, 2019). The discipline delves into the intricate history and behavioral patterns of human ancestors (hominins) and modern humans. It also encompasses an understanding of the similarities and differences between humans and other species such as our association with non-human primates in their genes, body forms, physiology, and behavior (Jurmain et al., 2014; Kovarovic, 2019). The fundamental goal of palaeoanthropology is to construct a comprehensive understanding of humankind, essentially narrating the story of our existence from long evolutionary processes by which humans originated from our apelike ancestors over the past seven million years (Blundell, 2006; Brunet et al., 2002, 2005; Campbell & Loy, 2000; Jurmain et al., 2014; Tuttle, 1988). Through comprehensive multidisciplinary approach, palaeoanthropologists have now unearthed thousands of human fossils, cultural materials, and environmental proxy data that provide insight into our ancient ancestors and the journey they undertook in becoming human.

The significance of paleoanthropological sites cannot be overstated, as they provide critical information that enhances our understanding of humanity's past. Consequently, the protection and preservation of these sites are of utmost importance. Without adequate safeguarding measures, the potential for discord among researchers and an overall lack of collaboration between different institutions could impede the thorough research, meticulous documentation, and essential conservation efforts required for these invaluable sites. In the end, a failure to address these conflicts could obstruct our ability to achieve a complete and nuanced understanding of the complex narratives that make up our evolutionary history. Globally, researchers have invested considerable effort in uncovering evidence that narrates our human past, allowing us to address misconceptions about evolution. Evolution is a gradual process characterized by change over vast periods, especially evident in complex organisms such as humans (Delisle, 2018; Holden, 1981; Jurmain et al., 2014; Kottak, 2011). The evolutionary journey leading to modern humans spans over 3.5 billion years, beginning with the origins of life on Earth.

Paleoanthropologists emphasize the importance of understanding that humans and chimpanzees have each evolved separately from a shared ancestral lineage (The Last Common Ancestor) (Brunet et al., 2002; Daver et al., 2022; Haile-Selassie & WoldeGabriel, 2023; Pickford et al., 2002). Recent genetic analyses, particularly studies of DNA mutation rates, suggest that the evolutionary split between humans and our closest relatives, the chimpanzees, likely occurred between seven million and eight million years ago. In contrast, it is estimated that the divergence between humans and gorillas may have taken place somewhere between 8 million and 19 million years ago (Blundell, 2006; Jurmain et al., 2014). This critical understanding plays a significant role in dispelling enduring misconceptions, particularly in regions such as Tanzania, where a common misunderstanding persists regarding the evolutionary relationship between humans and monkeys. Historically, these misconceptions have led to skepticism toward paleoanthropological research, fueled by questions such as why modern monkeys do not transform into humans if we share a lineage.

To put this in context, it is essential to note that the oldest known monkeys have existed for at least 60 million years (Campbell & Loy, 2000; Kottak, 2011). Old World monkeys are believed to have emerged around 40–50 million years ago, while the origins of New World monkeys trace back to approximately 25 million years (Campbell & Loy, 2000; Kottak, 2011). Even though both humans and monkeys fall within the primate family, it is essential to clarify that humans did not evolve from monkeys or any existing primate species (Campbell & Loy, 2000; Kottak, 2011).

The trajectory of human evolution is far from linear; instead, it resembles a complex branching bush, where many distinct species have emerged over time from common ancestors. Given these complexities, paleoanthropologists have meticulously assembled an exhaustive overview of human evolutionary history, culminating in a comprehensive "Timeline of our Evolution." This timeline encapsulates the major biological and cultural transformations that have occurred from our humble ancestral forms to the emergence of modern *Homo sapiens*. These findings are included in numerous publications detailing research from the 1920s to the present day. To simplify the presentation of this extensive information, I will outline the traits that define us as humans using the fossil human ancestors compiled by paleoanthropologists. Table 9.1 provides a review of key human attributes, such as bipedal locomotion, long periods of childhood dependency, large brains, and the use of tools and language, along with the fossil human ancestors to trace their origins.

TABLE 9.1 Traits marking Human Evolution – within the last eight million years ago (mya – million years ago, ka – thousand years ago)

Event	Brief description and names of ancestors recorded, so far	Source
Bipedalism	• Bipedalism characterizes human lineage since its split from the line leading to the African apes around 8–7 million years ago, many other "human" features developed later. • Pre-Australopiths: species show evolutionary significance when early humans evolved an upright posture and the ability to walk on shorter legs. Arguably, there is earlier bipedalism in *Sahelanthropus tchadensis* (6–7 mya), *Orrorin tugenensis* (6 mya), and *Ardipithecus kadabba* (5.6–4.4 mya). The brain volume was small; for example, *S. tchadensis* had a volume of 320–80 cc, comparable to modern chimpanzees (285–500 cc), and it featured a less sloping face. • Scientists have identified several advantages of bipedalism: the ability to see over tall grass and shrubs, carry items back to a home base, and reduce the body's exposure to solar radiation. Studies using scale models of primates indicate that quadrupedalism exposes the body to 60 percent more solar radiation than bipedalism does. • Fossil records confirm that upright bipedal locomotion preceded the production of stone tools and the expansion of hominin brain. While early hominins could move bipedally on the ground, they also retained sufficient apelike anatomy to be effective climbers (as seen in *Ardipithecus kadabba*). They could ascend into the trees to sleep and evade terrestrial predators.	(Brunet et al., 2002, 2005; Daver et al., 2022; Haile-Selassie et al., 2023; Kottak, 2011; Potts, 2013)
Brains, Skulls, and Childhood Dependency	• Compared to contemporary humans, early hominins like *Australopithecus afarensis* – a bipedal hominin that lived 3 mya – had a cranial capacity of 430 cm³, slightly exceeding the chimpanzee average of 390 cm³. The shape of the afarensis skull also resembles that of the chimpanzee, although the brain-to-body size ratio may have been larger.	(Jurmain et al., 2014; Kottak, 2013)

(Continued)

TABLE 9.1 (Continued)

Event	Brief description and names of ancestors recorded, so far	Source
	• Brain size increased during hominin evolution, particularly with the emergence of the genus *Homo*. In comparison with young primates, human children experience a prolonged period of dependency during which their brains and skulls expand significantly. Larger skulls necessitate larger birth canals, but the requirements of upright bipedalism impose constraints on the human pelvic opening. If the opening becomes too large, the pelvis cannot support the trunk, impacting locomotion and leading to postural issues. If the birth canal is too narrow, both mother and child may encounter complications. • Natural selection has established a balance between upright posture requirements and increased brain size, resulting in the birth of immature and dependent children whose brains and skulls grow rapidly after birth.	
Tools	• The first evidence for hominin stone tool manufacture is dated to 3.3 Ma, but significant production of tools occurred around 2.6 Ma. Upright bipedalism would have facilitated the use of tools and weapons against predators and competitors. • Bipedal locomotion also allowed early hominins to carry items, potentially including scavenged parts of carnivore kills. The primates have generalized abilities to adapt through learning. • Arguably, early hominins shared abilities to manufacture and use tools, certainly, a homology trait with the great apes.	(Bower, 2015; Kottak, 2013; Semav et al., 2003; Toth et al. 2018).
Teeth	• One example of an early hominin trait that has been lost during subsequent human evolution is large back teeth. (Indeed, a pattern of overall dental reduction has characterized human evolution.) • Once adapted to the savanna, with its gritty, tough, and fibrous vegetation, it was adaptively advantageous for early hominins to have large back teeth and thick enamel. This adaptation permitted thorough chewing of tough, fibrous vegetation and mixing with salivary enzymes to aid in the digestion of foods that would otherwise be indigestible.	(Jurmain et al., 2014; Kottak, 2013)

(*Continued*)

TABLE 9.1 (Continued)

Event	Brief description and names of ancestors recorded, so far	Source
	• The churning, rotary motion associated with chewing favored the reduction of canines and first premolars. These front teeth are much sharper and longer in the apes than in early hominins, which use their sharp, self-honing teeth to pierce fruits. Males may also display large, sharp canines to intimidate and impress others, including potential mates. Early hominin characteristics, such as large back teeth and thick enamel offer clues about who our ancestors were at that time.	

Contests in palaeoanthropology

The field of palaeoanthropology has a long history marked by some of the most intense and contentious debates in the scientific community, a trend that persists even in contemporary discussions (Holden, 1981; Reader, 2011). The very nature of researching human origins seems to ignite intense debates, partly due to the emotional nature of researching human origins (Holden, 1981). Across nearly every cultures and religions offer creation myths to explain humanity's beginnings, from rich narratives to biblical accounts (Delisle, 2018; Holden, 1981; Schwartz, 2018). The paradigm underwent a significant shift in the mid-19th century, notably with Charles Darwin's "On the Origin of Species," which challenged the view of humans as divine creations by proposing evolution from primate ancestors (Reader, 2011). A milestone came in 1856 with the discovery of Neanderthal fossils, igniting discussions on humanity's ancestry (Krause, 2012; Reader, 2011).

The early attempts at uncovering our human roots were significantly influenced by the efforts of Eugène Dubois, who is often credited as the first individual to deliberately search for fossilized hominins (Pyne, 2016; Reader, 2011). Driven by the predominant belief in Western Europe that humanity had likely evolved in Asia, Dubois embarked on an expedition to the region in the late 19th century. His 1891 discovery of a skull cap and femur in Java, initially classified as *Pithecanthropus erectus* and later recognized as *Homo erectus*, along with finds like the Peking Man (*Homo erectus*) in China, positioned Asia as a leading candidate for the cradle of humankind during the early 20th century (Krause, 2012; Reader, 2011).

Palaeoanthropology is fundamentally reliant on collections, measurements, methodologies, and fossils, with a unique characteristic of discoverers often retaining ownership of their finds (Reader, 2011). This can create power dynamics where senior researchers control access to specimens and interpret evolutionary narratives, which may lead to biased interpretations and controversies (Pyne, 2016; Reader, 2011). Historical struggle for access to fossil evidence dates back to Dubois and his discovery of what he thought was the "missing link" between humans and their apelike ancestors (Pyne, 2016; Reader, 2011). As skepticism arose about the classification of these fossils in the 20th century, Dubois became secretive and restricted access, ultimately concealing his *Pithecanthropus* fossils to protect his interpretations (Pyne, 2016; Rader, 2011). Thereafter, Africa witnessed intensive contextual disputes for the past seven decades among paleoanthropologists who focused on the search for the so-called "Oldest man" or the "missing links" fossils that show the evolutionary link between man and chimpanzee (Reader, 2011).

South Africa and the battle of australopithecus and *Homo naledi*

The case of Australopithecus africanus

Intense debates emerged in 1925 after Raymond Dart published the description of *Australopithecus africanus*, meaning "the southern ape of Africa," a fossilized cranium of an early human ancestor (Pyne, 2016; Reader, 2011). Dart claimed that this creature walked upright, leading to his conclusion that Taung represented a "missing link." The anthropological communities were not impressed because the specimen was said to be in a wrong place (Africa, and not Asia), and it had clearly an ape feature and not human in appearance (Pyne, 2016; Reader, 2011). Others condemned him for producing casts of Australopithecus for public display at the British Empire Exhibition in 1925 rather than for scientific appraisal (Pyne, 2016; Reader, 2011). This approach drew criticism, particularly from scientists who argued that access to the cast should not be restricted to exhibition visitors (Reader, 2011). Others proposed that the Taung skull belonged to a young anthropoid ape, showing clear affinities with gorillas and chimpanzees, disputing its status as a "Missing Link" (Pyne, 2016; Reader, 2011).

It took two decades for Dart's publication to be accepted, especially after the discovery of more adult Australopithecines in 1936 by Robert Broom and subsequently find of robust Australopithecines in 1946 (Pyne, 2016; Reader, 2011). Further discoveries by the Leakeys' a prehistoric human species of *Paranthropus boisei* in 1959 and *Homo habilis* in 1960 and the ability to accurately pin the fossils with radiometric dating of the volcanic ash layers drew extensive global attention including coverage by National Geographic (Reader, 2011). Leakey's work at Oldupai Gorge sparked interest from various research groups in East Africa, especially in Ethiopia and later in northern Kenya, contributing to the global expansion of palaeoanthropology.

The case of *Australopithecus sediba* and *H. naledi,* South Africa

Over the last two decades, South Africa experienced intense debate over fossil discoveries, particularly *Australopithecus sediba* in 2010 by Lee Berger and *H. naledi* in 2015 (Bascomb, 2015). Berger described *A. sediba* as a small-brained bipedal ape with both primitive and advanced features. He then proposed an evolutionary link to *Homo,* which sparked criticism for being overly ambitious given its recent age (Bascomb, 2015). Berger faced backlash for his rapid publication practices, contrasting with Ron Clark's meticulous 18-year excavation of the "Little Foot" fossils, raising concerns about the accuracy of Berger's findings (Bascomb, 2015; Pyne, 2016).

Berger faced another disparagement just four months after announcing the discovery of *H. naledi* in 2015 (Bascomb, 2015; Pyne, 2016). His team's excavation and publication of over 1,550 fossils from the Rising Star Cave sparked enthusiasm in South Africa but raised concerns about the speed of the publication process. Critics argued that findings might have been released without adequate peer review, advocating for more rigorous scrutiny (Bascomb, 2015; Pyne, 2016). Despite the backlash, Berger remained committed to advancing palaeoanthropology by promoting collaboration (Pyne, 2016). He brought together nearly 60 scientists to contribute to the project and published details of the fossils in the open-access journal *eLife*, which was known for its expedited peer-review process (Pyne, 2016). His discovery emphasized two key lessons in palaeoanthropology: the importance of open access in scientific publishing and the value of timely dissemination of research (Phyne, 2016).

Allowing access to fossil collections has traditionally signified power in the field, with some viewing restrictions as necessary for maintaining rigorous standards in fossil analysis (see also Pyne, 2016). Discussions about *H. naledi* highlight a conflict in anthropology regarding scientific standards and practices. This species not only challenges existing scientific paradigms but also promotes new social practices within the scientific community (Pyne, 2016). The *H. naledi* project represents a significant shift in how scientific knowledge is created and shared, reshaping definitions of "good science."

East Africa and the battle of "the oldest man"

The case of Australopithecus afarensis *and* Homo habilis

The 1970s witnessed another intensive contest dispute between Richard Leakey and Donald Johanson (Holden, 1981; Krause, 2012; Reader, 2011). They both directed expeditions which discovered important hominid fossils. Louis Leakey presented the 1470 skull from Lake Turkana, remembered as the "Oldest Man" even though the dating was disproved. On the other side, Donald Johanson presented the famous "Lucy" skeleton from Ethiopia but held opposing views on the status of those fossils in human evolution (Reader, 2011). The differences in opinion were suffused with personal animosity which the media whipped up into a grand old scrap. For example, the Life magazine named these contests the "Battle of the Bones" (see Reader, 2011).

Richard Leakey and Donald Johanson addressed the central question: When did the line that culminated in the evolution of *Homo sapiens* diverge from the Australopithecine line, which coexisted with *Homo* for perhaps several million years? Following in his father's footsteps, Richard holds that the *Homo* line is very ancient, having diverged from the main line between five million and eight million years ago (Holden, 1981; Krause, 2012; Reader, 2011). Johanson contends that the crucial events in the evolution of modern man occurred between two million and three million years ago (Reader, 2011).

The first examples of man's most immediate ancestor were a *Homo habilis* skull, the famous 1470, which was originally believed to be close to 3 million years old (Reader, 2011). Leakey and his co-workers had a major stake in the earlier date because it pushed the known evidence of the *Homo* line back for about a million year. The 1470 skull lay below a layer of volcanic ash, called the KBS tuff after the geologist, Kay Behrensmeyer, who identified it (Reader, 2011). Dating of the KBS tuff saw tiffs between different teams, but in the end, it was dated to 1.8 million years.

When Johanson's discovered his major fossil finds in the Afar triangle in northeastern Ethiopia in 1974, a collection whose star is the famous "Lucy," a skeleton said to be 40 percent complete, making it the most complete early hominid, as well as one of the oldest, ever found (Reader, 2011). In 1975, a French American expedition that set up a camp in Hadar, near the Awash River, recovered more hominid fossils, of varying ages and both sexes from approximately the same age as Lucy (Reader, 2011). Adding to the intrigue of Lucy's story are the fossil hominin jaws, teeth, and fossilized footprints uncovered by Mary Leakey in 1978 at Laetoli, Tanzania, which date to approximately 3.66 million years. These ancient prints suggested that multiple hominins were walking habitually on two legs (Reader, 2011). Over time, however, the interpretation of these footprints sparked significant debate among paleoanthropologists.

Johanson got together with Tim White who was familiar with fossils that Mary Leakey had found at Laetoli, 1,000 miles away from Hadar, and this introduced another disputed saga in paleoanthropology (Reader, 2011). Tim White noted great similarity between the Harder and fossil teeth and jaws from Laetoli, and ultimately concluded that the whole batch represented one species. The fossils from both areas were dated at over 3.5 million years old, which made them the oldest bipedal hominids ever found. Although they bore a strong resemblance to *Australopithecus africanus* specimens from South Africa, the two decided that aspects of the jaws and crania and teeth were even more primitive than *S. africanus* (Reader, 2011). Lucy's pelvis and leg bones suggested that the creature walked upright, or was bipedal. They (Johanson and White) therefore devised a new species name for it, *Australopithecus afarensis* (after the Afar triangle where most of the specimens were found), and declared that this could be the common ancestor of the Australopithecus and *Homo* lines (Reader, 2011).

Johanson firmly believed that the Laetoli tracks should be attributed to *Australopithecus afarensis*, the same species as Lucy. In addition to redrawing the human family tree, Johanson has established himself as one of the world's most visible anthropologists. Mary Leakey's reaction to the new species was vehement in private, but otherwise restrained (Reader, 2011). She did not agree with the White and Johanson conclusions, and when told that the announcement of the new species would include her (Mary Leakey's) name among its authors, she had demanded that it be removed (see Reader, 2011). Johanson professed to be surprised by this, claiming that the inclusion of her name was a generous gesture to a deserving colleague that required no permission or advance warning. The chapter was already in the press when Leakey's demand arrived; it had to be recalled, amended, and printed over again – which delayed publication.

At the Royal Society meeting, Mary Leakey questioned the wisdom of assigning specimens from localities more than 1,000 miles apart to the same species and said that including the Laetoli hominid specimens in a new species of Australopithecus did "nothing to clarify one of the most important issues in the study of man's evolution" (Reader, 2011). Informally, she reiterated her conviction that the Laetoli fossils and the large specimens from Afar should be assigned to *Homo* and expressed deep regret that "the Laetoli fellow was now destined to be called *Australopithecus afarensis*."

Equivalent, Richard Leakey did not accept the new designation; he believed that the collection represents at least two species, possibly including *Homo*. Richard Leakey agreed that Lucy's primitive outlook that the rest because of her small size and large back teeth and primitive jaw, she could be the last survival of *Ramapithecus*, an apelike creature that lived around eight million years ago. Richard Leakey together with Alan Walker attacked the scheme of hominid evolution that Johanson and White had constructed, and in his personal capacity insisted that Johanson had been correct in his very first interpretation of the Afar fossils as *Homo* and should not have changed his mind.

Leakey contends further that there were two distinct species among the Afar and Laetoli collections, one of them being an ancestor of *Homo* and the other an ancestor of Australopithecus. Richard Leakey, in fact, regarded the evidence of Johanson's Afar fossils as proof of his belief that *Homo* and Australopithecus were no more closely related than as the descendants of a common ancestor who had lived in the very distant past, some six million or seven million years ago (Reader, 2011). Meanwhile, Johanson was of the opinion that Leakey's 1470 and sundry other specimens from East Turkana were compelling evidence of his belief that *Homo* was of relatively recent descent from Australopithecus.

But worse than such derring-do and self-promotion, Johanson told how he had stolen a human thighbone from the burial mound of an Afar family – Muslimsall (Reader, 2011). It happened at the end of the first field season (1973) – Johanson had found a knee joint he felt sure was human but could only confirm by comparing it with a modern example. Apparently, his agreement with the Ethiopian authorities required that any fossils deemed important enough to take out of the country had to be described at a press conference before removal. The act was deplorable; boasting of it in a book, shameful – and angered the Ethiopian authorities. The Ethiopians were furious and responded predictably: Johanson's team were refused excavation permits for nearly a decade. Johanson finally secured permits again in 1991.

The battle of Tugen Hills and the discovery of *Orrorin tugenensis*

Another example of contests relates to access to the Tugen Hills (Kenya), where the *Orrorin tugenensis* was discovered (see Yale University's research group, active since 1985, clash with a French team led by Pickford). The Yale group, holding licenses from the president's office, warned that the uncoordinated French excavations could undermine their work. Pickford claimed that no additional authorization was needed, leading to a significant fossil discovery and a press conference in Nairobi announcing the find of Millennium Man. However, he was arrested for collecting without a research permit and spent five days in jail until the charges were dropped. Pickford threatened to sue for wrongful arrest, accusing Richard Leakey's family of dominating palaeoanthropological research in Kenya. Eustace Gitonga, Director of the Community Museums of Kenya, supported Pickford, stating, "No longer is palaeontology in Kenya the monopoly of a single family or institution." This "Battle of Tugen Hills" showcased the intense rivalries among researchers and their connection to host country politics (Reader, 2011).

Contests at Oldupai Gorge

Oldupai Gorge (OG) is a critical paleoanthropological site in Tanzania, renowned for its well-preserved fossils that span over two million years. It contains over 100 documented fossil hominins, enhancing our understanding of human evolution (Ashley et al., 2009; Albert et al., 2015; Dominguez-Rodrigo et al., 2024). Located in the Ngorongoro Conservation Area, OG is significant for both its fossil record and its cultural history, particularly for the Maasai people, who were moved to facilitate the Serengeti National Park in the 1950s (Lee et al., 2021). The name "Oldupai" acknowledges the local Maasai term for the wild sisal plant, emphasizing the importance of Indigenous knowledge (Lee et al., 2021). The Ngorongoro Conservation Area Authority oversees the site's ecological and archaeological integrity (Bushozi, 2019).

The site's scientific value was first noted in 1911 by Wilhelm Kattwinkel, who discovered fossil bones, leading to systematic investigations by geologist Hans Reck in 1913 (Reader, 2011). Reck collected over 1,700 fossils, including a significant human skull, which sparked debate about human antiquity (Reader, 2011). Although none of the fossils was found with tools, Reck's work attracted Louis Leakey, who discovered a handaxe shortly after arriving at the site (Reader, 2011).

Oldupai Gorge (see Figure 9.1) rose to prominence through Louis Leakey's research, inspired by Darwin's theory regarding Africa's role in human ancestry (Masao, 2005). Between 1935 and 1950, Leakey and his wife Mary uncovered significant early stone tools and fossils, particularly in Beds I and II, sparking debates about the nature of these "occupation sites" (Leakey, 1971; Bunn, 1981; Bunn et al., 1986). Critics like Binford (1981, 1984) and Potts (1982, 1984) questioned whether they represented intentional living areas, suggesting alternatives like scavenging.

Aside from the "Living Floor" debates, in 1959, Louis and Mary discovered the cranium of *Zinjanthropus boisei*, now known as *Paranthropus boisei* (Leakey, 1971; Reader, 2011). While Leakey admired researchers like Raymond Dart, he disagreed with their claims of Australopithecus as a direct human ancestor, viewing human evolution as a gradual process (Reader, 2011). While findings at Oldupai Gorge's FLK site complicated his views, evidence suggested that australopithecines might have made tools. He named the specimen *Zinjanthropus boisei* and claimed it as the toolmaker, asserting it was distinct from australopithecines (Reader, 2011). Despite criticisms from some scientists regarding its classification, the skull's preservation and association with ancient tools represented a significant milestone in understanding human evolution. Leakey's assertion that Zinj was the oldest known stone toolmaker remained largely uncontested, emphasizing the site's importance in the study of human origins. The Zinj specimen, originally known as "Nutcracker Man," was showcased in Kinshasa, London, and at the University of Chicago during the Darwin Centennial celebrations, where it gained notoriety as a significant "Missing Link" in human ancestry (Reader, 2011). Louis Leakey promoted the Zinj fossil during an extensive lecture tour in America, securing over $20,000 in funding for further excavations at Oldupai Gorge (Holden, 1981; Reader, 2011). After examination by Phillip Tobias, Zinj was re-classified as *Australopithecus (Zinjanthropus) boisei* and later, in 1965, it moved to the Tanzania National Museum (Reader, 2011) where it remains to date.

After Mary Leakey's retirement in 1984, research with the Institute of Human Origins and Tanzanian authorities continued, leading to significant finds like OH 62, attributed *to Homo habilis* (Masao, 2005; Reader, 2011). The Olduvai Landscape Palaeontology Project (OLAPP), established in 1989, unearthed thousands of stone tools and hominin remains, while also training a few Tanzanians in the field and establishing a palaeoanthropology lab in Arusha (Blumenschine et al., 2005; Njau, 2006). This lab aimed to curate a systematic collection of findings,

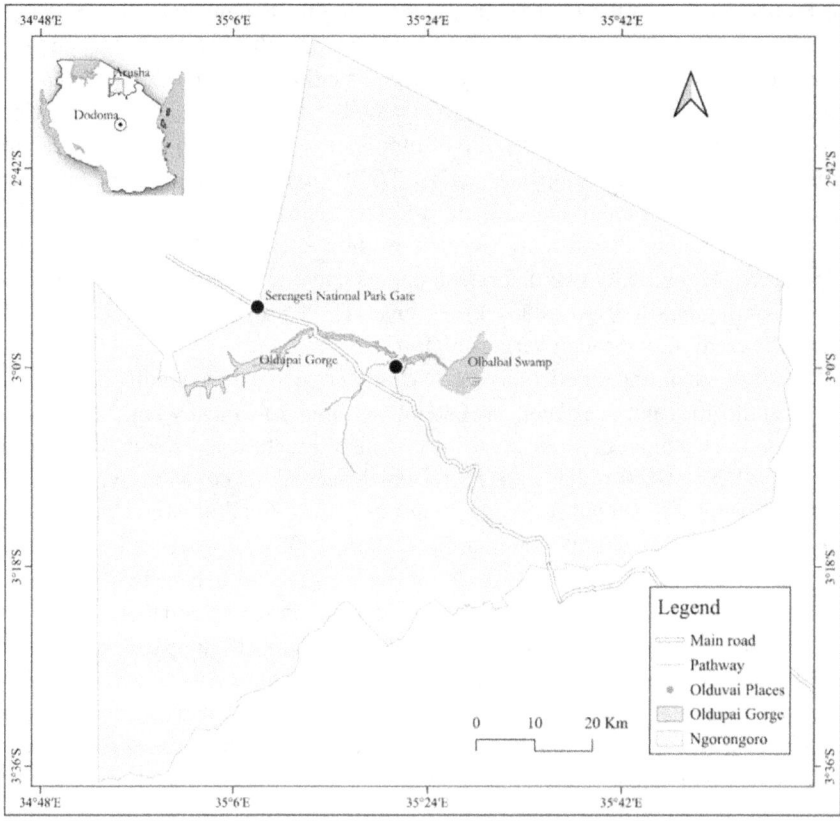

FIGURE 9.1 Mao of Tanzania showing location of Oldupai Gorge.

fostering collaboration and furthering the research at Olduvai Gorge (Blumen-schine et al., 2005).

For 17 years, OLAPP was the sole research team at Oldupai Gorge, a key archaeological site (Domínguez-Rodrigo, 2006). This changed in 2006 when the Tanzanian Olduvai Palaeoanthropology Project (TOPP) began its excavations, leading to tensions with OLAPP over accusations of disturbing previously exca-vated areas (Dalton, 2007). Complaints to authorities temporarily halted TOPP's work (Dalton, 2007). TOPP claimed to have thoroughly reviewed archaeo-logical materials at the National Museums of Kenya and sought to expand on Mary Leakey's earlier work in Bed I, which OLAPP was not actively studying (Domínguez-Rodrigo, 2006).

OLAPP opposed TOPP's research plans, reported them to Tanzanian officials, and temporarily suspended their work (Domínguez-Rodrigo, 2006). This prompted public criticism from TOPP, who accused OLAPP of unethical conduct and argued for broader access to the UNESCO site according to its guidelines (Domínguez-Rodrigo, 2006). TOPP criticized OLAPP in the media, alleging unethical conduct, their (TOPP) leaders alleged that OLAPP used its influence to block other researchers, including Gail Ashley, from studying at the site (see Domínguez-Rodrigo et al., 2007b). TOPP accused OLAPP of monopolizing access to significant areas of the gorge, effectively lobbying against TOPP's research permits and creating financial burdens for them (Domínguez-Rodrigo, 2006). TOPP criticized OLAPP's productivity, noting that despite over $2 million spent, OLAPP had published minimal work, with only two theoretical papers and one on a minor hominid fragment (Domínguez-Rodrigo, 2006). In response, TOPP vowed to publicly challenge OLAPP's credibility through various platforms.

The 2006 escalating conflict has significantly challenged the credibility of Tanzanian authorities and raised concerns about the future of ethical scientific research in Tanzania (Domínguez-Rodrigo, 2006). It also threatens the status of Oldupai Gorge as a UNESCO World Heritage Site, which depends on collaborative research. OLAPP strongly defended its stance, requesting an official apology for ongoing tensions within the research community (Dalton, 2007). However, a key government intervention has fostered a collaborative partnership between two research teams, paving the way for new guidelines to enhance research collaboration.

TOPP and OLAPP researchers have established labs at Oldupai for specimen storage and analysis (see also Blumenschine et al., 2005). Additionally, OLAPP trained a Tanzanian who is currently leading research at Oldupai, leading several postdoctoral researchers, including providing fieldwork opportunities for international students (Blumenschine et al., 2005). Although several labs have since been established at Oldupai, the current concerns remain about the impact of onsite conservation if every time a new research team emerged; they must be given camping areas and sites for lab contractions within the protected area. Efforts to build the capacity of Tanzanian paleoanthropologists have been progressing for over three decades now. The Tanzanian government launched an archaeology program at the UDSM in 1985 (Mapunda, 2005; Mturi, 2005); however, many sites, including Oldupai, remain underutilized by local experts. The country lacks infrastructure and trained personnel, leading to reliance on foreign project leaders, mainly from America, Spain, Canada, and Italy. Projects like Oldupai Gorge Geochronology and Archaeology Project, Conservation of Olduvai Gorge Project, OLAPP, Tanzania Human Origins Research (THOR), Stone Tools, Diet and Sociality (SDS), and Olduvai Gorge Vertebrate Palaeontology Project, among others, involve local training but often exacerbate conflicts rather than foster capacity building. Reports of mistreatment by foreign PIs have surfaced, including disputes involving local scholars in the SDS and THOR projects. Many local participants are engaged only to be sidelined later, undermining genuine capacity development.

To effectively preserve its unique archaeological and anthropological assets, Tanzania must invest in the development of well-trained local scientists and enhance its research facilities. This necessitates a collaborative effort that includes support from foreign experts who can provide guidance and knowledge transfer (Blumenschine et al., 2005; Masao, 2005). However, a significant challenge persists: the majority of training programs available tend to adopt a Western-centric approach (Ichumbaki, 2023). Such a framework often leads to a phenomenon I describe as "brain drain" where Tanzanian scholars return from their advanced training equipped with cutting-edge knowledge and technology but find it difficult to apply these skills effectively in their home context.

Based on personal observation, I argue that the existing model of paleoanthropological training frequently prioritizes individuals who hold less influence and authority within the academic and professional spheres. This hierarchical structure is often justified by the assumption that it will reduce competition with established experts. However, this mentality is rooted in colonial thinking and fails to recognize the urgency and importance of expanding the pool of trained professionals. With myriad unanswered questions surrounding our understanding of human evolution and the lifeways of ancestral populations, Tanzania is in dire need of a diverse and robust workforce that can tackle these various challenges. The implications of inadequate training are further compounded by the ongoing conflicts – some of which have severe psychological and societal impacts. The problem of underfunding and politics among researchers do also affect the research landscape. Consequently, many Tanzanian scientists choose to abandon their specialized fields in favor of more stable and financially viable career paths that require fewer resources and offer fewer complications.

An illustrative example of this problem can be seen in the recent repatriation of hominin remains. This event provides an opportunity for local training and research; however, the current situation is quite disheartening. There is a grave shortage of professionals specialized in biological anthropology within Tanzania, meaning that even when opportunities arise, there are not enough qualified local scientists available to engage in this essential work effectively. In summary, unless significant steps are taken to reform training models, enhance funding, and encourage local expertise, Tanzania risks losing valuable insights into its rich anthropological heritage.

Personal experience and recent scenario

The 2006 dispute at Oldupai Gorge (OG) is often cited as the most documented conflict in the area, but ongoing tensions have surfaced since then with the rise of various research teams. These disputes over site access have complicated collaboration and training opportunities, particularly for Tanzanian paleoanthropologists. Citing myself as a case study, I elaborate how contests at palaeontological sites such as OG cause problems, hence, affecting collaboration, publication, capacity building, and subsequently the sustainability of respective localities.

My journey at OG began in 2010 as an undergraduate at the UDSM, under Dr. Fidelis Masao's mentorship. This critical field school experience deepened my interest in Stone Age archaeology and the study of human origins. Dr. Masao emphasized the importance of "the use of an archaeological eye" in locating fossils. He promised students who discovered fossil hominins an opportunity for further studies in South Africa. Motivated, I focused on surveys and, during one visit to the Long Korongo site, I found a hominin cranial fragment, later confirmed by Dr. Masao. Although this discovery was exhilarating, my dreams of attending graduate school in South Africa did not come to fruition. Although I missed the opportunity to join a South African University, I managed to rejoin the UDSM to pursue postgraduate studies in Archaeology.

After graduating, I worked as Assistant Lecturer at UDSM. In 2016 and 2017, I returned to OG while pursuing a PhD under the SDS project. While progressing with my doctoral studies, a conflict with my former supervisor arose in winter 2018. After completing my first year and planning fieldwork, my supervisor halted my summer 2018 plans and banned me from going to OG for fieldwork. As I neared coursework completion and began my research proposal, issues with my supervisor intensified, forcing me to switch supervisors and change projects. I needed an extra semester in Winter 2019 for my new project, and I rescheduled my proposal presentation from Winter to Fall 2019. I completed my Faculty of Studies Exams in Winter 2020. During the conflict, I was removed as a co-author from a research paper on paleoenvironmental reconstruction in Northern Tanzania. They claimed I lost data, even though it was published within three years.

Narratives from UDSM academicians

To explore the ongoing disputes among Tanzanian paleoanthropologists, I conducted interviews with several academicians at UDSM who have worked at OG for over two decades. This interview process serves as the initial phase of a broader investigation into the social dynamics among these researchers. The face-to-face interactions with the selected colleagues allowed sharing of experiences freely (Berger, 2015; Moon et al., 2019; Sandelowski, 1991). To protect the respondents, alphabetical numerals such as A1, A2, and A3 are used for identification. Nearly all scholars I interviewed acknowledged the existence of misunderstandings at OG. Respondent A1, with over 15 years at the site, highlighted several causes of conflict, particularly the lack of equal partnership and inclusivity between global north and global south collaborators. A1 pointed out that researchers from the global north often possess more financial resources and advanced equipment, creating disparities in research opportunities.

To address these misunderstandings, A1 advocated for the use of local resources in education and the empowerment of Tanzanian faculty in decision-making regarding funding and equipment. A1 identified colonial attitudes, dismissal of differing perspectives, and competition for funding as key conflict sources among Tanzanian paleoanthropologists. Encouraging constructive dialogue among researchers was deemed essential by A1 to navigate these challenges effectively. This engagement could enhance collaboration and contribute to advancing paleoanthropological research in Tanzania.

Securing research funding poses a significant challenge at vital sites like OG. A1 advocates for increased collaboration among local and international researchers, arguing that building partnerships can foster innovative discoveries in paleoanthropology and that, recognizing diverse perspectives on early hominin behavior, is key to enriching the field. This researcher did also emphasize on the need for improved institutional frameworks in Tanzania to manage heritage sites effectively. Collaboration with local research facilities and support from organizations like the Commission of Science and Technology (COSTECH) can enhance research oversight, expand training for Tanzanian youth, and cultivate an independent research environment. Moreover, A1 encourages archaeologists and paleontologists to work with engineers, geologists, and other scientists to address multidisciplinary challenges. However, academic politics may hinder recognition and career advancement for collaborative researchers.

The misunderstandings at OG often stem from restricted access to sites and data, limiting local researchers' ability to share critical findings. The intense competition for fossil sites and funding can exacerbate conflicts, with some researchers reluctant to train students to avoid competition. Also, the scarcity of fossil-rich sites in the region intensifies this competition, leading to conflicts among local paleoanthropologists. To alleviate these issues, A2 suggests organizing meetings between academics and government authorities to discuss conflicts and facilitate resolutions. Workshops focused on conflict resolution could help promote better collaboration. A2 emphasizes that diversifying specialization could enhance contributions to national heritage and development. Additionally, restricted research funding exacerbates disputes because some researchers avoid mentoring students, fearing competition, which impacts knowledge sharing and the training of future researchers.

Another respondent (A3) is of the view that the disputes among research groups at OG are politically motivated rather than substantive rivalries. A3 argues that most collections from OG are accessible in museums and that cooperation among research teams could help uncover new archaeological insights regarding early human behavior. A3 stresses the importance of fostering partnerships to minimize redundant research efforts and ensure that all researchers see each other as collaborators. Furthermore, the recognition linked to hominid discoveries complicates dynamics at OG. Some established researchers hesitate to welcome newcomers or mentor students, fearing diminished recognition for their work. This has resulted in few Tanzanians receiving training in research at OG, despite its global appeal. With all these challenges, A2 suggests engaging in open discussions and mutual support frameworks within the academic community for resolving conflicts and advancing research on early hominins at OG and beyond.

Discussion

The study of human evolution is filled with exciting discoveries, immense promise, and contentious disputes. The study of human origins is often faced with disagreements or arguments because they rely on the results of the nature of limited evidence, such as skeletal fragments and artifacts (Delisle, 2018; Holden, 1981). This scarcity can fuel intense disputes, especially regarding the search for a "missing link" between humans and their ancestors. In many of the reported cases, arguments often occur between researchers displaying competition and desires to see their discoveries being used as either basis of classification.

Key studies conducted from the 1920s to the 1970s have significantly influenced both academic discourse and public media attention, creating an atmosphere where researchers often adopt defensive postures regarding their interpretations and findings (see Dalton, 2007; Dominguez-Rodrigo, 2006; Krause, 2012). However, controversy is common in science, and it is normal for scientists to debate and change the fundamental ways, pushing the boundaries of science (Bascomb, 2015). In palaeoanthropology, interpretations are sometimes subjected to personal personality (Holden, 1981). "If you have three paleoanthropologists in a room there will be five opinions" (Bascomb, 2015). Globally, the most heated cases reported are associated with the naming of a new Genus or Species, public display of fossil finds, access to site or fossil for studying (see Bascomb, 2015; Pyne, 2016; Reader, 2011).

Recent scenarios have shown that scientists are moving away from the traditional methods where fossils have been studied and published in a top-down way, where small team of senior experts spend years, and sometimes even a decade studying fossil hominins before publishing their discoveries in prestigious peer-reviewed journals (see Pyne, 2016). This implies that the fossils are carefully scrutinized, measured, compared, and analyzed before they reach a public audience (Pyne, 2016).

Oldupai's extensive research history and favorable preservation conditions not only makes it a prime location for understanding hominid behavior but also fosters conflicts driven by emotions rather than scientific inquiry (Holden, 1981; Reader, 2011). Key studies from the 1960s to 1970s shaped academic discourse and media attention, leading to defensive postures among researchers over their interpretations (e.g., Dalton, 2007; Dominguez-Rodrigo, 2006; Dominguez-Rodrigo et al., 2007b). The narrative discussions emphasize the critical role of funding in palaeoanthropology, particularly for Plio-Pleistocene projects that aim to uncover insights into human evolution (Delisle, 2018; Holden, 1981). However, previous discussion has shown that the significance of Oldupai goes beyond mere scientific inquiry; it also gives rise to emotional conflicts among researchers, driven more by personal stakes than collaborative exploration (see Holden, 1981; Krause, 2012).

Narrative discussions surrounding Oldupai underscore the crucial role of funding in the domain of paleoanthropology, particularly for projects focused on the

Plio-Pleistocene era that strive to unravel the complexities of human evolution. The competitive landscape is further complicated in Tanzania, where majority of people are concentrated in already known localities and those with archaeological visibilities. This scarcity intensifies competition among researchers, each vying for access to these invaluable locations, as noted by Holden (1981). Limited funding and a governmental focus on poverty alleviation further constrain Tanzanian researchers, who often collaborate with foreign counterparts due to high costs associated with sites like Oldupai Gorge (see also Ichumbaki, 2023; Masao, 2005). However, from my personal observation and experiences while working at Oldupai Gorge, I have witnessed the complexities of these collaborations first-hand. While some foreign researchers have unfortunately mistreated their local counterparts, creating tension and distrust, there are also commendable individuals among the foreign community who actively support and mentor younger Tanzanian scientists. This nurturing of talent is vital for the advancement of paleoanthropology in the region and highlights the importance of fostering respectful and equitable partnerships in the pursuit of scientific knowledge.

Scientific prestige and media attention drive competition for early hominin fossil discoveries over human remains (see also Delisle, 2018; Domínguez-Rodrigo et al., 2007b; Holden, 1981; Reader, 2011). This competitive nature can lead to disputes in the field (Domínguez-Rodrigo et al., 2007b; Gibbons, 2003), as evidenced by the long-standing public focus on figures like Richard Leakey and Donald Johanson (Holden, 1981; Reader, 2011). Also, the search for "Missing Links" the oldest fossils globally has been subjected to these contests' disputes, for instance, the debates and contests evolved around the discovery of *Sahelanthropus tchadensis* in Chad between Michael Brunet and Alain Beauvilain, and the Americas and French group disputes over the discovery of *Ororin tugensis* (Reader, 2011).

The limited and often poor-quality paleoanthropological evidence further complicates consensus (see Domínguez-Rodrigo et al., 2007a), with rare sites like Oldupai Gorge serving as focal points for ongoing debates. Paleoanthropologists now recognize the need for advanced research techniques, particularly at Oldupai Gorge, where multiple teams can work without scientific overlap (Domínguez-Rodrigo et al., 2007b). However, conflicts often arise with the emergence of new research groups (Holden, 1981). The COSTECH mandates foreign researchers to partner with local collaborators (COSTECH, 2022: 3). Unfortunately, some foreign researchers exploit this requirement, prioritizing their interests over local benefits, often neglecting to honor pre-established agreements.

Oldupai Gorge's rich fossil deposits necessitate multiple teams to fully explore its significance, as these resources are finite (Domínguez-Rodrigo, 2006; Domínguez-Rodrigo et al., 2007a). The future of Tanzanian palaeoanthropology depends on fostering local researchers who can contribute meaningfully to the field. Considerate the social dynamics and conflicts among scientists is essential, with institutions like the UDSM being pivotal for progress. The insights of Tanzanian paleoanthropologists are vital for the country's research in the field. This discipline, which began during the colonial era, carries its historical associations (see Ichumbaki, 2023; Mapunda, 2005). Understanding the factors behind misunderstandings is essential for decolonizing the field. Among others, the solutions include looking at the social interactions among Tanzanian paleoanthropologists and to listen to their perspectives and narratives. The younger generation holds the key to the future of palaeoanthropology in Tanzania, and seeking funding from organizations like the Leakey Foundation, Wenner-Gren Foundation, Gerda Henkel Foundation, and Palaeontological Scientific Trust, to mention a few, can help them acquire advanced degrees. Creating a supportive community of African scholars is vital for success (see Blumenschine et al., 2005; Gibbons, 2003). However, returning to Tanzania post-studies can present challenges due to a lack of infrastructure and employment opportunities (see Ichumbaki, 2023).

Conclusion

Currently, OG continues to see disputes as various research teams clash, often leading to the eviction of local researchers in favor of former students from different universities. While this shift may foster academic development, it has strained relationships and fostered friction within the academic community. For instance, we have seen the new initiatives from the University of Dodoma, while beneficial, have exacerbated tensions among researchers who previously collaborated with academics at the UDSM. Although new initiatives involving the University of Dodoma are beneficial for the country's development, they have strained former collaborative relationships. Allegations of unethical behavior and broken promises have emerged, impacting research permits and collaborations, with foreign researchers significantly influencing dynamics within the local research community at OG.

Recognizing the need for a localized approach to decolonization is vital for the palaeoanthropology community in Tanzania. Tanzanian paleoanthropologists are encouraged to leverage local facilities and resources to avoid colonial dependencies. Collaborations with other Departments at the UDSM and organizations like Tanzania Wildlife Research Institute and Sokoine University of Agriculture can enable palaeontologists and palaeoanthropologists to get access to lab facilities that can drive progress while minimizing reliance on foreign entities (see also Ichumbaki, 2023). As interest in palaeoanthropology grows among the youth, empowering them to take the lead and utilize local resources is essential for shaping the field's future in Tanzania. The current generation of Tanzanian paleoanthropologists should lead by example, focusing on cooperation and common goals, such as community engagement, education, and conservation. Decolonizing Tanzania's palaeoanthropology can reduce conflicts, and media plays a key role in promoting national pride through significant discoveries, like the celebrated find of *Paranthropus boisei*, or *Zinjanhropus* (Masao, 2005). Emphasizing local names is also essential. A recent initiative, discussed during the 2024 East African Association of

Paleoanthropologists and Paleontologists conference, called for the recognition of "Odupai" over "Olduvai" to honor the Maasai people and their heritage. Also, by acknowledging past errors and making changes, Tanzanian paleoanthropologists can conduct research harmoniously, engage youth, and contribute to the global understanding of human origins.

References

Albert, R. M., Bamford, M. K., & Esteban, I. (2015). Reconstruction of ancient palm vegetation landscapes using a phytolith approach. *Quaternary International*, 369, 51–66.

Ashley, G. M., Tactikos, J. C., & Owen, R. B. (2009). Hominin use of springs and wetlands: Paleoclimate and archaeological records from Olduvai Gorge (~ 1.79–1.74 Ma). *Palaeogeography, Palaeoclimatology, Palaeoecology*, 272(1–2), 1–16.

Bascomb, B. (2015). Archaeology's disputed genius: Archaeology's establishment hasn't always looked kindly on Lee Berger. Then he found a cave full of bones. *The NOVA Newsletter*. https://www.pbs.org/wgbh/nova/article/lee-berger/

Berger, R. (2015). Now i see it, now i don't: Researcher's position and reflexivity in qualitative research. *Qualitative Research*, 15(2), 219–234.

Binford, L. R. (1981). *Bone: Ancient Men and Modern Myths*. New York: Academic Press.

Binford, L. R. (1984). *Faunal Remains from Klasies River Mouth*. New York: Academic Press.

Blumenschine, R. J., & Peters, C. R. (1998). Archaeological predictions for hominid land use in the paleo-Olduvai Basin, Tanzania, during lowermost Bed II times. *Journal of Human Evolution*, 34(6), 565–608.

Blumenschine, R. J., Masao, F. T., & Peters, C. R. (2005). Broad landscape traces of Oldowan Hominid land use at Olduvai Gorge and Olduvai Landscape Paleoathropology Project. In Mapunda, B. B. B., & Msemwa, P. (eds.). *Salvaging Tanzania's Cultural Heritage*. Dar es Salaam: Dar es Salaam University Press.

Blundell, G. (Ed.). (2006). *Origins: The Story of the Emergence of Humans and Humanity in Africa*. Johannesburg: Juta and Company Ltd.

Bower, B. (2015). Earliest known stone tools unearthed: At 3.3 million years old, flakes, cores predate origin of *Homo*. *Science News*, 187(12), 6–7.

Brunet, M., Guy, F., Pilbeam, D., Mackaye, H. T., Likius, A., Ahounta, D., . . . & Zollikofer, C. (2002). A new hominid from the upper Miocene of Chad, Central Africa. *Nature*, 418(6894), 145–151.

Brunet, M., Guy, F., & Vignaud, P. (2005). Chad, Central Africa: Searching west of the Rift Valley for a new understanding of the hominid origin. In Lieberman, E. D., Smith, J. R, & Kelley, J. (Eds). *Interpreting the Past* (pp. 221–230). The Netherlands: Brill. https://doi.org/10.1163/9789047416616_019

Bunn, H. T. (1981). Archaeological evidence of meat-eating by Plio-Pleistocene hominids from Koobi Fora and Olduvai Gorge. *Nature*, 291, 574–577.

Bunn, H. T., Kroll, E. M., Ambrose, S. H., Behrensmeyer, A. K., Binford, L. R., Blumenschine, R. J., . . . & Wymer, J. J. (1986). Systematic butchery by Plio/Pleistocene hominids at Olduvai Gorge, Tanzania [and comments and reply]. *Current Anthropology*, 27(5), 431–452.

Bushozi, P. M. (2019). A multiple-institution corporation's engagement of local communities in conservation management. *The South African Archaeological Bulletin*, 74(211), 104–111.

Campbell, Bernard G., & James D. Loy. (2000). *Humankind Emerging*. 8th edition. Boston: Allyn & Bacon.

COSTECH. (2022). National Research Registration and Clearance Guidelines. https://costech.or.tz/Files/Documents/1684598463.pdf

Dalton, R. (2007). War of words erupts over fossil dig. *Nature*, 448(7149), 12–13.

Daver, G., Guy, F., Mackaye, H. T., Likius, A., Boisserie, J. R., Moussa, A., . . . & Clarisse, N. D. (2022). Postcranial evidence of late miocene hominin bipedalism in Chad. *Nature*, 609(7925), 94–100.

Delisle, R. G. (2018). The deceptive search for "missing links" in human evolution, 1860–2010: Do paleoanthropologists always work in the best interests of their discipline?. In Schwartz, J. H. (Eds.), *Rethinking Human Evolution* (pp. 1–30). Cambridge: The MIT Press. https://doi.org/10.7551/mitpress/11032.001.0001

Domínguez-Rodrigo, M. (2006). Sort out controversy over Olduvai research. *Business Times Newspaper*, August 25–31.

Domínguez-Rodrigo, M., Barba, R., & Egeland, C. P. (Eds.). (2007a). Preface. In *Deconstructing Olduvai: A Taphonomic Study of the Bed I Sites* (pp. xiii–xvi). Dordrecht: Springer Netherlands.

Dominguez-Rodrigo, M., Cobo-Sanchez, L., Baquedano, E., Mabulla, A., Gidna, A., & Diez-Martin, F. (2024). *Reconstructing Olduvai: The Behavior of Early Humans at David's Site.* New York: Academic Press.

Domínguez-Rodrigo, M., Mabulla, A. Z. P., & Bunn, H. T. (2007b). Olduvai fossils need more than one research team. *Nature*, 449(7160), 281.

Gibbons, A. (2003). Africans begin to make their mark in human-origins research. *Science*, 301(1178–1179).

Haile-Selassie, Y., & WoldeGabriel, G. (Eds.). (2023). *Ardipithecus kadabba: Late miocene evidence from the Middle Awash, Ethiopia.* Los Angeles: University of California Press.

Holden, C. (1981). The politics of paleoanthropology: Personalities and publicity enliven efforts to decipher the story of human origins. *Science*, 213(4509), 737–740.

Ichumbaki, E. B. (2023). Training and collaboration in African archaeology. *African Archaeological Review.* https://doi.org/10.1007/s10437-023-09560-7

Jurmain, R., Kilgore, L., & Trevathan, W. (2014). *Introduction to Physical Anthropology (2013–2014).* Wadsworth: Cengage Learning.

Kottak, C. P. (2011). *Anthropology: Appreciating Human Diversity.* 15th edition. New York: The McGrawHill Companies Inc.

Kovarovic, K. (2019). The realities of fieldwork: Embedding professional practice-a case study from palaeoanthropology. *Journal of Archaeology and Education*, 3(8), 1.

Krause, J. (2012). Human origins and the search for "missing links". *PLoS Biology*, 10(5), 1–3.

Leakey, M. D. (1971). *Olduvai Gorge Excavations in Beds I and II, 1960–1963.* Volume 3. Cambridge: Cambridge University Press.

Lee, P., Koromo, S., Mercader, J., & Mather, C. (2021). Enacting Maasai and palaeoanthropological versions of drought in Oldupai Gorge, Tanzania. *Science & Technology Studies*, 34(1), 43–64.

Mapunda, B. (2005). Two decades of archaeology programme at the university of Dar es Salaam: The ups and downs. In Mapunda, B. B. B., & P. Msemwa, P. (Eds.), *Salvaging Tanzania's Cultural Heritage.* Dar es Salaam: Dar es Salaam University Press.

Masao, F. (2005). Archaeological research in mainland Tanzania up to the 1900s. In Mapunda, B. B. B., & Msemwa, P. (Eds.), *Salvaging Tanzania's Cultural Heritage.* Dar es Salaam: Dar es Salaam University Press.

Moon, K., Adams, V. M., & Cooke, B. (2019). Shared personal reflections on the need to broaden the scope of conservation social science. *People and Nature*, 1(4), 426–434.

Mturi, A. A. (2005). The idea of archaeology teaching programme in Tanzania. In Mapunda, B. B. B., & Msemwa, P. (Eds.), *Salvaging Tanzania's Cultural Heritage.* Dar es Salaam: Dar es Salaam University Press.

Njau, J. K. (2006). *"The Relevance of Crocodiles to Oldowan Hominin Paleoecology at Olduvai Gorge, Tanzania."* PhD diss., Rutgers University.

Pickford, M., Senut, B., Gommery, D., & Treil, J. (2002). Bipedalism in *Orrorin tugenensis* revealed by its femora. *Comptes Rendus Palevol*, 1(4), 191–203.

Potts, R. (1982). "*Lower Pleistocene Site Formation and Hominid Activities at Olduvai Gorge, Tanzania.*" PhD diss., Harvard University.

Potts, R. (1984). Home base and early hominids. *Am Scientific*, 72, 338–347.

Potts, R. (2013). Hominin evolution in settings of strong environmental variability. *Quaternary Science Reviews*, 73, 1–13.

Pyne, L. (2016). Dear Paleoanthropology, *Homo Naledi* Just Shifted Your Paradigm. https://daily.jstor.org/daily-author/lydia-pyne/.

Reader, J. (2011). *Missing Links: In Search of Human Origins*. New York: OUP Oxford.

Sandelowski, M. (1991). Telling stories: Narrative approaches in qualitative research. *Image: The Journal of Nursing Scholarship*, 23(3), 161–166.

Schwartz, J. H. (2018). What's real about human evolution? Received wisdom, assumptions, and scenarios. In Schwartz, J. H. (Eds.), *Rethinking Human Evolution* (pp. 61–62). Cambridge. The MIT Press. https://doi.org/10.7551/mitpress/11032.001.0001

Tuttle, R. H. (1988). What is New in African Paleoanthropology. *Annual Reviews in Anthropology*, 17, 391–426.

10

BRONZE SOLDIERS

Cultural heritage as weapons and flashpoints
in the Baltic States' hybrid conflicts

Craig Ross

Introduction

The unique properties of cultural heritage are often deeply intertwined with a community's social and historical fabric (Bahrani, 2008). Adverse effects to heritage may, therefore, carry a profound psychological impact and, at extremes, can be used to attack the very cultural character of an enemy, degrading their will to fight back (Clack & Dunkley, 2023). As a result, the deliberate targeting of heritage has long been a strategic act in warfare, aimed at attacking identity and crushing the spirit of a people to resist external actions by removing their cultural reference points. This tactic is rooted in the history of conflict, from the ancient obliteration of Carthage to the systematic destruction of cultural sites in modern conflicts, such as those in Palestine today (Institute for Palestine Studies, 2024). Heritage has also been destroyed during internal shifts in power, with the destruction often subjecting a tyrant to *damnatio memoriae* (Humphreys, 2002), the damnation of memory. Leaders like Saddam Hussein and Joseph Stalin encountered iconoclastic moments towards the end of their reigns, much like how they had exiled those they viewed as enemies of the state to oblivion (Knaus, 2017).

The motivation behind such acts does not seem to have changed much, as cultural heritage remains a symbol of collective memory. However, more modern attacks on heritage, intentionally secretive and denied, use propaganda and deception to obscure the attacker's true intent. Studying such attacks in the Cold War reveals plots that might feature in a James Bond novel, such as the American Central Intelligence Agency (CIA) and the UK's Military Intelligence, Section 6 (MI6) teaming up against SMERSH to repatriate stolen valuable heritage items (Nemeth, 2015). However, this is not fiction, and the global superpowers realised and adopted the value of cultural warfare, weaponising many forms of cultural heritage in their

DOI: 10.4324/9781003623724-10

battle for superiority in the form of 'hybrid warfare'. Understanding these actions means one can spot patterns of heritage manipulation and clues as to the intentions of key players in the great power struggles between the North Atlantic Treaty Organization (NATO) and Russia today. Appreciating the nature of the problem also allows us to understand how to resist such attacks, which is important if we truly find ourselves in a new Cold War, as some would suggest (Ferguson, 2024).

Hybrid warfare is an essentially contested concept and, therefore, may be best understood in its parts and how they might apply to heritage. At this stage, it is important to clarify the NATO definition of hybrid threats for the readers:

> Hybrid threats combine military and non-military as well as covert and overt means, including disinformation, cyber-attacks, economic pressure, deployment of irregular armed groups and use of regular forces. Hybrid methods are used to blur the lines between war and peace and attempt to sow doubt in the minds of target populations. They [hybrid threats] aim to destabilise and undermine societies.
>
> (NATO, 2024a)

This chapter exposes research gaps, revealing how heritage might suffer from hybrid warfare and calls upon examples from the Cold War to question how heritage can be adapted to resist modern hybrid forms of conflict. In this chapter, I adopt the Baltic States as a case study due to their unique history of occupation by the Soviet Union, their armed and non-violent resistance to foreign aggression, and their current importance as independent states on the flank of Russia's border during a geopolitical unease. It discusses the Baltics' de-Sovietisation process, a term adopted for removing unwanted Soviet-era symbols. It draws out the Bronze Soldier incident in Tallinn as an example and prominent illustration of hybrid warfare in action against heritage. Data from semi-structured interviews with experts either in the Baltic region or directly affected by the current tensions, together with observations from visits to the region's various Cold War museums, are utilised to draw lessons for heritage and security professionals. The nations of Estonia, Latvia, and Lithuania are referred to collectively as the Baltics for their brevity. However, it should be appreciated that each country has its unique beauty, culture, and history. Their shared oppression by the Soviet Union and similar timelines in the struggle for independence merit examination in parallel.

The chapter is divided into ten main sections. Next to this introduction is a section that explores how both superpowers strategically used cultural heritage during the Cold War, with initiatives ranging from propaganda to theft of art and monuments to shape ideological narratives. Then, I discuss the Baltic States' historical experiences under Nazi and Soviet occupation, highlighting the severe repression, mass deportations, and efforts to reshape cultural identities during Soviet rule. A section on resistance and de-Sovietisation examines armed and non-violent resistance in the Baltic States. The issues discussed include the role of the Forest

Brothers, the Singing Revolution, and de-Sovietisation efforts to remove Soviet symbols and revive national identities. The Hybrid Warfare and Heritage Protection section analyses the evolving concept of hybrid warfare, focusing on Russia's use of cultural narratives and historical revisionism as tools of influence and subversion while highlighting NATO's strategic responses.

I then detail the research methodology, including interviews and museum visits, to explore heritage, resistance, and Cold War legacies in the Baltic States. In the Mimicking Hybrid Warfare Through Alternative Concepts part, I explore how hybrid warfare concepts like subversion and disinformation are perceived and communicated through language and museum narratives. Next to this is a discussion on how monuments and symbols hold layered meanings in the Baltic States, illustrating their emotional and political significance in public spaces. I examine how heritage can be manipulated to serve geopolitical goals, contrasting different approaches to contentious Soviet-era monuments.

Before ending my chapter, I highlight the use of stories, objects, and symbols in Baltic museums to communicate resilience, national identity, and the power of intangible heritage in resisting subversive narratives. My conclusion emphasises the dual role of heritage in resistance and its vulnerability to manipulation in hybrid conflicts. It calls for expanding heritage studies to include a security focus and underscores the need for 'cultural intelligence' to counter disinformation. The conclusion draws on Cold War lessons to develop strategies for safeguarding heritage and fostering resilience in today's polarised political environment.

Cultural heritage in the Cold War

The Cold War (1945–91) was a geopolitical struggle between the United States and the Soviet Union, representing a clash between capitalism and communism (Westad, 2007). Although it is likely that Bernard Baruch first coined the term, theorising that the Cold War was a peacetime arms race (Achcar, 2023), it is perhaps fitting that George Orwell is often attributed through his prophetic opinions on how possession of atomic weapons would create a peace that is no peace (Orwell, 1945). This concept of an ongoing yet undeclared conflict is rooted in the ideological battles of the 20th century, where propaganda, espionage, and manipulation played pivotal roles. The idea of 'Orwellian' control over information and truth became synonymous with tactics employed by both sides, reflecting the pervasive influence of warnings about the dangers of totalitarianism (Arendt, 1951; White, 2019). It is a term heard often in traditional and social media today as we reflect on state oppression and censorship.

War was never officially declared in the Cold War, but the tension between global superpowers profoundly influenced global politics, culture, and society. The term 'Cultural Cold War' has been used to describe the strategic use of cultural initiatives by the United States and the Soviet Union during this period to influence global public opinion and win ideological battles (Saunders, 2013). Heritage was often politicised, with the Soviet Union and the West using historical sites and narratives to promote their ideological agendas (Bastiansen, 2023). This exchange of cultural influences, with strong links to their respective intelligence agencies, was part of a broader strategy to win hearts and minds, with both sides seeking to demonstrate their adversaries' moral and cultural bankruptcy. It is here that we find heritage used intentionally as a weapon, with intelligence agencies and secret police units gathering cultural weapons while the atomic arms race developed in parallel. The CIA was closely linked with multiple intellectuals who were hired (even if they did not know it was the CIA hiring them) to fight the Cultural Cold War. In the CIA's 'battle for men's minds', it stockpiled a vast arsenal of unconventional weapons: journals, books, conferences, seminars, art exhibitions, concerts, and awards (Saunders, 2013, p. 2). Multiple tests were carried out using these new forms of cultural weaponry. Books such as George Orwell's *Animal Farm* were balloon-dropped into Soviet territory to subvert through literature, hoping to undermine the adversary using the printed word (White, 2019). Authors on both sides of the Iron Curtain spied and sometimes faced prison for their actions. The East German Ministry for State Security, known as the Stasi, developed poetry circles to improve agents' ability to detect subversive content and enhance their propaganda skills (Oltermann, 2023). The Soviets erected thousands of monuments and memorials to the 'Great Patriotic War' all over the Eastern Bloc; the narrative adopted emphasising the heroism and sacrifice of the Soviet people, portraying the Union of Soviet Socialist Republics (USSR) as the primary victor over fascism, and becoming a cornerstone of Soviet national identity in the process (Fedor et al., 2017).

Antiquities haemorrhaged from developing nations in a shift from 'accretion' to blatant theft (Merryman, 2006). The Russians confiscated over two and a half million art objects, books, and archival material during and after World War II (WWII) (Akinsha & Kozlov, 1995). This included German-owned material stolen from countries like France, Poland, and the Netherlands during the war. SMERSH collected works of art – a sinister counterespionage unit under the direct control of Stalin, with an abbreviation of the Russian words for 'Death to Spies', '*SMERt' SHpionam*'. SMERSH used special trophy brigades, somewhat like the Monuments Men, but instead of returning stolen artworks to their original owners, they directed artworks back to the USSR. Much of Russia's foreign heritage remains today (Akinsha & Kozlov, 1995).

Historical context in the Baltics

To understand the importance of cultural heritage and resistance in the Baltic region, it is imperative to understand its historical context. The Baltic States have shared similar troubles due to their strategic location on the Baltic Sea and proximity to powerful, expansionist neighbours. They also share similar periods of domination and occupation, and first declared their independence in the wake of World War I (WWI) in 1918. Despite a promising start as independent nations, the Baltic

States disappeared into the prison house of nations known as the USSR following the treacherous Molotov-Ribbentrop pact of 1939 (Nollendorfs, 2024). Between 1941 and 1944, in WWII, the Soviet-annexed Baltics became a battleground for the Nazis and the USSR. In June 1941, as part of Operation Barbarossa, Nazi Germany launched a massive invasion of the Soviet Union, which included Estonia, Latvia, and Lithuania. The Nazis were initially welcomed by some local groups, who saw them as liberators from the initial brutal Soviet occupation. However, Nazi rule soon proved to be equally harsh, marked by widespread repression and atrocities, particularly against Jewish communities (Lucas, 2014). By late 1944, the tide of war had turned, and the Red Army launched a retaliation that pushed the Nazis out of the region. By early 1945, Soviet forces had reoccupied the Baltics, leading to another period of Soviet domination. This is how the Baltic States entered the Cold War, remaining occupied until the dissolution of the USSR in 1991. Russia maintains to this day that the Baltics 'voluntarily' joined the USSR (Centre for European Policy Analysis (CEPA), 2020) and often uses any historical collaboration with the Nazis as evidence of fascism in all three countries (Institute for Strategic Dialogue (ISD), 2022).

Soviet repression began immediately upon re-occupation through the People's Commissariat for Internal Affairs (NKVD) and Committee for State Security (KGB), secret police institutions commonly known in the Baltics at the time as 'the Cheka'. They aimed to eradicate all anti-Soviet elements and used a vast web of informants in their efforts. The cellars of multiple Cheka buildings served as torture and execution chambers, subjecting people to interrogation and torture that could last weeks to gain a confession, real, or otherwise. Common sentences were death or long prison terms in Soviet Gulags. The Soviets also imposed mass deportations of people from their homes in the Baltic to hellish conditions in Siberia, with little to no time to pack or say goodbye. Deportees numbered some 200,000 in all, herded into railroad cars intended for cattle freight. Less than 70 per cent were eventually able to return, making the threat of deportation one of the most dreaded instruments of control through terror (Okupacijas Muzeja Biedriba (OMB), 2016). The destruction and manipulation of cultural heritage during the Cold War also served as a means of subjugating occupied regions through spiritual–intellectual terror. In the Baltics, the Soviets imposed their cultural symbols and narratives, systematically erasing local traditions and rewriting history to integrate these regions into the Soviet ideological framework. This cultural domination was not only about control through fear but also about legitimising Soviet rule by creating a historical narrative that aligned with contemporary political goals (Andrejevs, 2022).

Resistance and de-Sovietisation

Despite the severe oppression, the Baltic people resisted through both violent and non-violent means to preserve their national identities. An armed resistance group known as The Forest Brothers was active in the 1940s and 1950s and exemplified armed resistance against Soviet control. Rooted in their deep national identity, these fighters utilised the region's dense forests to wage an enduring campaign against Soviet forces (Blūzms et al., 2011). Non-violent forms of resistance also played a crucial role in the Baltic States' eventual independence. Communication of ideas was important, something the Cheka understood all too well and tried to counter by banning books and typewriters. Dissidents had to use cunning ways to conceal typewriters or mask the font, knowing that typefaces might be linked to the registered owner. Banned books, such as The *Gulag Archipelago* and *Nineteen Eighty-Four*, and regular resistance newsletters were often copied by typewriter or hand and distributed in a process known as 'Samizdat', meaning 'self-publishing' in Russian (Vabamu, 2019).

The Singing Revolution of the 1980s and early 1990s harnessed the power of songs, particularly folk songs and national anthems, to unite the population against Soviet rule (Vesilind, 2008). This demonstrated how cultural identity could be a powerful tool for mobilising people and asserting national sovereignty. Folklore and customs, through songs, stories, and literature, proved to be a valuable tool in the fight against oppression. It was a 'brilliant way of portraying the art of subversion in the everyday world of compliance under a repressive state' (Naithani, 2019, p. 39). Following the collapse of the Soviet Union in 1991, the Baltic States embarked on a path of 'de-Sovietisation', aiming to remove Soviet symbols, restore national languages, and revive pre-Soviet cultural practices. This process was crucial to removing physical reminders of oppression and reasserting national identity and sovereignty (Lewis, 2023; Bellentani, 2024). De-Sovietisation efforts included the removal of Soviet monuments, renaming or returning streets and public spaces to their originals, and reviving traditional customs and practices suppressed under Soviet rule.

This process of rejecting or neglecting historical reminders can be understood as disinheritance and has been a complex strategy which exposed a lack of shared agreement on heritage, therefore requiring careful consideration, especially when dealing with legally listed heritage (Krumberga & Storm, 2024). However, the resurgence of Russian influence in the region and invasions of Ukraine have heightened the urgency of these efforts. The Baltic States have responded by intensifying their de-Sovietisation initiatives, removing more Soviet War memorials, and focusing on further erasing the remnants of Soviet influence to reinforce their national identities (CEPA, 2020).

Hybrid warfare strategy and heritage protection

Hybrid warfare has become a popular term in modern conflict, but one of the core challenges in understanding the concept is the difficulty of defining it precisely (Johnson, 2018). The term encompasses a wide range of activities and targets that do not fit neatly into traditional categories of conflict. The term's popularity has soared following Russia's 2013 Crimea annexation and its 2022 'special operation' in Ukraine, which has led to various works considering how hybrid threats have developed. Propaganda and disinformation are typically key elements, weaponising narratives that manipulate public perception and create confusion among the target population. The intentions are typically to dismiss, deny, distort, distract, or dismay (White, 2016) and to create ambiguity and surprise by integrating unconventional tactics. These techniques might be boiled down further as *subversion*, referring to actions aimed at undermining or overthrowing established structures and ideologies. Subversion operates on a spectrum, from subtle manipulation of public opinion, a 'tool of the statesman' in international politics (Beilenson, 1972), to more sinister direct efforts to destabilise regimes. The latter end of the spectrum was often seen in 'active measures', a term used to describe a range of political warfare tactics employed primarily by the Soviet Union and continued by Russia today (Rid, 2020). While hybrid warfare is contested, it remains a valuable framework for understanding the potential Russian threat in the Baltic region. It has already witnessed influence operations targeting the psychological and informational domains. Here, hybrid warfare has taken advantage of existing vulnerabilities, proximity to Russia, and many Russian-speaking minorities (Radin, 2017).

Hybrid threats targeting heritage have become a growing concern because Russia is increasingly using cultural narratives and historical revisionism to support its geopolitical goals (Lucas, 2014). By promoting a nostalgic but distorted view of Soviet history, Russia seeks to foster a shared identity among Russian-speaking populations in neighbouring countries. Russia uses nostalgic ideas to justify its interventions and territorial ambitions while incorporating cultural property into its national security strategies (McGlynn, 2023). Russia's modern propaganda efforts, including its integration with the Foreign Intelligence Service and various presidential departments, demonstrate a swift adaptation to tools like social media, especially after effectively losing the Cold War (Pomerantsev, 2020). Even though Russia has long recognised cultural property as a component of hybrid warfare (NATO, 2024b), NATO has only recently acknowledged its importance and is lagging in its response (Rosén, 2023).

NATO is taking the Russian hybrid threat seriously, and other Western allies are adapting their strategies to counter such hybrid warfare, emphasising the need for resilience across military, government, and societal levels. Definite strategic shifts to counter hybrid warfare can be found through published strategic documents. The 'Resistance Operating Concept' (ROC; Fiala, 2020), for example, is a new framework aimed at enhancing the resilience of NATO member states, particularly those bordering adversarial nations, by preparing them to resist and counter occupation or subversion. The concept emphasises the integration of military and civilian efforts, including fostering national resistance movements and leveraging unconventional warfare tactics. The concept has been developed and refined with significant input from the US Special Operations Command Europe. It is considered a critical component of NATO's strategy to enhance national resilience and prepare for potential invasions or occupations (Friberg, 2020).

We might consider what these strategic changes mean to heritage and how heritage might be impacted should NATO's worst fears materialise. Concerns about a new Cold War have been raised for some time (Friedman, 1998; Mackinnon, 2007; Kaplan, 2019). The rise of authoritarianism, coupled with Russia's aggression in Ukraine and attempted subversion in the Baltic States, has led some analysts to draw parallels between current geopolitical tensions and the Cold War. If 'Cold War II' is already happening, as some strongly suggest (Ferguson, 2024), and if expansionism, historical distortions, and hybrid attacks do draw cultural heritage into the battlefield, we should begin to consider the lessons we can learn from the Cold War to grasp the new risks we face and what might be done to resist them.

Little research compares Cold War I to Cold War II, especially in the Baltic region, as a concept still lacking a broader consensus. Even though a review of existing literature shows some initial research into heritage and hybrid warfare, it indicates gaps in our current understanding of heritage and resistance to these techniques. Studies covering armed resistance or state-led de-Sovietisation efforts are evident, but there is far less on how heritage was or could be applicable in modern resistance efforts. A need for an updated assessment of the threats to heritage and how heritage might be exploited or attacked through modern hybrid techniques has been demonstrated (Ross, 2025; Clack et al., 2023). Nevertheless, we must understand where heritage might fit into the modern resistance concept and consider where heritage and culture-related studies may contribute to intelligence planning against such threats.

Exploratory study and field research

To address these gaps, an exploratory research methodology was adopted to develop an understanding of the subject and the potential for future directions of inquiry. This study was undertaken in two steps: semi-structured interviews and site visits. Semi-structured interviews with academics or those working in heritage fields, either from or living in the Baltics, who had first-hand experience of the general subject, or those who had carried out academic work on a similar area. Site visits to resistance or Cold War themed museums in Estonia, Latvia and Lithuania were undertaken for further contextual understanding. The interviews and site visits were undertaken in 2024. This methodology was adopted to triangulate the existing literature, interview opinions, and museum site visits' observations within the overarching case study of the Baltics to draw out meaningful themes with an enhanced degree of validity.

Interview participants were selected to explore the intersection of heritage, resistance, and Cold War legacies in the Baltic States, with representatives from each country. The selection criteria prioritised individuals with either academic expertise in these areas or professional experience related to heritage management, ranging from PhD students to senior professionals in their field. Interviews were undertaken remotely using Microsoft Teams, and, in some

TABLE 10.1 List of participants

No.	Pseudonym	Gender	Nationality	Country of Work
1	RU-1	Male	Russian	Estonia
2	BE-1	Male	Belarusian	Anonymised
3	EST-1	Male	Estonian	Estonia
4	EST-2	Female	Estonian	Estonia
5	LVA-1	Female	Latvian	Latvia
6	LVA-2	Female	Latvian	Latvia
7	LVA-3	Female	Latvian	Latvia
8	LITH-1	Male	Lithuanian	Lithuania
9	LITH-2	Female	Lithuanian	Lithuania
10	LITH-3	Male	Lithuanian	Anonymised

cases, follow-up discussions were held informally in person. Each interview was conducted in English and lasted approximately one hour using a semi-structured format. This approach facilitates in-depth exploration of key themes while maintaining the flexibility to discuss emerging topics. Given the subject matter and potential for published comments linked to a participant to expose them to future risk of reprisal, interviews were conducted based on agreed-upon anonymity with care taken to ensure that the participants remain unidentifiable personally in the published text. A list of pseudonymised participants is provided in Table 10.1.

Regarding site visits, exhibits at the following museums were examined to understand the look and feel of how the subject is displayed to the public, the type of items being displayed, and the narrative used to explain them.

Estonia:

- Vabamu, Museum of Occupations and Freedom, Tallinn
- KGB Prison Cells Museum, Tallinn
- Estonian Literary Museum, Tartu

Latvia:

- Museum of the Occupation in Latvia, Riga
- The Corner House KGB Museum, Riga
- The 'Book in Latvia' exhibition, National Library of Latvia, Riga
- Burning Conscience exhibition, Cēsis

Lithuania:

- Museum of Occupation and Freedom Fights/KGB Cells, Vilnius

The interviews and site visits revealed varying opinions and relevant lines of inquiry, which were then subjected to thematic analysis. These have been grouped into four main themes: the language used, how heritage communicates, weaponisation, and resistance. Despite a small sample size, the interview approach provided a significant amount of relevant material, not all of which can be captured here, demonstrating the possibilities for further research in this area.

Mimicking hybrid warfare through alternative concepts

All the participants required clarification of what 'hybrid warfare' entails, and very few used it thereafter in their discussions. This lack of widespread use of the term is understandable because, despite being an English term, it is linked with war; hence, it is inconsistently used in media reporting on the war in Ukraine. Additionally, 'hybrid warfare' is never found in the museum exhibits, most likely because the exhibits were created before the broad adoption of the term. This demonstrates how museums may capture opinions at a point in time, whereas modern events, like Ukraine, add extra layers of meaning to past events. There were, however, plenty of references to parts of hybrid warfare, such as subversion, deception, and disinformation, both in the museums and in the participants' dialogue. Two participants pointed out the problem with using the term 'warfare', as this suggests elements of conventional war between the Baltic States and Russia, which is incorrect and unhelpful. BE-1 outlined that 'resilience' might be more appropriate than resistance due to the latter's links to armed resistance and mentioned that more familiar and better-defined terminology is preferred, such as 'subversive activities'.

This scenario would agree with the literature that hybrid warfare might not be helpful due to its ambiguity. It suggests that further academic study or dialogue in a military–civilian partnership might best focus on precise strategic effects. Several participants used Cold War-like terminology to discuss current events, such as the presence of a new 'Iron Curtain'. When asked if they believed we were in a new Cold War, all but one agreed they thought this was plausible, with BE-1 noting that 'one cannot step in the same river twice'. LVA-3 and LITH-2 suggested that the Cold War atmospherics may be partly due to how the local media portray the current situation with Russia, which communicates an ever-present threat.

Several participants used militaristic language to describe actions taken with physical heritage. For example, when discussing how a Russian T-34 tank memorial in Narwa, Estonia, was removed and relocated to a military museum, this had 'diffused' it. EST-1 discussed how moving heritage from problematic areas had 'discharged' the statutes of power. RU-1 gave an example of how Russia acted like one of its statues in the Czech Republic had been 'held hostage for ransom'. LVA-1 suggested heritage could be 'encoded' with layers of meaning. There were similar examples of how heritage can be weaponised in museum narratives. For example, a table for printing letters and a typewriter displayed at the National Library of

Latvia are described as 'banned weapons', with everyday objects of heritage production becoming weapons of resistance.

The invisible heritage meanings in the Baltics

Many discussion points emphasised how monuments are more than just commemorative objects in the Baltics, holding power to communicate through the city's urban fabric. This is summed up well by LITH-3, who, when talking about de-Sovietisation, said:

> *If you keep it* [Soviet monument] *in a public space, it affects the urban environment. It affects our feelings, and I do not know how to say it, but I do not like it* [retaining Soviet public monuments] *because it reminds us of the Soviet past. In a way . . . I agree on being respectful, but it is a reason to be stuck for a certain period. It is not just an object; it* [the monument] *affects the environment.*

(Field notes, 2 July 2024)

Participants gave some examples of how physical heritage communicates. For example, in Lithuania, LITH-2 discussed the traditional architectural motifs added to buildings during the occupation as symbols that could be recognised as traditionally Lithuanian among the occupied cities. Abroad, LITH-1 explained how Lithuanian exiles in America added traditional woodcarvings to buildings, communicating their ongoing identity through their specific architectural style. In a situation where the Soviet occupiers were removing built heritage, these may be seen as actions of defiance in the physical space.

The Bronze Soldier of Tallinn (Figure 10.1) features in several studies of de-Sovietisation and was discussed with the participants as an example. Initially unveiled in 1947, the 6′5″ imposing statue on its plinth stood as a prominent Soviet war memorial in the centre of Estonia's capital. Officially, it commemorated Soviet soldiers who fought against Nazi Germany and for the Russian-speaking community. The monument was known as 'Alyosha the Liberator' in the Russian-speaking community, representing the heroism and sacrifice of the struggle against Hitler. For many Estonians, the monument communicated a painful reminder of Soviet occupation and repression. The imposing statue, along with the graves of Soviet soldiers, was situated in central Tallinn, making it a focal point for both remembrance and Russian-speaking gatherings (Haukkala, 2009).

By the early 2000s, as Estonia embraced its independence and European identity, the Bronze Soldier became increasingly contentious. The statue was often used ritually in Russian identity politics, and tensions escalated, leading to public debates over the monument's place in post-Soviet Estonia (Ehala, 2009). In April 2007, the Estonian government relocated the Bronze Soldier to a military cemetery on the outskirts of Tallinn. The relocation proposals triggered an immediate

FIGURE 10.1   The Bronze Soldier in its original location.

Source: Wikipedia Commons (2007)

and intense backlash from the Russian-speaking community, leading to the first large-scale ethnic riots in Estonia since 1980. This became known as the *Bronze Night,* resulting in one death, numerous injuries, and significant property damage (International Centre for Defence and Security, 2020). The events drew international attention, with Russia strongly condemning Estonia's actions and accusing the Estonian government of disrespecting the legacy of the war dead. Worryingly, the Kremlin not only refused to condemn the violence being inflicted in the name of Russian patriotism but also endorsed it, praising the looters as youthful patriots who were protesting about Estonia's 'fascist' vandalism of a sacred edifice (Lucas, 2014).

The statue was removed, and the Bronze Soldier was placed at a focal point in the military cemetery. Shortly after the relocation, Estonia faced many coordinated distributed denial-of-service cyberattacks that targeted government websites, financial institutions, media outlets, and other critical infrastructure. These incidents were widely believed to have been orchestrated by Russian actors, further straining relations between Russia and Estonia. In response to the cyberattack, Estonia swiftly implemented several measures to mitigate the damage and enhance its cybersecurity, becoming a global leader in the cybersecurity field and leading to the establishment of the NATO Cooperative Cyber Defence Centre of Excellence in Tallinn in 2008 (e-Estonia, 2017).

The fact that the strong emotional response to the removal of the statue by Russophones caught the government and the public by surprise indicates a misunderstanding of the complex set of social meanings that the statue embodied and the potential for hybrid attacks in reprisal. Its removal may have communicated insensitivity or indifference to Russophones' connection to the statue and its symbolism, which would appear to be a factor in the violent response. Participants supported its removal; however, feeling the statue and its location was an unwanted reminder of Estonia's treatment by the Soviets. In some cases, the feeling was apathy to Russian objections, and its central position insulted Estonians who suffered so severely during the Cold War. Indeed, the monument's removal was perfectly justified. However, moving the statue to a new position in a military cemetery was seen to be respectful. It involved removing the potential for flashpoints during gatherings in the centre of Tallinn while retaining the ability for Russians to pay their respects. The respondent EST-1 offered a parallel narrative of the Bronze Soldier. EST-1 described how, during the time of the singing revolution, when Estonia started to demand freedom, a tiny baby deer statue (Figure 10.2a) in the centre of Tallinn started to be vandalised:

> *The statue became a kind of symbol of a small Estonian nation, harmless and defenceless. Trying to stand for its rights and dignity was, and still is, very vulnerable. Everybody was afraid that the Russians could at any point turn back the Perestroika, and repressions could start. Most people feared showing their real attitudes because they knew what could not last. That freedom will soon be either turned back or an expression for which one gets punished. Consequently, a small animal statue became a symbol.*

(Field notes, 27 May 2024)

The small baby deer statue can be found in the Old Town in Estonia and starkly contrasts the Bronze Soldiers' imposing figure with its intimidating stare (Figure 10.2b).

These examples largely agree with Kruk's (2009) work on how heritage communicates politically through physical icons and how it may feature in cultural resistance by preserving local monuments and architectural styles. The Bronze Soldier incident exposed the potential for heritage as a tool in multi-pronged approaches of destabilisation tactics targeting societal divisions to undermine government authority. It is considered by some as a prime example of hybrid warfare in action (Šešelgytė & Bladaitė, 2020), highlighting how kinetic actions are intertwined with cyber operations and subversion to achieve strategic objectives without crossing the threshold of conventional military conflict. Indeed, Rid (2020) cites the Bronze Soldier episode as a milestone event for the 21st-century return of active measures, where we can see hybrid threat components in action against cultural heritage.

FIGURE 10.2   (a) Bronze deer statue, Estonia. (b) The Bronze Soldier in new position, Estonia.

Heritage weaponisation

The Estonian examples illustrate how heritage can be both weaponised and, conversely, neutralised. The Bronze Soldier in Tallinn and the Victory Park monument in Riga were also discussed as examples of how different treatments might be applied in different conflict environments. Both were weaponised during the Russophone public gatherings as focal points of identity and tension, but the treatment by Tallinn and Riga and the response from Russia differed. The Bronze Soldier was relocated and disarmed during relative quiet from Russia. The relocation resulted in coordinated violent and cyber reprisals. Likewise, the Victory Park monument was destroyed by Latvia in a bold statement following the 2022 Russian invasion of Ukraine. This incident evidenced a more diplomatically measured response from Russia, possibly reflecting their focus elsewhere. These scalable effects show that there can be options for neutralising weaponised heritage, depending on the broader political situation and the message.

Participants in the current research pointed out that because of the potential of heritage to be weaponised, one must be very careful about what is kept. Respondent LVA-2 highlighted the significant debates in deciding the fate of Soviet-era heritage. A 'bottom-up' approach was better received, where the population's will is used to gauge appropriate measures on contentious heritage. Participants also highlighted how the de-Sovietisation process was carried out in waves, with those deemed most oppressive removed in the years following independence in the early 1990s. As a book supporting the exhibition from the Museum of the Occupation of Latvia notes, 'When the blindfolds of oppression were finally removed, the people's eyes were confronted with the heavy material and spiritual legacy of the occupation everywhere they looked' (Nollendorfs, 2024, p. 238). Discussions also suggested that Soviet heritage was usually treated respectfully. Rather than destruction, pieces like the Bronze Soldier were moved to war graveyards, the Narwa Tank was moved to a military museum, Soviet war graves were left in situ, and large imposing statues were relocated to places like Grutas Park. All these interventions allowed the Russian-speaking population to visit their respective heritage without the insult of having them in the town centre, where memories of a painful past are not communicated daily.

These problems also highlight how the concept of 'Retain and Explain', as promoted by the UK Government following the Black Lives Matter attacks on statues in the UK, is not always a viable option for built heritage, where contextualisation or providing additional narratives is insufficient to diffuse heritage as a weapon. This is apparent in a Latvian friend's comment about the Victory Park Monument: 'My daughter and I used to drive past it every morning and wonder: why the hell is it here?' We should also consider Michael Billig's suggestion that nationalism can be reinforced through everyday reminders, symbols, language, and routines, which blend into the background while reinforcing our national identity, which is 'Banal Nationalism' (1994). Such Russian symbols may reinforce national belonging for

Russophones while simultaneously simmering resentment, subconsciously or otherwise, among Latvians.

All participants in the current study discussed the conflict in Ukraine and the effect this had on de-Sovietisation efforts. The new waves of de-Sovietisation were initiated following Russian invasions in Ukraine in 2013 and 2022. There was a general feeling that had Russia not been so aggressive, the remaining heritage would not have mattered and might have remained. Understanding what is happening in Ukraine is important, as this can indicate what might happen to heritage elsewhere. The looting of Ukrainian heritage back to Moscow, in a similar vein to what happened during the Cold War and the need for protective measures are crucial. Such understandings may be challenging to navigate as published opinions on Russia's targeting of heritage vary. For example, Bevan (2022b) casts doubt on the intentional targeting of heritage in Ukraine, while other sources, such as Data4UA, as mentioned by LVA-3, draw evidence to the contrary (Data4UA, 2024). Such variance in opinions may be partially attributed to disinformation campaigns, but regardless, we must be careful not to become 'useful idiots' of new cultural Cold War propaganda. Heritage scholars, practitioners, and other individuals whose views or actions align with the strategic goals of influencing power must be cautious, even though they might genuinely believe they are acting independently (Gaffikin, 2023). Suppose Hannah Arendt (1951) is correct, and the ultimate totalitarian threat comes from convincing people that the difference between true and false does not matter. In that case, a factual understanding of the threat is important. Understanding how and why physical heritage is targeted, which heritage has the potential to be weaponised, and how best to counter the threat at any given point in time is, therefore, important. We may consider this as 'cultural intelligence' (Nemeth, 2015), where heritage specialists can contribute to 'Intelligence Preparation of the Battlefield' (Clack & Dunkley, 2023), informing strategic response decisions.

Heritage space in hybrid war resistance

All but one participant agreed that there is a place for heritage in resisting hybrid threats, and the potential is demonstrated at the museums. Stories of individuals who have suffered terrible events at the hands of the Soviets and how they endured and resisted are prominent in all museums. Many feature the Forest Brothers and how they endured living in the forest for years, but most are of normal people and how their lives were sent into turmoil by the occupation. These stories support the exhibits, which are everyday objects or simple belongings: a vial of earth from the home country taken to Siberia, a suitcase used to pack for deportation hastily, and a typewriter used to create banned books.

Train carriages are also prominently featured in the museums. These are presented in different forms, but all are meant to convey the use of that everyday vehicle as a terrible symbol of oppression, transporting people from their homes in trains designed for cattle. Without the accompanying stories, these exhibits might appear as just everyday objects, and this would seem to be an important component of how museums with traumatic exhibits explain how everyday objects became components in the resistance effort. Testimonies and photos provided by people alive when the exhibits opened, who lived and suffered the experience, charge the objects with a deep and powerful meaning. Here, it should be noted that the museums and supporting textbooks do acknowledge there was collaboration with the Nazis and draw out the complexity of the time. This collaboration might be seen as resistance against the Soviets, but explanatory narratives highlight that assistance in collaboration has not been adequately researched to this day (Nollendorfs, 2024). Narratives are undoubtedly important in how a museum understands what has happened and communicates the intended message (Frykman, 2009), but museums do not communicate messages of hate and retribution. Instead, these are stories wishing to tell the truth, to demonstrate the indomitable spirit of the people who suffered, and to explain the importance of national identity in these efforts. The overarching narrative is deep sorrow, but a hope that could not be broken.

Truth, however, can be problematic, and heritage is often shaped by selective narratives that may obscure or manipulate historical truth – another problem for 'Retain and Explain'. The museums present a point of view from the Baltics, and it should be considered that this is one point of view that carries its discourse of cultural and social meaning. *Authorised heritage discourse* (AHD) as Laurajane Smith (Smith, 2006) refers to the dominant, official ways institutions understand, manage, and present heritage. However, in this case, the exhibits seem to provide evidence to support the narratives through the facts we can see physically in the photographs, belongings, keepsakes, and the scars of oppression they bear.

Additionally, AHD tends to focus on physical heritage, often overlooking the intangible. However, in the case of resistance, intangible heritage is important. The power of words and stories in resistance becomes evident in the examples in the museums. It echoes comments about the importance of folklore studies in resistance and recording oral histories by EST–2. One of the reasons that the Singing Revolution was so successful was that it elevated national stories with music to demonstrate a spirit impervious to Soviet oppression, infiltration, and countermeasures. Participants and museum narratives described how important the singing events were in resisting the occupation, growing bolder from grassroots to events with thousands of people. Unwilling to cancel the local singing festivals to appear culturally superior, the Soviets did not realise the power these song gatherings had and how they could stoke national pride to a boiling point until it was too late to ebb the flow.

A related component of resisting sorrow through levity via words is humour. The risk associated with telling jokes about the Soviet regime is often mentioned, but this does not prevent people from sharing them. An entire wall in Vabamu is dedicated to Cold War jokes, such as 'Why are coffee beans no longer sold?

You can't paint a portrait of Lenin on them'. Gamboni (2007) notes that resistance often comes in humour. Hence, the banning of jokes by the regime and humour is identified as a key strategy of 'Laughtivism' by Popovic and Miller in their book *Blueprint for a Revolution* (2023).

The power of words is also demonstrable in the physical exhibits. Diaries, notes written on pieces of bark, records kept by those in exile, flyers of the resistance passed from hand to hand, but especially in Samizdat, a concept discussed at length by LVA−2. 'Samizdat created an independent universe that tried to preserve a range of different cultural codes' (Museum of the Occupation in Latvia). Poems and songs often helped keep up spirits in the forests during times of hardship, and many poems, stories of heroism, and songs are found in written records that reflect the resilient state of mind of the authors. As an exhibit label in the 'Book in Latvia' exhibition emphasises:

> For centuries, the printed word has been a form of resistance, including violent forms of it, for a word can call to action, struggle and murder. Secretly and illegally printing anti-government publications, one can take a stance against the powers that be and challenge them.

Preserving books and the freedom to read them is an important tool in a free society. As Ovenden (2020) reminds us, the preservation of information provides reference points that we can trust and rely upon, and capturing those truths, including the actions that would deny them, defends the truth against the rise of 'alternative facts'. As Heinrich Heine suggests, 'where they burn books, they will, in the end, burn human beings too'. Perhaps banning books is an initial stage of this process.

All museums feature the country's flag in various shapes and sizes, often as a small, concealable item hidden during occupation or captivity. No narrative explains this practice; however, it is, perhaps, easy to understand how these treasured items were symbols of resistance and kept close by to remind the people of home. Vesilind (2008) describes how, for many young people in Estonia, the first time they saw their flag flown in public was at the large song festivals and how, sometimes, the flag was demonstrated covertly by showing separate white, black, and blue fabrics together. Tim Marshall, in his book *Worth Dying For: The Power and Politics of Flags* (2017), suggests that encapsulating a nation in a flag means trying to unite a population behind a homogeneous set of ideals, aims, history, and beliefs. The respondent LITH-3, in this regard, underscored the importance of emphasising the value system behind heritage rather than the physical object itself. Perhaps the flag ideally exemplifies this aspect, as a visual reminder that the people of the Baltic States belonged to a nation that celebrated freedom and did not conform to their Soviet oppressors' ideals. Indeed, in all three countries, at the time of research for the current study, Ukrainian flags adorned the streets, flown next to the home country flag, making a similar statement. Symbols of a home nation's values are important in resisting oppression. This is summed up well in the narrative describing how the Estonian coat of arms was scraped off a leather photo album at Vabamu:

> Symbols are very important to every regime, but the more totalitarian the rule, the more rigid the attitude towards symbols. Any symbols the authorities do not like are banned or destroyed; monuments are blown up, flags are burnt. Old symbols are erased because of their emotional power to unite people and to stand as a reminder of things that the authorities do not want to be remembered . . . manipulation through symbols enables the control of people.

Whereas the correlation between the suppression of symbols and increasing totalitarianism might not be proven beyond doubt, the Baltic States have certainly witnessed their fair share of this Orwellian tactic of controlling the past to control the future. If such attacks on heritage can be an early indicator of attacks on people, as Bevan suggests (2016), then resisting them is undoubtedly worthwhile.

Conclusion

Through these exploratory conversations and visits to museums related to the Cold War and occupation, we can conclude that there is no definitive way that heritage interacts with resistance. Physical heritage can be charged with meaning and communicate resistance through our urban fabric, but its recognisability makes it easier to target and neutralise conflict. On the other hand, intangible heritage works may be more resilient to oppression in the long run by providing resistance through people. It is also clear that resistance means different things to different people at different times. As acknowledged in an exhibit label in the Vabamu exhibition,

> In the 1940s, resistance meant that you hid in the woods and fought with weapons in hand against the Soviet regime. In the 1960s, it meant drawing up written appeals. In the 1980s, you accidentally hit your finger with a hammer and then cursed the Soviet regime under your breath. Was that resistance? There are no definite answers here in this room.

However, we can see that heritage undoubtedly has been important in resistance efforts, and looking at the Baltics, as a unique case study, provides an eyepiece for a theoretical lens from which to consider how heritage studies might contribute to resisting the modern resurgence of Cold War-style subversive actions. The research broadens the scope of heritage studies beyond preservation and management by introducing a security dimension, emphasising how heritage can be weaponised or targeted in modern conflicts. It shows we must collate folklore and physical heritage to provide genuine narratives.

In the current study, I define hybrid warfare as a tactic unlikely to disappear anytime soon. The World Economic Forum's *Global Risks Report* (2024) identifies several significant threats over different time horizons. Societal or political polarisation and disinformation are highly prevalent in the short and medium terms. It highlights how hybrid warfare might target fragile states, leveraging cultural and historical tensions to fuel conflict. In addition, the current trend of heritage-related discord in the West will likely continue (Clack & Dunkley, 2023) as authoritarian regimes find value in restricting images of cultural cracks. The Institute for the Study of War, based in the United States, concludes that the Russian military is openly and actively preparing for a whole-of-society hybrid war (Clark, 2020); however, as in Cold War I, we should be wary of assuming that only the Russians utilise culture in such efforts.

As Europe polarises between the Far Left and Far Right, and identity politics clash with nationalism, such divisions could be exploited in subversive operations at home and abroad. Therefore, we should consider how to create the best strategies for safeguarding physical and intangible heritage and countering subversive activities that exploit cultural narratives. This cannot and should not be carried out by giving politicians or militaries alone the potential for politicisation or weaponisation of our heritage to place humanity's history and its symbolism of the values we hold dear in danger of erosion.

As in the first Cold War, Orwell again appears as an appropriate reference as we find frequent claims of fake news on both sides of the political dichotomy, which bear an uncanny resemblance to the work of the Ministry of Truth. These are deliberate acts of subversion, and, unsurprisingly, the heritage critic Robert Bevan draws out the potential for heritage to be manipulated by such 'post-truth' forces (Bevan, 2022a). Therefore, heritage professionals can provide value by verifying the facts and material authenticity that physical heritage can provide to challenge such post-truth activities. The most significant benefit of exposing culturally subversive operations is increasing public awareness of the threat and how to resist it. Adopting cultural intelligence in this way makes culturally subversive operations against humanity far more challenging to achieve. Failure to understand the past and present 'silent movements' involving tangible and intangible heritage in the Baltics and taking appropriate initiatives to address the issues could have multiple implications. This could include endangering the future of heritage in the region and creating fertile environments for continued volatile situations. It is either now when authorities, broadly defined, must work up and address the challenges, or otherwise it will be too late.

As a final call to action, we should consider that many more 'bronze soldiers' are active in the field, waiting to be mobilised. They can start civil unrest or rally people around a cause. They can either attack with weaponised narratives or protect citizens with indisputable facts. They can either despair or sing in hope. They are spies who do not need to be brought in from the cold and can provide valuable cultural intelligence. Whether they fight for freedom or oppression is up to us.

Acknowledgements

The author wishes to express his sincere gratitude to all interview participants, the invaluable staff in all museums visited, and friends in the Baltics for their gracious hospitality during the research visits. Thanks also go to the author's PhD supervisors, Dr. Peter Lehr and Dr. Tim Wilson of the Centre for the Study of Terrorism and Political Violence, St Andrews University.

References

Achcar, G. (2023). *The New Cold War*. Westbourne Press, London.

Akinsha, K., and Kozlov, G. (1995). *Stolen Treasure: The Hunt for the World's Lost Masterpieces*. Orion, London.

Andrejevs, D. (2022). *Contested Monuments and Their Afterlives: The V. I. Lenin monument in post-Soviet Riga*. PhD Dissertation University of Manchester. https://pure.manchester.ac.uk/ws/portalfiles/portal/231426126/FULL_TEXT.PDF

Arendt, H. (1951). *The Origins of Totalitarianism*. Schocken Books, New York.

Bahrani, Z. (2008). The battle for Babylon. In Bajjaly, J., and Stone, P. (Eds.), *The Destruction of Cultural Heritage in Iraq* (pp. 165–171). The Boydell Press, Woodbridge.

Bastiansen, H. (2023). *Media and the Cold War: Cultural Narratives and Propaganda*. Bloomsbury Academic, London.

Beilenson, Laurence W. (1972). *Power Through Subversion*. Washington, DC: Public Affairs Press.

Bellentani, F. (2024). *Soviet and post-soviet monuments in Estonia*. In Saloul, I., and Baillie, B. (Eds.), *The Palgrave Encyclopedia of Cultural Heritage and Conflict* (pp. 1–9). Springer Nature Switzerland, Switzerland. https://doi.org/10.1007/978-3-030-61493-5_16-1

Bevan, R. (2016). *The Destruction of Memory: Architecture at War*. Reaktion books, London.

Bevan, R. (2022a). *Monumental Lies: Culture Wars and the Truth About the Past*. Verso, London.

Bevan, R. (2022b, 27 April). Reports say Putin is deliberately targeting Ukrainian heritage – but is that true? *The Art Newspaper* [Online] Available at: https://www.theartnewspaper.com/2022/04/27/reports-say-putin-is-deliberately-targeting-ukrainian-heritagebut-is-that-true

Billig, M. (1994). *Banal Nationalism*. SAGE Publications Inc., London.

Blūzms, G., Viļums, J., Turčinskis, Z., Dreimanis, I., Ābelnieks, R., and Jansons, R. (2011). *The Unknown War: The Latvian National Partisan Fight against the Soviet Occupiers 1944–1956*. Domas spēks, Riga. ISBN: 978-9984-9961-6-5.

CEPA. (2020). *The Evolution of Russian Hybrid Warfare: EU/NATO*. CEPA. https://cepa.org/comprehensive-reports/the-evolution-of-russian-hybrid-warfare-eu-nato/

Clack, T., and Dunkley, M. (2023). Introduction. In Clack, T., and Dunkley, M. (Eds.), *Cultural Heritage and Modern Conflict* (pp. 1–27). Taylor and Francis, Abingdon.

Clack, T., Dunkely, M., Gane, T., and Rotherham, L. (2023). Heritage as a focus in US-Iran tensions: implications for aspects of power and culture in modern warfare. In Clack, T., and Dunkley, M. (Eds), *Cultural Heritage and in Modern Conflict* (pp. 142–162). Routledge, Abingdon.

Clark, M. (2020). *Russian Hybrid Warfare*. Military Learning and the Future of War Series. https://www.understandingwar.org/sites/default/files/Russian%20Hybrid%20Warfare%20ISW%20Report%202020.pdf

Data4UA. (2024, 24 February). Impact of the two-year war on Ukraine's cultural heritage. *Data4UA*. https://www.data4ua.eu/news/2024/february24

Eberle, J., and Daniel, J. (2023). Introduction: The problematic politics of 'hybrid warfare'. In *Politics of Hybrid Warfare. Central and Eastern European Perspectives on International Relations* (pp. 1–28). Palgrave Macmillan, Cham. https://doi.org/10.1007/978-3-031-32703-2_1

E-Estonia. (2017). *How Estonia Became a Global Heavyweight in Cybersecurity*. https://e-estonia.com/how-estonia-became-a-global-heavyweight-in-cyber-security/

Ehala, M. (2009, March). The Bronze soldier: Identity threat and maintenance in Estonia. *Journal of Baltic Studies, 40*(1), 139–158. https://www.jstor.org/stable/43212867

Fedor, J., Kangaspuro, M., Lassila, J., and Zhurzhenko, T. (2017). *War and Memory in Russia, Ukraine and Belarus*. Springer, Cham.

Ferguson, N. (2024). Kissinger and the true meaning of détente. *Foreign Affairs, 103*(2), 120–133.

Fiala, O. C. (2020). *Resistance Operating Concept (ROC)*. The JSOU Press, MacDill Air Force Base, Florida. ISBN 978-1-941715-43-7.

Friberg, J. (2020). SOCEUR and the resistance operating concept (ROC). *SOF News*. https://sof.news/uw/resistance-operating-concept/

Friedman, T. (1998, 2 May). Foreign affairs; Now a word from X. *New York Times*. https://www.nytimes.com/1998/05/02/opinion/foreign-affairs-now-a-word-from-x.html.

Frykman, G. S. (2009). Stories to tell? Narrative tools in museum education texts. *Educational Research, 51*(3), 299–319. https://doi.org/10.1080/00131880903156898

Gaffikin, F. (2023). *The Human Paradox: Worlds Apart in a Connected World* (1st ed.). Routledge, London. https://doi.org/10.4324/9781003106593

Gamboni, D. (2007). *The Destruction of Art: Iconoclasm and Vandalism Since the French Revolution*. Reaktion Books.

Haukkala, H. (2009). A close encounter of the worst kind? The logic of situated actors and the statue crisis between Estonia and Russia. *Journal of Baltic Studies, 40*(2), 201–213. https://doi.org/10.1080/01629770902884250

Humphreys, R. (2002). The Destruction of cultural memory. *Middle East Studies Association Bulletin, 36*(1), 1–8. www.jstor.org/stable/23063229

Institute for Palestine Studies. (2024). *Israel Destroys Palestinian Cultural Heritage Sites in Gaza*. (n.d.). https://www.palestine-studies.org/en/node/1655264.

International Centre for Defence and Security. (2020). *The Bronze Soldier Crisis of 2007: Revisiting an Early Case of Hybrid Conflict*. https://icds.ee/en/the-bronze-soldier-crisis-of-2007/

ISD. (2022, 8 September). Recurring pro-Kremlin Rhetoric linking Baltic States with Nazism. *Institute for Strategic Dialogue*. https://www.isdglobal.org/digital_dispatches/recurring-pro-kremlin-rhetoric-linking-baltic-states-with-nazism/

Johnson, R. (2018). *Hybrid War and Its Countermeasures: A Critique of the Literature, Small Wars & Insurgencies, 29*(1), 141–163, https://doi.org/10.1080/09592318.2018.1404770

Kaplan, R. D. (2019). A New Cold War Has Begun. *Foreign Policy*. 10 January. https://foreignpolicy.com/2019/01/07/a-new-cold-war-has-begun/.

Knaus, J. (2017). *Stalin and Saddam: A Study of Iconoclasm in Totalitarian Regimes*. Princeton University Press, Princeton.

Kruk, S. (2009). Wars of statues in Latvia: The history told and made by public sculpture. *Revue belge de philologie etd'histoire, tome, 87*(fasc. 3–4), 705–721. https://www.persee.fr/doc/rbph_0035–0818_2009_num_87_3_7700

Krumberga, K., and Storm, A. (2024). Cold war heritage dissonance and disinheritance as a heritage alternative: The case of Soviet military remnants in the Baltic States. *International Journal of Heritage Studies/IJHS*, 1–14. https://doi.org/10.1080/13527258.2024.2334242

Lewis, J. (2023). *Regions of Memory: The Dynamics of Collective Memory and Cultural Identity*. Routledge, London.

Lucas, E. (2014). *The New Cold War: Putin's Threat to Russia and the West*. Bloomsbury, London.

Mackinnon, M. (2007). *The New Cold War*. Carroll and Graf, New York.

Marshall, T. (2017). *Worth Dying For: The Power and Politics of Flags*. Elliot and Thompson, London.

McGlynn, J. (2023). *Memory Makers: The Politics of the Past in Putin's Russia*. Bloomsbury, London.

Merryman, J. H. (2006). *Imperialism, Art and Restitution*. Cambridge University Press, New York.

Naithani, S. (2019). *Folklore in Baltic History: Resurgence and Resistance*. University of Mississippi Press.

NATO. (2024a). *Countering Hybrid Threats*. https://www.nato.int/cps/en/natohq/topics_156338.htm

NATO. (2024b). *Hybrid Threats and Hybrid Warfare Reference Curriculum*. https://www.nato.int/nato_static_fl2014/assets/pdf/2024/7/pdf/241007-hybrid-threats-and-hybrid-warfare.pdf

Nemeth, E. (2015). *Cultural Security: Evaluating the Power of Culture in International Affairs*. Imperial College Press, London.

Nollendorfs, V. (2024). *Latvia Under the Rule of the Communist Soviet Union and National Socialist Germany*. Museum of the Occupation of Latvia. SIA Brivs, Riga.

Oltermann, P. (2023). *The Stasi Poetry Circle. The Creative Writing Class that Tried to Win the Cold War*. Faber and Faber, London.

OMB, Latvijas Okupacijas muzeja biedriba. (2016). *The Three Occupations of Latvia, 1940–1991*. Museum of the Occupation of Latvia, Riga. ISBN 978-9934-8299-3-2

Orwell, G. (1945). You and the atom bomb. *The Orwell Foundation*. https://www.orwellfoundation.com/the-orwell-foundation/orwell/essays-and-other-works/you-and-the-atom-bomb/. Accessed 26 July 2024

Orwell, G. (1950). *1984*. Signet Classics, New York.

Ovenden, R. (2020). *Burning the Books*. John Murray, London.

Pomerantsev, P. (2020). *This Is Not Propaganda*. Faber and Faber: London.

Popovic, S., and Miller, M. (2023). *Blueprint for a Revolution*. Scribe Publications, London.

Pullin, E. (2013). The culture of funding culture: The CIA and the congress for cultural freedom. In Moran, C. R., and Murphy, C. J. (Eds.), *Intelligence Studies in Britain and the US: Historiography since 1945* (Edinburgh, 2013; online edn, Edinburgh Scholarship Online, 29 May 2014), https://doi.org/10.3366/edinburgh/9780748646272.003.0003

Radin, A. (2017, 23 February). Hybrid warfare in the Baltics: Threats and potential responses. *RAND*. https://www.rand.org/pubs/research_reports/RR1577.html

Rid, T. (2020). *Active Measures: The Secret History of Disinformation and Political Warfare*. Farrar, Straus and Giroux, New York.

Rosén, F. (2020). The dark side of cultural heritage protection. *International Journal of Cultural Property*, 27(4), 495–510. https://doi.org/10.1017/S0940739121000023

Rosén, F. (2023). *"NATO and Cultural Property: A Hybrid Threat Perspective."* PRISM 10, no. 3: 44–58. Institute for National Strategic Security, National Defense University. Stable URL: https://www.jstor.org/stable/10.2307/48743422

Ross, C. (2025). Terrorism and cultural heritage: An unconventional threat assessment. *International Journal of Cultural Property*. Published online 2025, 1–29. https://doi.org/10.1017/S094073912510012X

Saunders, F. S. (2013). *The Cultural Cold War*. The New Press.

Šešelgytė, M., and Bladaitė, N. (2020). How to defend society? Baltic responses to hybrid threats. In *The World of Small States* (pp. 73–86). https://doi.org/10.1007/978-3-030-51529-4_6

Smith, L. (2006). *Uses of Heritage*. Routledge, Abingdon.

Vabamu (2019). *Freedom Without Borders*. Vabamu Museum of Occupations and Freedom, Estonia.

Vesilind, P. (2008). *The Singing Revolution*. Varrak Publishers Ltd, Tallinn.

Westad, O. A. (2007). *The Global Cold War*. Cambridge University Press, London.

White, J. (2016). *Dismiss, Distort, Distract, and Dismay: Continuity and Change in Russian Disinformation*. Institute for European Studies – Policy Brief 13 (May 2016). http://www.ies.be/policy-brief/dismiss-distortdistract-and-dismay-continuity-and-change-russian-disinformation

White, D. (2019). *Cold Warriors: Writers Who Waged the Literary Cold War*. Custom House, New York.

Wikipedia Commons. (2007). *File: Tallinn Bronze Soldier – 24 02 2007.jpg*. https://commons.wikimedia.org/wiki/File:Tallinn_Bronze_Soldier_-_24_02_2007.jpg

World Economic Forum. (2024). *The Global Risks Report 2024*. https://www.weforum.org/publications/global-risks-report-2024/

11

HOLISTIC APPROACH

A strategy for sustainable management of Saadani
nature–culture heritage sites, Tanzania

Richard Nandiga Bigambo

Introduction

Worldwide, the protection of various natural and cultural heritage forms is prevalent among countries and communities (Jenkins, 2018). This interest stems from
the significance of such resources – for example, their role in identity construction
and social cohesion – and their irreplaceable nature as part of the broader community. Numerous systems have been established in these resources' management
structures and frameworks. However, these face multiple challenges, including
conflicts in managing sites where cultural and cultural heritage converge, often
called 'mixed heritage sites' (Young et al., 2005; Estifanos et al., 2020; Maczka
et al., 2021). These conflicts stem from differing priorities, stakeholder interests,
and the inherent tensions between preserving cultural identity and maintaining ecological balance (King, Cavender-Bares et al., 2015).

The concept of 'mixed heritage sites', introduced by UNESCO in the 1990s,
is significant in heritage management. It refers to sites where cultural and natural
heritage intersect, presenting unique challenges and opportunities for conservation
and preservation (Bridgewater & Rotherham, 2018). It was introduced to address
the underrepresentation of Africa, Southern America, and Asia in the UNESCO
World Heritage Lists and to recognise the global significance of these unique sites
(Said & Ichumbaki, 2023). Some of the famous mixed heritage sites in the world
include the Ngorongoro Conservation Area in Tanzania, where natural beauty
(i.e., the crater and wildlife) and profound cultural significance (i.e., localities
with evidence of early hominin biological and cultural evolution) meet (Lwoga &
Mwankunda, 2020); Mount Kenya National Park, where glacial peaks and diverse
ecosystems intertwine with the cultural traditions of the Gikuyu people; Tongariro
National Park in New Zealand, a volcanic landscape sacred to the Māori people

DOI: 10.4324/9781003623724-11

(Asher, 2014), and the Rice Terraces of the Philippine Cordilleras, a testament to centuries of sustainable agricultural practices (Cagat, 2018).

Despite resonating with heritage management efforts worldwide, the dual nature of mixed heritage sites often leads to competing priorities and potential conflicts in their management (Seila, Selim, & Newisar, 2025). Conservation efforts to preserve natural ecosystems may clash with the desire to protect and promote cultural heritage and vice versa (Li, Lau, & Su, 2020; Keitumetse et al., 2023). For instance, restrictions on visitor access to protect fragile ecosystems limit opportunities for cultural interpretation and engagement (Robinson, 2011; Baloch et al., 2023). Similarly, traditional practices integral to cultural heritage may adversely affect natural resources, necessitating careful negotiation and compromise (Robinson, 2011). The diverse stakeholders involved in mixed heritage site management, including government agencies, local communities, conservation organisations, and tourism operators, may hold different perspectives and interests, further complicating the decision-making process (Li, Lau, & Su, 2020). As a result, these tensions create what I refer to in this chapter as 'silent conflicts'.

'Silent conflicts' denote unresolved tensions, disagreements, or disputes among stakeholders, including governments, conservationists, archaeologists, local communities, and businesses. These conflicts frequently arise from the differing interests of stakeholders concerning heritage sites and natural landscapes. For instance, governments and conservation groups may prioritise preserving archaeological or natural assets. Meanwhile, local communities might value a site's everyday social, cultural, and economic functions. Consequently, conservationists may advocate restricting public access to protect sensitive areas, while residents may resent the loss of traditional rights and livelihoods. These divergent views can occasion conflicts and undermine effective site management and community engagement.

This chapter, therefore, aims to explore the complexities associated with mixed heritage site management and propose a comprehensive approach that encourages collaboration and balances competing priorities to ensure cultural and natural heritage sustainability. Using Saadani National Park as a case study and drawing examples from around the globe, the chapter enquires into the common challenges and conflicts encountered in managing mixed heritage sites and identifies successful strategies for their resolution. Specifically, it examines the role of community engagement and participation in decision-making, the importance of integrating traditional knowledge and practices into conservation efforts, and the necessity for adaptive management approaches responsive to changing environmental and social conditions.

The chapter is divided into six parts. This introductory part is followed by a section that explores the differences, similarities, and intersections between nature and culture in the context of natural and cultural heritage. The second part outlines the strategies for gathering the information presented in the chapter. The third part describes the case study, the challenges and drawbacks of managing natural and cultural heritage in the study area. While the fifth part presents the proposed holistic approach to managing the assets, the final segment summarises the chapter and offers recommendations for future actions.

The nature–culture divide

In different literature (e.g. UNESCO, 1972; Lowenthal, 2005; Harrison, 2013), heritage falls into two distinct categories – natural and cultural. In this sense, natural heritage encompasses landscapes, geological formations, and biodiversity, while cultural heritage focuses on human-made creations, traditions, and practices (Lowenthal, 2005; Harrison & O'Donnel, 2010). Notably, separating heritage into natural and cultural heritage is a Western conception that took hold during the Renaissance period (Delanty, 2017). Such perceptions were integrated into the existing heritage management discourse in what Byrne (2008) calls 'colonial baggage', forming what Smith (2006) calls 'authorised heritage discourse', referring to a Western-influenced heritage management system operating using trained experts, administrative institutions, and legal frameworks (Bigambo, 2021).

In international heritage management discourse, the idea of separating natural and cultural heritage was cemented with the introduction of the 1972 UNESCO Convention Concerning the Protection of World Cultural and Natural Heritage. Articles 1 and 2 of the Convention define cultural heritage to comprise monuments, groups of buildings and sites, and natural heritage comprises natural features, geological and physiographical formations, and natural sites (UNESCO, 1972). In individual countries, cultural and natural heritage separation has led to the formulation of various instruments that manage them separately. However, scholars from different parts of the world have questioned such segregation.

Harrison (2013), for instance, cites the Great Barrier Reef in Australia, which signals a significant connection between natural and cultural heritage. The Great Barrier Reef became a World Heritage Site in 1981 under criteria VII, VIII, and IX for its outstanding natural beauty and universal geological and ecological significance (UNESCO, 1972; Harrison, 2013; Pocock, 2021). However, the Reef has a deeper meaning for the Aboriginals and Torres Strait Islanders. Indeed, it remains a source of their traditional food, a platform for practising their living maritime culture, and a place for educating younger generations about traditional and cultural rules and protocols (Harrison, 2013, pp. 8–9). Cultural activities, such as rituals, ceremonies, and practices, further help sustain the Reef and its significance. Therefore, the strict separation of 'natural' and 'cultural' heritage can become increasingly untenable.

Similarly, Chirikure and colleagues (2016) present another scenario of the interconnectedness of the natural and cultural heritage of the Khami World Heritage Site in Zimbabwe. The Khami Ruins National Monument, west of Bulawayo, Zimbabwe, comprises complex platforms built with dry-stone walls. The site was nominated as a World Heritage Site under criteria III and IV. It is sacred to the surrounding communities and is protected through traditional custodianship.

The protection strategies include rituals and taboos that forbid repair, rebuilding, or even trimming surrounding vegetation, which is an integral part of the site's spirituality. Following the 'Western-influenced' conservation philosophy, vegetation around the site is considered a sign of neglect, hence warranting its removal. Meanwhile, for the local communities, such vegetation is an integral part of the site, and their removal or alterations might amount to disturbing the ancestors' 'home' and 'communication networks' among the inhabitants (Chirikure, Mukwende, & Taruvinga, 2016, p. 171).

These examples and others elsewhere continue questioning and invalidating the separation of natural and cultural heritage. Moreover, the rigid divide between these two forms of heritage has frequently fuelled conflicts and contests in various regions around the globe. For instance, in many areas of Africa, local communities have resisted externally induced conservation strategies that prioritise natural heritage over culturally significant practices tied to the land since time immemorial. Such tensions are evident in rifts related to land use, resource access, and the recognition of traditional knowledge systems encompassing natural and cultural elements. The failure to grasp and acknowledge the interconnectedness of these heritage forms can result in the marginalisation of local populations, provoking protests and movements aimed at reclaiming their cultural identity and heritage. This ongoing struggle emphasises the need for a more holistic approach to heritage management capable of respecting and seamlessly integrating local perspectives and practices into decision-making processes.

Following these discussions, recent scholarship has attempted to promote an integrated approach to managing mixed heritage sites to minimise recurring tensions and conflicts. This approach can allow stakeholders to participate actively in planning and management decisions. Moreover, this perspective recognises how cultural practices and beliefs are often deeply rooted in the natural environment and how human interactions imbue landscapes with cultural meaning. Even as the move towards a more integrated approach gains traction, challenges persist, including the issues of power dynamics and differing valuations. Research by scholars (e.g. Girard & Vecco, 2021; Azzopardi et al., 2023) has highlighted the risk of primarily valuing natural heritage for its cultural significance, potentially overshadowing its intrinsic ecological values. Additionally, questions remain regarding the most effective strategies for managing and preserving mixed heritage sites.

Generally, extant literature has shifted from dividing heritage into natural and cultural categories to a more integrated understanding. This shift acknowledges the interconnectedness of natural and cultural elements in shaping places and identities. To improve the overall understanding of these dynamics, research must address the challenges of managing and valuing mixed heritage sites while ensuring the equal representation and protection of natural and cultural elements. This chapter, therefore, establishes a more precise framework for understanding how these dual aspects influence the significance of heritage sites. By examining the complexities of mixed heritage, researchers aim to provide insights that will guide effective management strategies. Ultimately, this work seeks to ensure the representation and preservation of natural and cultural elements for posterity.

Research strategies

This chapter discusses data from fieldwork conducted in different seasons between 2012 and 2023. The strategies for gathering data included personal observations, interviews with local people and government authorities, and a review of various documents, including management plans, conservation reports, and proceedings of various meetings.

While doing fieldwork in the Saadani area over the years, I observed people's behaviours, events, and interactions in their natural setting. Such observation enabled me to gather first-hand information on the local community's interactions with wild animals, such as common warthogs. Observing behavioural patterns, social interactions, and the effects of economic activities on wildlife facilitated my analysis of how local customs and practices influence conservation and coexistence with these animals. Throughout my fieldwork in Saadani, I visited various villages, observing people's economic activities and animal movements within and around these areas. Furthermore, observing these happenings gave me valuable insights into the community and their environment, emphasising the importance and challenges of wild animals in the social and economic fabric of the local community culture.

I conducted face-to-face interviews with diverse respondents in all the villages I visited, including workers from Tanzania's Saadani National Park (SANAPA) and the Antiquities Department, local community members, government administrative officials, and tour operators. My primary semi-structured interviews allowed me to follow a series of guiding questions while also having the flexibility to adjust the structure or delve deeper when necessary. Through these discussions, my interviews uncovered how local communities and officials perceive and interact with cultural and natural heritage. Consequently, I managed to interview 176 respondents, all with a stake in the management of SANAPA. Table 11.1 summarises the categories of respondents who participated in gathering data presented in the current chapter.

TABLE 11.1 Categories of respondents

s/n	Respondents	Number
1.	Local community	123
2.	Village officials	11
3.	SANAPA officials	8
4.	Tour guides	27
	Total	**176**

Source: Field data

The document review entailed examining various published and unpublished materials related to the management of SANAPA and engaging local communities from the surrounding villages. I consulted various documents, including books, academic articles, newspaper features, theses, and dissertations, all of which shed light on the challenges of managing SANAPA. Moreover, reviewing these sources was essential for developing holistic approaches that effectively address these challenges, providing a comprehensive understanding of the complexities involved in heritage management.

I used thematic analysis to identify, analyse, and interpret patterns or themes within a dataset I collected and compiled. The thematic analysis approach was practical because it enabled me to examine complex qualitative data, including interview transcripts, open-ended survey responses, and observational notes. Applying this approach also required initially transcribing all interviews before reviewing the resultant transcripts to highlight recurring patterns and themes. These emerging themes fell into categories of primary and sub-themes, whose results inform the subsequent presentations and discussions.

Case study

The case study for this chapter is SANAPA and the six villages bordering the national park. As one of the national parks managed by the Tanzania National Parks Authority (TANAPA), SANAPA lies between 5°21'22" and 6°21'53" south latitude and 38°34'13" and 38°51'2" east longitude in south-eastern Tanzania (Figure 11.1). The park spans three districts, namely Handeni and Pangani in Tanga region, and Bagamoyo in Pwani region, covering an area of 1,062 square kilometres (Peter et al., 2020). Although established in the 1960s as a Game Reserve and Ranch area, the park was officially gazetted in 2005 as one of Tanzania's national parks.

Unlike any other wildlife sanctuaries in Tanzania, SANAPA borders the Indian Ocean. This unique location allows it to encompass both marine and terrestrial habitats. Marine habitats consist of saltwater environments containing diverse life forms, including the endangered green sea turtle (*Chelonia mydas*), the humpback whale (*Megaptera novaeangliae*), and over 40 fish species (Moshi, 2016). On the other hand, terrestrial habitats are home to mammals, birds, reptiles, amphibians, and invertebrates. The mammals include four of the 'Big 5' (lions, African bush elephants, Cape buffaloes, and leopards), Masai giraffes, sable antelopes, colobus monkeys, and porcupines. In contrast, reptiles include hippopotamuses, crocodiles, and Nile monitors. Meanwhile, the park is home to numerous bird species. The park is also part of a larger ecosystem that includes the Wami-Mbiki Wildlife Management Area, which allows for migrating animals such as elephants and buffaloes to continue flourishing (Mligo, 2017; Moshi, 2016).

This park is also important for the communities in its vicinity. Currently, the park borders 17 villages. These villages are in three districts, that is, Bagamoyo (Kitame, Saadani, Matipwili, Gongo, and Mkange), Handeni (Kwedikabu,

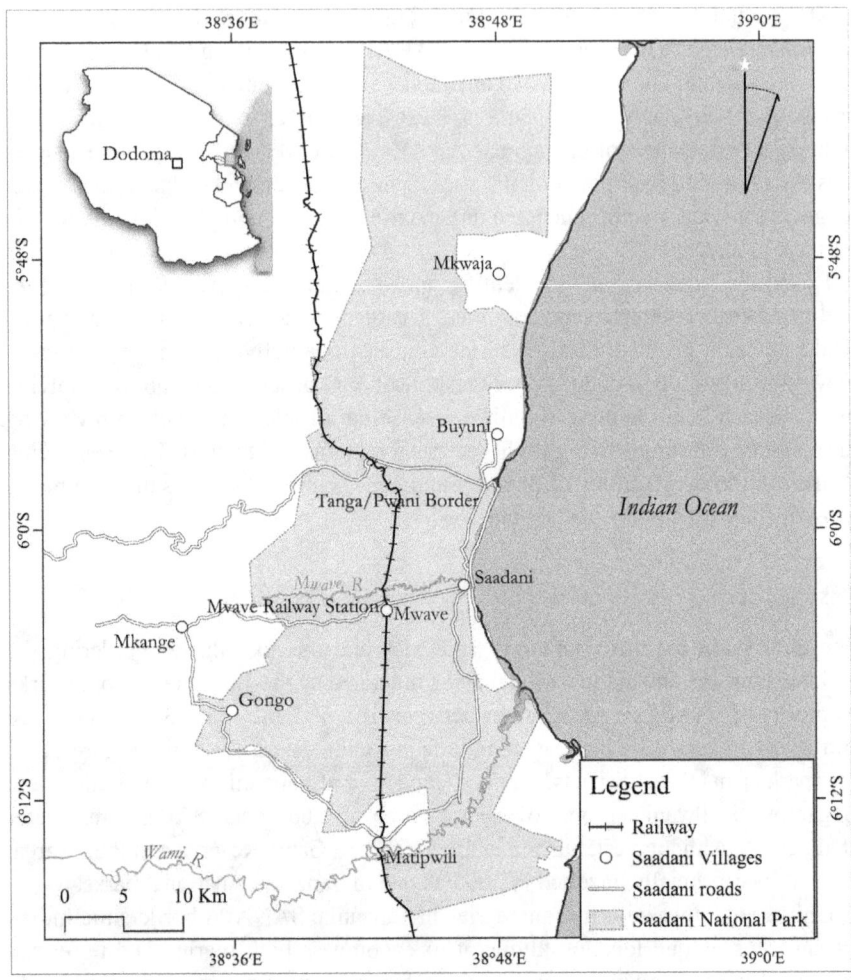

FIGURE 11.1 Map shows SANAPA and nearby villages.

Kwamsisi, Mkalamo ya Handeni, and Gendagenda), and Pangani (Buyuni, Mkwaja, Mikocheni, Sange, Kwakibuyu, Mbulizaga, and Mkalamo ya Pangani). The villagers engage in multiple socioeconomic activities, including tour guiding, fishing, animal husbandry, agriculture, salt mining, and small businesses such as restaurants and shops.

This chapter focuses on six villages: Saadani, Matipwili, Gongo, Mkange Buyuni, and Mkwaja, for they boast numerous elements that qualify as cultural heritage. These elements encompass oral traditions, traditional crafts, local ceremonies, ancestral rituals, and unique architectural styles that reflect the community's history and identity. Additionally, various monuments and structures indicate

FIGURE 11.2   German graves at Saadani village.

the interactions between the villages and the outside world, including remnants of Arab and colonial monuments, such as boma, graves, and tombs (Figure 11.2) (Bigambo & Mwitondi, 2024).

'Silent contests' in the management process

As highlighted earlier, in various parts of the world, areas rich in cultural and natural heritage are often characterised by silent contests among stakeholders, including between government departments legally mandated to care for heritage and local communities. In most cases, these conflicts arise when the management of these areas fails to accommodate the perceptions, needs, and aspirations of the communities residing near the protected areas (Bigambo, 2024). The SANAPA authority and surrounding villages are also embroiled in such disputes, manifesting in land-use priorities, unintended wildlife impacts, and challenges within the legal framework.

Conflicting land-use priorities cause misunderstanding between SANAPA and the surrounding communities, arising from the different activities and functions assigned to various land areas. In Saadani, both SANAPA and neighbouring communities assign different functions to the land and nearby areas. For SANAPA, like any national park, its primary function is to conserve diverse plant and animal species. Unlike game reserves, which permit licensed human consumptive use, national parks only allow controlled non-consumptive uses, such as game drives, walking safaris, and photographic tourism (Michael & Naimani, 2016). Therefore, conservation and authorised tourism-related activities are primary for the officials responsible for the park and its designated areas.

Conversely, the surrounding communities have designated different socioeconomic activities and functions for the land, including a sugarcane plantation in the southern part of SANAPA. This farm, which encroaches on the park, attracts elephants. These elephants damage the farms and threaten the workers and villagers. Moreover, in the north, at Buyuni village, the local government has established a significant salt farm right at the park's border. Some members, such as tour guides, noted that this area is home to elephants, where the concept of 'the beach meeting the bush' originated. As farming, animal husbandry, and fishing are vital for their livelihoods and contribute to the local economy, the residents believe that any available land should be utilised for socioeconomic activities integral to their way of life and the local economy.

In this instance, conflicts arise when each party assumes its land-use interests take precedence over those of others. Surrounding communities might prioritise socioeconomic activities that exploit natural resources, whereas conservationists advocate preserving the natural landscape for ecological reasons. Indeed, villages around the park engage in farming activities. Specifically, Matipwili, one of the villages adjacent to SANAPA, is well known for various farm produce, including maize, cassava, and the recently introduced paprika. Due to the increasing population and need for arable farming areas, the surrounding community tends to encroach on the park boundary areas, such as the wildlife corridors and dispersal (buffer zone) areas. However, this does not mean that a solution is unattainable. A sustainable solution can be found through a balanced approach that respects the park's conservation and the communities' socioeconomic needs.

Similarly, areas within the ocean are also protected by the park, for example, the Madete beach in Buyuni village. The park protects this area because of its potential for breeding green sea turtles, such as 'Chelonia mydas'. According to the IUCN, the green turtles are labelled as vulnerable (Seminoff, 2023) under criteria 2(b), that is, 'restricted geographic range and continuing decline, fluctuation, or other threats' (IUCN, 2012). However, for the surrounding communities, such an area is still a potential breeding environment for other fishes. Thus, the strict protection of the area can be translated as the preference for wildlife species' survival over their own.

The proximity between the park and the surrounding communities has led to instances of wild animals causing unintended consequences for the surrounding communities. The elephants and baboons sometimes destroy crops on the bordering communities' farms. Also, warthogs regularly roam close to Saadani village houses (Figure 11.3). Common warthogs are wild members of the pig family found in grassland, savanna, and woodland in sub-Saharan Africa. Some community

FIGURE 11.3 Common warthogs forage for food at the heart of a village.

members in the village have even reported instances of common warthogs entering people's houses, the mosque, and sometimes giving birth inside people's houses. This is a problem because many community members in Saadani are Muslims who treat animals of the 'pig nature' as dirty/forbidden or 'haramu' (Peter et al., 2020). Because of this scenario, continuously, the community complains to SANAPA about the presence of 'pigs' in their living area, which interferes with their religious beliefs.

Similarly, the blue and vervet monkeys pose significant challenges for wildlife in Saadani. These two species are abundant in the area and attract numerous visitors. They disrupt and annoy local communities by stealing food from households and streets. Numerous reports have been of these species attacking children found roaming in the village with food in hand. Although locals set traps and use traditional weapons to manage them, TANAPA officials prohibit harming these animals regardless of the havoc they wreak in neighbouring communities. There are also extreme cases of wild animals attacking both crops and community members. For instance, respondents farming near the SANAPA boundaries reported marauding crops raiding as the most frequent negative impact of living in the park's vicinity. Respondents in Mikocheni, Gongo, Mkwaja, and Buyuni villages have also complained about wild animals (e.g. elephants, baboons, and buffaloes) damaging their coconut farms. In rare instances, park animals have reportedly inflicted fatal injuries or even caused deaths among villagers. A case in point is the 2014 incident in Saadani village, where a resident of Matipwili village succumbed to a lion attack.

Another significant source of conflict in managing Saadani pertains to the legal framework. A system of rules, regulations, and laws governing the management of SANAPA is not well set to provide the structure and boundaries within which individuals, organisations, and the government, all with stakes in Saadani, must operate. Numerous rules, regulations, and laws governing the management of Tanzania's natural and cultural heritage have not been harmonised. Indeed, there is a pressing need for a unified approach to management, as natural and cultural heritage are often treated as distinct entities, each with its own set of rules and regulations. In this context, the Tanzania Forest Act No. 7 of 2002, the Antiquities Act No. 10 of 1964 [and its amendments No. 22 of 1979], and the Wildlife Conservation Act [CAP.283 R.E. 2022] must be interconnected. Each of these Acts separately addresses a specific aspect of natural or cultural heritage. Due to jurisdictional restrictions, some aspects of heritage – natural or cultural – may receive better attention and care than others.

Saadani, for example, is one of the villages bordering the park and is rich in tangible and intangible cultural heritage. Following the country's regulation, the village was supposedly protected by cultural heritage-related Acts (e.g. the Antiquities Act), whereas the natural heritage is under the National Park legislation protection. Inevitably, the imbalance in the attention given to natural and cultural heritage creates seemingly insurmountable problems. Furthermore, though natural heritage thrives as a part of tourism, cultural heritage suffers from a lack of proper management initiatives, leading to destruction.

Indeed, changes also stem from the recent enactment of new rules of Antiquities (2020), where different Tanzania Forest Authorities, Tanzania Wildlife Authority, and National Museum of Tanzania have become 'Honorary Antiquities Wardens'. These wardens care for selected cultural heritage sites and those within their jurisdiction. One of such wardens is TANAPA. Thus, SANAPA, as part of TANAPA, is now also the warden overseeing the cultural heritage resources in Saadani village. Although the cultural resources in the village are not yet gazetted, recent surveys and observations around the village revealed the presence of efforts to improve their management alongside the Caravanserai in Bagamoyo. However, without appropriate legal instruments, some of the challenges numerous tools pose might persist and hinder effective management of the heritage resources in the area.

Linking natural and cultural heritage for sustainable management

A holistic approach could become an alternative to managing mixed heritage sites in Tanzania and beyond. The approach ensures that all stakeholders, along with their practices and skills, are not merely involved but actively engaged in the decision-making and management processes. Active participation is crucial, making stakeholders feel valued and essential in management. The approach also guarantees the inclusion of various perceptions and perspectives in the management process. Specifically, it centres on three key aspects: the decision-making process, the design of management tools and guiding principles, and implementing the proposed principles. The discussion emphasises how the approach tackles the earlier challenges in each aspect.

Decision-making process

This first step in implementing any management practice establishes the foundation for managing heritage sites and clarifies participants alongside associated restrictions. In managing mixed heritage sites, this process must consider the complexities of balancing diverse cultural, natural, and economic values. Significantly, the decision-making process must be inclusive, transparent, and adaptive. Inclusiveness ensures that all stakeholders actively participate in decision-making. The stakeholders in mixed heritage sites include local communities, heritage experts, government agencies, and NGOs. Each stakeholder typically has reasons for interacting with the protected aspects. In Saadani, the local community values the site for its cultural or spiritual significance. Meanwhile, scholars from the University of Dar es Salaam – the oldest such institution in the country – treat it as a potential research and knowledge generation area. Conversely, government agencies – SANAPA – prioritise wildlife protection (Bigambo, 2024). As a result, government agencies make most decisions in favour of wildlife while overlooking the local community and their cultural heritage. A notable example is the SANAPA initiative to relocate some villages around the park, including Saadani village. This initiative protects the wildlife and site boundaries while disregarding the surrounding communities and their connection to their land and available cultural resources.

An inclusive decision-making process aims to incorporate diverse voices and interests into management. Such inclusivity guarantees that all valued aspects receive equal attention in the management process, rather than the current tendency to prioritise natural heritage (wildlife) at the expense of cultural heritage. For SANAPA, an inclusive decision-making process should ensure equal participation of local people from the surrounding villages, government agencies responsible for managing natural and cultural heritage, and heritage experts undertaking research in the area.

Regarding transparency, stakeholders ought to feel secure and informed about the decisions. Transparency emphasis is a process that guarantees stakeholders feel supported and knowledgeable regarding the decisions made. Ideally, numerous decisions should be made on managing a heritage resource. However, in some cases, only a few make decisions without effectively communicating them to all interested parties. For example, a transparent process involving all the parties on the plan and repercussions for relocating the villagers could have yielded different outcomes, attracting little resistance and acrimony. As it stands, many respondents were uncomfortable leaving their ancestral lands due to their deep-rooted connections. A holistic approach ensures that every decision is communicated to all parties. By promoting transparency, we eliminate feelings of being overlooked and mitigate the issues that arise when some stakeholders make decisions affecting others without their presence. A mechanism should, therefore, be established to facilitate this process and guarantee that decisions are conveyed through formal channels that reach all members effectively and promptly.

Finally, the decision-making process must be adaptive enough to recognise the need for flexibility and continuous learning. Adjusting strategies and plans based on new information, feedback, and emerging challenges is thus crucial. In other words, making numerous decisions about the protected aspects also required those involved to be receptive to change based on new insights or ideas. The rapid evolution of the heritage sector in Tanzania has regularly ushered in new practices and approaches. Although the preferred approach has been to relocate villages from within the park's boundaries to elsewhere, a new strategy could accommodate their presence in line with traditional practices ingrained in these societies. They could, for example, transform the village into a tourist hub, focusing on providing various services and amenities for visiting tourists instead of removal. Therefore, the decision-making process necessitates a holistic and adaptive approach, enabling the latest techniques and strategies to integrate seamlessly into management practices rather than sticking with a rigid system that fails to embrace new ideas.

Designing management tools and guiding principles

Management tools are strategies or tactics for making management choices and accomplishing conservation-related goals. Guiding principles, on the other hand, are values, ideals, and moral considerations that guide and inform the management process. Management tools and guiding principles provide a framework for day-to-day operations, decision-making, accountability, and the site's long-term sustainability. Moreover, these tools and principles are essential in balancing conservation needs and societal, economic, and cultural development. Management tools and guiding principles often do not consider the diversity of stakeholders. In many cases, the government's and experts' interests prevail over those of other groups. Consequently, the imposition of numerous restrictions in a designated protected area excludes other stakeholders' access to it.

Some promoted activities, such as conservation and tourism, tend to contradict the values imposed on other stakeholder groups. For instance, some natural forests used for ritual activities restrict access to groups based on either gender or age (Bigambo, 2021). However, such restrictions are usually violated once the area is open for tourism. This situation has been a source of conflict between the government and other stakeholders worldwide in many African countries, including Tanzania (e.g. Girard & Vecco, 2021; Azzopardi et al., 2023). Thus, in designing management tools and guiding principles, the proposed holistic approach underscores the importance of three key elements: the participation of all stakeholders, expert guidance, and flexibility in the proposed tools. In terms of the involvement of all stakeholders, as in the decision-making process, all stakeholders should be part of the design process.

Similarly, there should be a possibility of integrating perspectives from all stakeholders. Many heritage management frameworks have, in fact, not featured the traditions and practices of the local community (Bigambo, 2019; 2021), signalling a need to include such aspects in newly designed tools and principles. Involving trained experts in the design process is crucial for obtaining specialised guidance and ensuring the proper functioning of proposed tools and principles. Consequently, the design process should ensure the presence of experts throughout. Lastly, flexibility in the design process is necessary. Flexibility is vital as it allows for adaptation and ensures the tools remain relevant and practical. This adaptability also makes stakeholders feel that their input is valued and can contribute to creating practical tools.

Implementing the proposed principles

Executing the suggested principles is fundamental to the holistic approach proposed. This represents the concluding phase of this comprehensive method, guaranteeing the active engagement of all essential stakeholders. Four key aspects are crucial: (a) designing a collaborative governing structure, (b) capacity-building and awareness-raising programme, (c) conflict resolution mechanism, and (d) monitoring and evaluation programme.

(a)   A collaborative governing structure

A governing structure defines the connections, roles, and duties between the parties involved in the decision-making and execution processes for the site's conservation, preservation, and sustainable use. Moreover, it stipulates those responsible, how decisions are made, and how the parties involved collaborate. This framework ensures that each stakeholder and their interests participate in the management process. Therefore, the interests and roles of the local community must be accommodated in the management process, as is the case for government and heritage experts. The local community should also have a non-negotiable place in the decision-making process to have an active voice. Unfortunately, this is not the reality at present, as most of the decisions lack the active involvement of the local community. The village leadership has set up security and environment committees to oversee various aspects of the village. However, there is no committee to deal with heritage matters. Thus, in formulating an integrated management framework, there should also be a 'heritage committee' in charge of the cultural heritage in the village and providing a linkage between the community members and the village and park authorities, respectively.

The management process must also consider and support the various traditions and customs upheld by the community, which are vital for protecting heritage. Often, these customs and traditions among community members identify a feature as heritage and provide crucial mechanisms for its preservation and management. For example, Saadani village has a single well that supplies freshwater that the villagers and local wildlife use as a vital resource. Oral traditions inform that the well was created through a ritual and requires annual rites to sustain it (Bigambo, 2024). Thus, these traditions and customs should also be considered when creating an integrated management framework. Aside from fostering an active role for the community, accommodating these traditions will offer mechanisms for effectively protecting natural and cultural heritage.

Restricting or prohibiting local cultural practices may also alter the relationship between the protected aspects and the surrounding communities. In other cases, it might create conflict between the local community and the government authorities legally mandated to care for the sites. In implementing this proposal, one must know that some customs and traditions can be exclusive. There could be some taboos that limit access to specific elements or demand severe punishments for violators, such as public flogging. Therefore, proper attention must be paid to avoid harm than good when advocating for the role of traditions and customs in the management process.

(b)   Capacity-building and awareness-raising programme

To execute a holistic approach, all stakeholders must understand the strategies and techniques used in the process. A substantial capacity-building and awareness-raising programme is essential to achieve this. Capacity building entails training and educating stakeholders on best practices in heritage management, fostering skills necessary to address the complexities of mixed heritage sites through workshops, seminars, and professional development programmes. On the other hand, awareness-raising focuses on educating the public, stakeholders, and decision-makers about the value and importance of mixed heritage sites. This scenario might include educational programmes, media outreach, or public campaigns.

There is also a notable misalignment of values between SANAPA officials and the local community. The officials' primary responsibility is to protect the natural heritage. Wildlife is not more important for the community than its cultural values, which are tied to various aspects, including built heritage and natural features like ritual baobab trees and sacred groves. Against such a background, a well-structured capacity-building and awareness-raising programme should empower local communities, heritage professionals, and government officials to ensure sustainable and inclusive management practices. In addition to enhancing their understanding of current issues, such programmes would ensure that new techniques and strategies are effectively communicated to all parties, fostering a common understanding among everyone involved. It would promote dialogue and collaboration by engaging various stakeholders, including local communities, experts, and government agencies. This process helps develop a shared vision for the site and ensures that diverse perspectives are considered in management decisions.

(c) Conflict resolution mechanism

Due to the involvement of multiple stakeholders and interests, managing mixed heritage sites is often associated with numerous conflicts. These conflicts may arise from conflicting land-use priorities or contested values. A holistic approach should also establish a framework to ensure that such conflicts are identified and swiftly resolved without negatively impacting the relationships of the parties involved and the heritage values. Indeed, one of the ongoing conflicts involves relocating certain villages from their current locations. This relocation sparked disagreements among some villages long before the park's transformation. Likewise, the problem of wild animals attacking people, crops, and dwellings has been a persistent issue in the villages surrounding the park. Consequently, the holistic approach recommends the formation of a committee composed of representatives from each stakeholder involved.

The committee should address any misunderstanding emanating from the presence of diverse interests and stakeholders. Recognised rules, stipulations, and agreements should guide such an entity in ensuring fairness and transparency. These mechanisms might adapt to what is amenable to the fisheries sector in Tanzania, the beach management units. In Tanzania's Fisheries Act No. 22 of 2003, a Beach Management Unit (BMU) is a group of devoted stakeholders in a fishing community whose primary function is to manage and protect fish in their locality in league with the government (URT, 2003). One of the BMU's agreed-upon aspects is the 'provision for settlement of disagreement' (URT, 2003: 18[d]). A similar group should be an integral part of managing mixed heritage sites to ensure effective resolution of conflicts without any negative repercussions.

(d) Monitoring and evaluation

The last part of the implementation process is an effective monitoring and evaluation programme. The holistic approach emphasises collaboration across various dimensions, including individuals, committees, strategies, and multiple methods. Effective management necessitates ongoing monitoring and evaluation of these agreed-upon aspects. For instance, it is vital to assess all stakeholders' participation in the decision-making process and identify any associated barriers. Also, understanding the progress of the proposed strategies and pinpointing potential solutions to any challenges is essential. In alignment with the conflict resolution mechanism discussed earlier, I recommend establishing a dedicated monitoring and evaluation committee. However, there should also be a slight difference in the composition of the monitoring and evaluation committee. It should comprise experts from within

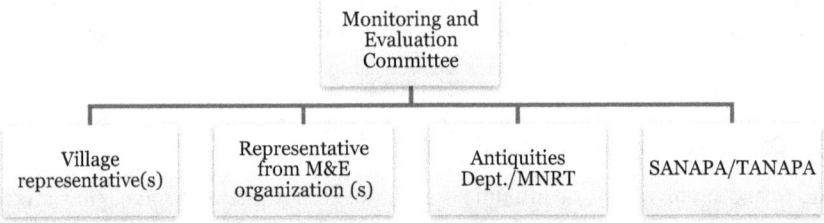

FIGURE 11.4 Proposed structure for the M&E Committee.

and outside the institutions. For Saadani, members can come from SANAPA/ TANAPA and the Antiquities Department in the Ministry of Natural Resources and Tourism (MNRT) and other independent members from institutions dealing with monitoring and evaluation in general (Figure 11.4). Expert officials are essential because of the professional nature of monitoring and evaluation. Likewise, members from outside the institution enable quality control to avoid complex scenarios whereby the person ostensibly under observation is also conducting the observation. This measure can ensure the impartiality of the proposed reports for existing institutional politics.

Conclusion

Saadani National Park highlights the ongoing challenge of balancing conservation efforts with the rights and livelihoods of local communities. The chapter illustrates the tension between preserving natural heritage and protecting cultural heritage, which arises from competing land-use priorities, economic pressures, and differing views on what constitutes valuable heritage. Consequently, the park's diverse ecosystems and historical legacies – ranging from remnants of the slave trade to traditional salt-making practices – are at risk. It has demonstrated how conventional conservation methods primarily focus on wildlife without necessarily adequately addressing the complex challenges. Furthermore, these methods frequently compound tensions with local communities that rely on these resources for survival. The ongoing tensions between the park management and surrounding communities highlight the urgent need for a more inclusive strategy that integrates nature and culture as essential heritage components. By recognising and valuing the interdependence of these elements, stakeholders can collaborate to develop sustainable solutions that benefit conservation efforts and local livelihoods. The proposed holistic approach that prioritises natural and cultural heritage equally is vital and likely to facilitate sustainable coexistence between conservation initiatives and local communities' livelihoods. Adopting such an approach protects the park's biodiversity and historical assets and nurtures a more equitable and resilient future for all stakeholders.

References

Asher, G. (2014). The tangible and intangible heritage of Tongariro national park: A Ngãti Tûwharetoa perspective and reflection. In S. Disko, & H. Tugendhat (Eds.), *World Heritage Sites and Indigenous People's Rights* (pp. 377–402). Copehhagen: Gundjeihmi Aboriginal Corporation.

Azzopardi, E., Kenter, J. O., Young, J., Leakey, C., O'Connor, S., Martino, S., . . . Koutrakis, M. (2023). What are heritage values? Integrating natural and cultural heritage into environmental valuation. *People and Nature, 5*, 368–383.

Baloch, Q. B., Shah, S. N., Igbal, N., Sheeraz, M., Asadullah, M., Mahar, S., & Khan, A. U. (2023). Impact of tourism development upon environmental sustainability: A suggested framework for sustainable ecotourism. *Environmental Science and Pollution Research, 30*, 5917–5930.

Bigambo, R. (2021). Challenges and solutions in the safeguarding of intangible cultural heritage in Tanzania. *South African Archaeological Bulletin, 76*(215), 135–139.

Bigambo, R. (2024). Residents' perception of the meaning and importance of conserving cultural heritage assets in Saadani village, Tanzania. *Journal of Cultural Heritage Management and Sustainable Development*, ahead-of-print.

Bigambo, R., & Mwitondi, M. (2024). Cultural heritage resources in shambles? An approach towards a proper conservation and management of Saadani village, Tanzania. *Journal of African Cultural Heritage, 3*(1), 234–255.

Bridgewater, P., & Rotherham, I. D. (2018). A critical perspective on the concept of biocultural diversity and its emerging role in nature and heritage conservation. *People and Nature*, 291–304.

Byrne, D. (2008). Western hegemony in archaeological heritage management. In G. Fairclough, R. Harrison, J. H. Jameson, & J. Schofield (Eds.), *The Heritage Reader* (pp. 229–234). London: Routledge.

Cagat, K. A. (2018). Mixed views on the Philippines' Ifugao rice terraces: 'Good' versus 'beautiful' in the management of a UNESCO World Heritage Site. *Journal of Southeast Asian Studies, 49*(1), 84–104.

Chirikure, S., Mukwende, T., & Taruvinga, P. (2016). Post-colonial heritage conservation in Africa: perspectives from drystone wall restorations at Khami World Heritage Site Zimbabwe. *International Journal of Heritage Studies, 22*(2), 165–178.

Delanty, G. (2017). *The European Heritage: A Critical Re-Interpretation.* London: Routledge.

Estifanos, T. K., Polyakov, M., Pandit, R., Hailu, A., & Burton, M. (2020). Managing conflicts between local land use and the protection of the Ethiopian wolf: Residents' preferences for conservation program design features. *Ecological Economics, 169*, 1–15.

Girard, L. F., & Vecco, M. (2021). The "intrinsic value" of cultural heritage as driver for circular human-centred adaptive reuse. *Sustainability, 13*(6), 1–28.

Harrison, R. (2013). *Heritage: Critical Approaches.* New York: Routledge.

Harrison, R., & O'Donnel, D. (2010). Natural heritage. In S. West (Ed.). *Understanding Heritage in Practice* (pp. 88–126). Manchester: Manchester University Press.

IUCN. (2012). *IUCN Red List Categories and Criteria: Version 3.1* (2nd ed.). Switzerland and Cambridge: Gland.

Jenkins, V. (2018). Protecting the natural and cultural heritage of local landscapes: Finding substance in law and legal decision making. *Land Use Policy, 73*, 73–83.

Keitumetse, S. O., Mwale, K. P., Satau, G., Velempini, K., Baitsiseng, V. O., Ntema, O. P., . . . Mgotsi, S. T. (2023). Exploring cultural values of African wetlands for sustainable conservation: Okavango Delta World Heritage Site, Botswana. *Journal of Cultural Heritage Management and Sustainable Development, 13*(3), 2044–1266.

King, E., Cavender-Bares, J., Balvanera, P., Mwampamba, T. H., & Polasky, S. (2015). Trade-offs in ecosystem services and varying stakeholder preferences: Evaluating conflicts, obstacles and opportunities. *Ecology and Society, 20*(3), 25.

Li, Y., Lau, C., & Su, P. (2020). Heritage tourism stakeholder conflict: a case of a World Heritage Site in China. *Journal of Tourism and Cultural Change, 18*(3), 267–287.

Lowenthal, D. (2005). Natural and cultural heritage. *International Journal of Heritage Studies, 11*(1), 81–92.

Lwoga, N. B., & Mwankunda, J. (2020). Comparing motivation and profile between archaeotourists in Ngorongoro, Tanzania. *Geo Journal of Tourism and Geosites, 32*(4), 1394–1401.

Maczka, K., Matczak, P., Jeran, A., Chmielewski, P. J., & Baker, S. (2021). Conflicts in ecosystem services management: Analysis of stakeholder participation in Natura 2000 in Poland. *Environmental Science and Policy, 117*, 16–24.

Mbise, F. P., Moshi, B., & Røskaft, E. (2021). Impact of protected areas on the livelihood of locals: A case study in Saadani national park, Tanzania. *International Journal of Biodiversity and Conservation, 13*(3), 98–108.

Michael, E., & Naimani, G. M. (2016). Implications of upgrading conservation areas on community's livelihoods: Lessons from Saadani national park in Tanzania. *Journal of the Geographical Association of Tanzania, 36*(1), 39–57.

Mligo, C. (2017). Diversity and distribution pattern of riparian plant species in the Wami River system, Tanzania. *Journal of Plant Ecology, 10*(2), 259–270.

Moshi, B. S. (2016). *Impact of Protected Areas on Local Livelihood: A Case Study of Saadani National Park.* Norwegian University of Science and Technology: Unpublished Master's thesis.

Peter, E., Mashuka, E., Githae, D., Okoth, E., Cleaveland, S., Shirima, G., . . . Pelle, R. (2020). Detection of African swine fever virus genotype XV in a sylvatic cycle in Saadani national park, Tanzania. *Transboundary and Emerging Diseases, 68*(2), 813–823.

Pocock, C. (2021). Great barrier reef world heritage: Nature in danger. *Queensland Review, 28*(2), 118–129.

Robinson, J. G. (2011). Ethical pluralism, pragmatism and sustainability in conservation practice. *Biological Conservation, 144*(3), 958–965.

Said, C., & Ichumbaki, E. B. (2023). Ours or yours? Localizing the 'mixed sites' concept for the sustainable preservation of heritage in Africa: The case of Chongoleani Peninsular, Tanzania. *International Journal of Cultural Policy, 29*(3), 299–313.

Seila, F., Selim, G., & Newisar, M. (2025). A systematic review of factors contributing to ineffective cultural heritage management. *Sustainability, 17*, 1–26.

Seminoff, J. A. (2023). *Chelonia Mydas (East Pacific subpopulation). The IUCN Red List of Threatened Species 2023.* Retrieved April 22, 2024, from https://www.iucnredlist.org/species/220970302/220970304

Smith, L. (2006). *Uses of Heritage.* London: Routledge.

UNESCO. (1972). *Convention Concerning the Protection of the World Cultural and Natural Heritage.* Paris: UNESCO.

United Republic of Tanzania (URT). (2003). *Fisheries Act.* Dar es Salaam, Tanzania: Government Printing Services.

United Republic of Tanzania (URT). (2020). *Antiquities (Management and Control of Monuments, Conservation Areas and Protected Objects) Rules.* Dar es Salalaam: Government Printers.

Young, J., Watt, A., Nowicki, P., Alard, D., Clitherow, J., Henle, K., . . . Richards, C. (2005). Towards sustainable land use: Identifying and managing the conflicts between human activities and biodiversity conservation in Europe. *Biodiversity and Conservation, 14*, 1641–1661.

12

COLONIALISM, AUTHENTICITY, AND THE SACRED

A museum perspective

Lars Frühsorge

Introduction

Heritage conflicts extend beyond physical sites since artefacts and human remains housed in museums can also spark disagreements. However, they possess the potential to highlight both historical and contemporary Indigenous agency. By examining the relationships between museums and descendant communities more closely, we can better grasp the dynamics behind heritage conflicts and explore possible ways to resolve them. This chapter focuses on objects and experiences related to my work as the director of the Collection of the Cultures of the World in Lübeck, Germany.[1] This ethnographic museum holds a collection of 30,000 objects from around the globe from 100,000 BC to 2024 AD. About 60 per cent of the collections were brought to Germany before 1945 in the global context of colonialism.

The head of the Hanseatic League, Lübeck, was one of the most important trading hubs in medieval Europe but lost its importance with the shift of global trade networks in the 16th century. A private collection of archaeological and ethnographic objects from beyond Europe can be traced back in Lübeck's history to the 17th century, and in 1893, an ethnographic museum was created. It was presented to the public in a building with a natural history museum and collections related to global trade and crafts. This combination reflects the 19th-century German colonial desire to explore all aspects of the world for economic benefits. During the bombing of Lübeck in 1942, the museum and about one-third of the ethnographic collections were destroyed (a number that needs to be remembered about statements that keeping objects in Europe was a way of saving them). In 1945, there were plans by the British liberators of Lübeck to use ethnographic objects in schools in their efforts at anti-Nazi re-education. Still, it took until the 1970s to start new exhibitions and until 1984 to reopen a museum which, for political reasons, was closed

DOI: 10.4324/9781003623724-12

again in 2008. There is no permanent exhibition; nevertheless, changing parts of the collection are exhibited in the other nine city museums once or twice yearly.

The objects and offices are still located in the museum building known as "Zeughaus", which symbolically reflects the problematic history of ethnography in Germany. The building is right north of the Cathedral, thus standing literally in the shadow of the church (just as many ethnohistorians and ethnologists depended on data collected by missionaries). Before becoming a museum, the building served as the headquarters of the notorious Gestapo. In the basement, there are still cells which were used to imprison and torture critics of the Nazi rule. Even the office of the museum director is the same one that was used by the head of the police, and the director's desk is very likely the place where the deportation of the Jews from Lübeck to the concentration camps was planned. Working in such a place evokes intense feelings of historical responsibility.

After becoming the Director of this collection in 2018, an important task was to study and inform the public about the colonial contexts in which the objects came to Germany. In a city of 220,000 inhabitants in the Northern German province with rather uncritical views of its glorious past and a migrant community of 160 nationalities, it was not easy to establish new discourses. Public discussion about the origins of museum objects turned out to be an essential motor to create a new awareness and to reconstruct the long-ignored role of the city in the global system of colonialism that continues to shape international relations up to the present day (Frühsorge, 2022). Self-critical reflections are essential to create a new vision for ethnographic museums in Germany, which are currently in the crossfire of critique in the media. Long-time ethnographic museums were mainly Eurocentric places where German curators explained "exotic" cultures to German visitors.

Although most of the progressive curators and directors of Ethnographic museums in Germany would agree that Postcolonial ideas influenced us, no author of specific importance and even less a fixed methodological or theoretical framework of our work can be stated at this point. Most museums currently embrace the idea of so-called "labs": temporary exhibition spaces, which serve as laboratories, where new ways of curating, displaying, representing and working with artists from Indigenous communities are tested (see, e.g. Balzar, 2022). Much of the need to find new approaches is, in fact, the result of external pressure, the influence of postcolonial movements of the political left and migrant communities in the big urban centres that demand museums to share information about the more problematic aspects of their history and to allow restitutions. In Lübeck's case, the situation was slightly different because there was no comparable awareness of the German colonial past, and the museums were free to address this topic without external pressure. Also, the basis for establishing dialogue was much better in Lübeck than in more prominent museums.

Between 2012 and 2016, the whole collection was photographed and digitised, which allowed me to easily get in touch with communities all around the globe via the Internet and share these data. I consider it a moral obligation that we actively inform all communities about which kind of material from their ancestors survived in Lübeck and invite them to share their thoughts on how to deal with it in the future. In these dialogues, the topics of restitution, sacred objects and human remains turned out to be the most important ones and will be addressed in the corresponding sections of this chapter. Bridging the gap between archaeologists and museums and Indigenous communities was also a subject of my earlier research in Guatemala, which I will briefly explain in the next section. A more recent topic that I will address at the end of this chapter came from research within the museum. All ethnographic museums hold many replicas of archaeological and spiritual objects or souvenirs from the historical tourist trade. They are easily discarded as "fakes" and hardly studied or exhibited. Our research, however, shows that they can be important sources to better understand Indigenous agencies in colonial and postcolonial heritage conflicts.

From Guatemala to Germany

Authors from Europe and North America have dominated the debate on the future of museum collections. However, important voices and ideas from the communities predate the current debate but attract less attention (Paczensky, 1984). Years before becoming part of the museum world, I documented during my first fieldwork (2004–07) the role of archaeological sites for descendant communities of ten different Maya groups in Guatemala (Frühsorge, 2011, 2010, 2007).[2] After visiting various sites, I became aware of the complexity of the relations between the people and the mounds containing the remains of pyramids and palaces of their ancestors surrounding their villages. Some communities struggled with growing populations and a lack of farming lands (partly because the national government gave their traditional territories to international farming companies). Under this pressure, some Mayan farmers wanted to remove the mounds to allow more crops to be planted. Others saw no other way to escape poverty than "mining" the mounds for artefacts to be sold on to the international art market. During my research, archaeologists of North American universities excavated some sites, although some other ruins were already preserved as national heritage sites. Those sites provided some income to the community members either as part of the excavation teams or in various businesses of the tourist sector. Besides, there was still a conflict between local needs and the management of the ruins as national sites, with numerous non-Indigenous people having economic benefits.

There were also sites which were still "undiscovered" (from the Western archaeological point of view) even though local communities knew very well about their existence and preserved some memories of their history passed down through oral traditions, which archaeological and linguistic research verified later (Frühsorge & Wölfel, 2009). Despite these differences in every place studied, at least some mounds remained untouched because they had spiritual importance to the people. This "spiritual monument protection" was based upon tales of cursed magical treasures, sleeping kings ready to defend their people or other supernatural events observed there.[3] In most places, the remains of the old temple pyramids also served as stages for contemporary rituals honouring the ancestors' spirits.

The latter was particularly true for Q'umarkaj, the former capital of the powerful K'iche Maya kingdom, during the Spanish invasion in 1524. Despite 500 years of colonisation and missionary efforts, this site, with its ruined temples, palaces, ball courts and artificial caves, remained an important focal point of K'iche's identity, historical memory and spirituality. When I visited the site's small museum, I was surprised to find a burial with the remains of an ancient Maya ruler laid out in a showcase with a small altar and various candles in front of it (Figure 12.1). Being aware of the importance of the ancestors in Maya spirituality and the unequal relationship between national heritage institutions and local communities I immediately speculated, that this altar had to be a sign of protesting the exhibition of that ancestor to ignorant tourists. However, during an interview with one of the traditional Maya priests who performed ceremonies in the ruins, he appeared rather happy about the museum. He called it a "good compromise" and insisted that the ancestor was protected and honoured by being displayed in such a nice glass showcase. He also added that he would light the candles at the altar each morning when the museum opened, but the guards stepped in if he was unavailable. I am not sure

FIGURE 12.1   Museum of Q'umarkaj, Guatemala, in 2006.

if everyone in the community would still feel the same amount of agreement about this arrangement today. Anyway, this example has always remained in my mind. It helped me to understand that there was no need for a museum to be a purely colonial institution and that the peaceful coexistence of science and Indigenous spirituality was indeed possible. Instead of seeing a rather humble museum in a developing country, Q'umarkaj provided me with a remarkable intellectual "development aid" for debates which would only attract large-scale public attention in Germany more than a decade later.

The question of restitution

Claims to return museum objects such as African masks or the famous portrait of Nefertiti from German museums to their countries of origin date back to the creation of the first postcolonial nations after World War II but remained unheard for a long time (Paczensky, 1984). Because museums saw themselves mainly as institutions to preserve cultural heritage, just talking about restitutions appeared to many like opening Pandora's Box. Only a few progressive museums pioneered opening dialogues and faced many political challenges before returning at least some human remains. However, most ethnographic museums ignored postcolonialism as a possibly short-lived trend and felt it safer to remain silent about their colonial past.

This only changed around 2018 when a considerable debate in the media erupted about the Humboldt Forum in the German capital, Berlin. This building is a modern recreation of an imperial German palace, which was planned to be a new venue for exhibitions of Berlin's non-European museum collections. Promoting such an imperial building crowned by a Christian cross as a future place of intercultural respect seemed implausible to many observers. Further critique focused on the involvement of sponsors related to right-wing political parties in the construction of the building and on the new permanent exhibitions, which, in many places, remained silent about the problematic ways many of the objects on display had reached Germany. In the heat of this debate, calls for the return of looted art, especially to former German colonies, gained growing public awareness and acceptance.

Even before the debates surrounding the Humboldt Forum, there was growing attention in the media for claims to return human remains from former German colonies, which are still stored in various museums, universities and medical research institutions. A cataclysm for this debate was the 100th anniversary of the German genocide committed against the Herero and Nama peoples of Namibia (1904–08). Herero demands to have their ancestors back for a respectful burial, public apologies by various German representatives for the crimes committed, and the still unresolved conflict between the Namibian and German governments over financial compensation brought out the darkest sides of Germany's colonial past to the attention of many Germans for the first time. They changed many attitudes in the museum world, too.

Today, most curators and directors in ethnographic museums favour dialogue and certain restitutions. Museums also enjoy more media attention and funding from the German federal government to explore their colonial past than ever before. In the end, however, it turns out that the ethnologists who make great personal efforts to establish good community relations are not the ones to decide. Especially in communal and national museums, the last decision about restitutions is often in the hands of ignorant superior heads of the administration or politicians with limited willingness to accept historical facts and even less non-Western perspectives.

Whenever museums try to establish the proverbial "dialogue on an eye-level", they must face the truth of postcolonial inequalities. As the administrations running the museums are (at least according to European law) the legal owners of the collections and successful restitution usually requires written historical proof that the objects were stolen, Europeans remain pretty much in control. However, beyond legal questions, ethical aspects must be valued. For example, many African archaeological and ethnographic collections are still not found on the continent but remain in European and North American museums. As citizens of many African nations have, in terms of both visa restrictions and financial resources, only limited possibilities to travel to Europe and study the material heritage of their ancestors, it should be no surprise that some communities talk about injustice. Community members involved in restitution debates must also accept mixed feelings. They feel obligated to be diplomatic to achieve their goals but need a space to express their anger. Also, some communities feel that giving back some masks could turn out to be a cheap way for the Germans to get rid of their historical responsibilities and ask for much bigger financial compensation for all the adverse effects of colonialism. Others even argue that the objects should remain in Germany for some time to serve educational purposes in exhibitions as proof and a memorial of the colonial injustice. They should only be returned after the German society has accepted its historical responsibility.

A big challenge even for museums willing to support restitutions has to do with objects from ethnic groups that, after the creation of colonial borders and postcolonial states, are now divided between different nations. Other problems may arise because restitutions usually require cooperation at the national level. Some of the claims come, however, from groups which are ethnic minorities, people who still face discrimination or fight for public recognition in their own countries. To them, involving national actors can be rather unacceptable. Moreover, not all communities prefer restitution. Some community delegations who visited the Lübeck collection saw the objects as "cultural ambassadors", informing people abroad about their history and achievements. They thus prefered to leave the collectiions in Germany. Other communities faced with experiences of corruption have no trust in their governments or museums and find it easier and safer to work with collections in Europe. Countries such as Kiribati, whose very existence is heavily endangered through rising sea levels and climate change, prefer to keep objects of their ancestors in museums all around the globe as a kind of deposit, a focal point of identity for future generations in the Diaspora.

It would also be very misleading to think that communities always agree and speak with one voice. This can be illustrated well by Lübeck's collection of objects from the Fang people who live today in parts of Cameroon, Equatorial Guinea and Gabon. These objects came from an expedition of the Amateur Ethnologist Günter Tessmann in 1907–09 and have been recently researched in a project funded by the German Lost Arts Foundation (Schütte, Frühsorge, & Igouwe, 2021). The masks and statues in this collection are considered the most important and valuable holdings of the Lübeck Museum. However, a study of Tessman's diaries and other historical documents revealed that he used problematic ways to "collect" objects of spiritual importance. Initially, he tried trade but later turned to violence, such as raiding villages and taking local chiefs or their wives as hostages. However, he still did not manage to get the desired pieces. Then, he moved to another area of the Fang territory and pretended to be a colonial governor. Ultimately, he received the statues and masks in return for forged letters that should have guaranteed the chiefs that their territory would never be colonised (Schuette, Igouwe, & Frühsorge, 2021, pp. 48–57).

In parallel to this historical research, members of Fang communities in all three countries provided statements about the objects. The majority favoured restitution. Some saw these objects as a potential source of a new self-awareness in postcolonial times or to reunite their people divided between the countries. Some Fang ethnic members saw the objects as a possible inspiration for local artists or to re-create religious traditions lost through Christianisation. Only two people who identified as Christians opposed the idea of a return of those objects, saw them as a threat to the will of Jesus Christ and suggested they should be destroyed in the case of repatriation. Other people had the impression that Germans only wanted to return objects to get rid of the evidence of the crimes of their ancestors. Some stressed that these objects once had spiritual power and that giving them back so much later, with no power left (or the knowledge of the rituals to handle them long lost), would be disrespectful. Others, however, argued for restitution because of their continued spiritual power. One person explained that such objects were a kind of telephone to communicate with their ancestors and that it made no sense to keep such a thing in a museum, where no descendants lived, and no one knew how to make the call. Another person even showed concern for the Germans. He argued that the Europeans could suffer severe damage from handling such powerful pieces and thus felt it would be safer to bring them back home.

When publishing these results, the Lübeck Museum administration wanted to dialogue with museums and governments in all three countries, but only with a political authorisation that a possible outcome of these negotiations could include restitution. However, some politicians and other influential citizens of Lübeck ignored or reinterpreted the historical facts. They argued, for example, that the objects were not the kind of "looted art" you read about in the newspapers (because they came "only" from fraud and not plundering). They also argued that Tessmann was still a good scientist, respected in Africa and thus an innocent victim of posthumous discreditation by some woke leftist activists. They even paid a person from Equatorial Guinea to come to Lübeck and speak in defence of Tessmann without letting him know about the conflict he was about to be involved and without informing him about the recent findings of Tessmann's crimes, his brutality and the racist conclusions of his work that was eliminated in the translated version of his work being read in Central Africa. Opponents of restitution also complained about the low quality of African museums and the lack of democratic structures. They insisted that such pieces were "too valuable for Africa". For two years, there was no political majority available for any restitution, including the objects and human remains from the genocide in Namibia, and research in the same project. Only in 2024 was the museum authorised to return human remains and collections of limited value, but under the condition that the unlawful act of collection for each object had been proven through historical sources.

The spiritual dimension of museum collections

Artefacts with assumed spiritual powers are a kind of signature object for ethnographic museums, and it is not an exaggeration that they have always created mixed feelings. Starting with early missionary "collectors"[4] who did not deny their spiritual power but attributed it to the devil. Moving on through history, we can mention short stories of renowned writers such as Edgar Allen Poe, rumours about cursed tombs and mummies that killed archaeologists, the 1990s bestseller novel and movie *Relic* about a vindictive deity from the Amazon or even the Disney "Nights at the Museum" franchise. Like the display of Egyptian mummies or shrunken heads, the exhibition of sacred objects generated many Western visitors' uncertainty and doubt about how the museum got them or whether they should be displayed. However, the same feelings also generated excitement, like watching a horror movie, which made these exhibitions fascinating for uncritical visitors and profitable for the ethnographic museums.

On the other hand, spiritual aspects can be important arguments in Indigenous claims for restitution. The previously cited worry of spiritual harm, which might affect the museum or its visitors, is not unique. For example, a female member of a Native American group from the United States, very friendly, suggested to us not to exhibit objects in the presence of women because that could very negatively affect their fertility. Moreover, a priest of the traditional religion of the Ashanti in Ghana saw no need to return spiritual objects but offered to come to Germany and perform a ceremony of desecration if anyone ever had terrible feelings or illness that these objects could cause. These cases show how a spiritual discourse can help to invert the usual Eurocentric power structures that dominate museum debates.

Visits of members from the community also may have strong spiritual undertones. When, for example, such a visitor voices specific requirements, such as performing a ritual before allowing anyone to enter the archive, the museum staff can enjoy a good lesson on inverted power structures. However, moral dilemmas are everywhere. Two female visitors from Canada and the United States told us that racism and bureaucracy are still so intense in the museums of their countries that they found it easier and cheaper to buy a plane ticket to Germany and enjoy the new openness here. Both also stressed that part of their motivation was to see spiritual objects that women are usually not allowed to see according to the traditions of their communities. Several spiritual authorities of communities have no problems with having objects exhibited when they are only shown to male museum visitors. This, of course, creates a moral conflict between respecting Indigenous traditions and the European idea of gender equality.

Viewing the objects as living beings can create unsettling guilt and injustice. When we asked a spiritually sensitive guest from a "First Nation"[5] in Canada about his impression of the archive, he expressed that the object would feel like a person barely awaking from a long sleep, unconscious where they are, a feeling of being locked up in a dark room with iron bars at the windows, wondering how they came there and looking for a way to escape. However, he also highlighted that things happen for a reason and that there might be a divine plan. These objects might have come to Europe because they would have been needed here for an unknown reason. So, who are we to interfere? His answer was plain and straightforward when asking our guest about the dilemma of restitution. Why not ask the objects themselves where they want to be? The same answer was also offered in the 2024 production "Repatriation Nation" by the South African choreographer Jessica Nupen and found a surprisingly large amount of support from the audience (Figure 12.2). The idea is indeed an important re-shifting of perspectives. However, the question remains: Who would be qualified to communicate the will of the objects who usually do not speak to German curators?

Again, we must acknowledge that restitution is not a quick and universal solution, especially when the exact origin of a sacred object is unknown. A good example is the *tjurungas* from Central Australia, which are said to contain the souls of ancestors or even the powers that created the universe (Balzar, 2022, p. 71f.). Such powerful objects should only be handled by clan members who produced and owned them, precisely, by the male adults who underwent a training of several years. Some of the *tjurungas* in German museums were certainly only given away by the communities under the pressure of colonialism. For example, missionaries "bought" them in exchange for food after Aboriginal people had been moved to reservations where they could no longer survive as hunters and gatherers. Other *tjurungas*, however, seem to be just replicas made to satisfy the hunger of European collectors for sacred and secret things and thus helped to protect the real ones. German museums agree that *tjurungas* are no longer exhibited but kept in archives. Returning them is problematic, too, when the family of origin cannot be determined. An unprepared return has been compared to bringing a "spiritual

FIGURE 12.2 Folks symbolizing the spiritual idea of letting objects decide on restitution.

atomic bomb" into the community (cf. Balzar, 2022, p. 176). When making such a radical comparison and suggesting that keeping is the only provisional solution so far, it might also be justified to compare the museum archive to a quest for a "Spirituelles Endlager".[6]

We must even consider the possibility that objects came intentionally into museum collections because of their spiritual power. Possible examples are the Malanggan carvings from New Britain (Papua New Guinea), which were traditionally made to serve as temporal containers for the spirits of the dead and which had to be thrown away after the Malanggan festival to depart in peace. The living can take over the position of the deceased. At some point, Malanggan carvings were also carved to be exported. Looking at the enormous numbers in European collections, there can be little doubt that most of them were probably never used in a ceremony. In some early instances, however, used ones were also traded, and community members might have concluded that selling a carving to a European, who would bring it to a place at the other end of the world, could substitute the tradition of throwing it in the bush and letting it rot away. This is just speculation, but at least we can be sure that in the Malanggan trades, a lot of Indigenous Agency was involved, as particular objects were actively offered for sale. In other cases, Europeans could not purchase them at any cost (Barsch, Frühsorge, & Günther, n.d).

Another example would be a Sami shaman drum from Northern Sweden. It came to Lübeck as one of the earliest objects in the collection, probably around 1700. At this time, missionaries very aggressively fought Sami's pre-Christian spirituality. Not observing church services could result in financial fines or even imprisonment. Shamans were suspected of performing witchcraft and, for this reason, sometimes even executed. It is possible that a missionary confiscated the drum, which is now stored in the Lübeck Museum. However, it is not less likely that the former owner or his family actively gave it away because keeping it was considered too dangerous. It is not only persecution through the church that might have played a role. In many cultures, shamanic objects are considered very private and attached to their first owner and creator. When a shaman dies, his paraphernalia cannot be used by another one, who would probably get hurt from the uncontrolled powers. Some communities, like the Mam-Maya in Guatemala, traditionally laid out such objects in nature to ensure that wind and rain would cause their natural disappearance. In the case of the Sami drum, which shows several signs of extended use, damage and repairs, one can imagine that it also came from a deceased shaman whose family gave it away to protect themselves from both church persecution and its spiritual power (Frühsorge, 2022).

A modern example of an Indigenous agency behind such a transfer is a statue of the Maya deity Maximón, which was brought from Guatemala to the ethnographic museum in Hamburg for an exhibition that opened in 2010. It could only be purchased because the leader of the religious brotherhood in charge of venerating Maximón had not found any successor. Unable to continue the necessary rituals but convinced that the statues would contain spiritual power, he gave them to the museum. However, he demanded that Maximón be treated with respect. He even carved a non-functional pipe to ensure the deity would have some entertainment in the dark transport box. When Maximón finally arrived in the museum, a few unexplained things happened that were attributed to his agency and even involved other figures of the same god. Only after the Latin American students working in the museum offered a sacrifice of chocolate to Maximón did the incidents stop (Frühsorge & Schmelz, 2011). Although this example comes from a postcolonial context, similar thoughts might have influenced the transfer of colonial collections and archaeological artefacts.[7]

Many spiritual objects in European museums come from communities where Christianity was established when traditions declined. People most likely still felt that these objects could contain certain powers and should not be thrown away. Giving them away may be a good compromise to ensure that the objects continue to exist and receive a certain degree of good treatment. Furthermore, if the objects were still powerful, the curse of the ancestors would rather affect that museum in a country far away than their community.

Human remains and pictures

Apart from spiritual objects, we also need to discuss human remains as another case of what the contemporary secularist museum jargon refers to as "culturally sensitive holdings". There are skulls and bones of 25 people[8] in the Lübeck Museum, which has been recently researched by Claudia Kalka (2024).[9] After having a closer look at their provenance, there is good reason not to treat them as objects but to honour them like living persons. This is partly because they have a problematic way of coming into the museum. Also, they tend to cause much more conflict and hurt feelings than other holdings. I, therefore, decided to distinguish these remains from the regular collection and thus contribute to their "dehumanisation". They are now stored in a separate room in the archive, which resembles the design of the storage areas of urns in German funerary companies. Electric candles and black blankets mark this area as distinctive from the rest of the archive. Special handmade boxes are exclusively used in this room, and varying sizes should reflect the individuality of the different persons. Photography is not allowed there; whenever possible, the place is only entered by or with the community's permission. Respect for the deceased is also reflected in our working language. We avoid using the inventory numbers once given to these people and, whenever possible, refer to them not as objects but as indiividual persons (e.g. "the infant from Peru"). Anyway, we must acknowledge that there is also the problem of Eurocentrism in this separation of humans and objects. While many museum holdings would also qualify as subjects according to the view of some descendant communities, Western science has trouble adapting to this way of thinking. It simply cannot offer the same individual treatment for all 30,000 holdings. Here, the concept and resources of a museum just come to a limit.

In the case of the 25 human remains in Lübeck, we can distinguish between "archaeological" remains, like an Egyptian mummy or the part of an infant's skull that was returned to Peru in 2024, and recent individuals. Archaeological remains are sometimes considered unconnected to contemporary communities and thus less problematic than, for example, individuals taken from a more recent grave without the permission of the living family members. As it will become apparent later, this distinction can also be controversial. In terms of historical injustice, we can distinguish three cases of persons from Chile, the Democratic Republic of the Congo and Namibia who were taken from graves during the times of colonial genocides. None of them can certainly be identified as an actual victim of these atrocities (in the sense of having physical marks of having been murdered by a colonist). However, all of them refer to a time when the pseudo-science of the "Rassenkunde" (racial studies) collected human remains to "prove" the assumed superiority of white people over the rest of the world's population and thus legitimised the system of colonial rule. Taking these people from their graves for such an ideological purpose was a highly racist act of double abuse. It is more than understandable that returning these people to their countries of origin is a special priority for descendants. However, despite the best intentions, there are still obstacles to overcome.

A good example of the complexity, but also the potential for mutual collaboration, is an ancestor of the Selk'nam from Chile. We have good reasons to believe that he was taken from his grave during the time of the genocide on the island of Tierra del Fuego and that the motivation to rob his grave was racist, as Charles Darwin had called the Fuegians the most primitive people on earth and, thus, generated much scientific interest in them. Because of the genocide, Selk'nam survivors decided to hide their identity. They were considered an "extinct tribe". Only about ten years ago did their descendants return to the public. Finally, in 2023, the Chilean government recognised them again as a living Indigenous group. The first reactions were somewhat reluctant when we established contact with the Selk'nam and had to tell them about their ancestor in Lübeck. A private journey to Tierra del Fuego and personal talks in their hometown were seen as a sign of honest interest and brought change. It was explained to me that it was not my own decision that had brought me to their island, but the ancestors' will. They were convinced that our collaboration would be good for the same reason. We agreed to create an exhibition and a bilingual publication (Frühsorge, 2023) to inform the public in Europe and Chile that the Selk'nam continue to exist. The culmination point of this collaboration was a delegation's visit to the Lübeck exhibition. They also visited their ancestor and gave him a new name, "Hoshkó", to be able to address him as a person.[10]

It was clear from the outset that bringing him back to be buried on his home island was the goal. Partly not only to restore his dignity but also to make sure that his remains can never again be displayed or abused for research. The Chilean government also offered to help with such a restitution. According to Chilean law, Hoshkó is, however, an archaeological artefact and thus a national property to be managed by the cultural ministry, which would do DNA tests on him before deciding if he will be released for burial or not. To the Selk'nam, these conditions were unacceptable. They argued that performing even more tests on their ancestorts would be a continuation of their colonial mistreatment and requested that we not cooperate with the national government After two years, they finally asked the museum to bury their ancestor in a German graveyard instead. The funeral took place with both national and international media attention in October 2024, as this was the first case of an Indigenous victim of a colonial genocide being buried by his descendants, not in his homeland but in Europe. With the grave remaining in Lübeck, a new memorial for our historical responsibility is created; for the Selk'nam, the funeral was an important step to officially turn back their ancestor from a museum object into a person. Hopefully, this example will help other museums in Germany and beyond hand over more Selk'nam ancestors to the community.

Though the injustice of people being robbed from their graves for racial studies is undeniable, ethnographic museums also hold certain remains that come from Indigenous traditions of exhuming and modifying bones. These include musical instruments made of human bones in the Buddhist tradition of the Himalayas. Providing your bones for such an object is considered a good act that will positively influence the subsequent rebirth of the person. As with other human remains in Buddhist countries (e.g. victims buried in mass graves of the Killing Fields in Cambodia), the idea of their sensitivity is somewhat limited when you imagine that, according to the concept of rebirth, the person is already walking on earth again in a new body. In the case of the musical instruments of the Lübeck collection, no place of origin could be determined with certainty. They also show signs of damage, concluding that they were no longer used by the time they came into the possession of the German traveller Kurt Boeck. They were probably sold voluntarily in one of the monasteries he visited in India and Nepal in the late 19th century. A Buddhist expert consulted during this research felt restitution unnecessary, as the country of origin cannot be established. However, we followed his advice not to exhibit the remains anymore and to store them with respect in a regular box, wrapped in cotton cloth.

Little local interest is also related to returning human remains to Papua New Guinea. Here, a burial is only feasible when the exact village or family of the deceased is known, details that the colonial "collectors" hardly found necessary to write down. In most cases, we deal with the decorated skulls of honoured ancestors who were liberally shown publicly as a special sign of respect. Another question is whether the deceased would have loved to be shown in a German museum and how they ended up on the international art market. Some of them were confiscated by colonial soldiers plundering villages, but there was a general European desire to purchase human remains even by private persons not related to the military. This was partly to prove the assumed primitivity of the people and, thus, legitimise their colonial subjugation. The public display of human remains was often mistaken as proof of cannibalism and could result in violent actions of colonial military forces.

On the other hand, there is also plenty of evidence that some communities actively offered decorated skulls to European sailors and researchers. We even found evidence that some were produced exclusively to serve as a commodity. There are also individuals whose skulls were decorated as part of headhunting traditions. In one of these cases, the village where one skull was purchased is known, but this is, of course, only the home of the enemies who killed him and thus hardly a good place for restitution and reburial. It is hard to distinguish between ancestral and enemy remains. However, we can speculate that the skulls manufactured by some communities exclusively for the trade are more likely not to be remains of individuals from their own village. Altogether, our dialogues with people in Papua New Guinea produced no interest in returning those ancestors and no restrictions in displaying them. A former national museum director even encouraged us to take additional ones into our collection, as a private person offered one.[11] Therefore, the fact that we no longer show skulls from Papua New Guinea in exhibitions is not a community demand but rather a result of German sensitivities concerning death and ethnographic collections. That skulls from archaeological excavations in Germany or the famously well-preserved bog mummies are still rather freely exhibited leads some ethnologists to believe there is a kind of moral double standard in the museum world.

Another problematic case is a shrunken head from Latin America. Traditionally, these heads were produced by the Shuar people of Amazonia during headhunting rituals. Technically, we are talking about a person from another group turned into a sacred object by a Shuar. As the original group is primarily unknown, restitution for the sake of the deceased's dignity is difficult. Notably, this tradition underwent heavy commodification. The enormous European fascination for shrunken heads created a market that first resulted in a need to kill many more people than before, and quickly also motivated non-Indigenous people to produce such remains, mostly by using bodies robbed from non-Indigenous urban cemeteries. There are also in the Lübeck collection the late 20th-century replicas of shrunken heads made from animal skin that one can still buy in Ecuador for a few dollars. For the only human shrunken head in Lübeck, experts suggested that a Shuar neither produced it nor is the deceased one an Indigenous person. It is, therefore, no surprise that the Shuar who we contacted during our research showed limited interest and pointed out that they had more urgent problems to deal with then helping a German museum overcoming his problematic past. To them – as to many Indigenous groups globally, colonialism is not only a thing of the past but very much part of their present life. They still face racist discrimination, conflicts with their national governments, struggles with the pollution of their natural environment and international companies taking over their territories. Unsurprisingly, helping a remote German museum understand its history might not be a priority in such a context. Thus, the current boom of postcolonial research in Germany needs revision if it is ultimately not also trapped in Eurocentrism and how much it benefits the communities.

A good example of such conflicting views of sensitive Western scientists and Indigenous communities is colonial photos. Just like human remains, they somehow represent deceased persons whose dignity must be discussed. There is little doubt that most pictures were taken without the depicted person's consent. Another problem is the way people are portrayed, which may trigger certain racist stereotypes. Most museums and researchers, therefore, avoid showing colonial photos of Indigenous people at all. When talking to various guests from the African continent, this self-censorship is criticised every time. To some, these pictures are important illustrations of a way of life now lost, a valuable view into the world of their ancestors. But for most of our African guests, these pictures are solid proof of the cruelty of colonial rule. They highly recommend publishing even the most explicit ones with people in chains to inform Europeans about the crimes of their ancestors. Only very few of our guests confirmed that seeing these pictures in an exhibition would hurt their feelings.

A few other guests insisted that such pain be taken and displayed to reveal the historical truth. They also emphasised that the persons depicted had been dead long enough, so their feelings were no longer important. Therefore, the current German reluctance to exhibit these photos is not seen as a sign of respect but as another excuse to avoid discussing historical responsibility. The accusation of double moral standards can also be attributed to art museums in this context. Paul Gauguin's Polynesian paintings, for example, can tell a lot about his paedophilic relations with local girls. Emil Nolde's portrait of an angry-looking man from Papua New Guinea who was forced to be his model with a gun pointed at him is equally unsettling. However, no museum would even think of removing the works of such renowned artists from the display.

Authenticity and agency

Replica objects deserve our attention because they reflect different views of heritage and Indigenous agency, hardly visible in the written colonial sources. Ethnographic museums and art collectors have long championed the view that "their" objects are "authentic" in the sense of having been used in rituals (or other daily activities) of the communities. However, doubts must arise when comparing the vast number of masks and statues from Africa and Oceania in public and private collections to the sizes of the populations who supposedly created and used them. Museums realised that many of their holdings were exclusively created for the European market (Barsch, Frühsorge, & Guenther, n.d). Indeed, communities all around the globe realised the 19th-century European obsession with collecting things and started production to fit this early tourist market. In some cases, this globalised souvenir production even predates the formal colonisation of the areas (Figure 12.3). Miniature-sized objects such

FIGURE 12.3   Ivory carving of nude couple symbolizing European desires for African resources and sexualized bodies.

as boat models or replicas of ritual objects with designs that make no sense from the point of view of the cultures are just two examples of this production (Figure 12.4). Professional museums with scientific "collectors" looking for "authentic" (pre-industrial, pre-Christian, etc.) objects tended to ignore pieces produced for the early tourist market. They also avoided reporting too many details about Indigenous people actively engaged in the trade of objects or the production of replicas because such information would have challenged the sense and value of museum collections. In the Lübeck Collection, which comes mainly from non-scientifically trained private persons, those early souvenirs and replicas appear in even larger quantities and thus reflect the realities of 19th-century globalisation more honestly and accurately.

This early production also includes early replicas of archaeological pieces (Kelker & Bruhns, 2010). The manufacturing and sale of these pieces as assumed originals to inexperienced tourists continues, for example, in Nigeria, Mexico, Guatemala and Peru. Artisans have developed remarkable methods to make new pieces look old or to upcycle genuine, undecorated ceramics by adding new layers of fancy paintings. In Nigeria, for example, old ceramic materials are sometimes

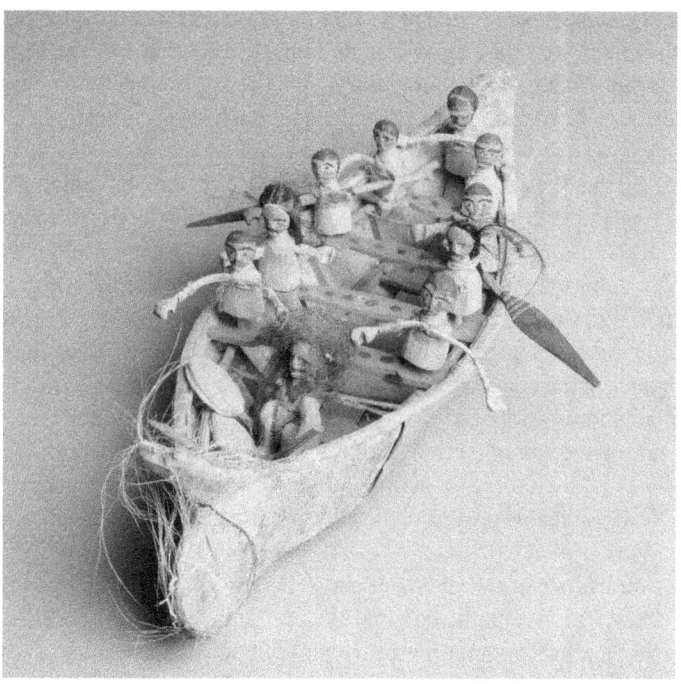

FIGURE 12.4   A boat model from Alaska representing advanced boat building tradition the Russian and US-American colonialists forbade.

included in new pieces, right at the bottom of the objects where European laboratory tests would take a sample for dating. My research and comparative evidence elsewhere (Brulotte, 2012) indicate that community members involved in these activities do not consider themselves criminals. They argue that removing artefacts removing artefacts from local sites to national museums is a way of taking the heritage of their ancestors away from them. Similarly, UNESCO's concept of a World Heritage Site is seen as a colonial construct because heritage sites often produce less income for the community than expected. It is often not the local economy but the non-Indigenous people who get the more significant share of the economic benefits of tourism. Making replicas and selling them as assumed originals is a legitimate form of cultural resistance, a method of reclaiming something taken away from them. Artisans also insist that they are descendants of the original producers and, thus, have the right to create such things.

When I noticed in one Guatemalan Maya community that not only in the local museum but also on an altar of ancestor worship, both old archaeological pieces and new replicas were mixed, my interview partners did not understand my confusion and stated, "Pero es la misma cultura" (but it is the same culture). It took me some time to understand this simple quote's whole meaning. In fact, since the colonial period, there has been an idea to see archaeological sites as something unrelated to contemporary Indigenous communities. Archaeologists, journalists and heritage institutions have created ideas like the so-called "Classic Maya Collapse" in the 10th century AD or assumed that the impact of colonialism and Christianisation was so significant that contemporary Maya is not "authentic" anymore. This allowed the nations to claim those sites as a national heritage. Creating new objects in an old tradition and placing old and new ones together on the other side is a way of challenging this Western concept of "authenticity" and reclaiming their history.

Interpreting souvenir production as a form of cultural resistance is also true for colonial times. In a context where colonial powers and church officials tried to change local cultures, producing replicas was a good way to preserve specific production techniques and pass knowledge of religious symbols to the next generation. In the German colonies, the core of exploitation was the introduction of a head tax, which each person had to pay in cash. Since the currency was hardly available, German plantation owners had a good excuse to recruit people for forced labour. Souvenir sales were one of the few ways to get cash from travellers and thus avoid slave work. It is, therefore, no surprise that, in some instances, ancestral skulls in Papua New Guinea were sold precisely for the price a person had to pay as an annual head tax (Kalka, 2024).

Indeed, souvenirs can tell us much about heritage conflicts and ways to resist the colonisers or survive in the colonial system. They prove that Indigenous communities were neither ignorant nor powerless but active participants in the global networks of their time. As positive as this sounds, research in this direction requires much care. Some people fear that this could distract from many objects being stolen. Instead of celebrating their ancestors' agency, they fear that, once again, the line between perpetrators and victims of colonial injustice might be blurred, and a

European museum is just looking for another excuse not to return its collections. One visitor even wrote in the guestbook of our colonialism exhibition that it is too early to confront the public with such complex topics as Indigenous agency. He felt that we should instead keep a simpler picture of [almighty] white aggressors and [powerless] non-white victims until the broader public has recognised all the atrocities of the German colonial rule.

Conclusion

Reflecting on my recent experience as the director of an ethnographic museum, it is evident that the questions of restitution regarding sacred objects and human remains will not find a general solution like those applicable to other types of museums. For example, some internationally accepted rules exist for handling exported archaeological collections. Also, for objects that came from Jewish families between 1933 and 1945 (and no matter if sold or stolen), there is a consensus among German museums that these transactions must be considered unlawful and restitution requests should be accepted. Such a generalising view would certainly not be accurate for the diverse collections of ethnographic museums. Understandably, a general injustice shapes all transactions within the framework of colonial power structures. The current state of separation of objects from their communities of origin is a global imbalance and a moral injustice that cannot be ignored any longer. The first step might be an agreement or a national law requiring museums to open dialogues and to offer for restitution specific categories, such as human remains, objects of specific spiritual or cultural importance to the descendants or entire collections which came from military "collectors" or left their countries of origin in times of war and genocide. In contrast, the current trend in provenience research to look for written proofs of unlawful acquisition remains problematic. Colonial "collectors" hardly cared about the origins of their pieces, and if they acquired them unlawfully, they were usually not eager to write this down. Museums, too, were not very active in documenting and sharing information about their sources. This was partly because they competed to build up exclusive collections.

Also, museums must find new ways to deal with restitution claims that are not based on historical facts but rather on contemporary cultural or spiritual needs. However, looking for such generalising solutions may still be too early.

The first and most important lesson learned from our dialogues is that every single case requires an individual approach and consultation of all actors involved. Restitutions are not always the best or only way to go. A possible alternative already in use is the transfer of ownership. However, this step also requires consent. Not involving all parties interested might quickly lead to the conclusion that this is just another half-hearted European idea of avoiding historical responsibilities. Nevertheless, even without a formal transfer of ownership, museum curators have the power and obligation to respect the veto rights of the communities in every decision concerning the storage, exhibition and publication of all objects belonging to their ancestors. Even if political and other obstacles remain, museums do not need to consider themselves the owners of their collections. I would rather call myself a caretaker who is as responsible to his administration as to the Indigenous communities. Working together should be a primary goal, and joint exhibitions in various places also provide a good context for a (at least temporal) circulation of heritage between museums in Europe and the communities of origin.

Another important insight might be that we will need to create bridges between what we call "Western science" and "Indigenous spiritualities". While Western scientists still try hard to distinguish between the sacred and the profane and thus classify objects as sensitive or non-sensitive, such a division does not necessarily make sense in other parts of the world. Looking at the Lübeck collection not just as 30,000 objects but as an equal number of living beings, spirits or souls can give a whole new dimension of respect and meaning to our work. Moreover, while restitutions are complicated, curators will have fewer problems talking with community members about their spiritual needs. Consulting communities, respecting religious feelings and thus not showing objects usually do not require political authorisation and can be a good way to show at least some basic respect and start a longer-lasting partnership.

Dialogues and collaborations not only offer benefits for the source communities but also are the only way to overcome the crisis of ethnographic museums in Germany and beyond. If ethnographic museums want to remain relevant institutions for the future in our globalised world, they must embrace a new ideal of openness. They need to replace Eurocentrism with new forms of dialogue and exchange with the communities that produced the objects. An important first step for museums is informing communities about what cultural objects their ancestors stored there. Museums can benefit significantly from learning more about the communities' views of the collection and spiritual issues that need to be respected when handling them. Learning more about traditional knowledge related to the objects (that colonial "collectors" were unaware of) can make a collection much more valuable to both sides. Communities can study the objects to reinforce their identity or heal at least some of the damage colonialism has caused. Exhibitions should make these Indigenous perspectives available to the European public and thus help to create a new balance between Eurocentric history and Indigenous self-representation. Museums must also serve as a platform for voicing contemporary concerns of the communities in terms of economy, ecology, racism and climate change, as well as inform about traditional knowledge and current achievements the communities wish to share with the world. Lastly, museums may not be shy about making the community's demands for the return of objects transparent to the public.

In the end, maybe it is not all about finding a solution for European museums but offering themselves as an area of discussion where our Indigenous partners can be loud and angry. Some activists note that the complexity of colonial history and the museum's efforts to deal with it are not their concern. They know very well that the big problems of our postcolonial world, like continued racism and economic inequality, cannot be solved overnight. Demanding the return of a specific mask is a goal more likely to be achieved, and a good opportunity to get attention from the media to point out all the other things. Some radical authors (e.g. Balzar, 2022) go so far as to suggest that ethnographic museums should not even try to get better. They could only be helpful if one builds a fence around them and presents them as a tragic example of historical injustice, a place of memories like a Nazi concentration camp. It is doubtful if all Indigenous communities would agree that the heritage of their ancestors should be used in such a way, and looking at a globalised world, the ethnographic task of creating and visualising dialogues between cultures is more relevant than ever.

Notes

1 Unless otherwise cited, all information provided in this chapter comes from two decades of personal dialogues with Indigenous communities from around the globe. I am very grateful that most individuals shared their opinions openly, although they prefer to remain anonymous in the academic world and with their national governments. However, I would like to thank David Seven Deers (Canada), Hema'ny Molina and Fernanda Olivares (Chile), Julian Jerónimo, Lalo Velasco Ceto and Diego Reanda Chiquival (Guatemala) as well as Samuel Kwashie Ametewee (Ghana) who helped me to organise my fieldwork or had an important influence on the ideas developed in this chapter. Claudia Kalka and Michael Schütte mainly researched the historical background of the Lübeck collection with research positions at the Zentrum für Kulturwissenschaftliche Forschung Lübeck. Both received funding from the German Lost Arts Foundation and the Cultural Ministry of Schleswig-Holstein to research Human Remains and collections from Namibia and the Fang people. Drossilia Dikegue Igouwe performed ethnographic fieldwork among the Fang. I also want to thank Brigitte Templin, Elke Krüger, Angela Hess, Stella Barsch, Lukas C. Saul, Dipika Nadkarni, Indira Piwko, Gisela Schliebs and Marianne Steup for their research in the colonial history of Lübeck.
2 By that time, NAGPRA had already created some awareness in the United States. However, ideas of Indigenous Archaeologies, such as integrating oral traditions into archaeological research, were still rather new and met with a lot of scepticism by many archaeologists in Europe. There was only limited interest in Europe in discussing colonial history or even considering the return of museum artefacts.
3 Very similar stories are told by rural people about neolithic burial mounds in Northern Germany as well.
4 The term "collector" commonly used to describe a person who brought objects from another country and donated them to a museum must be used with critical reflection. In many cases, the act of acquiring objects included violence or other methods ignoring or violating the rights of the source communities.
5 "First Nations" refers to Indigenous peoples in Canada, who are neither Inuit nor Métis.
6 The German term Endlager "final deposition place" is used for a permanent storage place for nuclear waste. The German government never found any place qualified to keep such dangerous material for millennia, just as keeping spiritual in objects in museums can hardly be a final solution.
7 For example, archival records in the Hamburg Museum inform us of a collection of Ancient Maya ceramics taken in the early 20th century from a cave that was still sacred to the descendants of the community. In this context, the German landowner who looted the cave explained in a letter to the museum that he had talked to a Maya priest and that man concluded that the objects themselves had agreed to be taken away; otherwise, the White man would have never been able to remove them.
8 The museum also holds some objects decorated with hair, which also qualify as human remains. The cultural sensitivity of them, however, depends on the views of the different

cultures. In some cases, it is still unclear if human or animal hair was used. Therefore, they are excluded from the following discussion.

9 Funding for this research was provided by the German Lost Art Foundation. The title of the research report soon to be published on the museum website "Hanseatics as head-hunter?" refers to the European obsession of collection human remains and inverts the view of communities as the "primitive others".

10 In the old Seklk'nam tradition, there were a lot of taboos related to the death. Burial places were not visited by the community and all the belongings of the dead given away or destroyed to leave to trace of him. Because of this traditional avoidance of death handling human remains in museums is a particularly challenging experience for them.

11 The person showed up with a decorated skull and told us that it was in his family for a long time. As we told him a museum cannot accept human remains so easily, he threatened to destroy the ancestor with a hammer and throw him in the trash bin. In the end, the police were informed and took care of the case and took the skull in custody.

References

Balzar, C. (2022). *Das kolonisierte Heiligtum. Diskriminierungskritische Perspektiven auf das Verfahren der Musealisierung*. Transcript.

Barsch, S., Frühsorge, L., & Olaf Guenther, O. (Eds.). (n.d.). *Beiträge zur Tagung "Koloniale Objekttransfers und Indigene Agency"*. Lübecker Museen.

Brulotte, R. (2012). *Between Art and Artefact: Archaeological Replicas and Cultural Production in Oaxaca, Mexico*. University of Texas Press.

Frühsorge, L. (2007). Iximche: Indigenous Perspectives on Archaeological Heritage in Guatemala. *Archaeologies* 2(3), 39–58.

Frühsorge, L. (2010). *Archäologisches Kulturerbe, lokale Erinnerungskultur und jugendliches Geschichtsbewusstsein bei den Maya*. Kovač.

Frühsorge, L. (2011). Memory, Nature, and Religion: The Perception of Pre-Hispanic Ruins in a Highland-Mayan Community. In C. Isendahl, & B. Liljefors-Persson (Eds.), *Ecology, Power, and Religion in Maya Landscapes: Proceedings of the 11th European Maya Conference* (pp 177–190). Saurwein.

Frühsorge, L. (2022). *Spuren der Lübecker Kolonialgeschichte*. Lübecker Museen.

Frühsorge, L. (2023). *Hoffnung am Ende der Welt: Von Feuerland zur Osterinsel/Esperanza en el fin del mundo. De la Tierra del Fuego a la Isla de Pascua*. Lübecker Museen.

Frühsorge, L., & Schmelz, B. (2011). Maximón: un santo milagroso, incluso en Hamburgo. *Mitteilungen aus dem Museum für Völkerkunde Hamburg* 42, 348–384.

Frühsorge, L., & Wölfel, U. (2009). Salt, Sites, and "Mythology": Cultural Memory in San Mateo Ixtatán (Huehuetenango, Guatemala) from Pre-Hispanic to Modern Times. In G. Le Fort, R. Gardiol, S. Matteo, & C. Helmke (Eds.), *The Maya and their Sacred Narratives: Text and Context of Maya Mythologies, Proceedings of the 12th European Maya Conference, Geneva, December 7–8, 2007* (pp. 157–173). Saurwein.

Haakanson, S. (2018). The Luebeck Angyaaq model from Alaska. In E. Krüger, C. Kalka, & L. Frühsorge (Eds.), *Searching the Key Festschrift für Brigitte Templin* (pp. 118–120). BoD.

Kalka, C. (2024) *Hanseaten als Kopfjäger?* https://vks.die-luebecker-museen.de/provenienzforschung

Kelker, N., & Bruhns, K. (2010). *Faking Ancient Mesoamerica*. Left Coast Press.

Paczensky, G. (1984). *Nofretete will nach Hause: Europa – Schatzhaus der "Dritten Welt"*. Bertelsmann.

Schütte, M., Frühsorge, L., & Igouwe, D. (2021). *Erforschung von Objekten der Herero und Fang in der Lübecker Völkerkundesammlung*. https://vks.die-luebecker-museen.de/provenienzforschung-2

13

CARE, PEOPLE, AND ARCHAEOLOGY IN A RESILIENT WORLD

Exploring community processes and networking in cultural heritage and museums in Europe and Latin America

Alicia Castillo Mena, Constanza Segovia Quinteros, Ana Pastor Pérez, Nekbet Corpas Cívicos, Sonia Menéndez Castro, Citlalli Reynoso Ramos, and Eloisa Pérez Santos

Introduction

The role of local communities in managing cultural heritage has continued to gain ground in recent decades due to implementing strategies of co-management, shared governance, and involving people at different levels (Pastor Pérez & Colomer, 2024), mainly driven by academia and the administration (Castillo et al., 2014; Castillo, 2015a, 2016). In collaboration with local associations, these agents have overseen reviewing and adapting the proposals that have emerged from organizations such as UNESCO, ICCROM, and ICOMOS, partly due to the need to integrate institutions into the perspective of cultural landscapes (e.g., Council of Europe, 2000). We assume that participation establishes democratic spaces, but if it is organized in such a way that few agents can participate or with top-down perspectives, its results will not be significant in the long term. To combat these difficulties, localized participatory actions can be proposed, which include under-represented agents and allow for studying how to reproduce these actions in other spaces and levels.

Working with spaces that allow intergenerational dialogues involves an investment of time and space that is not always possible due to economic and reproductive reasons. Undoubtedly, these are complex tasks, especially in terms of the interests and agencies of those involved for they are not free from conflicts, which can be addressed through methodological innovation. This chapter presents an approach to managing archaeological heritage, drawing from a multidimensional viewpoint (Castillo & Querol, 2014), a care perspective (Fisher & Tronto, 1990; Tronto, 1993), and an intersectional gender perspective (Hankivsky et al., 2014;

DOI: 10.4324/9781003623724-13

Hooks, 1981). The chapter emerges from the framework of a project called "CIPA-MUR: Care, People, and Archaeology in a Resilient World: Innovating from Community Processes and Networking in Cultural Heritage and Museums for the Latin Context."

The project team has been researching heritage space management in Latin American and Spanish contexts since 2007 (Castillo & Menéndez, 2014), as well as studying local communities' relationships with museums and archaeological sites at a management level (Rodríguez and Menéndez, 2021; Menéndez & Castillo, 2021), including conflict resolution (Almansa-Sánchez & Corpas, 2020; Castillo & Corpas 2024; Corpas 2020a; 2020b; 2023). In addition to these basic studies, there is also research based on lengthy experience in public studies in museums, mainly from evaluation (e.g., Pérez Castellanos & Pérez Santos, 2023) and the traditional field of heritage didactics (e.g. Fontal & Marin, 2016), which has been inclusive in considering local communities from as early as infancy and childhood (Martín Cáceres et al. 2014; del Mazo et al., 2018; Pérez Santos, 2020a, 2020c). Initiatives have been undertaken to raise public awareness of the scientific and technical values of heritage (Pastor Pérez & Remacha Acebrón, 2024).

The CIPAMUR project

This international project, which has been carried out simultaneously in three countries (Cuba, Spain, and Mexico) for four years, was developed as a laboratory of care experiences and active listening with local communities. Specifically, the project seeks to provide a diagnostic analysis of the connection between a museum and archaeological heritage site and its community of reference in the three selected case studies. Based on the results of this analysis, steps will be proposed to strengthen the territorial context as a sustainable ecosystem that is inseparable from the surrounding social discourse and realities.

Inclusive strategies must be adopted to ensure that the experiences outlined in the objectives become spaces shared between locals and visitors. This project aims to establish the foundations of such shared spaces through studies and proposals that cover different phases: diagnosis, participatory action research, and evaluation. This, in turn, will allow us to design participatory research strategies that foster a sense of co-creation or co-responsible participation in heritage management (see Figure 13.1). Thus, CIPAMUR is a project that seeks to connect heritage spaces, such as museums, with local communities so that they become more inclusive, safe locales. At the same time, heritage spaces can become proactive agents in social and cultural sustainability policies, in line with the sustainable development goals and from a people-based approach. The project rests on Participatory Action Research (PAR) and an iterative strategy of self-evaluation and transfer. It prioritizes the multilevel dissemination of results from the perspective of social innovation while considering the transfer of results to the business sector, the generation of new job opportunities, and a focus on people and social agents to address

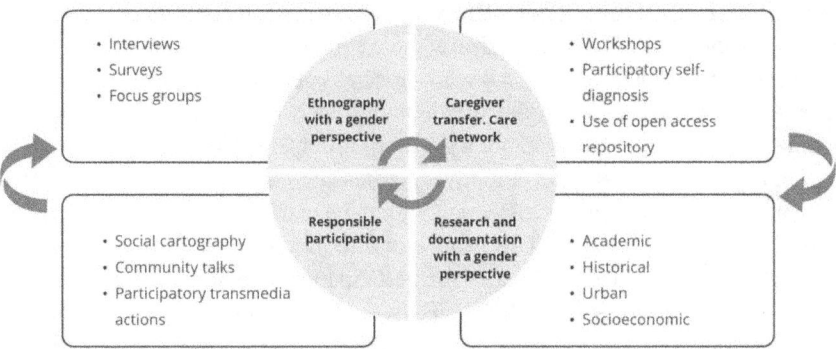

FIGURE 13.1   Theoretical–methodological conceptual summary of the project.

Source: CIPAMUR (2023)

heritage management. In this chapter, we present some methodologies that allow us to reflect on the limits of participation and co-creation strategies for heritage management, through case studies in museums in urban contexts and the formulas to improve them.

Trends in archaeological heritage management, including different local actors, have become entrenched in globalized discourses that do not always consider evolving cultural contexts (Laužikas et al., 2018; Waterton, 2005). The expert groups in archaeology and other heritage sciences seek to mitigate these distances through participatory studies (Tully et al., 2022; Colomer & Pastor Pérez, 2024; Tully et al., 2022). However, we do not always work at methodological levels capable of generating short- and long-term solutions for diverse actors while simultaneously empowering surrounding communities (Castillo Mena, 2018). Moreover, care and gender perspectives are rarely integrated into these studies (Esteban, 2017), and they mostly lack elaboration from complex thoughts (Morin, 1994). Therefore, this chapter explores how to enhance management methodologies to foster well-being and care within the main heritage knowledge transfer spaces, thus minimizing tensions and contests among various stakeholders at historic towns (see Ichumbaki, this volume) at the nature–culture locales (see Bigambo, this volume, Saldin and Zarandona, this volume) and in museums (Frühsorge, this volume). We apply these methodologies to museums and archaeological sites in urban areas, aiming to prevent the reification of heritage spaces.

In the context of CIPAMUR Project, heritage is understood as an additional element that must be integrated into urban life to create a city. This progress involves combating epistemic extractivism, which has grown as global issue and social voices that have become necessary. Currently, an authorized academic discourse seems to prevail (Pastor Pérez & Ruiz Martínez, 2020), leading to authorized participation (Pastor Pérez & Colomer, 2024) with the same effects as authorized heritage discourse (Smith, 2006). This way of approaching discourse has expanded in recent decades, primarily through academic conferences and publications. Activities such as traditional educational workshops or open days at archaeological sites have been presented as examples of community participation. In those cases, the population is mostly a receiver, not a giver or participant. There is no convergence toward knowledge creation or initiatives to measure participation level or format. In some limited cases, only satisfaction with the experience is evaluated (Castillo, 2016; Pérez Santos, 2020b). This academic role has come to replace administration and has also turned the spaces for participation into something imposed or imperative (Sánchez-Carretero, 2022). Thus, the backing of a symbolic community agency is sought to justify public policies that are still far from being effective in practice (Pérez Santos, 2019).

The CIPAMUR project is part of a bigger picture of heritage management that includes everyone and encourages participation to fight against extractivism and fake or symbolic participation in cultural heritage (Castillo, 2016; Ruiz-Blanch & Muñoz-Albadalejo, 2019). With a marked holistic character, it proposes to create situations of dialogic co-research (Buraschi & Oldano, 2022) at the intersection of individuals, museums, sites, and communities. The project aims to strike a balance between the various aspects of archaeological heritage, thereby promoting a less asymmetrical management approach that justifies the preservation, protection, and safeguarding of cultural assets (Castillo & Querol, 2014). This initiative will foster the development of "caring communities" around museums and archaeological sites and the parallel birth of "caring museums or sites." Consequently, museums and sites will place the needs of local communities that surround, inhabit, and transit these territories at the center (Puig de la Bellacasa, 2017). Incorporating PAR techniques into the caregiving framework and considering gender and intersectionality as structural and cross-cutting issues (Díez-Bedmar, 2020) is expected to enhance social cohesion in archaeological heritage environments, in both the short and long terms.

The proposed strategy to forge links between institutions and local communities focuses on exploring the relationships between a series of co-created archaeological and anthropological discursive proposals (filtered through the lens of gender and care) and analyzing their consequent impact on participating citizens. In this way, cooperation methods are sought between the professional and academic sectors and local associations (Saladino et al., 2021; Stendardi et al., 2020). The aim is to turn passive visitors and surrounding communities into key assets for renewing the studies and discourses of sites/museums based on a joint interpretation of memory. These aspects of co-creation had already been partially experimented with by team members (Castillo 2012, 2015b, 2018; Corpas & Castillo 2020; Martín et al., 2021), with satisfactory results in terms of the representation of different voices and the construction of collective knowledge. In this case, as mentioned earlier, the selected case studies are Castillo de La Real Fuerza Museum, Havana (Cuba), National Museum of Anthropology of Madrid (Spain), and the Regional Museum of Puebla de los Ángeles (Mexico). In the following sections, we will describe the actions carried out protectively.

Museums and heritage sites as augmented space: actions for local empowerment and the creation of caring spaces

The research was developed around four pillars. First, to outline the augmented spaces of museums and sites in inhabited spaces at different scales and with repercussions in the closest territory. Spaces in this context draw on social archaeology, feminist ethnography as an applied methodology, and the historical dimension. Second, we considered it relevant to introduce prior, formative, summative, and corrective evaluation as the main methodological axis of the whole project, thus generating a dynamic of Action–Evaluation–Action. Third, we propose to analyze the results in a way that contributes to bringing heritage education closer to more iterative proposals that are inclusive and gender sensitive. Introducing the constructivist paradigm aims to turn the community into the protagonist of heritage discourse, promoting elements that shape identities. This would strengthen social cohesion and the promotion of "community resilient" attitudes. Finally, we hope to establish a network of *caring cultural ecosystems*: museums and archaeological sites that care for people through shared actions and dialogue between the community and cultural heritage.

The methodology implemented for this proposal focuses on the following points: (1) To approach participatory actions in museums and heritage sites from an intersectional perspective, foregrounding gender, age, and sociocultural background. The actions were co-created by different agents while also considering how to evaluate them. (2) Facilitating and monitoring the development of participatory actions focused on aspects linked to heritage discourses. (3) Reviewing the actions and their results through proactive evaluation and action interpretation to understand the social perception of co-creation tools of narratives and discourses (i.e., museum discourses and those of archaeological sites in various case studies) and to investigate how these can enhance networks between agents (serving as networks of care).

Conflicts rest on long-term processes and patterns of relationships beyond concrete public manifestations of disagreement (Lederach, 2003). As such, any meaningful work to address them should be directed toward root causes such as inequality, marginalization, exploitation, and all types of indirect intensity, including cultural violence (Galtung, 1996). Drawing on the perspective that conflicts are part of all human relationships but can be conducive to positive social changes, this project works with dispute prevention by dealing with exclusionary discourses in museums.

CIPAMUR works in two conflicting areas derived from the museums' discourses and the lack of connection between them and the communities. The participating museums present echoes of a colonial museographic discourse, exhibiting objects as identity vehicles, often decontextualized from the present, leading to a disconnection between the heritage and the visitor. Furthermore, museums can be perceived as inaccessible, distant, or unappealing spaces by some groups, such as children, adolescents, or older people, who often do not perceive themselves as legitimate groups to contribute to heritage discourse.

We aim to configure a methodology based on participatory testing that listens to and considers all voices in decision-making. The methodology should enable the construction of a series of indicators that facilitate the case studies' political and management strategies and their extrapolation to other spaces with similar characteristics. The goal is to change the meaning of museum spaces and cultural assets by using participative and proactive strategies to create multivocal and multifocal dialogues that allow, at the same time, co-responsibility among all social actors that constitute and give meaning to museums and archaeological and cultural heritage. The hypothesis is that a shift in discourse and consequently in the heritage values under consideration will inevitably impact all forms of caring management measures, ranging from conservation and cataloging to more sustainable ways of publicly exhibiting cultural assets.

Heritage consensus: weaving networks of care through PAR

As with any participatory process, creating a care network between agents first requires mapping these agents by collaborating with the associative fabric, entities, and key individuals. This enables the identification and characterization of the social, educational, cultural, tourist, and business agents that partake in the activities and channels of participation and make up the museum and archaeological site's ecosystems. The research methodology is grounded in the social and human sciences. Therefore, the team has carried out important documentary work through a model that incorporates prior, formative, and summative evaluation, along with PAR strategies. Since museums and their relationship with the surrounding territory constitute heritage, the methodological strategies of participation in museums play a significant role. Our approach and timetable are flexible, as we work based on continuous, cumulative, and growing results over time, adapted to the particularities of each case study. This, in turn, allows and encourages the independent reproduction of the working group and the case study, promoting the use and enjoyment of other public spaces and cultural centers. It is not merely a matter of replicating the actions of each case study but rather contextualizing them, thus multiplying results and improving the productivity of knowledge, sustainability, and the ultimate meaning of scientific research, including its social transfer.

At a human group level, we operate at various scales, with teams in each city taking responsibility for implementing and designing actions at a local level. Due to its size and proximity to the coordinating team, the Madrid group serves as a facilitator and repository for the project's general information. The leadership of this group can result in the decisions made being somewhat biased toward colonial logic at the epistemic level, but this is compensated through regular meetings where situated experiences are shared. Also, case study researchers stay in and visit sites outside their home city to participate and give their opinions.

Dialogue is quite fluid during this project's intermediate phase, enabling us to share our thoughts on methodological corrections effectively. This phase, which is linked to the state of the art and PAR designed for each case, is devoted to diagnosis. PAR has been promoted in two cycles in the participating museums through experimental workshops that transversally address issues such as gender perspective, tolerance and dialogue between communities, empowerment, resilience, inclusion, and social cohesion. The actions are aimed at local communities that may be intergenerational or culturally diverse: school groups, migrants, Indigenous people, tourists, neighbors, and older people, among others. The PAR work relies on the fundamental role of participating agents in the research process. To this end, we have included museum teams and representatives from nearby communities that act as liaisons in designing the experimental actions that are subsequently applied and evaluated. There is a marked interest in applying PAR from an intersectional perspective. This is why we began to implement a gender and care plan to contribute to existing paradigms in heritage management practices and methodological research approaches. Although the implementation of this plan is in its early stages, it serves as a valuable tool in designing strategies for interaction between heritage, people, and territory from an ethical care perspective. As agents, it also enables us to self-evaluate our network of care.

The management of heritage spaces in Spain and Latin America

Havana, Madrid, and Puebla were chosen because the team members live in these cities, allowing for simultaneous and comparative work. They were also selected because of experiences and results from previous projects that sought to reveal the disconnected relationship between museums and cities (see Mora et al., 2015; Corpas & Castillo, 2019). Moreover, in each city, we work in spaces that are located in World Heritage Sites and are, therefore, highly sensitive to heritage issues. Two case studies – one museum and one archaeological site – were proposed for each city. In this chapter, we present results from the first experiences in the Castillo de La Real Fuerza Museum of the Office of the Historian in Havana, the National Museum of Anthropology of Madrid, and the Regional Museum of Puebla (Mexico) (Figure 13.2). The three cases are at different stages in the development of their PAR, which has been structured in two cycles for each participating community (see later). The results we are obtaining are still awaiting detailed analysis. While Madrid has completed the practical part of the experience with one of the chosen communities, Havana is still completing the second activity cycle, and the first PAR cycle at the Regional Museum of Puebla has not been completed.

FIGURE 13.2 Case studies: Castillo de La Real Fuerza Museum, Havana, National Museum of Anthropology in Madrid, and Regional Museum of Puebla (from left to right).

Source: CIPAMUR (2024) and María Fernanda Rodríguez García (2023)

Castillo de La Real Fuerza Museum in Havana, Cuba

The Castillo de La Real Fuerza Museum is one of the archaeological museums run by the Office of the Historian of the city of Havana. Its building, located in the city's historical/colonial center, is Cuba's oldest bastioned fortress. Havana is regarded as an urban nucleus with a high historical–archaeological heritage value. In 2016, it was recognized as one of the Seven Wonders Cities of the World, while Old Havana was designated as a World Heritage Site in 1982. This museum was chosen because of its long history of working with the territory and other institutions, as well as being recognized for carrying out multiple heritage dissemination activities. Its collection comprises historical and archaeological items, focusing on themes and goods related to underwater archaeology and naval history.

The National Museum of Anthropology in Madrid, Spain

The National Museum of Anthropology (MNA) is in a historic and highly touristic area in the center of Madrid. It is next to the historic Atocha railway station and the museum circuit of Paseo del Prado and Retiro Park, a designated World Heritage Site since 2021. Founded in 1875 by Dr. Pedro González Velasco, it has undergone significant changes in name, mission, and values (Ayuntamiento de Madrid et al., 2020: 186). Its collection is composed mainly of ethnographic and anthropological objects, mostly from Africa, America, Oceania, Asia, and, to a lesser extent, Europe. As Spain's administrative capital, Madrid oversees economic, administrative, and social activity. The city has undergone numerous transformations to become a cosmopolitan, diverse space with a broad cultural legacy.

In recent years, the MNA has taken a notable social turn. Within the framework of the Spanish Ministry of Culture's "Museo + Sociales" national plan, the museum has redefined its lines of work, directing its actions to serve as a space and tool for the community. It has positioned itself as an open, participatory, and reflective place of intercultural coexistence, primarily visible through its temporary exhibitions. The museum has not yet updated its permanent exhibition, which, aside from some guided activities and children's workshops, still adheres to the functionalist and positivist discourse, a hallmark of this type of museum in Spain during the 1980s and 1990s.

The Regional Museum of Puebla, in Puebla, Mexico

The Regional Museum of Puebla (MUREP) belongs to the National Institute of Anthropology and History (known as the INAH) and is in the spot where the historically relevant battle of May 5, 1862, took place (Enríquez, 2012). This museum, a public cultural institution, houses an important archaeological and prehistoric collection from the State of Puebla, along with a history and ethnographic room that highlights the intangible expressions of the cultural heritage of the various Indigenous groups that inhabit the state, including their festivities, customs, clothing, and worldview. UNESCO added Puebla's historic center to the World Heritage Sites list in 1987, and it is currently one of Mexico's most important tourist destinations.

The motivation for including the MUREP in this study is that all the pieces on display are results of research projects, some emblematic of Mexican archaeology (e.g., García, 1997; Marquina, 1970). In addition, this museum has an educational services team and is open to exploring new forms of dissemination. Furthermore, according to a survey carried out as part of our previous project (2019–21), the local population considers MUREP one of the most visited museums and representative of the city in terms of archaeology.

An iterative methodology from a people-based approach

Configuring a network of care of agents that enhances the museum's role as a hub for social interactions is a complex process that necessitates empathizing with each agent/person and establishing a procedure and roadmap that can be modified as needed. The methodological format chosen in the project is an iterative flow of action that allows for evaluations and adaptations for each case, as well as a spirit of rectifications and adjustments. All this was directed toward a way of working based on PAR (see Figure 13.3).

Working with experimental workshops situated and configured from an inclusive, intersectional, and integrative contextual diagnosis is one of the main methodological goals of the project. The workshops target specific population groups designed jointly by the research team of each city. The workshops are organized in consultation with all project members, who have contributed from each of their fields of knowledge on an interdisciplinary level. Participants' specialties include heritage management, museology, conservation of cultural property, anthropology, archaeology, and architecture. The first drafts of the workshops were shared with the teams working on management, conservation, education, and dissemination at

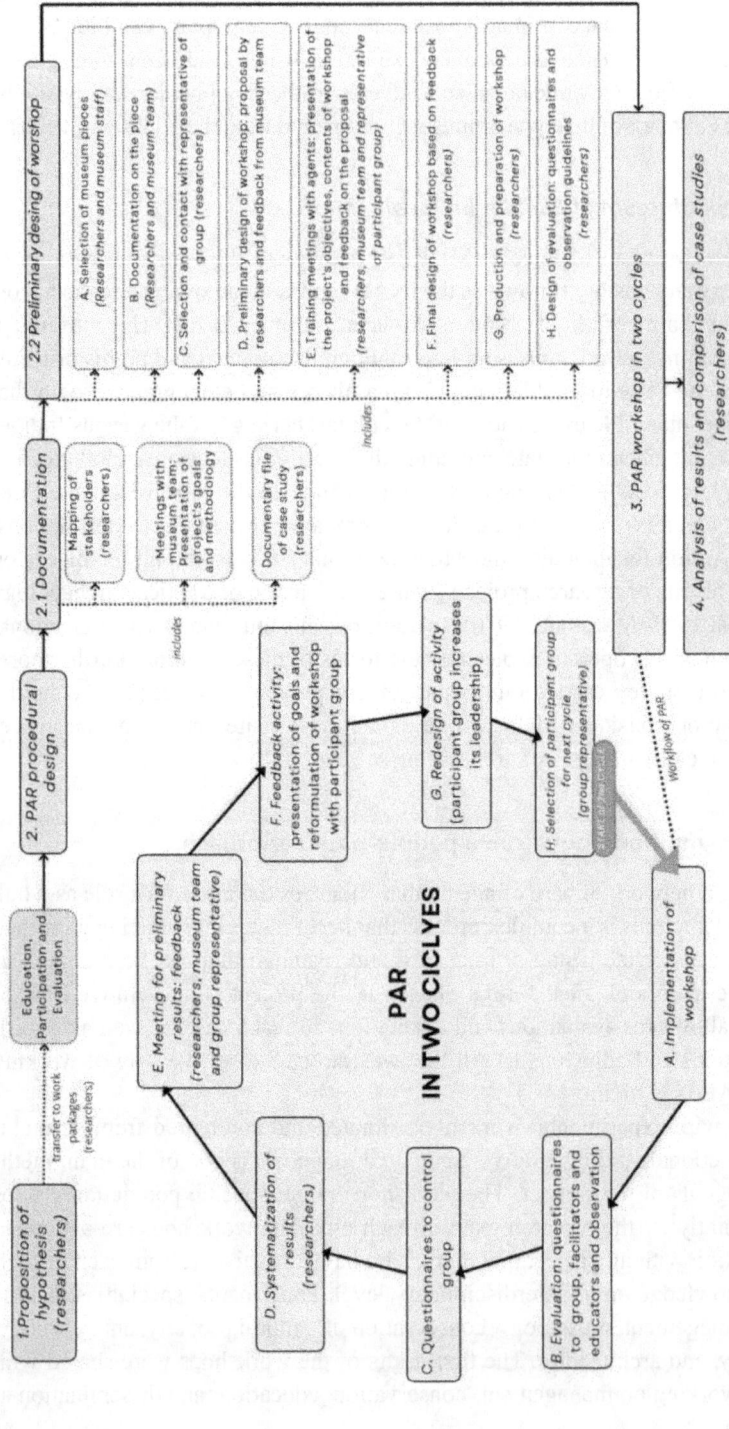

FIGURE 13.3 Methodological flow from the overall project to PAR in the case studies.

Source: CIPAMUR Project 2024

each museum. Dissemination was also done in local communities, school groups, university students, and the wider public.

Before developing the PAR's specific actions, a context study was conducted to create an information file adapted to each case study. This file, which was co-designed by different project members and focused on an intersectional perspective, aimed to establish a general diagnosis of the territory, the selected museums, and the urban communities as part of the case studies. This file contains contextual data on the regulations applicable to cultural heritage, tourist, and sociodemographic characteristics. It also has details of productive spaces associated with the case study and the main establishments in the immediate surroundings. Our team also explores the museums' missions and values, main works and objects, and permanent and recent temporary exhibitions. Other issues explored include resources, teams, services, and equipment. We also investigate accessibility, attention to diversity, collaboration networks, audiences, educational programs, and the profiles of visiting schools and institutes.

In addition to serving as a basis for comparison, this detailed study is adapted to worksheets and used in the PAR to shape activities and address the following common objectives:

- To know a culture with ancestral anchors and customs through its community.
- To present other ways of life connected to nature today.
- To recognize women's roles in other cultures, as well as their own.
- To achieve respect for diversity and difference.
- To foreground an active role of museums as intermediaries between societies, fostering intercultural dialogue, thus improving human coexistence in their areas of influence and close territories.
- To provide tools for citizen participation in museum exhibitions.

Workshop design and the actors involved: selecting the pieces

The activities designed for PAR focused on pieces selected by museum teams that could be approached from various discourses and through various resources while fostering a dialogue among agents. This approach intended to facilitate a subsequent analysis that could be compared across each case study. A further information file was created for each piece that the interdisciplinary museum team selected. This file provided details about the piece, including its name, location, historical and archaeological information, connection with the immediate environment beyond the museum, and colonial issues. Specifically, the file also offered information on the social archaeology of the piece in relation to the project's objectives, including gender perspective, social cohesion, tolerance, and dialogue between communities, empowerment, and resilience and well-being as health.

Next, we held workshops on the chosen piece(s) (see Table 13.1) and introduced the participating community to the process. Our team selected agents from the

TABLE 13.1 Summary of cases of studies

Case of Study	Selected Piece	Stakeholders	
The Havana	Gold Earring, made by aboriginal communities that inhabit Colombia Gold Pendant, 16th century, and Fragments of Gold Bars. Ground Floor, New World Riches Collection. Room B, showcase 4.	Castillo de la Real Fuerza Museum	Antonio Quevedo (Director of the Archaeological Museums of Havana, Office of the Historian of the City of Havana) and Arlene Cordero Alfonso (Archaeology Office, Office of the Historian of the City of Havana).
		Simón Rodríguez Primary School	Magalys Cordoví, teacher, who acted as a facilitating agent. Class of 5th year of education.
		Colegio Universitario San Gerónimo de La Habana, University of Havana	Dr Rosalía Oliva, acted as a facilitating agent, and second-year undergraduate students in Management and Preservation of Historical and Cultural Heritage.
Madrid	*Mukawa*, ceramic bowl made in 2008 by Melva Shiwango (Kichwa and Shuar cultures from Ecuador), located in the America Room, second floor of the permanent exhibition, showcase 24.	National Museum of Anthropology	Fernando Sáez, director, Patricia Alonso, curator, Susana Álvarez, museum assistant and Beatriz Estirado, museum assistant.
		Caligrama (outsourced education services company to MNA)	Alberto Cuetos, María Redondo, Raquel Lozano and Priscila Becerra acted as educators in the activities.
		San Isidro Secondary School	Nuria Torregimeno, facilitator of the group. Two classes of students in second year of compulsory secondary education.
		Retiro municipal day center and flats for the elderly	Nuria Ruiz, occupational therapist, facilitator of the group. One group of 11 elderly residents of the day center.

area close to the museums, including agents from different institutions, especially educational ones. Together, we built a database according to the types of agents: educational communities, migrants, neighbors, and tourists, among others. Data were collected by contacting associations and schools, previous experiences of the museums, and from other associations and local councils. We also conducted a physical territorial exploration and a netnography, which included searches on Google Maps, social networks, and various web environments.

We envisioned creating an expanded community space for museums by identifying groups capable of establishing a network of care or a network of agents in the short, medium, and long terms. As facilitators who transcend academia and cultural heritage management from a technical and static point of view, we aimed to explore the idea that co-created sustainable knowledge originates from safe spaces. These spaces allow different stakeholders to confidently express their needs and ideas, knowing they will be proactively considered. This has led to close collaboration with various stakeholder groups.

The agents involved in the Castillo de La Real Fuerza Museum case were primarily from the conservation and education fields. Work has been carried out in Madrid with local community, educational, and neighborhood agents, as well as with an education company providing services to the museum. These groups of agents helped to create alliances to strengthen workshops. In this way, training meetings were held between the researchers, museum agents, educators, and social agents, with the latter represented by either the teacher or the psychosocial therapist, depending on the group. These meetings allowed us to improve the activities, receive feedback from the groups, and define the materials and resources available in each experience (Figure 13.4). The workshops were developed so that the agents

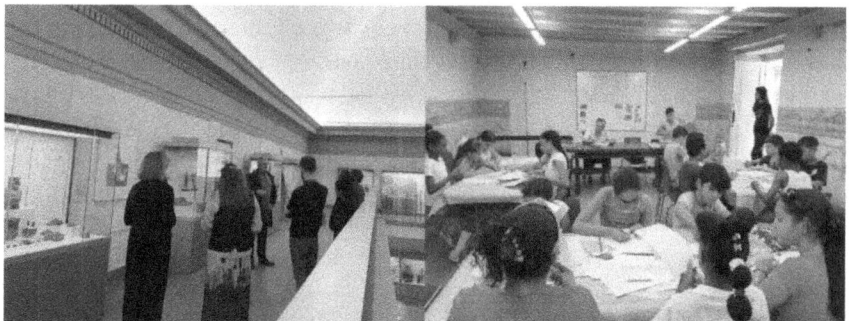

FIGURE 13.4   Meeting with educational and local community agents, along with the team of the National Museum of Anthropology, December 12, 2023, and Students and teachers working co-creatively during the first PAR cycle, April 1, 2024, Museum of Archaeology, Old Havana (from left to right).

Source: CIPAMUR Project, 2023–24

had complete knowledge of the project and what actions would be derived from their feedback, seeking to limit possible biases derived from epistemic extractivism.

The co-created workshops in Madrid and Havana involved participatory and multisensory experiences through gamification. Most participating communities were unaware of the project's objectives until they attended the first PAR workshop. The museum agents and those facilitating community contact and participation helped design the activity. Based on the selection of one or several pieces from the museum's permanent collection, multiple narratives were constructed to give an account of the use, tangible and intangible values and discourses on which participants reflected. During the discussion, overlapping themes of gender, tolerance and dialogue between communities, empowerment and resilience, inclusion, and social cohesion were addressed. The role and opinion of the agents who facilitated access to the workshops for the participating communities were also considered.

The rationale for not disclosing the project to the entire participating community served a dual purpose, enabling the application of constructivist techniques. First, we believed it was crucial to learn from practical experiences rather than rely solely on theoretical explanations, particularly on topics like interculturality and the perception of the museum as a local cultural hub. Second, we could verify if the project's objectives were achieved through the participating communities' narratives, co-created by the research team, museum, and liaison members. Our team avoided creating bias in the opinions of the participating community so they would be influenced as little as possible by the project's objectives. Instead, participants would offer opinions based on their own experiences. In this way, we indirectly introduced the project's objective themes through the workshop, whose discursive axis was created based on what was revealed about the pieces, their cultural origins, and how they were made.

In this sense, pre- and post-activity questionnaires have been designed to evaluate the different points of view of all those involved in the process: participants, mediators, and facilitators; and control groups have been included to analyze differences that may occur due to both the activity and visiting the museums. To obtain common data for comparison, all team members in different cities and museums agreed on the evaluation instruments, questionnaires, and observation guidelines. The team also decided on the distinctive features of each activity and context. The results provided relevant information for monitoring and redesigning the workshops carried out throughout the process.

Additionally, the research team, the agents who have been liaising with the participating community and the museum team scheduled meetings with the community after the workshop to discuss the findings (Figure 13.4). Similarly, the research team presented the partial results in an understandable way to the entire participating community. Through direct disclosure, the project's objectives and techniques are reinforced, seeking a non-academic transfer and formulating them in a didactic tone. This approach allowed for feedback to all parties involved in the PAR, thereby redefining the activity for the second cycle. Thus, we reformulated the workshops to align with our objectives, which are now directly co-created. This decision led to the start of the second cycle of PAR, which strengthened the partially achieved objectives and further progressed toward them by including the participants' perspectives. All this has empowered the participating community, which now takes joint responsibility for the second workshop and the discourse created for it. The research team is progressively relinquishing its leadership role in the project, allowing the participant community to take charge and modify the discourse and the first workshop cycle in creating the second. The team now assumes a facilitating role for the new workshop, following the guidelines and changes the participant community proposed.

In Puebla, although the participatory activity has been designed, it has not yet been applied to the target group. However, project meetings have been held with the MUREP's management and its cultural promoters. Also, contacts have been made with social agents such as the local school community at the secondary education and university level, as this represents the main public.

This case study is ideal for implementing improvements derived from evaluating previous workshops in Cuba and Spain. It generates space for well-being and inclusive transfer; we must always begin by understanding and rectifying our mistakes. This is a fundamental part of co-learning and knowledge construction. Each workshop has evaluation tools and feedback spaces for reviewing actions and designing contingencies. The actions and contingencies can be used during all the stages of workshops.

Regarding conflicts between stakeholders, the project has promoted a space for dialogue between agents in which the exponential involvement of the communities has been fundamental for them to experience the museum space more closely and to perceive their voices as legitimate. Multivocal discourses have linked heritage values with relevant social issues such as gender, connection with nature, sustainability, and cultural diversity, among others, allowing a comprehensive approach and understanding of heritage and its associated cultural aspects. This has strengthened the vision of the museum as participatory, diverse, and a learning space. In addition, the experience can be replicated by museums in their own practice of designing both exhibition discourse and visits. This generates a new space for communication among multiple agents with the possibility, depending on how it is managed and conducted, to channel future tensions and disputes between these groups and the museum institution.

A conscious and situated PAR?

We have discussed the limitations and scope of applying PAR in cultural heritage co-management projects. Participation and participatory techniques in cultural heritage have always been subject to debates about agency and endorsement by the powers that be, sometimes becoming mere tools at the service of the authorized heritage discourse (Smith, 2006). This raises the question of whether we are heading toward more symbolic participation, directed by us as researchers, which does not always support the interests of local communities. What CIPAMUR proposes is to counteract these erratic practices through co-creation processes in an iterative format and to produce spaces of active listening where academics, curators, and educators become facilitators at the service of social needs.

This role of researchers that CIPAMUR proposes is possible because of several methodological approaches implemented through phases that emphasize characterizing the links between museums, territories, and communities. The initial diagnosis, which focuses on institutional social commitment and explores the most complex aspects of the agencies, is key to weaving future alliances between agents. This allows for an articulated community transfer that leads to renewed approaches and heritage strategies in formal and non-formal education. This transfer of experiences brings the museum or heritage space closer to the rest of the agents, generating diverse and inclusive cultural discourses. New transversal axes are thus promoted, where through the shared bonds of sense of place, belonging or shared custodianship, knowledge and heritage transfer programs can be articulated in an intersectional and multivocal key.

Thus, progress is being made toward a more conscious and caring PAR that rectifies and listens to itself while focusing on intersectional issues, from configuring activities from an intergenerational perspective to addressing a non-discriminatory cognitive and educational diversity. Cultural heritage as a backdrop to these actions also enables progress to be made by creating a series of new future memories that weave new collaboration networks between agents and improve the management of cultural assets from a people-based approach.

Paradoxically, these proposals would not have been possible if not for previous practices, in which we have also been and are complicit as researchers and as part of the scientific system embedded in a neoliberal model in which knowledge construction occurs. Indeed, these erratic practices and academic or patrimonial discourses in which a lot of heritage management work is done today have been and still are necessary; hence, they continue. Therefore, we are aware of our experimental, theoretical role in improving them. The disruption they instigate, based on critical and self-critical inquiry, has created opportunities for innovative methods of knowledge and action that would have been unattainable without previous methods. The challenge, therefore, is to transfer these new forms, still in a pilot phase, to everyday heritage management contexts.

Final reflections

CIPAMUR is a project for improving heritage management through care networks and spaces of well-being between cultural heritage management authorities and communities of interest. The project is a vehicle and a proactive agent that can elicit these changes. It brings together the expectations of members from different institutions, countries, and professional backgrounds. The project members have networks and knowledge to bring different institutions and communities together. In this way, we hope to establish new connections with the local population and its museums and heritage sites through citizen participation, bringing the agents together and enabling museums to provide a larger space to their visitors while becoming more projective tools for social cohesion in the long term.

Establishing new networks of caring agents linked to cultural institutions who work with mutual respect to achieve objectives and build more inclusively may seem excessively ambitious. However, the iterative methodological configuration and the involvement of agents with solid experience in the environment make the proposal more realistic. Furthermore, the project considers museum management practices and citizen involvement from the perspective of PAR and in a comparative, cumulative, and scaled-up manner. It is therefore hoped that the results obtained from the project will have repercussions on museum management, integrating cultural heritage as a fundamental part of the social, economic, and political development of the territory in which our case studies are located. We also believe this process will develop through an initial deconstruction of current management structures, starting with the discourses that may support some of the pieces analyzed in the case studies.

By working from PAR and connecting different actors at a local and international level, each case study is established as an interactive and glocal learning space. This allows its transfer and adaptive replication in the educational, tourism, urban, social, and environmental sectors internationally. In this way, the research will be sustainable and extend beyond the project scope, yielding direct and indirect benefits by generating spillover effects:

- Training professionals and encouraging creative entrepreneurship in the cultural heritage sector.
- Transferring experiences through formal education at all levels, from early childhood to higher education.
- Building the capacity of alternative discourses in museums and heritage sites from the co-creation and co-responsibility of citizens.
- Encouraging changes to governance models in asset management toward more horizontal and inclusive working structures.
- Pointing out the need to foster spaces for social inclusion using a caring and conscious PAR that provides solutions in line with society's challenges.

We hope that the results obtained in this project, including the workshops, will improve and strengthen the existing networks of agents in cultural heritage management from the citizen science perspective. Building bridges between society and academia is always a challenge that lacks the necessary support in terms of time, listening, and objectives. Achieving realistic sustainability and a balance between and among institutions is one of the greatest challenges facing the agents involved. For this reason, the tools CIPAMUR proposes can be key in the co-management of cultural heritage.

Acknowledgments

We are part of a transdisciplinary and international group of researchers from Spain, Cuba, and Mexico who have been collaborating on cultural heritage research for more than ten years. We thank each member of the CIPAMUR team: Arturo Ruiz Taboada, Luis Benítez de Lugo Enrich, Esther Jiménez Pablos, Gloria Pérez, Raquel Caerols Mateo, Mª Ángeles Querol Fernández, Beatriz A. Rodríguez, Francisco Vélez Pliego, Erik Chiquito Cortés, and Gemma Muñoz. Also, we would like to thank Dr. Manuel Villarroel, manager of Centro INAH-Puebla, Manuel A. Melgarejo, manager of MUREP, and the museum staff. For the Havana and Madrid case studies, we are grateful to the staff mentioned in this chapter.

Funding

The research and results presented are part of the CIPAMUR research project of the competitive call for grants for "Knowledge Generation Projects 2021," within the framework of the "State Program to Promote Scientific-Technical Research and its Transfer" included in the "State Plan for Scientific Research," funded by the Ministry of Science and Innovation of Spain. Execution period: 2022–26. Principal Investigator: Alicia Castillo. https://www.ucm.es/cipamur/

References

Almansa-Sánchez, J., & Corpas Cívicos, N. (2020). Vanishing heritage, materialising memory: construction, destruction and social action in contemporary Madrid. In V. Apaydin (Ed.), *Critical Perspectives on Cultural Memory and Heritage. Construction, Transformation and Destruction* (pp. 111–127). UCL Press. https://discovery.ucl.ac.uk/id/eprint/10091628/1/Critical-Perspectives-on-Cultural-Memory-and-Heritage.pdf

Ayuntamiento de Madrid, Comunidad de Madrid Madrid & Ministerio de Cultura. (2020). Paseo del Prado and Buen Retiro. A landscape of Arts and Sciences. *Nomination Dossier Update.* February 2020. https://whc.unesco.org/en/list/1618/documents/

Benetti, F., Möller, K., & Ripanti, F. (2022). Working with communities: Public participation from the archaeologists' perspective. *Journal of Community Archaeology & Heritage*, 9(4), 287–303. https://doi.org/10.1080/20518196.2021.1953320

Buraschi, D., & Oldano, N. (2022). Paulo Freire's legacy in dialogic participatory practices. *RES, Revista de Educación Social*, 35. https://eduso.net/res/wp-content/uploads/2022/12/res-35.miscelanea.5-daniel.pdf

Castillo, A., & Corpas, N. (2024). Participatory processes and conflict resolution in archaeology and heritage. In *Encyclopedia of Archaeology.* 2nd Edition. Routledge.

Castillo, A., & Menéndez, S. (2014). Managing urban archaeological heritage: Latin American case studies. *International Journal of Cultural Property*, 21(01), 55–77. https://doi.org/10.1017/S0940739113000313

Castillo Mena, A. (ed.). (2012). *Proceedings of the First International Conference on Best Practices in World Heritage: Archaeology. Mahon, Minorca, Balearic Islands, Spain 9–13 April 2012.* Complutense University of Madrid. https://www.ucm.es/data/cont/docs/3-2013-02-07-1-58974.pdf

Castillo Mena, A. (2015a). Mapping stakeholders in archaeological heritage management. In M. H. van den Dries, J. van der Linde, & A. Strecker (Eds.), *Fernweh: Crossing*

Borders and Connecting People in Archaeological Heritage Management. Essays in Honour of Prof. Willem J. H. Willems (pp. 64–67). Sidestone Press.

Castillo Mena, A. (ed.). (2015b). *Proceedings of the Second International Conference on Best Practices in World Heritage: People and Communities. Mahon, Minorca, Balearic Islands, Spain. 29–30 April, 1–2 May. 2015.* Universidad Complutense de Madrid. https://docta.ucm.es/entities/publication/72a9eb5d-addf-4a82–92eb-ae939b21b1c7

Castillo Mena, A. (2016). Relations between citizens and heritage agents from the perspective of academic research: Pending challenges in the management of cultural heritage. *PH90 Journal.* https://doi.org/10.33349/2016.0.3802

Castillo Mena, A. (ed.). (2018). *Proceedings of the III International Conference on World Heritage: Integral Actions/Actas del III Congreso Internacional de Buenas Prácticas en Patrimonio: Acciones integrales. Mahon, Minorca, Balearic Islands, Spain 2–5 May 2018.* Complutense University of Madrid. https://docta.ucm.es/entities/publication/c68aa74d-8074–45bc-9aee-142035175cf7

Castillo Mena, A., & Querol, M. A. (2014). Archaeological dimension of world heritage: From prevention to social implications. In A. Castillo (Ed.), *Archaeological Dimension of World Heritage: From Prevention to Social Implications* (pp. 1–11). Routledge.

Castillo Mena, A., Yáñez, A. Dominguez, M., & Salto-Weiss, I. (2014). Citizenship and heritage commitment: Looking for participatory methodologies adapted to the urban cultural heritage context. *Symposium Heritage and Landscape as Human Values. Firenze, Italy. 9–14 Nov. 2014* (pp. 415–422). Edizione Scientifique Italiane.

Colomer, L., & Pastor Pérez, A. (2024). City Governance, participatory democracy, and cultural heritage in Barcelona, 1986–2022. *The Historic Environment: Policy & Practice,* 15(1), 81–100. https://doi.org/10.1080/17567505.2023.2298546

Corpas, N. (2020a). El Patrimonio cultural y el conflicto. In M. A. Querol (Ed.), *Manual de Gestión del Patrimonio Cultural* (pp. 520–522). 2nd Edition. Akal.

Corpas, N. (2020b). Alternatives in conflict resolution in archaeological heritage. The case of looting and illicit international trafficking. *Revista d'Arqueologia de Ponent,* 30, 337–348.

Corpas, N. (2023). Archaeological heritage, conflict and immigration. A reflection on its management. In E. Pérez (Ed.), *El patrimonio cultural sin límites: los retos de la corresponsabilidad social en su gestión y uso* (pp. 158–163). Ayuntamiento de Buenavista.

Corpas, N., & Castillo, A. (2019). Tourism 3.0 and archaeology: approaching tourists' generated content of World Heritage sites. *Pasos. Journal of Tourism and Cultural Heritage,* 17(1), 39–52. https://doi.org/10.25145/j.pasos.2019.17.003

Corpas, N., & Castillo, A. (2020). Towards an archaeological heritage management for the city of Puebla: Archaeological interventions and citizen valuation. *Cuetlaxcoapan,* 24, 8–13.

Council of Europe. (2000). *Landscape Convention.* Treaty No.176. https://www.coe.int/en/web/conventions/full-list?module=treaty-detail&treatynum=176

del Mazo Fernández, S., Pérez López, R., & Rufián Fernández, F. J. (2018). Didactics and dissemination of historical and archaeological heritage. In A. Galán Pérez (ACRE), & D. Pardo San Gil (GE-IIC) (Eds.), *Las profesiones del Patrimonio Cultural. Competences, training and knowledge transfer: Reflections and challenges in the European Year of Cultural Heritage 2018* (pp. 136–139). Ministry of Culture and Sport.

Díez-Bedmar, M. del C. (2020). Heritage education, intergenerationality and intersectionality from a gender perspective. Experience and conclusions for initial teacher training. Revista *Investigación en la Escuela,* 100, 55–70. https://doi.org/10.12795/IE.2020.i100.05

Enríquez P. A. (2012). *A 150 años de la Batalla del Cinco de mayo de 1862. Revisiones y Valoraciones.* Government of the State of Puebla.

Esteban, M. L. (2017). Care, a central concept in feminist theory: Contributions, risks and dialogues with anthropology. *QuAderns-E,* 22(2), 33–48.

Fisher, B., & Tronto, J. C. (1990). Toward a feminist theory of caring. In E. K. Abel, & M. K. Nelson (Eds.), *Circles of care. Work and Identity in Women's Lives* (pp. 35–62). SUNY Press.

Fontal, O., & Marín Cepeda, S. (2016). Heritage education in museums: An inclusion-focused model. *The International Journal of the Inclusive Museum*, 9(4), 47–64. https://doi.org/10.18848/1835-2014/CGP/v09i04/47-64

Galtung, J. (1996). *Peace by Peaceful Means: Peace and Conflict, Development and Civilization*. International Peace Research Institute Oslo; Sage Publications, Inc.

García Cook, A. (1997). Richard Stockton MacNeish and the origin of agriculture. *Arqueología Mexicana*, 25, 40–43.

Hankivsky, O., Grace, D., Hunting, G., Giesbrecht, M., Fridkin, A., Rudrum, S., Ferlatte, O., & Clark, N. (2014). An intersectionality-based policy analysis framework: Critical reflections on a methodology for advancing equity. *International Journal for Equity in Health*, 13(1), 119. https://doi.org/10.1186/s12939-014-0119-x

Hooks, B. (1981). *Ain't I a Woman*. Routledge. https://doi.org/10.4324/9781315743264

Laužikas, R., Dallas, C., Thomas, S., Kelpšienė, I., Huvila, I., Luengo, P., Nobre, H., Toumpouri, M., & Vaitkevičius, V. (2018). Archaeological knowledge production and global communities: boundaries and structure of the field. *Open Archaeology*, 4(1), 350–364. https://doi.org/10.1515/opar-2018-0022

Lederach, J.P. (2003). *The Little Book of Conflict Transformation*. Good Books.

Marquina, I. (1970). *Cholula Project*. INAH.

Martín, J., Domínguez, M., & Castillo, A. (2021). La activación de la ciudadanía como estrategia para la sostenibilidad turística en lugares patrimoniales cercanos a la gran ciudad. El caso de la región madrileña Pasos. *Revista de Turismo y patrimonio cultural*, 19(4), 695–711. https://doi.org/10.25145/j.pasos.2021.19.045

Martín Cáceres, M., López Cruz, I., Morón Monge, H., & Listán Ferreras, M. (2014). Heritage education in museums. Analysis of didactic materials. CLIO. *History and History Teaching*, 40. http://clio.rediris.es/n40/articulos/martincaceres.pdf

Menéndez, S., & Castillo, A. (2021). Cultural heritage, citizenship and management from preventive archaeology. La Habana Vieja, espacio para repensar y dialogar. *Gabinete de Arqueología*, 14 (Year 14), 31–41.

Mora, S. Castillo, A., & Rubio, N. (2015). Presentazione al pubblico del sito urbano: uno sguardo critico dall'osservazione delle Città Patrimonio Mondiale. *Osservare il Patrimonio Culturale Valutare lo Stato di Conservazione e Comunicarlo al Pubblico*. (pp. 58–60). Herity.

Morin, E. (1994). *Introducción al pensamiento complejo*. Gedisa

Pastor Pérez, A., & Colomer, L. (2024). Dissecting authorised participation in cultural heritage. *International Journal of Heritage Studies*, 30(2), 226–241. https://doi.org/10.1080/13527258.2023.2284741

Pastor Pérez, A., & Remacha Acebrón, S. (2024). Recovering the memories of the capdella cardboard hospital through community archaeology. *Archaeologies*. https://doi.org/10.1007/s11759-024-09504-w

Pastor Pérez, A., & Ruiz Martínez, A. (2020). Are we the authoritative academic discourse on heritage? In A. Pastor Pérez, M. Picas, & A. Ruiz Martínez (Eds.), *21 Assajos al voltant del Patrimoni Cultural. 21 Essays on Cultural Heritage* (pp. 63–67). JAS Arqueologia. https://doi.org/10.23914/book.001.12

Peréz Castellanos, L., & Pérez Santos, E. (2023). La evaluación de resultados e impacto en los museos: una misión posible y necesaria. *RdM. Revista de Museología*, 86, 46–49. ISSN 1134–0576.

Pérez Santos, E. (2019). Good practices in audience research in museums. In Pérez Castellanos, L (Coord.), *Estudios sobre públicos y museos Volumen III. Referentes y experiencias de aplicación desde el campo*. (pp. 26–56) ENCRYM Digital Publications.

Pérez Santos, E. (2020a). Best Practices in visitors studies. The permanent laboratory of museum audiences (Spain). In A. A. Tak, & Ángel Pazos-López Socializing Art Museums (Eds.), *Rethinking the publics experiences*. De Gruyter.

Pérez Santos, E. (2020b). Investigaciones de públicos en los museos: Evolución histórica, problemas actuales y retos futuros. In F. Bayón, & J. Cuenca (Eds.), Públicos en transformación. Una visión interdisciplinar de las funciones, experiencias y espacios del público actual de los museos (pp.16–36). Dykinson.

Pérez Santos, E. (2020c). Jóvenes y museos: una revisión crítica de los principales informes, estudios e investigaciones sobre el tema. In *Laboratorio Permanente de Público de Museos: Conociendo a todos los públicos: Los jóvenes y los museo*s. Ministerio de Cultura. http://www.culturaydeporte.gob.es/dam/jcr:a673f725-f0a7–48f1–8566-c21d2f-ec6ac2/dest-conociendo-jovenes.pdf

Puig de la Bellacasa, M. (2017). *Matters of Care: Speculative Ethics in More Than Human Worlds*. University of Minnesota Press.

Rodríguez Basulto, B., & Menéndez Castro, S. (2021). The city we are: Co-responsible condition for a dialogic space in heritage management. *Complutum, 32*(2), 347–364.

Ruiz-Blanch, A., & Muñoz-Albadalejo, J. (2019). Citizen participation: from Welfare to Do It Yourself. In C. Sánchez-Carretero, J. Muñoz-Albadalejo, A. Ruiz-Blanch, & J. Roura-Expósito (Eds.), *El imperativo de la participación en la gestión patrimonial* (pp. 41–57). Consejo Superior de Investigaciones Científicas.

Saladino, A., Castillo, A., & Nara, J. C. (2021). Arqueourbanismo como instrumento de gestão das Cidades-Patrimônio: reflexões sobre desafios e possibilidades em cidades Patrimônio Mundial na Espanha e na América Latina. In A. Nakamuta (orgs.), *Arte, cidade e patrimônio: futuro e memória nas poéticas contemporâneas*. Automatica Edições.

Sánchez-Carretero, C. (2022). The silent transformations of the heritage regime. Participation and conflicts around cultural heritage. *AIBR, Revista de Antropología Iberoamericana, 17*(2). https://doi.org/10.11156/aibr.170205

Stendardi, D, Pérez, E., Castillo, A., & Garci, J. (2020). Isolated identity, tourism and heritage: Social perception and participation in cultural heritage management for the transformation of tourism governance in Buenavista del Norte (Tenerife, Canary Islands, Spain). *Revista ESPACIOS, 41* (17), 24 ff. https://www.semanticscholar.org/paper/Isolated-identity%2C-tourism-and-heritage%3A-Social-and-Stendardi-P%C3%A9rez/e9a474548720ef5f2b4a8b697a3ac42b0352d19c

Smith. (2006). *Uses of Heritage*. Routledge.

Tronto, J. C. (1993). *Moral Boundaries. A Political Boundary for an Ethic of Care*. Routledge.

Tully, G., Anés, L. D., Thomas, S., Olivier, A., Benetti, F., Castillo Mena, A., Chavarri Arnau, A., Rizner, M., Möller, K., Karl, R., Matsuda, A., Martín Civantos, J. M., Brogiolo, G. Pietro, Corpas Cívicos, N., Ripanti, F., Bautista, J. S., & Schivo, S. (2022). Evaluating participatory practice in archaeology: Proposal for a standardized approach. *Journal of Community Archaeology & Heritage*, 1–17. https://doi.org/10.1080/2051819 6.2021.2013067

Waterton, E. (2005). Whose sense of place? Reconciling archaeological perspectives with community values: Cultural landscapes in England. *International Journal of Heritage Studies*, 11(4), 309–325. https://doi.org/10.1080/13527250500235591

INDEX

Note: numbers in **bold** indicate a table. Numbers in *italics* indicate a figure.

For Product Safety Concerns and Information please contact our EU
representative GPSR@taylorandfrancis.com
Taylor & Francis Verlag GmbH, Kaufingerstraße 24, 80331 München, Germany